THE GOOD PRIEST'S SON

BOOKS BY

REYNOLDS PRICE

THE GOOD PRIEST'S SON 2005

A SERIOUS WAY OF WONDERING 2003

NOBLE NORFLEET 2002

FEASTING THE HEART 2000

A PERFECT FRIEND 2000

LETTER TO A MAN IN THE FIRE 1999

LEARNING A TRADE 1998

ROXANNA SLADE 1998

THE COLLECTED POEMS 1997

THREE GOSPELS 1996

THE PROMISE OF REST 1995

A WHOLE NEW LIFE 1994

THE COLLECTED STORIES 1993

FULL MOON 1993

BLUE CALHOUN 1992

THE FORESEEABLE FUTURE 1991

NEW MUSIC 1990

THE USE OF FIRE 1990

THE TONGUES OF ANGELS 1990

CLEAR PICTURES 1989

GOOD HEARTS 1988

A COMMON ROOM 1987

THE LAWS OF ICE 1986

KATE VAIDEN 1986

PRIVATE CONTENTMENT 1984

VITAL PROVISIONS 1982

THE SOURCE OF LIGHT 1981

A PALPABLE GOD 1978

EARLY DARK 1977

THE SURFACE OF EARTH 1975

THINGS THEMSELVES 1972

PERMANENT ERRORS 1970

LOVE AND WORK 1968

A GENEROUS MAN 1966

THE NAMES AND FACES OF HEROES 1963

A LONG AND HAPPY LIFE 1962

REYNOLDS PRICE

THE GOOD PRIEST'S SON

SCRIBNER

NEW YORK   LONDON   TORONTO   SYDNEY

SCRIBNER
1230 Avenue of the Americas
New York, NY 10020

SCRIBNER and design are trademarks of Macmillan Library Reference USA, Inc., used under license by Simon & Schuster, the publisher of this work.

For information about special discounts for bulk purchases, please contact Simon & Schuster Special Sales: 1-800-456-6798 or business@simonandschuster.com

Set in Electra

Manufactured in the United States of America

1   3   5   7   9   10   8   6   4   2

Library of Congress Cataloging-in-Publication Data
Price, Reynolds, 1933–
The good priest's son / Reynolds Price.
      p. cm.
      I. Title.
PS3566.R54G66 2005
813'.54—dc22   2004065383

ISBN 0-7432-5400-7

FOR

JONATHAN USLANER

THE GOOD PRIEST'S SON

ONE

9 . 11 . 2001

9 . 13 . 2001

The whole three weeks in Italy had felt like the rescue Mabry hoped for—not a single moment of cloudy vision and almost none of the maddening jangle of threatened nerves in his hands and legs. Even the two quick days in France, despite the routine Parisian rudeness, had failed to crank his symptoms. So he'd stuffed his ears with the airline's free plugs and sunk into a nap in what he suspected was half-foolish hope. *Maybe my body isn't ruined after all. Maybe Rome has cured me.* And the nap was so deep that the pilot's first few news reports didn't reach him at all. What finally woke him was the huge plane itself—a steep tilt northward, a wide swing, then a man's calm voice as the wings leveled off.

It said "Ladies and gentlemen," not the usual jaunty *Folks*. Then it took a long pause. "The latest news is even more impressive. At the World Trade Center, the second tower has also collapsed. As many as six thousand people may be lost. The plane that crashed into the Pentagon has taken maybe three hundred lives, and a fourth plane has crashed in a Pennsylvania field with all hands aboard. All U.S. airports are now closed to traffic, and we have our orders to divert.

We're headed for Halifax, Nova Scotia. No further plans are available at present. I'll keep you posted."

Mabry had removed his earplugs by then; but he'd still never heard such silence in an airplane as what swept through in the wake of that voice. Before he could look around—the plane was half empty—the pilot said four more words that were worse than all the rest. "I hope I can." When had any of them heard such desolation?

Behind, a single voice sobbed distinctly. It seemed to be a man.

But since no other passenger was near in the first-class seats, Mabry rang for help; and a rattled steward told him the little they knew. Both of the World Trade Towers had been hit by full-sized jets, and both had now fallen. The collisions had come just after work started. Some reports said a plane had struck the Pentagon; a fourth plane had crashed in rural Pennsylvania. Mabry sipped at the double gin the steward brought, unasked. Then he shut his eyes to think, if thinking was possible. He knew just enough American history to calculate that, if six thousand human beings were dead, then this was the most disastrous day since the bloodiest day of the Civil War—the battle at Antietam when, almost surely, nearly four thousand died. And this day had barely started. Whoever had done this and what else was planned?

Yet when he opened his eyes again, he looked to the jittery steward alone in the all-gray galley and saw him as clear as a stark photograph—or grim as a Goya torture victim. Mabry gave him a brief consolatory wave, a windshield-wiper side-to-side gesture (he was in first class, courtesy of years of frequent-flier credits).

His wave brought the steward back; he leaned to Mabry's ear and whispered. "My partner works fifty yards away, across the plaza. He's an architect. Say a hard prayer for him. Me as well—he's all I've got on the planet Earth."

Somehow Mabry felt he knew the truthful thing to say. "Your friend's OK. I'm all but sure." When he looked, the steward's name tag said *Larry Leakins*; so Mabry took the further risk of saying "He's truly safe, Larry. I live down there, just three blocks south."

For the moment at least, Larry seemed to believe him. He squeezed Mabry's shoulder and went back to work.

Then Mabry scratched his palms deeply to check for numbness. He was hurting himself; the feeling was normal. And his legs were still calm. So in his mind he stroked the curious peace he still felt, like a cooling wound in the pit of his heart. He was tired, God knew, but not drunk or drugged. All his life he'd been a buoyant soul. *Why on Earth now?* From the time the Towers had first been bombed in 1993, he'd known the Muslims would try again—and likely succeed. Now he was right, way righter than he could ever have guessed. And aside from the blow his city and country had suffered today—and the future was botched for years to come—he'd surely taken hits of his own.

His loft was in actual sight of the Towers. It was bound to be damaged if not destroyed. How many friends were dead? Likely the client who sent him to Paris. His daughter lived and worked uptown but was she safe? He'd never surrendered to the cell-phone plague, and he'd had no luck with airplane phones, so there was nothing he could do before landing—if there was still land in Nova Scotia. He looked out and tried to imagine nothing but *water water*. It was easy enough to think that the heaving steel-blue plain stretching beneath them was all there was or ever would be, from here on at least. Well, he'd shut his eyes and try for more sleep.

Sleep took him straight in, no nightmares or frights. And even as early darkness settled round him, hours later, in Halifax—and while he was waiting to learn where he'd roost till U.S. airports opened again—he was still a calm man. By then he'd guessed that the small painting he'd brought from Paris, cushioned in socks and T-shirts in his suitcase, was the cause of his peace; but he couldn't know why. That understanding, and the help it would bring him, was weeks away.

*   *   *

With all the diverted flights, every hotel was filled before his plane touched the runway; so Mabry was seated in the living room of the Wilkins family, who'd offered him a tidy room, before he learned from their television that no private citizens were being allowed anywhere near his part of lower Manhattan. And after a welcome Irish-stew dinner, with healthy lashings of good rye whiskey, his eerily quiet hosts left Mabry alone in the kitchen to try once more to reach his daughter. After six tries he managed to speak with her brusque roommate on the Upper West Side. Yes, Charlotte was safe but at her yoga class.

When Mabry hung up he laughed for the first time since leaving Rome and Paris. Why should a world-class catastrophe disturb Charlotte Kincaid in the higher reaches of mind-bending yoga she'd now attained? He helped himself to another drink from the quart Tim Wilkins had left beside him and tried again to call the numbers of a couple of friends who lived in his building on Rector Street—endless unanswered rings. Then he tried his father; and at last the phone in North Carolina gave its ancient cranky ring. It had been as busy all day as the White House.

Eventually an unexpected woman's voice answered. "Father Kincaid's residence. Who's calling please?" It had only been recently that Southern Episcopal clergymen were addressed as *Father* by their more fervent parishioners, and no one representing his father had ever asked to know who was calling. So when Mabry repeated his full name twice and was still apparently unrecognized, he raised his voice to a civil near-shout. "Just say I'm his son—his last living child. I suspect he still knows me."

The woman thought through that as slowly as if she were testing the claim between her teeth for gold. Then her voice went lower, a sudden and disarmingly beautiful pitch. "Oh good, Mr. Kincaid, he's truly been worried. Next time, call him sooner." The words were slow and oddly accented—an almost surely American black voice but distinctly altered by life abroad or by earnest intent.

For a moment a patch in Mabry's chest warmed to her sound. Even in Italy no woman's voice had sounded that welcoming, but the whiskey made him snag on her orders to call sooner *next time*. Before he could ask what plans the woman might have for further chaos, she set the receiver down. Mabry could hear the trail of her footsteps wandering off and at last the sound of his father's new wheelchair.

There were the usual thirty seconds of fumbling and wheezing; then "Darling Jackass, *where* is your butt?"

The big surprise of the long entirely incredible day came instantly. Tears filled Mabry's eyes. For another half minute, he couldn't speak. Then he said "Oh Pa, I'm almost up in the Arctic—Halifax, Nova Scotia."

The Reverend Tasker Kincaid paused to test the truth of that. Was this truly his son? Was his only near-kin somehow safe in Canada? At last he said "This new TV you so rashly sent me?—it's saying all the flights that weren't hijacked are skewed around badly. You're intact though, boy?" The rust was clearing from the old man's voice. By now he was sounding priestly again. Not the holy-Joe fraudulent timbre so rife in the Christian clergy but an almost trustworthy confident beat. He also sounded more nearly in control of his faculties than he'd been for months.

Mabry had thought that the day's disasters would have shaken his father. He'd stumbled only three weeks ago and broken an ankle; and at best lately, his memory had seemed more fragile by the week. But this voice now was encouraging. So Mabry said "Pa, I'm in full possession of all my limbs and most of my wits, such as they are. A kind family up here has taken me in for as long as I'm grounded—two days at most, they say."

Tasker said "Who is *they*? You're assuming the airports will open, *ever*. I'm assuming worse trouble is barreling toward us than anything we've seen today. These Muslim lads know what they're doing and we plainly don't. They've got *H*-bombs."

Mabry laughed again, now pleasantly weary. "Why is it that a hea-

then like me takes the rosy view while my favorite clergyman fore-
sees the worst?"

"—Because your pa *is* a priest, dear Hotdog. God is famous for
smiting us, hip and thigh, just when we think He's our best friend."

Mabry said "He's holding four aces today, that's for sure. He or
Allah."

"Don't knock Allah. Allah's got our phones tapped—and don't
forget, Allah's just the Arabic name for our God."

There was some consolation in learning that, whatever else the
day had destroyed, his father still held on to monotheism; so Mabry
took another deep draft from his tumbler of rye. He was not a big
drinker under normal conditions, but surely he was past his limit
today, so he tried to steer the talk to saner zones. "The airline says we
may fly out tomorrow. Lord knows, there are ten million things I've
got to check on." He'd been on his first real vacation in years.

Tasker said "Your zillion things can wait forever. Where are the
things these people treasured who perished today? What good did
things do them?" The old man heard himself mounting the pulpit
and he chuckled apologetically. Then he said what he thought was
his most important truth. "You don't have a home, son. Not in
New York. You never did."

For an instant Mabry feared his father might know some awful
fact; and the dim Canadian kitchen around him, with his hostess's
cookie-jar collection, threatened to be a permanent prison.

In Mabry's pause, Tasker gouged his point deeper, though he kept
his tone down. "You've never made a home since you left your
mother. And you know that."

Again, for a moment, it seemed a mere fact. He'd never let his
marriage be a home. Then his anger at his father's endless large-
and-small condemnations rose in his throat. "Listen, Pa, you don't
know that. You've spent as little time with me in the past forty years
as you could possibly spare." That much, anyhow, was true.

And Tasker had the sudden grace to grant it. "It's been years, if ever, since I claimed to be a father. But I also know you've failed your own child, as lately as today."

"Pardon me, Preacher, but how do you know that?"

"I've talked to your daughter—my one grandchild—two or three times today. Talked to her, not ten minutes ago. She's not heard from you."

"You must have her cell-phone number then. I refuse to use it. And she won't respond to calls anyhow from the midst of a perfect yoga position with both heels locked behind her neck."

Once more Tasker laughed and, this time, his chuckle had become more nearly the giggle from the rare times he'd roll on the floor with Mabry and Gabriel (the golden brother who'd died at age eighteen). When Tasker had caught his breath, he took a new tack. "The weather down here is so damned gorgeous you'd barely believe it."

And Mabry saw a splendid Carolina late summer day—he still loved the gripping damp and the blazing light like year-old brass. But he couldn't risk yielding to what reeked suspiciously of one more urge to fly down and visit the Aged Laid-Up Solitary Parent. He launched his own tack. "Reverend Kincaid, sir, who was the damsel that answered your phone? She didn't seem to know you had kinfolk. Have you found some chunky new girlfriend from Poland or an anorexic model from Mazatlán?"

"Audrey—you know her." Tasker clearly believed the claim.

"No, Pa, I don't."

"Don't lie to me. *Audrey*—you grew up with her. Well, very nearly." Tasker's mind was balking on the woman's last name. "She's close kin to us, old Cooter's grandchild."

Mabry said "You mean *Thornton*? Wasn't Cooter a Thornton?" Cooter had been Mabry's grandmother's cook, an antique—but nonetheless rail-straight—figure from near slavery days. She wore a perpetual black cloche hat that made her head look like a cooter shell, the dark safe house of a ground turtle, a terrapin. And she'd only retired, with hard-earned dementia, at ninety-odd years old, when Mabry was maybe five or six. But even with his adult knowledge of the local miscegenation rate, any chance that they were kin to Cooter or her numerous clan was more than unlikely, however intriguing.

Tasker said "Thank you—yes. She's Audrey Dell Thornton."

Mabry said "If she's who I think, she's bound to be Cooter's great-great- or great-granddaughter, Pa. She's something like twenty years younger than me."

But Tasker only said "Not quite." Then he said the full name again, rolling it out like a phrase from the grandest litany in the prayer book—the old prayer book before they made it sound like something Xeroxed on cheap copy paper. And the nicely imposing sound braced the old voice even more strongly. It sounded almost as firm as it had, oh thirty years back—the days when Mabry would call from college and try to ease out a few extra dollars for one more trip to a Vietnam protest in D.C. or Boston or down to Key West for "a spring break of painting." (Tasker might say "Painting what exactly?—frescoes of luscious oases around girls' quivering navels?" And Mabry might say "You sound like you've seen more navels than me." Then Tasker would snort but shake loose a small piece of cash from the little he had.)

If Mabry had ever seen Audrey Thornton, he couldn't remember a face or voice. And what was this about being kin to her? At last report, his father was tended by Nelson Summers, an elderly black man of sumptuous dignity, reliable as any granite hillside. The family had known him since before Mabry's birth. "Where's Nelson tonight?"

Tasker paused till Mabry thought he was gone. "Nelson decided I was too hard on him. Audrey bailed me out. She's sleeping here now. You know all this."

There was no point in another denial, but Mabry had to ask "Can she handle your weight?"

"I beg your pardon?"

With a genuine mildness, Mabry said "Can she lift you onto the john; and what about that deep bathtub?"

"I haven't gained a pound in sixty years."

"I understand that, sir. But Nelson was Goliath. He could heave you over his shoulder and burp you."

Tasker said "I'm glad to hear your Sunday-school facts at least have stayed with you. But Audrey can handle most of my needs. And her son can manage the rest."

"Does the son also live with you now?"

"He comes in at bedtime, just long enough to help me."

There were whole new layers of important information here, but plainly tonight was not the right time to sort them out. Still, Mabry pushed on. "So she's treating you *right*?"

"Adequate, yes. She's an interesting cook." Tasker had always been a man who could easily engulf ten thousand calories any day—on their rare family vacations—and never gain an ounce. Other times, he'd never seemed to care what he ate.

Mabry said "So what did yall eat tonight?" *Yall*, as the second-person plural pronoun, was almost the only vestige of his native tongue that Mabry still clung to, after years in the north.

"She's brought in a five-foot shelf of cookbooks from around the world. We're working our way, by degrees, round the globe."

Since the most exotic foods of Mabry's childhood had come from his mother's inherited copy of *The First Ladies' Table*—say, Dolly Madison's fricasseed chicken with boiled stuffed turnips—this was interesting news: a dining tour through the entire planet, presided over by a woman whose family his own forebears had used like a rag? Mabry said "How on Earth did you find her?"

Tasker said "She found *me*—unless the Holy Ghost called a cab and poured her in it. She heard how Nelson walked out on me; and she turned up, bag and baggage, two minutes before I started howling."

Mabry understood his father's tendency to endless hyperbole. It frequently cast an amusing light on whether or not the Reverend Kincaid believed a word of the lifetime's theology he showered on hapless congregations. But for now, Mabry let the Holy Ghost ride. Another question mattered more. "Have you got that leaking roof fixed yet?" Back in the spring, when Tasker retired from substitute priesthood and—out of the blue—announced he was moving back to the home place alone, a distant cousin phoned Mabry and warned him the roof "poured water like Niagara."

But all Tasker would ever admit when Mabry inquired was what he said now. "Those Mexican boys say they'll fix it tomorrow—or someday soon. I'm mainly dry. I can still dodge water." Then, as if he were dredging an admittedly feeble memory, he found this to ask—"Those strange pains of yours, son: they with you still?"

Mabry could barely recall ever telling his father about the strangeness that had worried him in the past few months, and he knew he hadn't told Charlotte yet, so was this just coincidence or some brand of blood-kin telepathy? Whatever, this man was the only human being left who could rightly call him son; and all the long day's fatigue and horror poured in behind the word. "Pa, they think it may be multiple sclerosis. Wouldn't that be a pisser?"

Tasker took an audible long dry breath. "Oh Jesus, that would be—the whole waterworks. Darling boy, who is they?"

Mabry said "I've seen my personal physician and the two neurologists he recommended. They say it may take another few weeks, or even months, for a final diagnosis." In his father's next pause, Mabry took another slow look around him. This Canadian kitchen, that had just now seemed his prison, might be a place he'd beg to stay in forever. Nobody here could revel in his plight—no one he'd hurt or cheated on. He could stay here and slowly freeze in each joint, and no one would feel either pity or blame.

Tasker said "You better come down here, to Duke or Chapel Hill, and get more opinions. They're both hospitals with world-class care. Or so I read."

"I've thought of that—thanks. But I've got so much to do in the city right now; and if it's M.S., it's incurable anyhow."

Then Tasker said the most surprising thing of all. "You in need of any cash?"

Mabry knew his father had precious little cash—a minuscule pension, the pitiful savings from more than a decade of fill-in services at pastorless churches, plus Social Security. In fact he even returned the occasional check Mabry tried to send, or he mentioned the charity to which they'd been forwarded. Was he sliding back now to those college-boy days, thinking his feckless son was broke? Anyhow, Mabry said "A world of thanks, sir. I'll tell you when I am."

Tasker said "I can sell what I've got. This house is a treasure."

Gently, Mabry said "Oh stop." The place was a hundred and twenty-odd years old, a likable one-story late Victorian but hardly a treasure to anyone who hadn't been born or reared there (and several of them had fled it like the cholera). When Tasker didn't speak, Mabry had to say "All I'm concerned for, here and now, is that you get the care you need and can handle in that no-doubt-lovable but rickety building."

A silence spread down both ends of the call till Tasker broke it. "You'll be the first to know, boy, when they find my cold corpse." Then without another word, the old voice burst into the finest laughter Mabry knew.

It had been so long since he actually heard it that the boy—a man fifty-three years old—sat a long minute more, better than calm at the end of this nightmare, and longed to see the father who'd deviled his mind from the age of six onward: a thoughtful good man, still propped more or less upright on various items of a faith (that Mabry couldn't share) and never relenting in the drive to save this helpless son, this child who was all Tasker Kincaid had to leave to a world of

demons, cutthroats, and simpletons, ready to kill in the name of
God.

When the Wilkinses came to the kitchen to see if Mabry had further
needs before bedtime, he thanked them and said that—with their
permission—he might sit up awhile longer. He was hopelessly jet-
lagged. Kind as they'd been throughout the day, it had got embar-
rassing by now—the extent to which they'd begun receding into the
carpet, yielding their home (like so many kind locals in the crisis) to
this tall American as if he owned it and they were only the overnight
gypsies. And here they were, as early as ten o'clock, turning in like
two aging sitters of a giant distressed baby they couldn't outlast.

Mabry was on the verge of saying "Look here, I can try the yellow
pages one more time for a motel room." But Agnes Wilkins was in
the act of setting beside him a plate of cheese biscuits so rich they
were already oiling the lacey doily beneath them.

So, touched, Mabry thanked them with a quasi-formal bow.
Then for another silent hour, he sat back down and wrote thank-you
letters to friends in Rome—two museum conservators of staggering
skill, who always shared their knowledge with him as open-handedly
as desert saints, and an even more dazzlingly gifted forger of Greek
and Etruscan marbles and bronzes (an art that Mabry genuinely
envied but had never quite attempted). Old as he was, those three
colleagues still taught Mabry more on each short visit than all his
American teachers had managed in the three decades of work
behind him.

When he sealed the letters, he opened Tim Wilkins's rye again,
then paused to consult the health of his brain and his actual vision.
Though he drank so seldom, he'd inherited Tasker's cast-iron head
for spirits; so he poured another shot. Then he took his journal and
began to bring it up to date. At half past eleven, he'd almost finished
describing the telephone talk with his father when his hand quit on
him. As surely as if a crucial motor nerve had severed, the fingers of

his right hand wouldn't make more words to describe Tasker's prankish good sense or to sketch the outlines of what seemed a promising mystery—Audrey Thornton, the new strong woman in the family. Surely it was understandable fatigue. But he looked beyond him to the wall to check his eyes. He could read the text of the stitched motto on the yellowing sampler—*You Are The Cause Of Everything*. His eyes were working then. But, Lord, was this the chosen message of some long-dead Presbyterian maiden with too much needlework time on her hands? He noticed that both his feet had started the awful tingle that would only increase till he slept.

At last the right hand moved on its own, so he turned to his journal; and instead of describing the end of his conversation with Tasker, his hand wrote quickly what (for whatever reason) demanded recording—in a compact italic script with exaggerated care for spacing and straightness—*An Inventory of Loss and Failure*. Then it made the list.

> —*Frances Kenyon Kincaid dies, medulloblastoma*
> —*Mabry K. commences neuro weirdness*
> —*MK likely to inherit disastrous funds from FKK*
> —*MK rejects Tasker K*
> —*Charlotte K likely to reject MK*
> —*New York assaulted by Allah*
> —*MK's loft rightly stove-in*

The hand paused there, then returned to the list and made the child's symbol for rays of light around two words—straight lines emitted by the words *disastrous* and *rightly*. Only then did Mabry's sense of control begin to return. He laughed a little. Now the words were like something in one of his junior-high-school notebooks—*love* or *peace* with garlands and flowers and kissing doves. Still he wondered what the rays meant. Were they only, at the end of this hard day, a switch-back to the corny codes of his boyhood?

Before he could think, a whisper spooked him. "Mr. Kincaid, may I bother you?"

It was Leah Wilkins, the daughter of the house, sixteen years old and even better looking now than she'd been at dinner. She was in a dark burgundy bathrobe, holding a hushing finger to her lips. But her straight ash-blond hair and the pale blue eyes were no bother at all.

Mabry whispered "By all means" and cleared a space for her.

She went to the refrigerator first, found a Coke, and asked what Mabry wanted.

He flourished his glass of rye.

And Leah frowned before she managed to suppress her regret at one more imbibing adult. Then she silently refused the space he'd cleared. She stood in the midst of the room, a good ten feet from the overnight American. "I'm desperate to *sleep*. See, I've got an exam tomorrow at school. But after all this tragic stuff today, I'm wide awake."

No doubt he'd heard the word *tragic* fifty times since leaving his room in Paris before dawn. Coming from this lovely child, though, it had the instant weight of a verdict without appeal. He'd weigh it further once she left the room. For now he said "And the caffeine in that Coke will guarantee you're wide awake till your teacher hands out the dreaded exam. Then you'll plop right over." He let his head fall forward on the table, then felt as silly as he no doubt looked. So when Leah still resisted a chair, he lured her gently. "What's the exam? Maybe I can help."

Quickly her face assumed the solemn gravity that haunts the border between late childhood and what it hears from the land ahead—the high notes of hope for the long onward life and the harsher chords that promise sure failure. Then she nodded, almost fiercely. "You could *absolutely* save my neck! It's in studio art—you remember I mentioned art was my thing. Tomorrow we have to draw a brilliant still life in an hour-long class."

Had she mentioned art? Mabry anyhow said he remembered and got to his feet. "You sit down here. I can show you something right down your line, for better or worse." His bedroom opened off the far kitchen wall. He ducked in there and came right back with the package that had maybe fueled his peace all day.

By the time he returned, Leah had sat and laid both hands—palm down—on the table. When Mabry stood in his former place to open the package, she actually whispered "If we don't make a lot less noise, the two of us'll be pitched out in the night. Beyond a certain point, my dad's a major dragon."

Mabry said "He trusts me, darling—he gave me this entire bottle of whiskey." Before it had fully sounded in the room, he knew the *darling* was likely wrong, this far north anyhow. And it did strike a definite silence around them. Within three seconds they'd both gone quieter than Leah could have hoped as Mabry peeled off layers of paper and tissue from the mystery object. At last he held the canvas in its heavy frame, maybe eighteen by twenty. He'd never seen it till now and had heard very little about it from his client, who was maybe dead—almost surely, if he'd gone to work as early as usual this morning.

Nothing to do now but hold the picture at arm's length before him, with Leah to his right. Its age was immediately clear to see, especially at the top and sides where a wide matting liner invaded the image. Especially there the linen itself was almost uniformly discolored and splotched. Mabry stared for so long that Leah finally stood again, came round and looked with him. A good deal of surface was almost the color of bitter chocolate, and Mabry's fingers were stroking the surface, uneven as a child's flour-and-water relief map of a country with low hills and crooked valleys, all exposed to floods and lava flows.

At last Leah said "*Is* it a picture?"

He said "It's meant to be a picture of the château at Auvers near Paris. Or so we were told. But sorry, I'm afraid it's no art lesson. My client *heard* it was a picture, a charming one at that." Mabry sat and went on feeling the canvas, even sniffing it in spots.

Leah was standing behind him now. "You work for a museum?"

"Not regularly, no. I'm a private conservator—the gent you hire, if you're rich enough to have a collection of your own or are in a hot rush to get your great-grandmother's awful portrait cleaned before your pregnant daughter's wedding, just to show off your few blameless ancestors to the reception guests."

By then Leah was closing the door between the kitchen and the rest of the house.

Mabry said a quick "Don't—" but his hand had just found an envelope tucked between the canvas and the frame on the underside. It was the size that mostly accompanies gifts of flowers, big baskets of roses. He couldn't suppress a conspiratorial "Ah-ha!" and that brought Leah back to her seat.

With the same slow care which had marked his inventory of loss and failure, Mabry opened the envelope and drew out a stiff card folded once on itself. It was crowded, both sides, with a message in a tiny script so eccentric it might have been beamed down from deep outer space. For whatever reason, he leaned back and looked toward the ceiling with shut eyes.

So Leah slipped the card from his fingers and whispered "May I?" When Mabry nodded, she read out softly but with perfect eyes—

"This small treasure was painted by a twelve-year-old American, a native of Charleston, South Carolina, with M. Vincent van Gogh beside him on the evening of 27 July 1890. The picture shows the château on the edge of Auvers-sur-Oise. In the field behind the mansion, M. Vincent suffered by his own hand while the boy, unaware, continued this image which sadness prevented his ever completing. The boy's name was Philip Adger, who—at the age of seventy-two, and sixty years after M. Vincent's necessary death— signs his name. What he says is the plain truth, though precious.

Philip Adger, 29 July 1950."

When Leah finished, Mabry was still facing upward, his eyes still shut. Now he suddenly rocked his chair back down, looked to the girl and almost whispered "Surely you just invented that."

As suddenly, her sense of insult flared; and her eyes and cheeks went ten degrees hotter. "I *didn't*. It's all right here in plain English." She held the card toward him, absolute proof.

The ring on her forefinger caught the overhead light, and the sight of it hooked in Mabry's heart with more pain than anything earlier today. *Why?* Then the answer all but floored him. He'd given Frances, his now-dead wife, a literally identical ring the first evening they spent together—an inexpensive replica of a ring the Queen of England had worn at her coronation in 1952. He'd found it at a flea market in Key West two days after meeting Frances there, and he'd bargained the dealer down from twenty dollars to a little over ten. That evening, Frances joined him as promised for the sunset on Mallory Pier; and as the surrounding hippies burst into applause for the sinking sun, Mabry reached for her hand and found that the ring would only fit her right forefinger—her hands were that small from the start. Too small, he might have guessed, for the several huge handfuls he'd prove to be in the years before his repeated sad cheating forced her to ask him to set her free.

He wouldn't tell Leah that story now. It might do him in. So he smiled and took the card from her. When he'd studied it a moment, he said "Wonder why he wrote this in English, after sixty years in France? Who did he think could ever read it?"

Leah's curiosity was calming her. "God, Mr. Kincaid, what *is* this?"

Mabry said "I didn't know we had that note. But it more or less describes what my client thought he was buying—for a song, not more than five hundred dollars."

"Who's your client?"

"His name's a little funny—Baxter P. Sample, Esquire. I should likely say *was*, unless he slept later than usual this morning."

Leah said, with a child's indifferent candor, "Did he die today?"

Mabry held out his hand for the envelope; and Leah returned it, almost reluctantly. Only then, somehow, could he answer her question. "Baxter had his office in the World Trade Center. I honestly don't know which Tower. The second plane hit just after nine, and the first Tower fell just after ten. Unless he answers his home phone in the next few days, I'll have to wait for a list of the missing. To the best of my knowledge, he had no family. And he made no bones about being a gay man who didn't need a partner and whose parents were dead. I'm almost sure he was an only child too. He seemed to crave loneliness, in his after hours—just him and his pictures and a few absolutely first-class Greek marbles and vases, madly pornographic vases!"

Luckily, the girl ignored his *pornographic*. She said "Oh *no*, it'll take days, won't it?—just finding all the bodies?"

Mabry nodded, suddenly sadder than he thought he'd be for a man he'd found even more reptilian than the average lawyer—a reptile, though, who paid his bills almost before you sent them. "They won't find many bodies. That many thousand gallons of jet fuel has cremated almost everybody who didn't start running at the first explosion. And Leah, what started today won't end before you die of old age." When he looked up at her, he saw how hard his last sentence struck her—like a hand on her teeth. He took a new tack. "So far I've restored Mr. Sample's smashed ceramic Tang horse. I only just mounted his very nice Rembrandt drawing of a boat on a river. And I cleaned his small Degas head of a baby boy—you hardly think of Degas and babies, much less baby *boys*. He heard I was spending some recent time in Rome and hired me to loop through Paris just yesterday and pick this up from a small hotel he discovered on his last trip."

Leah looked at Philip Adger's picture again. "Mr. Sample paid good money for this? Then he's truly loaded."

Every assaulted nerve down the length of both Mabry's legs was roaring now; and for the first time, he was fully convinced. *Baxter Sample is gone.*

But the canvas held Leah more closely than further news about lawyers. She followed Mabry's lead and felt the surface gently, intent as any blind girl in serious need of instruction. At last she looked up and said "Is there much of a picture under all this—fudge?"

Mabry smiled. "Or peanut butter. But do they make either one in France? If Mr. Sample's alive, he'll have to see it before I decide on how to proceed. Between you and me, now that I see this, I'm not at all sure he'll want to fork out my standard fee for a clean-and-varnish job. If it were mine, I doubt I would. I might just hang it somewhere in a half-dim corner of the kitchen and call it a dubious relic of a bibulous visit to a Left Bank hotel."

Leah said "So you don't believe an American boy painted this while poor Mr. Van Gogh shot himself?" Plainly she knew a little, at least, about the event.

Mabry registered that but pushed to tell her more. "It's sometimes one of my jobs to be a stubborn doubter, when a client thinks he's found a cheap treasure that's just a cheap fake (and I've bought the occasional fake myself when it proved truly fine—I've got a fake Renoir that beats a third of the genuine Renoirs I've ever cleaned; and I've cleaned fifty thousand, or so it feels sometimes when I'm brought another adorable Renoir girl in Easter finery). All I know about Philip Adger at present—and I just read a new life of Van Gogh—is that Auvers did indeed sport a number of resident American would-be painters at the time of Vincent's death. The old woman who runs the hotel told Mr. Sample that her long-dead father-in-law was the boy himself and that he'd kept the picture behind the hotel desk till his death some forty years ago. Then her own husband took it down and stored it in the cellar. Late one night, while Mr. Sample was staying there—he always stayed in little dark hotels where he tended to run across interesting souls or so he claimed—he and the woman somehow began to talk about Impressionist painters, and she told him the story of her father-in-law's contact with Vincent. As a boy, young Philip had gone with his wealthy parents from steamy Charleston to cool Auvers, precisely to paint—the whole family were amateur painters, and the father was even more ambitious than the rest. None of them had the slightest knowledge of who Monsieur Vincent Van Gogh was or where he lived—I mean, *nobody* knew him, not even in France. You know he was Dutch; he'd never sold a painting and barely would, not while he drew breath. Anyhow Baxter Sample offered to buy this picture, sight unseen once he heard the story, and he gave the woman his trusting personal check on the spot. She told him she'd have to hunt it down but would ship it right away. It didn't arrive for several months, which is when he asked me to turn up and claim it on my way home from Italy. I think he'd begun to suspect she meant to abscond with his funds and keep the picture. I met her all right. She's the kind of monstrous crone of a sort Paris specializes in. I stood her down, though; and she coughed up the picture. But as you say, it's hardly a picture."

Leah had already found a roll of masking tape and was setting the canvas back into its wrappings.

Mabry stopped her for one more look at the painter's card. "Philip Adger—" He said it in French first—*Ad-jay*—then in English, *Adger* to rhyme with *badger*. "It's a Charleston name all right. I knew an Adger from Charleston in college, and I know his father was rich as Croesus; but they couldn't have painted a basement door, much less a landscape."

By then the parcel was wrapped again. Leah was standing across the table, facing Mabry with a combination of a wary child's *What next?* and a young woman's frank readiness for whatever came.

Mabry went so far—she was that lovely now—as to list in silence the dangers involved in reaching toward her. The table was narrow. Even without her reaching toward him, he could brush at least the back of her hand. But how could he stop that process if his interest was shared? He was not a firm believer (nor a full-fledged doubter); but he actually spoke his relief out loud—"No, thank God."

And Leah seemed partly to understand. Whether she'd offered him a single thing more, she nodded and looked to the watch on her arm. "Oh crumbs, it's two o'clock!" In another three seconds, she'd opened the kitchen door to leave. At the final moment, she turned, faced him once more; and when he only waved, she blew him a kiss that likely meant no more than the XXs and OOs at the ends of school valentines.

Yet, as she left, Mabry felt he'd made one more of the billion mistakes of his life—the stingy denials he'd learned to make in a Protestant minister's household fifty years ago. *Granted, I'm a year or two older than her father, but more than a few girls wouldn't turn down a kindly cuddle with a substitute dad who'd promise to vanish in a day or two. Oh, go to bed, Mabry—your own safe bed, you sleazy bugger. You're a fifty-three-year-old piece of damaged goods that the worst raddled whore wouldn't stretch out for, much less this pure girl (maybe not pure as the driven snow; but when was the driven snow pure, here lately, traffic and pollution being what it is?). She could almost be your grandchild anyhow; and here you're baying at her as if she were a harvest moon—and all at the end of a day when your country had its throat cut, right through to the spine.*

At least he was all but exhausted now, and going through the minimal rites of preparation for sleep had sandbagged him further. But once he'd finally switched off the pink-beribboned bedside lamp at 2:38, Mabry wasn't too tired to feel what he'd felt at the end of his conversation with Tasker—an actual longing to see the old man and a sudden chill of fright that his father might die before Mabry reached him and said whatever he might find to say. *Is there one last single thing that needs saying?* As best he could, that near sunrise this far toward the Arctic, Mabry racked his brain. Nothing volunteered as remotely urgent—*Which truly means nothing in a mind as wild as mine is now.* Then, even on his thin hard Nova Scotian pillow, he was gone in a perfectly harmless dream—not murderous Muslims, not even a pit bull dog as unpredictable as his nearest neighbor's (a bull named Rodney).

TWO

9 · 13 · 2001
9 · 14 · 2001

As he turned his rented van over the tracks, Mabry waited for the comforting lift and thump of iron rails beneath him. But he crossed as smoothly as a rowboat on a pond. *Damn, these new cars have got plush shock absorbers!* When he slowed and looked back through the mirror, he reminded himself. Maybe five years ago the railroad had come through and torn up the tracks from here to Raleigh, more than sixty miles. They could ship the old iron to Japan for scrap and let these little railroad towns die.

As he moved on forward, the Methodist church was there in place, with the tacky steeple his cousin had donated thirty years ago. It sat on the honest squat brick building like a well-earned dunce cap, but any one of the three new houses in the grove of oaks that stretched past the church — the site of his play in a childhood happier than he tended to recall — would make a feasible vacation house for occasional visits to the scenes of his youth. A hundred yards more, though; and Mabry braced himself for his goal.

He hadn't seen the homeplace in nearly three years; and he'd heard sad reports of neglect and rot and the depredations of migrant workers, here for a season of tobacco or pulpwood, renting the old place and mailing their savings back to families in Mexico or Guatemala. As he pulled into the drive, though, the first impression was better than he'd feared. The tin roof had rusted in broad streaks, some palings were gone from the long porch rail, and the porch floor seemed to be rotting in spots. Still, as he stopped, the low rambling house felt like the only home he'd known, despite the fact that—even since leaving his father's various parish housing as he headed toward college—he'd lived in at least a dozen rented slots. Well, his father had more than hinted at that deep rootedness, two nights ago.

And in fact this was home. Though Mabry was born in a bright bedroom in the far west wing, and though his father brought the family here for the rare times he could leave his parishes, the only substantial stretches Mabry had spent in the house were a visit approaching two months each summer with Tasker's mother, whom the boy loved without reservation—from maybe age five till the jaws of puberty closed around him, hauling him off to the fleshpots of Raleigh or Nags Head or Myrtle Beach. What made it home was a small set of things, most of them people—in addition to his Kincaid grandmother, there were always the black men and women who'd made it possible for her to live, and a small clutch of neighbors. The other vast component was solitude—aloneness and silence in the green fragrant depths that lay not more than five hundred yards in any direction from the bed he was born in: growths of oak and pine, hickory and sycamore, endless yards of honeysuckle and thickets of cow itch and poison ivy that often gripped the finest trees in vines as thick as a growing boy's wrist. Mabry wondered, as he sat now, *What child in ten million has such gifts today? Silence and lone time—ultimate blessings on Earth at least.* For all his real errors, the ones that had left lasting hurt on his family, it was still the time in solitude here that had taught him whatever good he'd known and done.

Then he killed the engine and waited another slow moment as the late sun crept through the window and bathed his face and arms, a private welcome. He could sit here till dark, easily, letting the jangles of a day in the air between Nova Scotia, Baltimore, and Raleigh-Durham bake away before he tackled the Reverend Kincaid, guns loaded (doubtless) and in a new wheelchair with an otherwise unknown woman at his side. Mabry took his new Italian eyeshades and looked through the thirty yards toward the front door.

There in what looked like dark bell-bottom trousers and a man's white dress shirt, with the tail hung out, stood a tall woman with skin the color of mocha ice cream and a long plait of black hair over one shoulder. She was holding a broom upright like a battle tool; and her big eyes were drilling the space between them with no apparent effort—the face was neutral, not smiling or frowning. Would the broom convert, with ease, into a shotgun or sprout with early fall red roses or four-inch thorns? Mabry tried to laugh but, when he reached to open his door, for the first time ever he felt uneasy to touch this ground. Some weird but unmistakable signal from the base of his brain seemed to say the ground wasn't *there* or that he wouldn't feel it if his foot went out. But when he put his whole weight on it—yes it was there, simple earth. *Thank God.*

As he walked toward the porch, the woman came forward a slow two paces. Then she held her own. Within five seconds she looked like a handsome natural object somehow grown by the boards she stood on—that natural, in place, guaranteed to last. And by now her face had turned against him.

When Mabry reached the white river rocks that paved a landing at the foot of the steps—the rocks that Mabry and his brother had brought here one Labor Day forty years ago—he felt a shock of the energy generated by this woman's frown. Maybe a good fight could start here and now and clear the air. It was maybe what he needed, after all the suspensions and doubts of these recent days. He climbed the four steps, moved carefully over the few rotten porch planks and got to within almost an arm's reach of the woman before he stopped. "Miss Thornton?"

"Ms. Thornton, yes." The face was a sturdy blend of the watchful strength of the local African genes and the local English/Scottish/Welsh with their forthright guile. The eyes were the killer.

All his life, Mabry had heard of golden eyes. This woman's eyes were a shade of old gold. Or numerous shades. The irises were larger than any he recalled; and from where he stood, the gold was edged with strokes of brown and what he thought were dots of an emerald green—he was that close to her. She held her place so he took a step back.

The eyes were searching his entire body like an almost comically avid squad of the new police who were already gathering to frisk the country fiercely in the wake of its alien devastation.

Mabry tried to smile but couldn't. He said "You don't seem to know me, do you?"

"That's correct, sir. Have you got some business here?" She lowered the broom that had been upright.

It was the voice that had seemed so strange on the phone two nights ago. And coming from this blended face, even the few tense words seemed familiar, though more carefully schooled than nine-tenths of the whole population. But when her eyes hadn't begun to relent, he finally said "I'm Reverend Kincaid's only son, his only living child. Ms. Thornton, I'm Mabry." He held out his right hand.

She was in no hurry to take it, if ever. She studied it, though, through the distance between them. She might have been reading his creases and folds and finding only *lies lies lies*.

Mabry had never touched a woman with the least thought of violence, but now he quickly assessed this woman's standing position. She was only two inches shorter than he; but no question, she was lean as a finely polished gun-stock. Very likely her strength was an honest match for his, give or take a little gouging—especially with all his recent weirdness in body and mind. And she clearly saw herself as a paid security guard for the place and the wheelchaired man behind her indoors. Yet she had no pockets in her trousers. She couldn't be packing any serious weapons. Mabry wondered *Am I game for a few seconds' tangling?* But then he shook himself. *You're a full-grown white man, with a master's degree in art conservation; and here you're planning to tackle an impressive young black woman? You're exhausted, boy, and more than half crazy—this woman didn't even know you were coming.*

Still, this was his homeplace as much as his father's. Audrey knew who he was; he'd claim his own rights. So he slowly walked past her, and she didn't reach to stop him. He opened the screen door and stepped up the one step into Tasker's dim front hall. Despite all the years, and the mixed lot of tenants in the recent past, the smells in the air were still familiar and surprisingly welcome—a likable bookish mustiness, the light-colored smells of flour and meal, maybe buttermilk and okra. But when he heard nothing, and when the woman didn't come in behind him, he called out "Pa?"

No answer at all.

Once his eyes had opened to the indoor dark, Mabry slowly walked toward the back of the house. The hall was nearly thirty feet long, and the pictures on either side were windows into Mabry's childhood. He'd often thought that his early plan to be a painter and, failing that, a patient caretaker of damaged old pictures had dawned in the presence of these few almost-amateur paintings—the five-foot lady-angel with her single impossibly long-stemmed lily offered to someone outside the frame, the inexplicably cross-eyed buck elk posed with would-be menace in a deep snowdrift at sunset, the piney branch with a cluster of cones and the state's official toast—

> Here's to the land of the long leaf pine,
> The summer land where the sun doth shine,
> Where the weak grow strong and strong grow great,
> Here's to "Down Home," the Old North State!

Then came the wide span of family photographs that stretched back at least to the Civil War and paused with the beautiful face of his brother Gabe and the mother whom Mabry still bitterly missed every day of his life. The Latino tenants had been kind to the pictures. *Aren't country people always?*

Then he was at the open door of what used to be the kitchen. When he entered, it still seemed to be a working kitchen. And the air here was brighter, though no lights were on. Only now did the fullness of the fact press on him—*This may not work out the way I planned*. He hadn't phoned his father to say he'd made this last-minute choice to fly here today instead of New York. After the one conversation with Tasker, Mabry had thought he'd check on the local situation and give Manhattan time to sort out at least a few strands of its present confusion before he faced whatever had happened to his studio (it was also where he'd lived and slept for the past four years).

But oddly the thought of its total destruction—*total* seemed unlikely—didn't hurt as much as he might have expected. On the contrary, when he'd paused to consider how he'd feel if he got reliable word that his entire building was ruined past salvage, he might feel remarkably younger and lighter. That was part of why he was standing here in Wells today. If anything remained of his loft—a few good sticks of furniture, a dozen or more admirable pictures, a life-size Roman copy of a Greek torso of the Venus Anadyomene (which he was still trying to believe was genuine but which a smart friend claimed had been made in Naples by yet another friend twenty years ago)—if any of that was still intact, he could give it to his daughter with the greatest ease. Tasker at least would applaud the gesture as conforming to the will of God, while others (even Charlotte) might see it as one more expensive show-off—an imitation Buddhist event.

Again he said "Pa?" No answer. Well, if Tasker was alive and in this house, he'd hardly be angry to be surprised by his one close kinsman. Hadn't the Reverend Tasker Kincaid long since earned an old-aged calm from a lifetime's duty in sanctuaries where dead-drunk vestrymen keeled over at the altar rail, strewing whole plates of communion wafers, and buck-naked choir ladies occasionally lurked in the organ pipes to lure a beloved clergyman aside for a frantic merger? So this time Mabry raised his voice distinctly, broadcasting each syllable as if it were an urgent seed to feed starving children. "Reverend Kincaid, urgent help is required." It was not an entirely untrue announcement.

And in fact it worked. From closer by than Mabry expected, the most memorable voice in a lifetime of voices said "*Pitiful* Hotdog, how did you get here in this week of woes? God bless your sinful hide." Then the usual chuckle.

It seemed to come from the newest bedroom in the house, the one Uncle Buddy had built ninety years ago when his young wife died. Bereft, Bud meant to move in with his niece, Mabry's grandmother; but when he was told the awful truth—that there were truly no available beds in the packed house—he turned up the next day with two black men. And in under three weeks they built him a sizable room with numerous doors and windows (Bud was claustrophobic and required as many fire escapes as the laws of stable architecture could permit).

Mabry walked past the kitchen table to the door that opened on the bedroom. Compared to what he'd seen of other rooms, passing through the hall, the atmosphere here felt habitable. The walls were unstreaked by rain or age, the old tan rug was mainly intact, Uncle Bud's engravings of scenes from the tales of Thackeray and Bulwer-Lytton were in their places trapped behind wavy glass. There were—Mabry counted—six windows that ran from floor to ceiling. No curtains or shades, so the evening light fell mercifully in. Bud's old iron double bed, still painted white, was made up to strict hospital standards. But Mabry looked all around and saw no trace of any live human. He turned to face the kitchen again. "*Sir?*"

At last Tasker said "You're way too old to call me *sir*." He was tucked in the farthest corner in his wheelchair—a clean pale-blue shirt, open at the neck (a major concession to slacker fashion), and dark gray trousers. He was almost smiling, a far better sight than even his only child had expected.

Mabry went straight toward him and dropped to his haunches to be at eye level.

Tasker reached for his son's neck—the too-long hair—and pulled him inward. For a long time, he rocked his chin in the crown of Mabry's head. Then not releasing him, Tasker said "Which one of us now is the Prodigal Son?"

It puzzled Mabry. He knew the famous parable, and he'd more than once thought of himself as the son who ran out on his father and surrendered himself to riotous living. But Tasker had never been remotely riotous, except in his wit. So what was his father's uncertainty now? When Tasker's grip slackened, Mabry leaned back and said "*Prodigal*'s hardly the word for you, Pastor."

Tasker said "Did you know *pastor* means *shepherd* in Greek?"

"I think you've mentioned that before, a few thousand times."

Tasker smiled. "Does that make you a sheep?"

Mabry said "A lamb anyhow—a tough old bunged-up lamb but still learning."

Tasker laughed. "I very much hope you are. A few times you've tried to impersonate a ram. I've heard that rumor anyhow. Am I badly wrong?"

Mabry ignored the ram joke (too true to discuss) and pushed ahead on the prodigal line. "How have you turned prodigal, Pa?"

Tasker took his time, deciding whether to answer. Then he pointed behind him toward the kitchen and grinned his patented grin, the live equivalent of sunrise over Bryce Canyon or Yosemite. And then he whispered "Audrey was sleeping in your old room, but we had a deluge while you were in Rome, and she woke up soaked— the roof sprang a leak. So I urged her to move her bed closer by. She sleeps in the kitchen now, in sound of my voice. I really needed that. See, once you lay me down at night, with this broken ankle, I'm like an upended turtle on the Interstate—" He paused as if for some subtle effect, then grinned again.

Mabry was still hunkered down by the wheelchair. He hadn't noticed a cot in the kitchen, but now he was actually testing his brain. *Is this as peculiar as it sounds? Can the old fellow mean what I think he means?* Mabry's mother had died twelve years ago, ending an apparently ideal marriage. Tasker had never so much as hinted at subsequent rumpy-pumpy with the church ladies, however fervently devoted to his welfare several had been.

And Tasker was among the few Protestant ministers in the whole upper South, not to mention the Deep, who'd steadily spoken from the pulpit against racial injustice. He'd lost two churches—and been forced to move his family—for that indubitable brand of Christianity. Surely now he hadn't somehow persuaded this woman to join him after dark. But what else could these recharged grins begin to suggest?

Mabry leaned forward again, took his father's earlobe, and asked a question that was maybe forty percent serious. "Who's the president of the United States—today, right now?" He knew that was often the first question asked in emergency rooms to test a patient's sanity.

Tasker plainly knew the same. But with a suddenly blank face, he said "Grover Cleveland, praise the Lord."

Mabry said "I voted for him too and proud to have done so, even if he did have a bastard child." Before any more could pass between them, both men heard ice rumbling in the kitchen. Mabry stood and took a minute to look round the room again. At his first look, he'd failed to check for any signs of Audrey in the room. And now he saw nothing, not till his father noticed him checking and pointed toward the mantel.

There, on the dark honey-colored heart pine, were two photographs, maybe six by eight, in dimestore brass frames—two teenage boys who were clearly kin to Audrey, one maybe three years older than the other. Despite the fact that they were plainly school pictures, in the saturated colors of mass-produced photos, Mabry could see that their skin matched hers for color and grain; and their eyes were an even brighter gold. The younger boy's picture had a small Christmas sticker in the lower right corner, a thorny rose with a deep crimson bloom, all but funeral-black. The only thing that might have made him wonder about the boys' genes were their outright smiles. They were both grinning, broad and easy, with heads tilted slightly back. But he'd yet to see Audrey part her lips except in the taut words she'd said on the porch.

And between the two pictures was the only object which Mabry recalled as belonging to his father, the crucifix Tasker had bought on his college trip to Palestine in 1938. It was maybe nine inches tall, pale olive wood with the body of Christ in handcarved ivory. No other corpus known to Mabry in all his studies of Western art, even the terrible Grünewald Christ, could compare with what this anonymous carver had made to clarify the plain fact that a human body can be forced to suffer almost to the limits of imagination—almost but not quite. This six-inch-tall man, pegged to real wood, was being asked—through the past sixty-three years at least (and counting)—to bear an agony to end all agonies.

Then behind Mabry, a fine voice spoke. "Mr. Kincaid, will you be dining with your father?"

Dining was not quite what Mabry had in mind. But he turned toward the woman's voice; and before he could say so again, his father said "Audrey, this man is my beloved son."

Mabry registered the word *beloved* with some surprise, so he didn't offer his hand again, but Audrey came forward offering hers.

He took it then gladly—a warm dry palm and the faint smell of maybe rosemary (could it be?). Whatever, she was plainly at home in this room, this pleasant air. Otherwise, why are her sons' pictures in here?

Tasker said "Of course he's eating here. He's staying here too, as long as I can hold him. Where can we bunk him though? We got a dry bed?"

Mabry suddenly thought to say "Oh Pa, I'll bunk at the Creech Motel. I can see things here are in fairly bad shape."

Audrey smiled for the first time, the same broad spread that her two sons showed in the pictures behind her. The smile partly sweetened what she chose to say next. "*Bad shape?* Mr. Kincaid, you ever see my grandmother Cooter's house in the years she worked here?"

Tasker's voice went into a tender pitch that Mabry could hardly remember hearing. "That's ancient news. That's behind you, Audrey."

And Audrey took it, for now at least. Her eyes shut, hard.

Mabry thought *I very much doubt she's flushing that away.* But he said "Yes ma'm. I recall Cooter's house vividly. No hyena should have had to live there."

So she faced him. Remnants of her smile were still in place, and she said "I'll fix you a private room. The mattress is old but you know that—you were born on it, weren't you?"

Surely she was too young to know such a fact. "I was," Mabry said, "but how did you know?"

"Old Cooter," she said.

Mabry said "You can't have known Cooter, young as you are."

But by then she'd turned to face Tasker; and all she said was "Supper at the regular time, Father?"

Tasker asked Mabry "How starved are you, son?"

Mabry said "Those airline snacks are thinning out."

Audrey said "It's four-thirty now. Is six still OK?"

Her jaunty OK seemed to trigger a glitch in Mabry's vision (in Mabry's boyhood the word OK was frowned on by his father). So he saw two images of Audrey, both clearer than a moment before, though slightly overlapping. He waited to study the lines of her face.

So Tasker said "Son, is six too early for a metropolitan like you?"

Mabry came back to normal. "Oh no, Pa. Please. Any time's

good with me." He looked to Aubrey again and said "Ms. Thornton, I hope you'll be joining us. I'd like to know you."

Her chin tucked down in a firm assertion of her prior place here. "I plan to, Mr. Kincaid. Your father wants me."

As she moved out of sight, Tasker cleared his throat theatrically. When Mabry looked toward him, he gave a blank wink.

Mabry couldn't read it. Or wouldn't let himself. If, again, it meant to loop him into some collusive knowledge of hijinks between this aged priest and a young black woman, with ties to this family's ancient error, then Mabry wouldn't bow to the loop. He said "Is there anything I can do for you, Pa, before I find this room Ms. Thornton is setting up for me?"

Tasker spread both hands before him in the air, as though he'd levitate in a moment. But he stayed in place, gaining power by the instant in his son's needy eyes. And the hands did beckon to Mabry once. Yet before Mabry could choose to go toward them, they slipped back down to the arms of the wheelchair. Tasker had only meant, again, to bless his first child. But that could wait till bedtime or, no doubt, morning when Mabry might leave him, likely forever. As his son left though, Tasker tried to whisper—whispering was almost impossible now for a long-term priest—"You smell mighty sweet. Nothing wrong with you. You're not a sick man. I can see that from here."

Mabry wanted to believe him; so he said "Thank you, sir. I wish you were a doctor."

Tasker said "I'm better than a doctor."

They left it at that.

For now, while Audrey was making the bed, which he'd helped her move from under the leak, Mabry went to the front hall and dialed a New York number. It was neither his daughter's nor Baxter Sample's nor the friend's who lived above him on Rector Street but the number that—if it was working again—would instruct him to punch in a short set of codes. Then it would tell him, in canned tones, his current savings balance. He'd tried it last night from Nova Scotia but got the same automaton's voice, saying "By tomorrow we hope to be up and running. Please call us then."

Mabry took his time now, got the numbers right, and yes the bank was running. His checking balance was $838.76, and his savings balance was $796,443.32.

It's actually come through. Christ, she truly did it. When the bank's voice gave him the further option of pressing #1 and hearing the balances one more time, Mabry took the chance. The figures were the same, no hallucination. It was far more cash than he'd owned at one time in his whole past life, and the news left him stunned. Before he went to Europe, he'd paid all the taxes and arranged this deposit for future investment; but this was the first time he heard the net sum. All but frozen, he sat in the straight chair by the phone table. Mabry had never lived for money, not for five straight minutes; but the news crashed down on him now, a hot wave. He understood it could drown him in six weeks or bear him onward through whatever transformed hard new life would face him soon and everyone he honored in this newly bent world, only two days old. When he looked up, he could hear Audrey working in the bedroom he'd use. His bags were still in the car in the yard. He'd go get them.

Once he was out of the front door, though, he was drawn toward the big tree standing straight ahead, almost at the road. Before he was born, lightning had struck it and stripped a wide tongue of bark off the trunk from top to bottom. Everyone told his grandmother to cut it down fast; it was sure to die. She'd said "So am I. Chop *me* down and haul me off at the same time then. You're bound to save money." More than fifty years later, the tree was healthy. The leaves were only beginning to redden for the winter rest. His grandmother saw him once in early childhood, straining to stretch his arms round the trunk, a hopeless ambition. She told him to quit. "But once you're a man, then maybe you can ring it. *That's* a reason to last."

Now he knew his arms would never grow another quarter inch; and they still couldn't circle this solemn girth, though they tried it again. He stepped back to look at the lightning scar; and recalling how often he'd come here in boyhood and stroke the healing edges of the burn, he thought this was surely his introduction to the fact that the bland sky concealed real havoc. Was it one more reason the twin New York catastrophe, so near his loft and all he owned, seemed natural to him—as it plainly didn't to so many of his countrymen? By now he'd sensed that neither his father nor Audrey Thornton, nor anyone he'd met in Nova Scotia, had shown any sign of really deep involvement in the huge event. Despite the big new TV in the corner, the awe hadn't truly reached this house at least. And would it ever? Though New York called itself the Capital of the World, it was five hundred Interstate miles from here—maybe twenty minutes in a new fighter jet but numerous light-years otherwise (it was doubtless also the solar system's capital of narcissism).

Mabry himself, even he had yet to register the past few days as tragic, despite his still unmeasured losses. Forget his loft, who did he know who was dead in the rubble? And how many months or years would go on, bruised from this? How much callus was involved in his present numbness? How guilty were they all of simple indifference and normal self-absorption? Tasker and Audrey could tend their own consciences. Mabry had fewer genes for converting others to his own opinions than almost any human he knew; he very seldom gave a damn in that department. People in general could go their own way, just a good way out of his please. But his old first sureties were boring up from his heart to his mind as he stood here now. *I'm nothing still but a soft-brained ex-hippie, aging and alone and with no more banners or placards to carry.* As a joke for himself alone, he hugged the tree and, sure enough, found he'd need at least one good-sized child to fill the space he couldn't engulf. He laid his head against the warm bark and hoped he could hear the kind of life he could hear in plants—and the rest of nature, local non-human mammals included—when he was a boy, staying here in the summers. No sound at all now, not at first anyhow.

Then a deep welcome voice came from a distance—"Mr. Mabry?"

Tired as he was, he knew it couldn't be coming from the tree. But he tried to think of the very few people still alive here who even knew him, and it didn't sound like any of them. The use of *Mister* with just his first name seemed to mean some older black person, surely not proud Audrey. His head and body were concealed from the house, though his hands might show; but some trace of playfulness had seeped into him. He pulled his hands back, meaning to hide.

Then the voice said "I see you. I can see through almost anything but rock." It had also risen to an almost playful pitch.

He looked and it was Audrey after all. She was on the porch, at the outside door that led straight to his bedroom, and was spreading an antique blanket on the railing. He remembered it from way back, a dark green favorite from his early boyhood. Though she hadn't smiled yet, she seemed to be waiting for him.

He trotted on toward her, paused ten feet away and said "Did you know that's my world's-favorite blanket? Is something wrong with it?"

"Not a thing," she said. "I just washed it this morning. Let it lie here till bedtime, to get good and dry. Can't have you sleeping under any damp cover. My grandmother said that would give you *arthuralis*."

At the sound of Cooter's word for *arthritis*, Mabry recalled her saying it a thousand times when she was surely past eighty years old—bending over at the woodstove door as she watched a blackberry cobbler bubbling or stooping to a puppy's mess on the porch. When did Cooter die? He knew he hadn't attended her funeral, and he couldn't recall the last time he saw her. He said "You got any idea when old Cooter died?"

Audrey barely paused. "August twenty-seventh, 1966. Four-thirty in the afternoon, hot as boiled Hell."

"Surely you can't remember."

Audrey looked down on him, shook herself hard as if ditching a burden, then smiled toward the empty road beyond them. "I remember. I was there, playing paper dolls at her feet. By then she thought I was her own baby, though I was at least her great-grandchild. I think I was three or four years old. She was over a hundred. Nobody really knew how much over."

Mabry's math was always weak, but now he felt sure his sum was right. Audrey had to be near forty years old, though she looked in good shape for five years younger. Surely then he'd known, or seen, her in her childhood. He said "Aren't we bound to have known each other long before now?"

She shook her head slowly. "I very much doubt it. My mother was compelled to raise me in D.C. We didn't get down here except for short visits, and I don't think I ever set foot in this house till two fast weeks ago. At least I don't recall it." She actually turned then and looked at the length of the house behind her, as if trying to place it in her early life. Her hands had stayed on the railing though, atop the green blanket.

By then Mabry had moved almost within reach. He was suddenly driven to take the last step and cover her hands. Not that he knew what the gesture meant. God knew he was lonesome. In Rome he'd had one long but fairly chaste night in bed with an old friend from graduate school, a woman from Texas who'd risen so far in art conservation that she managed to make a good living in Italy, an all but incredible achievement. But she was the only woman he'd touched in anything resembling outright desire since awhile before his ex-wife needed his presence by her deathbed. He'd made a silent vow, there beside Frances Kincaid, to lay off sex till he'd seen her through to death (his infidelities had ruined their marriage). And somehow the vow had extended now through nearly half a year. So nothing in Audrey—fine as she was—had stoked sex in him, not yet anyhow.

At that same moment, she faced him again and said "I think it would have hurt Mother too much to bring me down here." But she also smiled.

Then Mabry laid both his hands over hers—lightly, no pressure.

And she let them rest there long enough to study them as if this man's sinews and knuckles, and the old wedding ring he'd worn in the weeks he nursed his wife, might tell her as much as the lines of a palm could tell a good Gypsy. Then she slid them toward her, into her own keeping, for two or three seconds before recalling her hands to herself.

Mabry said "Thank you kindly."

Audrey nodded. "Your room's ready now. If it rains we'll put a bucket under the hole—or you fix the roof." Then as he turned to go for his bags, she said "You don't seem worried at all about what's happened to your hometown."

"In New York, you mean?"

"Yes. And wherever else these men strike next."

Standing that close to the room he was born in, Mabry suddenly seemed to know a full answer; and it almost shocked him. He said "On a scale of one to ten for disaster, I guess this is—what?—maybe an eight?" His voice suspended at that point. *What the hell can I mean?* But before he could laugh, Audrey seemed ready to take him up on his foolery.

Serious-eyed, she said "You think it's truly the start of the Last Days?"

He thought *Oh God, she may be in graduate school; but she's a Holy Roller.* He couldn't help a slight smile. "They're not claiming that down here yet, are they?"

She also smiled. "No, but your dad's been speaking about it."

"You mean his talk about hydrogen bombs? I doubt those Muslims have got one yet. If so, why didn't they use it this week?"

Audrey said, as calm as the tree trunk behind him, "I thought about killing my son, while he was asleep two mornings ago. I could take him on out of this whole business." She shut her eyes and again shook hard.

Mabry thought *Are we safe in a house with this woman?* But he said "Audrey, is it truly that bad? Are you that sure?"

She said "I was axing you, Mr. Mabry. You s'posed to tell me." She blared her eyes open like terrified Prissy in *Gone With the Wind*, then batted them fast, then gave a high laugh and turned toward the house. "I don't know nothing 'bout no H-bombs, Mr. Mabry."

As she left, the whole back of her head and body, her long legs, looked more than worth following to any destination. And Mabry felt mildly but rightly punished by her earnest joke. *How much more of this has she got stored up?* But he didn't try to call her back, and he didn't pursue her. He went for his bags. What was most important now was the hope to steal, between now and supper, a little of the sleep he badly needed.

When he woke, deep dark was all around him; and the air felt chillier than Halifax this morning—odd for mid-September down here. September in eastern Carolina could be as hot as Lumum-baville. *I'm down here, right?* In the pitch dark and drowsy as he was, Mabry couldn't guarantee his whereabouts—what day or hour, even what house. Or maybe he was somehow outdoors. As a first probe to test his location—not to mention whether he was living or dead—he spread both arms out straight at his sides. He was on a mattress, yes; but neither hand reached past the edge.

He rolled to his right side and fumbled to find an absolute margin. When he found it, the mattress was hardly more than a dense pad—dense yet thin enough to pinch between his thumb and forefinger. *The bed I was born in.* All because his father had loved the place so much that he managed to persuade Mabry's mother to come here—with the Kincaids' old MD and a younger black midwife—and deliver her first child "at home" as late as 1948. It had gone without incident, as it did after all in most of the world. And here now he was, all but six decades later. *Was it for good, for anybody?*

With all his recent weird symptoms, that possibility—or inevitability—hadn't crossed Mabry's conscious mind till now, not for maybe two whole days. If he was truly entering the long hallway of multiple sclerosis—anything from a lifetime of mildly annoying moments of numbness and double vision to eventual total and incurable paralysis—where better could he go than here, assuming of course that he put a big part of Frances's legacy into restoring this house, making it wheelchair accessible and securing strong help? He tried what he hadn't tried for an hour. He rubbed both thumbs and forefingers together hard. He could feel the pressure and the pain. *There's still a little time, at least.* But then whatever symptoms he'd had were intermittent to the point of mystifying his doctors.

There was no lamp near the bed, so he got to his feet and felt his way toward the string that hung from a single bare lightbulb far overhead. It worked. His watch said ten past six. He stroked his face, rough again with stubble. Then he found his shaving kit, went to the house's only bathroom—well-preserved, considering the years of wear—and shaved for the second time today. Watching his face, for even that long, was somehow easier than it had been since the moment he held on to Frances's wrist and marked her last heartbeat five months ago.

In the kitchen Audrey was still by the stove. At the sound of Mabry's footsteps, she turned and looked toward his father's room. "He's in there, guarding his gallon of whiskey." But then she grinned. "The ice is in here, and all the glasses we've got are in the cabinet."

As Mabry looked round, he saw the new tan refrigerator. The cabinet was the old canary-yellow cupboard that had been here forever. Like the bathroom, it showed few signs of wear, though it had weathered tens of thousands of meals. Maybe those Mexican farm-boy tenants had been gentler than he'd heard. When he opened the cabinet, though, there were only five or six glasses—mostly chipped leftovers from the peanut butter and jelly of his childhood. He took the biggest glass and half filled it with the doll-sized ice cubes he hated from the automatic ice-maker. Then just before he crossed his father's threshold, he thought to turn back and say to Audrey "How can I help?"

She never looked up from the biscuit dough she was laying in discs on the old black baking tray. "I'll let you know if something arises." Smiling to herself, she made a big rising gesture with both arms, almost an orchestra leader's crescendo.

Mabry saw it as at least mildly strange, but he thought he knew better than to ask more questions. He looked round the corner to where Tasker had lurked the last time he saw him.

And yes he was there, same clothes but nodding off in the wheelchair, the evening news droning on beyond him, obsessed as it was with downtown New York and however many thousand dead people and their desolate survivors.

Mabry stepped forward, turned the TV off, then saw the bottles of Scotch and bourbon on the floor by his father. He chose the bourbon and poured a stiff portion before Tasker woke.

As ever, he was wide awake, first pop. He aimed his pistol finger at Mabry and said "Bang. You're *right!*"

"How *right*, Pa? In my choice of potation?"

Tasker said "Absolutely. I just keep the Scotch to test my visitors." He motioned Mabry to the one other chair, then rolled himself to face it.

Mabry sat and lifted the glass in a toast. "Nothing wrong with Scotch, though—half our family was Scottish, as I recall."

Tasker thought a long moment. "That's a fact I'm struggling to suppress in my old age. The Celtic blood got us into this gulch we'll *never* get out of—Scotch, Irish, Welsh, Huguenot, on and on."

Mabry said "I don't recall hearing of any Celts lately flinging themselves into big jet planes and onward toward the World Trade Towers."

"Of *course* they were Celts, the real men who caused it. Who in hell runs the foreign policy of God's Own Country, ever since red-headed Thomas Jefferson commenced it? We've rammed our country down every other throat on the planet till they all rightly hate us."

Mabry had traveled widely—with Frances—in all of Europe, the Middle East, and North Africa. On his own he'd been to China, Thailand, Vietnam, and Malaysia. So his answer flipped out immediately. "That's not been quite my experience." And the thought that followed was automatic, this near his father. *But then I'm just fifty-three years old. What can I know?* He couldn't help laughing.

And Tasker joined him, amazingly.

When they'd quieted again, Mabry said "What was funny?"

Tasker rattled his ice, then took a long swallow. "There were two good reasons for general laughter—first, you and I both know you don't *have* much experience. Mainly, though, we're laughing at you being home again—how right it feels."

Mabry thought he wouldn't contest that yet. He said "You're back here too, old pal. How right does it feel to be in a wheelchair and stalled in a leaking house you haven't truly lived in since you were a child?" (for the past eight years, Tasker had bunked in a pokey set of rooms in Episcopal retirement quarters in Winston).

Tasker knew at once. "It feels like I should never have left." He searched his son's eyes and the powerful hands that were copies of his own. "And neither should you."

As always, Mabry couldn't tell how seriously to take his father's words. So he turned and looked out the brightest window—the fig tree was still there, gigantic now and fifty yards beyond him, one of the leafy caves of his boyhood. Then he laughed again. "Maybe you're right. But who would I be now, assuming I'd stayed?"

Tasker said "A good man."

That stung. Then Mabry said "Like somebody's harmless gentleman gardener or a truly hotshot crossroads mechanic?"

"Yes, along those lines—with a wife that you'd have been loyal to and a daughter you wouldn't have left like a dog in the midst of a very busy road."

Despite Tasker's priestly duties, he'd hardly said ten words — in all the years — to blame his son's choices in life and work. So these words seriously waylaid Mabry. He finished his bourbon in a last deep swallow and said "I was hoping you'd relish a visit from the last close kin you've got on Earth, but now you're trying to drive me off. Another ten words in that direction and you'll succeed. I'm full grown, you notice, with my own bank account. I can leave right now." Then he found himself chuckling.

His father said "I'm *relishing* you. But you're getting deaf. You didn't hear this, son — *you should have stayed here.* You can stay here now. It's not too late."

"Pa, what in the world is waiting for me here? Have you looked around at the actual present? It's a nearly dead village with half as many people as when I was born. What? — a hundred twenty people with a twelve-times-bigger county seat five miles away? And the main pipeline to the ongoing world is on that TV screen beyond us?"

"You might yet find a soul here, Mabry — an actual soul for yourself anyhow." Again, though, Tasker grinned, all but dismissing the chance he might have meant what he said.

For the first time since the New York disaster two days ago, real fear struck Mabry. Through a long moment he couldn't draw a rewarding breath. Then it came. He rose and bent to pour a second drink. Tasker's hand stayed on his wrist all the while, though he knew that drinking was a problem this son never had. So Mabry knelt again beside his father's wheelchair and faced the floor, not Tasker's eyes which were bright as a lizard's. "Pa, where are we headed, this country anyhow?"

"The country's going to come *all* apart."

"You truly believe that?"

Tasker said "I believe it every minute I'm awake in the dark — and long before those crazy boys struck."

Mabry said "And *me*? What's likely to become of me?"

Tasker said "As you can easily guess, I think the *big* ruin started more or less when World War II shut down—that was the country's likable hour, the summer of 1945. I was twenty-seven; you were not quite born. Several fine things have happened since then—*starting* to end American slavery was surely the best. But we've gone on claiming to be such loyal Christians and Jews while we've let the balance of mankind starve and tear each other to shreds like always—" His voice suspended.

Since this was a sermon, Mabry waited for the ongoing thought. When nothing came he quietly asked "We're compelled then to solve every problem on the face of the globe?"

Tasker slowly returned from his pause. His right hand went to the back of Mabry's neck and squeezed it lightly. "We could have fed every starving human and taught them how to farm or earn a decent wage. We could have stood between the howling packs of wolves called men. And women as well. We could have done all that—every penny—and had *plenty* left. Otherwise we shouldn't have claimed to be Christian, which we still mainly do. Hell, old as I am, I'm starting to reach for my gun anytime a stranger tells me he's a Christian— he *or* she (sometimes women are the worst). I've all but planned to become a Jew."

When the hand released his neck, Mabry thought it was time to come back to the business at hand. "So we're being punished now, for all our sins?

Tasker agreed. "Our *crimes*. I seldom think about *sin* anymore. But your big city? Sure, those servants of Allah will level New York yet. How can they help it? They'll buy an atomic bomb somewhere or breed a plague virus; and within ten years, they'll turn New York back at least six centuries—just rocks and maybe a few tough weeds, a dozen or so men as durable as the Manahatta Indians."

It sounded at least half sane to Mabry; but his fear had passed, for now at least. "Did that revelation come straight from God or the bourbon you and I are presently swilling?"

Tasker couldn't see Mabry's face dead-on, but he knew he could hear a tease in the voice. "No, son, I got it from the last remains of my common sense. Get you a TV big as mine. It'll tell you what to think, and it makes good sense."

Mabry stayed in place. "Say you really don't believe that."

Tasker waited till he knew what it meant. "No, I really don't believe it; but I think a good many of the pictures shown on any TV are bound to be true. How wrong is that?"

Mabry finally heard he was serious. "Somewhere between maybe forty and a hundred percent. Notice — everything on that giant screen looks a million times too simple. Somebody's always winning or dying, wailing or cheering — nothing else."

Tasker took his longest wait. "I can grant you that, but Fate sometimes thinks in idiot-straight lines, just like TV. Still, whatever happens to New York City or you or me may prove more interesting. The likely thing is, *nothing* will happen — nothing new."

What seemed newer to Mabry than daybreak was the sound of Audrey's voice from the kitchen.

"Supper for three grown people is ready."

Mabry had spread his napkin in his lap — an ample blue cloth napkin — before his father gently stopped his almost-reaching hand. "Son, I've recently learned a new blessing. It's John Wesley's blessing, a Methodist of course but likewise an Anglican priest to the end." When all heads were bowed, Tasker said

> *"Be present at our table, Lord;*
> *Be here and everywhere adored.*
> *These creatures bless and grant that we*
> *May feast in Paradise with thee."*

The notion of feasting in Paradise was good enough for Mabry, with the Lord or whomever. And the spread before him was, to his eyes and mind, paradisal at the least. How had Audrey known his boyhood favorites? And when had he last eaten country-style steak (pounded round steak, dredged in flour and slowly simmered in onion gravy), mashed potatoes smooth as the butter and cream lavished in them, green beans cooked with tiny cubes of smoky pork, cold sliced ripe tomatoes from somebody's carefully tended garden just down the road, cucumbers baptized in peppery vinegar, and thin pones of salty cornbread lightly fried with lacy edges? Just eating alone kept Mabry grinning but mainly silent for the first ten minutes. He'd loved good food all his life, though gluttony had never been among his major sins.

Yet despite his pleasure in first-rate cooking, he'd never learned how to make anything more complex than a soft-boiled egg (no mean chore, in fact) or a baked potato. It had been his luck—and sometimes his curse—to live beside women with caretaking genes, and they'd kept him well-fed, a part of the bargain to *have and hold*. But he couldn't recall an earlier meal that had moved as benignly through his veins as this one. It was almost as if he could feel real damage—like hacked-out chunks down the arms and legs of a marble statue—being gradually filled, from the inside out. And it kept him from looking directly to Audrey or speaking to her yet. He didn't want to blub, not this early in their acquaintance.

In Mabry's silence, Tasker and Audrey had talked ahead with the quiet ease of family members—a peaceful family, that condoned each other. Every few sentences they'd lapse into a plainly foreign language for a phrase or two; it was nothing Mabry had heard in his travels. At first he assumed it was some private tongue in which they were trading remarks about him, secrets anyhow. Finally, though, he couldn't resist. First he laughed in his father's direction. Then he said "Sir, am I really so bad yall discuss me in code?"

Tasker paid him no mind but turned back to Audrey and reeled off a long calm strip of the code. Was it just a nonsense language of the sort small children manufacture? But then he faced his son.

"No, darlin' lad, it's New Testament Greek. We're showing off for you."

Mabry looked mildly stunned.

So Audrey said "Father Kincaid is helping me learn my Greek. I'm a graduate student at Duke University, the Divinity School. Working on a PhD. I've finished my course work and am studying for my prelims—just five thousand books to read between now and next fall."

Tasker said "Truth is, she's helping me. I haven't read or spoken a word of Greek for a million years."

To Mabry's own surprise, once he'd paused for an overdue napkin-wipe of his lips, he burst into the opening lines—in Italian—of the *Divina Commedia*. His Italian had never been especially accurate; but owing to the Kincaid gene for mimicry, his accent was apparently impressive, even to native Italians. He'd more than once seen the facial shock on waiters and shopkeepers, not to mention curators, when he addressed them in wretched grammar but with an impeccable Roman accent. Neither Audrey nor Tasker knew enough Italian to order so much as a respectable pizza, so they listened to him reel out the first twenty lines of Dante in patient respect. Then Tasker said "I'm guessing it's Dante."

And Audrey said "Me too. But the first two pages of the Roman phone book would sound just as good, in your voice anyhow, Mr. Mabry."

He said "*Mr.* Mabry one more time? I know you're teasing but—"

Tasker rushed in. "Worse than teasing. She's punishing you for American history—the Southern division anyhow."

Audrey smiled but didn't deny it. Still, she faced Mabry. "I believe I can see you're enjoying your supper."

Mabry's mouth was full again so he nodded fiercely. "*Your* supper, lady. You cooked every morsel or am I wrong?"

Tasker said "Dead right. Give her five minutes' notice, she can cook every cuisine known to me or you—or any spy satellite soaring above us."

Audrey said "I cooked in Baltimore a number of years, at a number of restaurants, before I came down here."

Mabry leaned back from the table and bowed his upper half in her direction. "I've held off complimenting your art, lest I burst into tears. You've sure-God mastered the joys of my boyhood."

"You're kind," she said with a slight excess of solemnity.

Mabry said "*Accurate*, far more than kind."

Tasker said "Amen."

Mabry said "Careful, Pa. You're in danger of wearing *Amen* out. I thought you'd retired from the active priesthood."

Tasker struck the air with a half-frantic hand. "Don't ever retire from anything. Die panting in harness or bleeding at the joints. Just don't let anything retire you but Death."

Audrey said "I thought you were enjoying your rest—all the reading you do, the drives we take, the movies we watch." Her left hand was flat on the table before her.

Tasker covered it, then grasped it lightly (it was getting unusual attention today).

She let him hold it maybe five seconds, then drew it away.

Only then did Mabry wonder again if anything bound this mismatched two except the care that Audrey was paid to give an old man's weakness—slim pay, no doubt. He said "Seems like I heard the evenings down here make swinging Manhattan feel soporific."

Tasker said "When was the last time I swung in New York—thirty-odd years?"

Audrey said "I've never even seen New York."

Mabry said "You're kidding me."

"Not a bit. I've had two sons to raise and a good many other debts on my hands."

Mabry said "Then we go to bed right now? Where's the Ovaltine?"

Tasker gave no answer but deferred to Audrey.

She smiled at Mabry and by now her face had partly agreed to welcome him into his own birthplace. "Father and I are watching our way through the hundred best American movies from a rental service we subscribe to."

Mabry noticed the *we* but didn't comment. "Lord, how many do you have to watch per night?"

Tasker said "Three a week. I think it's *American in Paris* tonight." He looked to Audrey with no hint that their choice might not be a normal night's viewing in the wake of recent events.

And she assented as gravely as if Ingmar Bergman had directed a little-known Swedish version of the Gene Kelly caper.

So Mabry laughed. "Considering I myself was a Yank in France just three days ago, I think I'll go for a ride, if that's agreeable."

Tasker said, of all things, again "You got plenty cash?" (he meant did Mabry have American money, though Mabry heard it as a patriarchal question).

He said "Thanks, Pa. I changed some lire and francs in Baltimore." He pushed his chair back. "What time is lights out on the local scene?"

Tasker said "Anytime your city-dwelling heart requires."

Audrey said "My son comes in at ten o'clock and helps Father Kincaid get ready for bed."

Mabry said "I can save him that duty for a few nights anyhow."

Tasker shook his head. "You can't lift me, son. I need brute lifting—on and off the john, in and out of bed. I know what tricks your back's played on us since you were the pee-wee soccer goalie."

Mabry said "I'll be back to say good night at least." He almost stood to thank Audrey once more.

Before he could rise, though, Audrey said "You don't want even a taste of dessert?"

Before he could think, Mabry said "What is it?"

By then she was on her feet, taller and even finer looking. She narrowed her glinting eyes on Mabry.

Tasker held out arms in both directions. "Easy now, children—"

But before Mabry could apologize for rudeness, Audrey said "How about you name your favorite, kind sir?"

Mabry knew right off. "Brown-sugar pie with cold whipped cream or forty-five more homemade heart's delights from the same department as what we've just had."

Audrey said "I can't guarantee your heart's going to be entirely delighted with the butter content of what I've made next; but it's hand-made chocolate pie, with whipped cream, in a hand-rolled crust."

Mabry bowed again, deeper still. "Oh bring it *on*. And don't slice it too small, kindly, ma'm." His eagerness was thoroughly real.

"*Ma'm* is the same thing as *Mr.* Mabry from here on out," Audrey said. By then her back was turned to the men; she was already slicing pie at the sideboard with all the commitment she lavished on Greek of the first century AD.

After the pie, Mabry dialed a new Manhattan number on the hall phone.

A man's voice answered. "Miles Watson speaking."

It rang no immediate bell with Mabry. He thought he'd dialed wrong.

But when he said he was sorry for the error, the man said "Mr. Kincaid, is that you?" It was Baxter Sample's butler. But till now the butler had always said "Mr. Sample's residence. This is Miles, his butler."

Mabry said "Right, Miles. Yes, it's Mabry Kincaid. Is Mr. Sample in?"

Miles waited a good while. "Sir, I've had no word from Mr. Sample since he left Tuesday morning at seven for the office."

"No word whatever?"

"None whatever, sir, from him or any of his office staff. Oddly enough, the main office number rings normally; but no one has answered since Tuesday morning just after the first crash."

"And you're sure Mr. Sample got to the office?"

"Are you still in Europe, Mr. Kincaid?"

"I'm in North Carolina actually."

"But you must have seen, sir, what the situation's like in New York—absolute hell up here. Still, I'm sure you'd agree that Mr. Sample would have rung me if he were able. I'm here in the duplex, hoping for *something*." What was left of Miles's former voice was a whiff of his familiar Australian brass. He'd been the only actual butler Mabry had encountered in years of working with the rich; and Miles had seemed entirely impeccable, though no more than thirty. Whatever had happened to Baxter Sample, Miles would land on his big broad feet and with a legacy maybe—Baxter had shown him considerable affection.

Mabry said he'd call again tomorrow; then he tried to hang up.

But Miles said "Sir, are *you* all right?"

Mabry could only picture Miles as he'd been—a tall, brick-outhouse-solid ex–rugby player with an army record—but now he heard a sudden note of genuine forlornness. So he said "I'm safe, thanks. I had a good trip but am glad it's over." Somehow he didn't quite want to mention Paris or the picture he'd fetched on Baxter's account. "I'm at my father's place in North Carolina. He hasn't been in good health. And as you may know, my neighborhood's still quarantined. I'll likely be here then till I can get home." Mabry heard his voice denying his father's claim.

He passed a few more moments of provisional sadness with Miles, learning incidentally that the butler knew of no close kin or dependents of Baxter's. Even Baxter's whole office staff was missing—four adults and a teenage Xeroxer.

Finally Miles reverted to his own present state—he was all but a boy, still, and a long way from the Antipodes, hired no doubt as much for his looks as his stamina. He took a long pause; then said "Mr. Kincaid, what if they find a corpse?"

That last word was the most shocking single thing Mabry had heard all week. How many Americans now would use as real a word as *corpse*? Most people, even the police on TV, were substituting *passed on* for *dead*.

Before Mabry could answer, Miles rushed ahead. When should he close the duplex for good, what would become of all the contents, and to whom should he turn for any last bills and his own last wages?

Mabry urged calm patience for a few more days. Then he gave him Tasker's phone number and promised he'd check back every evening. When he hung up, he heard muffled laughter from the kitchen—Audrey's and Tasker's voices joined in a way which seemed so enviable that a chance at temporary rescue occurred to Mabry's lonely mind. He went to his room, took the wrapped painting from among the sour T-shirts in his suitcase and rushed toward the evening.

What was out there, first, but the twenty-odd houses that had made up the village—a village from which the old life had been uprooted by the death of tobacco, the blessed end of segregation, and the railroad's abandonment? All Mabry's kin, but his father, were gone. And it took him no more than twenty minutes now to pass two white-folks churches, three black-folks churches (a little farther out), a new post office as faceless as all recent federal buildings, one live grocery store, three abandoned stores, a dead filling station, and one tiny beer-hall with a damaged neon sign in the window, a pool table, and (surely) the standard clutch of post-adolescent bikers trying hard to look like threats to all other humans. The dead public school still stood on the edge of the field that had been a Confederate drill ground, but the sizable timber depot where his father's father had been stationmaster—and where he'd died, at nearly a hundred, on the telegraph key substituting for a youngster—had been moved bodily five hundred yards to sit by the house of one old boy who had a good deal more feeling for the place than the Seaboard Railroad itself.

Likely, some of the few dozen men, women, and children who lived now in the pleasant old houses—plus a few "mobile homes"— were laying down cellars of memory and feeling that might eventually rival Mabry's own for depth and thanks. The solitude and stillness were near at hand for anyone reckless enough to tear his eyes and ears away from the TV and wander the thickets and weedy fields. What was mainly gone was what had seemed the eternal richness of the monstrous relation between whites and blacks that had nonetheless yielded more than two centuries of a daily tolerance far more complex than anything visible now in schools and stores. Well-gone, God knew, but not yet replaced with anything richer—anything with half a chance of pressing, from human pain and guilt (slightly more of each than the average province), the arts of poetry, fiction, drama, music, dance, and the riveting sacred rites of the Southern past.

When his car had clocked off all those memories, Mabry hedged a little longer. He headed east, parallel to the dug-up rail tracks. And in two more pitch-dark miles he'd reached the white graveyard and negotiated the narrow entry, moving twenty yards onward and stopping by his family's large plot. He stayed in the car and tried, in his mind, to count the graves and recite the names—four of them dated before his birth, yet he'd known six others: aunts, uncles, cousins, and the one grave too hard to visit tonight.

Of the six, he'd loved at least three—Tasker's mother, his own, and Gabe, his brother. And there was only one person whom Mabry had truly despised—a drunken abuser of wife and children, an average demonic man-in-the-street who happened to be Mabry's second cousin. Normal as the demon was, and though he'd never laid a hand on Mabry, the buried nearness of his corpse was one more presence keeping Mabry in the car. And in twenty more seconds, another high wave poured through his whole body—cold dread this time. Again he heard Audrey Thornton's question—*Are these the Last Days?*—and his grin that had followed. Whether or not she thought there might be some irrevocable plan in the mind of a possibly demented God to shut down the universe—or this speck of a planet—in thermonuclear fire here soon, for Mabry the question had a sudden force. He stayed in place till that one possibility faded. Still he couldn't help thinking *Tasker's likely right—these madmen won't stop till they've finished off New York.*

He switched on the map light long enough to check his watch and see that he couldn't go back to his father and Audrey yet, not with this many hours left before sleep was feasible again. The friends he'd thought might be in town and welcome him no longer seemed a good idea. Then he'd drive five miles to the county seat anyhow and see if, by chance, a bar had opened or even a café was still in business as late as eight p.m.

No such luck of course, not this deep in the toils of the Bible Belt. There was only the same eternal pool hall—twice the size of the one in Wells—with its own *Cold Beer* neon in the single window, this one with a hint of imagination—an apparent mermaid poised between the two words. He went in there and, before he could choose his brand, he saw—through air like a literal smoke pudding—a face he thought he recognized from adolescent summers. Surely it was Vance Scott.

Whoever it was, the man grinned in Mabry's direction but gave no further real sign of recognition.

And when Mabry went toward him, the man leaned way forward to take his next shot with the cold focus of a fighter pilot.

Hadn't Vance been an actual pilot, in some war or other? Yes, Vietnam.

But the shot went askew; and the man said "Christ Almighty," then looked straight at Mabry. "You're still Mabry, right?"

Mabry laughed. The *still* was peculiar but he let it pass. "I was, last time I checked a mirror."

"You look enough like him anyhow."

Mabry said "And you're still Vance—almost, anyhow. Didn't we go to summer camp together, back when the world was younger than now?"

Vance nodded solemnly. "Oh Christ, yes we did." It seemed like a real discovery for him, one that might yield rewarding results. "Was it you or me that wet the bed the first night out?"

There seemed to be three other men in the place. Each one of them looked up to Mabry at that point and waited for his answer. And Mabry knew. He grinned and said "I'd never have brought it up myself; but since you did, old son, it was you. After that, I told you my bedtime secret—eat a handful of salt in the mess hall with supper."

Vance said "And it worked—or am I wrong again?"

Mabry said "Right as rain."

So Vance held out a hand that made untanned gator hide feel silken.

But to Mabry it felt like an unexpected form of protection.

Vance's face, though, belied the hand. The eyes were bleared, and the skin of the face was all but trenched. Still, he held Mabry's hand longer than expected; and he searched Mabry's eyes as if he'd lost something that was maybe hidden there. Finally he found it. "Didn't somebody tell me your Frances had died?"

Mabry couldn't think how that plain fact had reached Vance Scott in here. But he wouldn't ask. He said "Yes, Frances died in April."

Vance said "Cancer." It wasn't a question.

Mabry managed a Yes. It hurt a good deal more than he'd have guessed.

Vance said "I hardly knew her, as you recall; but in memory she's still a damned good woman. She loved you anyhow. I could see that much." Vance's facts were facts, wherever they'd come from.

Mabry nodded again but put up the flat of his hand in the air. They'd gone as far as he could handle, here at least.

Vance also nodded. "You're bound to need you at least a semilegal narcotic."

Mabry was glad to hear that, and it left him feeling he should pause here awhile.

But when Vance returned with the icy bottle, he faced Mabry earnestly again and said "Bad as you cheated, she left you well-fixed. Spend it all, boy. Don't leave a *cent* behind you when you truck off."

It was hard to resist either slugging Vance — he was so far gone, a punch would be easy — or engaging him in a point-by-point grilling. Where the hell had he got his information, and how much of it was drunken guessing from a few scraps of half-educated memory? But Mabry resisted. He wanted to stand here — a space that was not his father's house and was surely as safe this week as any room in the continental U.S. — and drink his free beer before heading out. As Vance turned back to take his next shot at the billiard table, Mabry suddenly knew a reason to stay.

Vance had maybe saved his life in the summer-camp lake in 1959. They'd been learning to dive on the buddy system — you and your buddy were each other's lifeguard. Mabry's buddy was named Stan Seaman, and Stan as ever was entirely absorbed in showing off to a small knot of snobs a whole year older. Mabry successfully executed his first required dive from the medium-high board. But before he surfaced, his trick left shoulder dislocated — nauseating pain, helplessness, then the onset of panic as he struggled to reach the shallows on one arm without revealing his trouble or his fear. Before he reached a safe depth, though, he heard a level voice beside him in the mountain-cold water — "I got you, Mabe." It was Vance and so he had. Though Vance was only a few months older, he was already two sizes bigger than Mabry; and with an amazing minimum of effort, he swam beneath Mabry, surfaced like the Navy's most trustworthy submarine and bore him to the edge.

Somehow tonight seemed Mabry's last chance to return the
favor—to stand a quiet guard on Vance as he fumbled the evening
away in solid smoke and the mortuary shine of a long fluorescent
tube overhead. So Mabry stood his chosen guard for over half an
hour, saying no more than fifty words to answer questions from
Vance and the manager and the one or two raddled boys who
deigned to acknowledge his ongoing life. At first there was consolation in standing in the kind of world he wouldn't have guessed
had survived outside nostalgic movies—not only the pool tables, the
cue sticks polished to an antique beauty by at least three generations
of serious hands and the underwater light, but even an actual
smoke-cured original example of the calendar from circa 1953 with
Marilyn extended in air-brushed grandeur, "Nothing on but the
radio," as she'd later said (he could sell it in New York tomorrow for
several hundred dollars).

Even more calming was the fact that no one said a single word
about the recent disaster or gave the least hint of suppressing any
knowledge of the horror. Their calm devotion to the job at hand—
an old, entirely honorable game involving considerable harmless
skills—was as reassuring as anything Mabry had met with in three
days of efforts from all sides of the Western world. He consulted his
mind for the current vital signs and realized that he might have been,
at that moment, in the grip of a previously unknown sublime drug
and concealed in a well-fitted cavern on the far side of Mars—and
with nothing more than a beer in his belly—till at last Vance looked
up from the somehow literally triumphant shot that completed his
game. Of course his smile was as wide as the exit gates from Heaven.
"Gwyn Williams is back too. But you knew that."

Mabry said he'd heard it. In fact he'd only heard such a rumor
before he left for Italy. But Gwyn had been his main target of the
evening—the final hope for a little relief and the reason he'd
brought Baxter's now-orphaned painting in the trunk of the car. He'd

only stopped here to pass a little time and let dark settle around the town. Through the one high window, he could see that now it was all but night. So he offered to drive Vance on home.

Vance said "I thank you but, if I can't drive when I finish up here, Betty Ann'll come get me."

God, is Betty Ann still hauling this kindly embalmed souse around? Mabry went up to him and held out his hand, just to touch that inexplicably durable hide again. Then he headed for the door.

His hand had barely touched the knob when Vance raised his voice. "You're safe to drive, right?"

Mabry turned and grinned. "I'm as right as a fifty-three-year-old scoundrel can be when he's lonely as any sidewinder in the sand and has almost surely got multiple sclerosis to add to his joys."

Vance had started a whole new beer. "You're bound to be kidding, good as you look." He clearly needed consolation of his own, not Mabry's bad news.

So Mabry said "You bet I'm kidding—*praying* to be."

Just before he entered the night, though, Vance called behind him. "Let me buy you a barbecue plate between this minute and the day you leave. Hey wait—you take the combo, don't you, with Brunswick stew and unsweetened tea?"

Mabry said he'd welcome the gift, any day. *But imagine Vance recalling the details. We can't have eaten a meal together in forty years, and how much of that soaked brain can be left?* It suddenly came to his own aging brain—*Any way at all I can step back in there and rescue him, the way he did me?* What? Haul Vance off to an AA meeting or a de-tox facility? Where would one be? Maybe nowhere nearer than twenty miles.

By then, though, his mind had tilted more toward the scent of Gwyn Williams. She'd always offered more various and more desirable odors than anyone else he'd ever been near.

*   *   *

When she finally answered his numerous raps on the front door and then the tall wavy-paned windows, the main odor—and the taste on her lips—was good champagne. He'd have known it, even if she hadn't appeared with an open bottle of Veuve Cliquot in hand and gazed up at him in the deep porch darkness for a trustful long time before she said "Kiss these withered ole lips, honey baby, and step indoors. I've been praying for you, by the instant, here lately."

The lips were still long years from withering, though the black evening dress was torn down one side and gave off the smell of long decades in her mother's cedar chest. When the first kiss ended, sooner than she wished, she set the bottle beside her on the floor. Then she peeled the long white kid glove off her right hand—she wanted to touch Mabry's actual skin and he gladly complied.

A second kiss followed and a thorough massage of both his hands by her own soft fingers. By then she'd pulled him backward inside, and he'd shut the door behind them. He said "Lady, I'm looking for Ms. Gwyn Williams; but I seem to have stumbled on Zelda Fitzgerald or Blanche DuBois. Can you give me some directions?"

Gwyn looked down at herself and tried to tug the torn seam together. She was hardly drunk but when she spoke at last, she was on the verge of tears. And she couldn't look up for fear of blubbing. "Sad as both those girls wound up, they'd have never answered the door like this; and you're bound to know it. But then you were ever a gentle soul."

"Right about those poor girls," Mabry said, "wrong about me. But we could just call each other's names. That'd prove we don't have Alzheimer's anyhow."

Gwyn finally looked up. She was only nine months younger than he, but those green eyes were finer than ever. She took up the champagne bottle again and said "I was Margaret Gwyneth Williams before I started drinking." Then she launched the smile that she could make more gorgeous by the moment, if she really tried. "And you'd be who, kind sir?"

He said "I was Mabry Kincaid in Paris last Tuesday; then I set out for home and the world half ended. So who am I now?"

"You're the same sweet boy. Or you look like you are. But you need some champagne." Gwyn turned her back on him and walked down the hall toward the dining room and kitchen.

When she was twenty feet away, Mabry said "Am I meant to follow you or just stand here and die?"

She didn't look back. "Child, when have I ever leaned on your free will? Do what you choose." By then she'd entered the dining room, and the sound of her feet was still moving on.

So Mabry chose to follow. And by then every step of her trail was what he hoped—perfumed by a good deal more than champagne. A little artificial scent (French, to be sure), a trace of the mayonnaise she'd recently hand-made, the acid of an over-ripe tomato, and his main hope—the strong assertion of her sex, an odor he'd kept on storage in his mind since the last time he'd been in bed beside her, both of them naked. What? Twenty-eight years ago?

Her destination was the kitchen worktable. And by the time he reached her, Gwyn was slicing bread for the sandwich she'd meant to make from the fresh mayonnaise and the big tomato when he interrupted her supper plans. She'd forgot about her prior conviction that he needed champagne.

He reminded her. "You once seemed to think I was under-spirited."

It was not the clearest remark of the evening and she didn't understand. The sandwich had her full attention.

Mabry went to the cabinet, found a champagne glass and reached for the bottle.

That got her attention. She still didn't face him, but she spoke very softly. "I know you've had kitchen privileges here since you were an infant; but you might just renew your license, don't you think?"

"How would I do that?"

"Try saying this—'Signora Becchi, may I steal a glass of wine?'"

"Signora Becchi?" Was she suddenly married, after so much long and unbroken single life? *And where's Signor Becchi?*

Gwyn tore a strip of high laughter from the air that lay between them. "Ignore that please. No, help yourself, Mabry. My hands are wet."

He poured the champagne (it finished the bottle, which he stashed in the garbage can). "Permission to sit?"

"End of joke, dear friend. Let's get back to normal—as if we could. Any-way, what's this about you in Paris?"

She silently offered to make him a sandwich; he omitted the pool-hall potato chips and told her he'd filled way up at his father's. Then he told her the story of Rome and Paris, Halifax and Wells. Something had told him to leave the painting out in the car, so he didn't mention that. And by the time he'd finished the lengthy story of his trip, Gwyn had consumed her sandwich and brought out a bottle of near-frozen Châteauneuf for him to open. As he worked with the antiquated corkscrew, he reminded himself that you asked for Gwyn's news at your own peril—as her own mother had once warned, "Gwyn is garrulous to a fault." So he silently slid through what he knew of her past.

In the years since he'd seen her, she'd spent a good deal of time in *bas Italia*, south of Naples (the home of Signor Becchi?), and before that, with a serious rancher in upper Montana. Mabry pretty much knew what lay before that—what a stone-freak hippie she'd been in the Sixties, the dead-earnest campaigns she'd waged against Lyndon Johnson and the war in Vietnam, and her howling grief at the deaths of Martin Luther King and Robert Kennedy. Then once the war ended, she'd gone to North Vietnam and slaved herself almost to the bone with various short-lived international agencies that were hoping to feed the victims of U.S. bombing and find good homes for the battle orphans, especially those with American GI fathers.

After that, he was vague—yes, didn't she wind up in some fairly decent hospital in Hanoi that nursed her back from near-starvation? And then there was the episode where she lived in Hong Kong for a few years and tried to launch an export business, selling highly dubious "ancient" Chinese ceramic horses and carved jade Buddhas to hapless tourists and State-side dealers. She'd contacted him at some point in those years in the hope that he'd accept a partnership with her and provide certificates of authenticity for her often handsome but quite likely fake items.

When he begged off involvement in any such career-ending venture, Gwyn's letters—and occasional trans-Pacific phone calls—stayed good-natured and always epic in length and personal specificity. There'd never be less than a full account of her ongoing love life, with frequent snapshots of the various men—all mostly Anglo, all ultimately terminated (to hear Gwyn's version) when they proffered engagement rings with plans for rooted lives and well-to-do in-laws in Asia, Europe, or Iowa and Nebraska. But here was this hint of a husband named Becchi, though at the moment she was wearing no wedding band.

So while she was still rinsing her dish and cutlery at the sink, Mabry told a lie in hopes of hearing where she'd been lately. "Pa said he heard you were fixing this place up and planning to stay on."

She finished her chore, came back to the table and filled both their glasses. "I have both hot and cold flashes on the subject, but what in the hell would I use for money? It's a sweet old place, but don't you just know it would take several fortunes to bring back to life?"

Mabry looked round slowly, as if he knew a lot more than he did about restoring anything bigger than a medium-sized oil painting or a portable urn. At last he said "I hear there are one or two boys in town who're not at all bad at the restoration business."

Gwyn said "Robo Ketcham and Randolph Baynes—they've both just given me estimates. Want to guess what they'd charge?"

Mabry grinned. "I'm from New York, remember. Their sights may be set a good bit lower. What? — under two hundred thousand, I'll guess."

"— By about ten cents. And both their bids are suspiciously similar. They're brothers-in-law, recall." Gwyn knocked back the first two inches of her wine, but then she'd always had a hollow leg.

"So's everybody else between here and Raleigh." Mabry crossed his eyes and twisted his mouth, a suggestion of the local inbred monstrosities.

Gwyn thought that through and at last broke up in her unique laugh, maybe the thing that had brought Mabry here. Or so he felt, as the promising waves spread out and rung his head and shoulders like orchid leis in a 1950s Hawaiian movie.

Both her hands were spread on the table.

Mabry reached out and she let him take them, so he leaned and lightly kissed both — backs and palms.

Then she brought them inward and down to her lap. One of the straps of her gown had broken, just since he'd been here. But she let it be. She half-suspected, and was underestimating, that her youthful beauty had partly survived the heavy wear she'd inflicted on her mind and body.

Mabry saw clearly, and for the first time tonight (or for years), how lovely she was — and with a whole new stillness. He took a long pause to let it sink in. Then he said "So what are we celebrating then, if not a restored house and you back in town?"

"Oh I was just cleaning out Mother's cedar chest. This is the dress she wore when Father won his little term in the State legislature — remember how Earth-shattering that seemed? Anyhow, I tried the dress on. And I thought it fit till I heard a seam split while I was making mayonnaise. That called for the champagne I'd had in the pantry for several weeks, and then you turned up. Don't you think you're worth a celebration?"

Mabry said "I'm glad at least one soul thinks I am. But if I'd waited another ten minutes, the champagne might easily have disappeared."

Gwyn frowned at his eyes. "You could have sat here all night, sweetheart, and not said that." Then she laughed again. "Mother spoke that maxim about twice an hour, if I was in earshot anyhow."

Mabry said "So did mine."

"What's the hound-dog meanest thing you ever said to your helpless mother?"

Mabry wondered why that had come on her suddenly. But he said "Oh, God, how much time have I got?" Then he rummaged across an apparently endless screen of possibilities.

"—Till both of us sit right here and starve." Gwyn laughed again but she plainly meant it.

It occurred to Mabry that she might be crazy, genuinely mad. As a college student, he'd worked the late shift in the mental ward at Duke Hospital; and he knew how often lunacy, in various forms, left women's beauty oddly intact. All the more reason, then, to try to be honest to this girl now. He said "Mother called me in Washington in the spring of '89 and asked me to meet her in Petersburg the next afternoon. She was up there to see her oldest sister. I was extra pleasant in the hope of finding out what was on her mind. Why should I quit work on a vast icon I was repairing for Dumbarton Oaks to drive three hours down the Interstate for Cokes and peanuts with two old ladies I'd known forever and would know forevermore? So I said 'Ma, I'm busier than I've ever been,' which was not quite a lie but—what?—a severe exaggeration. She said 'I've begged you nine thousand times not to call me *Ma*. Call me *Mother* or, since you're now full grown, you're free to call me *Eunice*.' So for the first time, I called her Eunice; but I still begged off." His voice shut down at that point; and he reached for the last of Gwyn's tomato that was still parked beside them on the edge of the table.

Once he'd swallowed and wiped his mouth with the back of his hand, Gwyn said "And what was so mean about that?"

Mabry said "She wanted to tell me the last thing she thought I needed to hear, from her at least—that she had the worst kind of brain tumor known. By the time Pa called me, three weeks later, with the bleak news, she'd gone past speech."

Gwyn's wide eyes were brimming. When she could speak, she said "Promise you don't want to hear mine now."

Mabry tested himself—was he even half drunk? *No, cold sober. Or maybe cool sober.* So he reached for her hands again. Then he said "Girl, you started this. Haven't I just done my share?"

Gwyn had to agree. Then she brought both hands back to the tabletop and said "You have gutted me like a hog on a rack in a cut-rate stockyard." She edged her hands toward him.

But he couldn't yet touch them. "Gwyn, what can you *mean*? I—"

"Oh not you, sweetheart. That was what I said to Mother once."

"It's elegant—I'll give you that much—but maybe it's way too elegant to believe."

Gwyn smiled but insisted. "I guarantee I said it."

"How old were you?"

"Let's omit my age," she said. "But it happened too goddamned recently. Like you, I saved the worst I could possibly do or say for last. Of course, she was on her own deathbed when I said it."

He kept his voice down; but he said "Gwyn, what the hell did you mean?"

"How can you ask that? You knew Mother." When Mabry nodded, Gwyn said "Then you know I was telling the absolute truth. I might have turned out fairly well if I'd been born from Father's belly, not Mother's. My mother was a *slaughterhouse*." She seemed entirely serious.

But Mabry had to laugh.

And Gwyn was suddenly too tired for anger. She just said "Remember my five-minute naps?"

He did. She'd always been able to put her head down anywhere and fall into a sleep deep as coal mines, then wake up exactly three hundred seconds later, refreshed and alert. So he said "Be my guest." He thought she'd head upstairs to a bedroom or maybe one of the living room sofas.

But no, she laid her head on the table—still damp with tomato pulp—and was instantly gone.

Mabry saw it as a relief at first. He could quietly stand and leave her to sleep off the flood of wine. He could phone her in the morning and come back by in the afternoon, well before either of them had commenced the evening drinks. And he was on his feet and into the hall when he suddenly thought *I brought her the picture. Sad as it is, she'll love the story. As much as me, she needs all the cheer anyone can supply.*

He went and was back in under five minutes, just time enough to untie the string and be in the midst of loosening the tape when—bang on schedule—Gwyn raised her head, knew right where Mabry was, and looked straight toward him. "I dreamed you flew out of here with great long powerful sweeps of your wings."

He had to say "Your dream was merely correct, O priestess—and I went to the far side of Planet Earth to fetch a small treasure for your delectation." He gave a sweeping bow from the waist. "But here I'm back. I couldn't leave you long." He reached for a towel that lay nearby and dried the tabletop. Then he laid the package between them and carefully unveiled the picture.

Gwyn found her granny glasses—she'd worn them even before John Lennon made the style urgent—and she studied the picture slowly, from near and far. At last she said "I could almost guarantee it was once a painting. What is it now, though, and why's it a treasure?"

Mabry quickly told her the story of Baxter Sample's finding the picture and buying it, sight unseen; then of his own loop through

Paris to collect it from the raging harridan who meant to steal it and now of what seemed more likely by the hour—that Baxter lay somewhere under a billion pounds of New York rubble. Mabry's first sob—oddly delayed for a man with such feelings—rose and died, unheard.

Gwyn stroked the surface of the canvas with her left hand; and though she was almost forty years older than Leah in Halifax, like Leah's her fingers seemed as knowing as the most alert blind woman's. Still, she said "Let's talk about New York in a minute; but first I want to know what this *is*."

At that, Mabry gave her the small envelope with the note from Philip Adger. When he told about Leah Wilkins finding it, she read it aloud, raising her eyebrows high at the name. "You know Mother had Adger cousins in Charleston. You'll need to meet them, if they're alive, and see what they know."

Mabry said "That's an idea at least."

"Considering the fact that the thing is *yours* now, almost surely, your priestess—*moi!*—hereby informs you." She held both hands an inch above the canvas, shut her eyes, faced the ceiling, and said "I'm telling you, child, that this dim picture is a real Van Gogh, not an Adger at all."

Mabry looked down at the peanut-butter reality. "Wouldn't *that* be fine?"

"*Fine?* You could sell it and restore every house in the county to pristine condition—and that would just cost you the interest on your profit for about four days." Sensing that she needed to get more serious, Gwyn paused. Then she said "It could also be the worst curse of your life."

Mabry said "Tell me how."

"You're bound to know, short as we've always been on cash—money is the source of all hatred, treachery, violence, fleas, ticks, mice, and all other horror in the history of man."

He said "Woman too—"

"I'll allow that," Gwyn said.

"Mighty handsome of you." When Gwyn gave a bow of her own in his direction, Mabry knew he was sober enough to say the two things that were heaviest on him. "A couple of things I want you to know—"

"I'm your best ear," she said. "Remember when you used to call me that?"

"More than a century ago."

Gwyn reached with both hands beneath her real gold hair and cupped her ears. "They still work, darling."

So Mabry said "I guess you know that Frances died, in dreadful pain, five months ago." He waited till Gwyn shut her eyes in agreement. "But I don't think even hyper-psychic *you* can know that modern medicine has apparently detected that I have multiple sclerosis." His description was a little more certain than any doctor had agreed to yet. Here and now, though, it felt right.

Gwyn shut her eyes again, then rose and slowly went to the sink. She drank a full tall glass of water and washed her eyes before she came back. When she sat down she said "We've both been a little drunk here, right?"

Mabry nodded, though he'd never felt less than sober lately.

So Gwyn said "Please tell me you made that up."

"Oh I wish I could. No, I had the first slight symptoms when Frances was dying—some numbness down my right leg, night sweats, cold flashes. You see, I'd treated Frances so badly wrong before we parted; but we never lost touch—weird as Charlotte can be, she forced us to have fairly frequent contact. Then when Frances learned that the doctors had run out of treatments for her kind of cancer, she called me with the news—it was two in the morning. Thank God I was alone and still up and cleaning a tiny Degas. Anyhow I'd been in New York more than ten years by then—even when Frances ditched me—and I knew right away that she'd soon need somebody with her, night and day. Charlotte couldn't easily quit the job she'd only just got with her Episcopal adoption agency. I knew Frances had the money to hire a whole houseful of maids and nurses for as long as it took. But suddenly I heard my voice telling her I'd come down to D.C. the minute she wanted me—if she ever could again—and I'd stay till she didn't need me a minute longer. I mean, my line of work can mostly be done anywhere there's decent light and a small box of tools. She thanked me, to be sure; but when we hung up a few minutes later, I thought I'd likely never see her again."

When Mabry went for his own glass of water, Gwyn said to his back "You surely don't feel she owed you one goddamned copper penny?" Gwyn had been—briefly, to be sure—one of the women with whom Mabry had cheated on Frances.

Mabry stayed at the sink but turned on her, almost frighteningly. "You planning to specialize in meanness in your menopausal years?"

It hurt, as it was meant to. Gwyn shrugged it off with a literal shake of her head and shoulders. She whispered *"Touché."*

So he came to the table, took a long look (over Gwyn's shoulder) at the muddy little picture—a wide stretch of architecture maybe or so Adger claimed. He put one hand on Gwyn's shoulder. "You guarantee it's a Van Gogh?"

Gwyn leaned down and smelled the surface. "I guarantee that pitiful Dutch soul had *something* important to do with it anyhow."

Mabry well understood the limitations on Gwyn's expertise in matters of authentic art—all those surely fake Buddhas she'd sold. This gluey dimness, distinguished only by a handsome old frame, plainly had nothing to do with the tormented Vincent. Still, Mabry all but longed to credit Gwyn's hunch; and the money that might be involved if it were a masterwork didn't mildly faze him. He already had more money than he needed for at least four or five years to come, thanks to Frances; and surely this picture would always be Baxter's, however dead he was. In another moment, Mabry brought up his other hand and caressed the crown of Gwyn's head.

She reached back and took the hand on her shoulder.

So he said "Can we go upstairs and lie down awhile? I mean, I'm *dead tired* and probably shouldn't drive home without a nap."

Gwyn laughed a little. "Is *rest* all you've got in mind, old chum?"

"Girl, I'm still too young to know my mind." He also laughed.

"Then call your father first, or he'll think you're bleeding in some country ditch—people are dying in droves this week."

The kitchen clock said ten twenty-five. A call would be a good idea. But who would he wake up? He dialed Tasker's number anyhow; and after the usual excess rings, a man's voice answered—a black man's baritone. "Preacher Kincaid's house."

Mabry was stumped. *Who the hell is this?* He gave his name and asked to speak with his father. The man said "Mr. Kincaid, your father's watching a movie and asked not to be disturbed. Can I give him a message?"

Mabry still couldn't think who this was—clearly not Nelson, the former caretaker. But a strain of anger was mixed with his voice when he said "I have no idea who you are, sir."

The man said "Oh, I'm Audrey Thornton's son—the live one, don't you know? I'm Marcus, sir."

Ah, sure. Audrey said he'd come at bedtime to help with Pa (so the younger son is dead after all). He said "Then Marcus, I'm glad you're there. And I hope to meet you soon. For now, please tell Pa I'll be late; but I'm perfectly fine. Just having a pleasant reunion with a friend."

Marcus said "I'll tell him but you don't need me to come get you, do you? You in any trouble?"

Mabry grinned to himself. *I could easily be—or headed there.* Still he only said "No, son, thank you. Me and my car are in good shape." He regretted the word *son*; how condescending might it sound in this world down here?

Marcus ignored any possible mistake, for now at least. "I hope you'll be staying on a good while. I need to meet you. You could really help me."

Whoa a minute. Mabry couldn't imagine what *help* would mean, with this young man—money or what? All he said, though, was "My plans are mighty unsure with all this awful stuff in New York, but I guess I'll be here a few more days—sure. Maybe tomorrow night?"

Marcus said "Right, Chief. I'll see you soon after dark tomorrow, OK?"

Where did the *chief* come from? Was it Marcus's dry response to Mabry's word *son*? Whatever, Mabry chuckled. "After dark tomorrow. Now be sure to tell my pa I'm safe and will see him at breakfast."

With no further word, Marcus was gone.

The hole he left in the air was bigger than Mabry would have guessed. He held the phone ten seconds and then said "Marcus?" twice before he conceded the boy was gone. *Or is he a man? Whatever his age, better call him a* man.

Then from the head of the stairs, Gwyn said—in her richest Tallulah Bankhead voice—"Darling, wasn't this lie-down your exclusive idea? You ready or not?"

Mabry said "Ready," not knowing what for, and walked on toward her. When he'd climbed the first four steps, great blooms of light exploded through his eyes, in a cushioned silence but over and over at terrifying yet intriguing intervals. He could barely see through them, so he stopped in place and thought an enormous understatement—*This is something new.* Should he call Gwyn down and ask her to drive him to the nearest hospital, which was twenty miles away? When he'd stood still there for half a minute, the lights slowly faded, in his right eye at least.

And Gwyn called again. "You all right, friend?"

So he reached for the stair rail to steady his legs; and hand over hand, he slowly pulled himself to the top. *Very likely I'll be dead in a year. Well, what the hell? Nothing to it apparently. No place to run, even if your legs work. It comes to get you whenever it's ready, as Baxter Sample already knows.*

＊　　＊　　＊

When he woke, it was dark still. But enough street light slatted through the blinds to let Mabry gradually establish his whereabouts. A big high bed with four tall posts, a big room around him with a ceiling so distant it might have been the sky, a warm presence beside him on his left. *Surely it's Gwyn*. She was turned toward him, but her breathing sounded very much like sleep. He turned to face her. And she smelled like Gwyn, yes. The hair that fell across most of her face still seemed to be Gwyn's—and it felt like hers when he brushed the ends lightly with his nose—but she'd shed the evening dress and was wearing only what seemed to be a slip or a short nightgown.

He didn't remember what had happened, though, between the time he dragged himself up the stairs and now. He looked down at himself—he was also in his underwear—and a quick frisk suggested that his cock had undergone no recent activity, whether pleasure or simple humiliation. So he had a quiet minute to consider what should, or might, come next. Since Gwyn was far gone, he could try to find his clothes and the picture downstairs and head for his father's. He could roll to his right side—the side he mostly slept on—and rest till morning. Or being this near to an all but life-long friend and partner in occasional undemanding pleasures, he could bring her awake with his voice and hands and hope for at least the kind of welcome he'd been starved of for so long.

Starved? When he'd sat by Frances through her last hard weeks and made his silent vow to hold his body back from any real sex for some appropriate stretch, he knew that any stretch beyond a month would be unlikely; but now one month had gone into five. The early days had been truly a strain. Within a month, though, relief like a trickle of clean springwater welled up in him and freshened both his mind and his body. At the gym he visited three times a week, four younger women and a middle-aged gay lawyer had made frank approaches or left their numbers on scraps of paper in the door of his locker.

In considerable amazement, he'd nonetheless discarded the

women's numbers and thanked the lawyer cheerfully; and while—
at his age—he was unavoidably pleased by the interest, he felt no
serious pangs in his rapid retreat into steady work, regular meals with
old friends, and a few trips out to Montauk for weekends with an
older widowed playwright friend who'd bought an oceanfront house
back when such property was in the reach of actual human beings.
His vow hadn't included masturbation, but he had little trouble in
cutting way back on even that likable domestic reward. So now he
moved close enough to Gwyn's lips to touch them with his own—
an intended goodbye, for tonight anyhow.

He'd barely drawn back when her voice said "Darling, it's all
gone, ain't it?"

She didn't sound fully awake, but apparently she knew who was
with her. So Mabry propped himself on his left elbow and said
"What's gone, other than our youth, thank God?"

She waited long enough to leave him almost free to head out,
then she said "You don't miss our beautiful youth? We were both
damned lovely."

"—Lovely enough to make an endless stream of trashy mistakes
that hurt other people." He wanted to laugh at the end of that, but
his mind wouldn't let him. It agreed with his voice, agreed in *spades*.

When her own mind had managed to process his claim, Gwyn
once more whispered *"Touché* again, dammit."

Mabry figured he could make an acceptably graceful exit at that
point, but she'd raised his curiosity anyhow. "Anything else gone?—
I've lost a wisdom tooth, and I think it took my last trace of wisdom
with it."

Gwyn punched her pillows, sat half-upright and thought a good
while as she looked out through the still dark window. When her
voice came eventually, it had very little of her old tiresome Cas-
sandra delight in telling him terrible news. "The world ended two
days ago."

It honestly took him the better part of half a minute to understand.

"I very well may have lost my home and all the contents. I may have lost a good client, as I told you. My daughter's safe, though maybe she'd rather not speak to her pa again, not anytime soon. But the world appears to be trotting along."

Gwyn had quit smoking eight months ago, longer ago than Mabry quit sex; yet her longing for a cigarette at this moment all but swamped her ability to forge ahead with this self-absorbed post-adolescent friend beside her in her mother's best bed. When she spoke, she sounded the way she felt—more or less benignly exasperated. "The whole of Western civilization—plus many thousand lives—ended this week on native ground, and all it means to you is your own piddling business?"

That seemed to deserve a considerable wait. Then Mabry said "You may have nailed it, yes ma'm."

"Then maybe you better just haul your sorry ass out of my house." There was no indication she was not dead earnest.

So Mabry said "Wait. Let me say what I mean."

"I think you've said it in very clear fashion—you're a self-enraptured maniac." But oddly she laughed.

He knew she was right—her words, not the laugh. At least half right. He went on, though, to try to explain. "I mean, what else can we do but lie here, or stand up tomorrow, and do our business? You don't plan to head for New York—do you?—and start slinging rubble off the heads of dead folks?"

"I don't, no," she said, "but—" Again she faced her window.

"And don't you know Western civ. has withstood the Visigoths, the Nazis, Joseph Stalin, and all their soul-stunted grinning henchmen, plus the endless procession of child molesters?—"

"Including our parents." Even in the dark, she turned to Mabry at last.

He said "My parents never laid a finger on me. I wish they had. I *craved* molestation."

Gwyn was fierce by now. "They sure as hell touched sixty zillion *black* kids from the day the first slave ship docked in Jamestown, a hundred and fifty miles northeast of here." She actually pointed northeast. "And of course I don't just mean your and my ma and pa but *all* our people, our lily-white forebears."

Mabry's voice was sincerely calmer—he was not only tired but strangely at peace. "Gwyn, your old friend Western civ. could never have crawled up out of the chasms of Asia and Europe without a liberal supply of slaves." Before she could reach to claw his eyes out, he went on. "I'm not defending the practice for an instant, just pointing out that almost everything you and I've loved in art and literature and cooking and you-name-it would almost certainly not have happened without the hard-forced service of men and women and children. Homer and Sophocles and Vergil and Horace were riding, soft as down pillows, on slaves as wretched as Dachau inmates."

Gwyn said "Name a great woman that depended on slaves."

"Sappho," he said.

"Sappho had all those willing girls."

"Most of whom she owned."

Gwyn said "There's no proof of that—I just read all her poems (you can read them in an hour). Anyhow, this much is past even your pissant intellect—this week has changed us all forever in ways we can't yet begin to feel."

Mabry said "I may not doubt a syllable of that—can we be sure yet? Tell me what else to do, though."

She sat even farther upright and covered both her eyes long enough to think she knew the answer. "Take the money Frances left you and rebuild your homeplace. I'll do the same here. Then we'll both hunker down for eternity in the walls where we first glimpsed daylight—and hell, we could meet for drinks every month or so, if you'll share the bar tab."

Mabry thought *Does everybody in this whole county know what I just learned about my bank account?* "What makes you think Frances would be fool enough to leave me a dime?"

Gwyn said "I knew Frances Kenyon Kincaid well enough to know she did. Who did we ever know that had a better heart? And to think I snuck around, stealing pieces off of you, back in the first few years you knew her. Me and several dozen more."

In the dark Mabry nodded.

Since Gwyn couldn't see him, she said "How wrong am I?"

"Not very," he said, "if *several dozen* can mean fourteen."

"Agreed," she said (men always knew their exact box score—every man she'd known, though few would give her a truthful total). She fumbled for his right hand and found it, cooler than the room around them.

The truths they'd released into the same air were way too painful to confront, not tonight. And whether Gwyn was serious about restoring the houses, Mabry was hardly likely to accept her challenge. By now, though, he was roused enough to move closer toward her. They'd confessed their guilt. Frances was as far gone as she'd ever be. Wasn't it time for a little mutual self-reward, albeit on the smoking ruins of Western civ.? He hadn't entirely bought Gwyn's dismissal of him as nothing but a narcissistic brat. Hadn't she herself, after all, been trooping round the Earth, eager to press her political convictions on the widows and orphans and titans of other lands? And—despite all his waste and outright deceit—hadn't a few hundred beautiful objects left his hands more beautiful, and safer, than they'd been before he touched them? He rocked toward Gwyn, laid his right arm across her sensible hips and pulled his own body closer still.

She said "Say more please about your M.S."

"Maybe I went a little too far. It's not a medical certainty yet— that'll take awhile longer—but the chances are better than sixty percent. And if it's not M.S., then something weird's got a foothold in me and scares me to death when it suddenly raises its various heads."

Gwyn reached over and began very lightly to ruffle his scalp. "I'm going to deliver another fearless prophecy, here and now—you're just undergoing a normal response to Frances's death, all those weeks beside her and all that pain. Not to mention the guilt. You'll slowly walk on away from whatever's wrong now."

Mabry said "I'll do my level best to believe you." Then sensing he'd been given some sort of permission, he began to explore her in accordance with his memories of their times together in a far distant world.

She helped him along, gently correcting his occasional mistakes and adding her own soft hands on his body.

They worked in full silence.

And Mabry truly enjoyed the minutes, though his cock had been out of service so long that it never quite hardened. Still, it gave a respectable performance, all things considered; and what it couldn't accomplish, his knowing hands did. Or at least he got thanked.

When they'd drawn back a little and calmed awhile, Gwyn said "I know I'm saying this, here, on unreal time; but the way I feel, I could wish we didn't have to leave here again."

Mabry's mind joined her enough to let him say "Who says we do?"

"We will of course. But it's been first-class while it lasted, sweet child." The voice was hers, no mimicry. In another few seconds, she'd sunk fast asleep.

Mabry took a short snooze of his own, then covered her with the nearest quilt and made his way out with Philip Adger's sad little picture under his arm.

The dim porch light was on at his father's, but no window was lit—it was nearly one-thirty. Despite the dark prospect, Mabry knew he was sober enough to feel the way toward his bedroom. The rest at Gwyn's had helped, but the whole long day's trip down from Nova Scotia remained to be slept off. Tasker had given him a front-door key; but when he got there, the door was unlocked. He stepped in quietly and paused long enough to let his eyes adjust to the blackness. Then he turned left to cross the sparsely furnished living room. Even the generally creaky floorboards cooperated nicely, and he was almost ready to enter the back hall when a deep voice said "Welcome home." Mabry stood in place and waited for the sudden chill to run through his bones. It was not his father's voice, not Audrey's surely. And firmly secular though he was, he considered briefly the chance that this was something spooky—some spirit messenger, called up in his father's bedtime prayers and bent on convincing Mabry that this house was *home*. When he was calm enough to speak, Mabry said "I was born here, yes. But who please are you?" At that point, he thought he could see a form sitting upright on the sofa, against the starlit bay window.

The form said "Mr. Kincaid, I talked to you on the phone. I'm Audrey's son, Marcus."

Mabry stayed in place, eight yards from the man. "I didn't know you spent the nights here."

Marcus said "I wasn't asleep. I was waiting for you."

"In this much dark?"

Marcus turned on the small table lamp beside him. He was fully dressed in a burgundy shirt and khaki trousers, and he looked wide awake. If Audrey had actually borne him, he was a darker shade of African than she; and he had a more up-to-date head of hair—a nicely planned design of tight braids and bare rows that set off a likably homely face with eyes as alive as a fast young threatened thing back in the trees, one of the taller antelopes maybe—threatened but not afraid and surely not cowed. Marcus said "I can think a lot better in the dark."

It was only then that Mabry fully registered another fact. His father had brought in a good deal of the furniture Mabry grew up with; and someone had arranged it in the old familiar order—useful chairs and tables and floor lamps, even the old enormous radio. Mabry sat on the edge of the overstuffed footstool. "Thinking anything good in this hard week?"

Marcus finally delivered what seemed like a carefully arrived-at grin. "You mean do I think I'll be drafted by Sunday? I guess I could be. Should I head out right now for Canada or Ghana?"

Mabry said "Considering our last war was mainly fought by men of your color, you might want to think about running right now — before sunrise." But he also smiled, though a little less broadly than Marcus had managed. Then he suddenly knew he was tired to the bone. He got to his feet. "Now that you mention it, I actually slept in Canada last night. I need to turn in."

Marcus stood up too; he was medium-height but strongly built, and his big ears fanned out as widely as if he'd set them on *patrol*. "I was hoping I could know you somehow, Mr. Kincaid."

Mabry said "How about we talk at breakfast then?"

Marcus shook his head hard. "I can't be here at breakfast time. Audrey would kill me. She doesn't know I'm still in the house." He was speaking at normal volume, though the kitchen was not that far away. "But see, I didn't know how long you'd stay; and I need to talk to you about my art. I can't get the kind of advice I need anywhere around here."

Whatever that meant, and most people's art was more than hard to take, it was news to Mabry. And maybe it was the lateness and his exhaustion speaking, maybe it was one of the reckless good patches that survived in his mind, maybe it was the fact that Marcus was the only fully *live* human being he'd seen since Leah Wilkins last night in the Halifax kitchen. In any case, the next thing he heard himself say was "Are you free from, say, ten o'clock tomorrow morning till you're due to come back here and help my father go to bed?"

Marcus said "I can sure-God arrange to be."

Mabry's lunge kept going. "And you've got a valid driver's license?"

"Since the age of sixteen —"

"Then come back at ten and drive me to Raleigh. You ever been to the State Art Museum?"

Marcus said "Just nine times or more, since I was a schoolchild. I worship that place."

Mabry heard himself take the next step of a plan that he had no idea his mind had made. "I want to see a friend of mine who works in the conservation department. He can lend me a few of the things I need to start work here on a picture I'm cleaning for a man in New York who's likely to be dead in the World Trade Center."

Marcus said "I'm sorry to hear it. I hope you didn't know him all that well."

Odd as it sounded, it was still a winning sentence. So Mabry said "He was the only lawyer I've known with a real sense of humor, but my friendship with him was mostly professional."

Marcus tried to look interested, but his young eyes were impatient. He was plainly hoping to push on toward the kind of advice he'd already mentioned. "Mom told me about your trade awhile back."

Mom was another all-but-universal modernism—TV born and bred—that Mabry loathed (he still said *Mother*). But he tried to push past it and return simple courtesy. And *trade*? Mabry hadn't thought of what he did as a *trade* for years, maybe ever. But he liked the sound. This young man might be an artist after all. Well then, Mabry Kincaid was a practiced *tradesman*. He needed to get his ass to work. With a weary flap of his hand, he told young Marcus "Good night for now."

When Mabry was fully out of sight, Marcus could no longer hold back. "*Yes!*" he whispered loudly.

Mabry heard him. *Have I started something I can't finish?* But he was too tired to walk back now and change the plan.

Mabry dreamt all night, the kinds of fearsome pursuits and entrapments that ride you hard and leave you more hungover at dawn than any drunk evening. When he woke at five-fifteen, his room was still dark; but he knew there was no hope of sleeping again. Yet he couldn't get up. The bed he was born in felt safe at least, for an hour longer. Though the starlight was strong enough to outline a few family pictures on the walls, he tried not to look. Each one portrayed a face he'd loved or liked—or enjoyed anyhow—and the sight of them now might plunge him deeper into wet self-pity than he already was.

My city's been poleaxed and far more people than we know are dead, including Baxter. The whole country's struck in a way that may last, the rest of my life anyhow. My loft is knee-deep in poisonous dust, maybe ruined past fixing. My only child will barely speak to me, and I'm caving downhill into blind paralysis. My gimped old pa is all I've got. So who the hell can take care of me when I'm a cold cod, bent double in a wheelchair? And I'm still a young man. I could last forty years.

That—and one or two naps, plus the scraps of prayer he'd say when the cards were down—kept him in bed till he heard the first real human sounds from the kitchen. Pots and pans and the rasp of an actual coffee grinder. Even his grandmother hadn't ground her own coffee since, oh, the Depression. *Is it Tasker or Audrey? One or the other.* So he dragged himself upright, washed his face and stumbled his way into yesterday's funky clothes, intending to head for the kitchen and whomever. When his hand was on the china doorknob, though, there was Baxter's French picture in its wrappings, leaned on the wall. Suddenly it seemed the next urgent thing.

He untied it again and took it to the window. His watch said six-twenty; and even this close to the fall equinox, there was light enough to let him see the dim surface again. Why hadn't he wondered what might lie under the wide linen matt that covered at least the edges of the canvas? He took his Swiss Army knife with the thousand tools and gently pried out the retaining nails at the back of the picture. When he'd laid the frame on the foot of his bed, he went to the brighter window and studied the larger picture. *Fool, you failed the first challenge here. But maybe it was good you didn't know last night. You'd have fed Gwyn's fantasy*—for now he could see that the frame had covered more than an inch of the canvas, all around. And what was covered was considerably cleaner than the rest. Maybe the signs of quite a different subject—was it clouds and occasional tortured tree limbs? In any case, young Adger's effort had left uncovered a different hour in the French countryside (this was surely not Charleston)—an even darker moment maybe that set in motion an older painter's ending. Was there something really interesting here? Had Baxter thought so? But Baxter had never seen the canvas.

Too groggy still to feel anything more than mild curiosity, Mabry propped the unwrapped picture back on the wall and went to the kitchen.

Audrey had already set the table and was working at the stove. She looked toward Mabry but offered no greeting.

"Your father's in his room."

"Is he awake?"

She didn't face Mabry; she was scrambling eggs. "He's been awake since five o'clock—every morning, five sharp." She didn't seem especially happy with the fact.

So Mabry said "I guess that doesn't give you much sleep." He wasn't aware of any deeper meaning.

But Audrey turned with a hot-eyed frown. "I get as much sleep as I need, thank you, yes."

His father's voice called him then. "Step here, baby boy."

Mabry was not the baby son. The actual baby—Gabriel, Gabe—was thirty-one years gone, killed at eighteen in a hunting accident, a few miles from here. It was still a sizable hole in Mabry's heart and surely in his father's. So he stepped on forward, not meaning to correct his father on the point.

Tasker was fully dressed in a jumpsuit—battleship gray with burgundy piping down his arms and legs. At the sight of his son, he assumed a droll grin and stretched his extremities out before him. He looked like a long-retired admiral, one who'd never lost a battle and wouldn't today. "Audrey bought me this getup at the new mall in Roanoke Rapids. She says it's the latest in fetching attire for elderly gents. Don't tell me she's wrong."

Mabry did his best to match the grin. "Not *wrong* at all. It's the height of male snazz but—" He dropped his voice to a stage whisper. "Did she truly say *fetching?*"

Tasker paused as though he were actually searching. Then he called toward the kitchen. "Audrey, didn't you say my new suit was fetching?"

No answer at all, though the sounds of cooking were plain to hear.

Tasker gave the quick shrug of a boy caught in mischief. "Did you get a wink of sleep?"

"I got home late but, yes sir, I slept a good two hours."

"You must have met up with some old friends then." Tasker had never been a probing father; this was the closest he was likely to move into Mabry's private life.

Hell, tell him the whole thing. It might cheer him some. "I stopped at the pool hall and saw poor old Vance Scott."

"Not sober surely?"

"When was Vance last sober—1965? No, but sober enough to tell me Gwyn Williams was back in town. So I went to see Gwyn."

Tasker's face was still not serious, but he said "I heard she was here. Gwyn may be the poorest girl I know."

That didn't ring right. Surely Tasker hadn't seen her in thirty years. "When was the last time you saw her, Pa?"

Quickly, Tasker's eyes went grave, caught in a small lie. "Four or five days ago."

Gwyn surely hadn't mentioned such a meeting.

"You ran into her somewhere in town?"

Tasker drew back again. "She came to the house here."

Mabry said "I spent several hours with her last night; and she never mentioned laying eyes on you, much less coming here."

"Son, it was a pastoral visit in reverse. Gwyn wanted communion, she came to this house, and I gave it to her. It's part of my job, very nearly the only part left."

"Gwyn's a Methodist—or was, right?"

Tasker said "I'm not a Roman Catholic priest. I don't recall ever turning away any human being who asked for the sacrament. I *did* have a gorgeous Irish setter turn up at the altar rail one warm Sunday morning. I had to refuse her, gently of course."

Early as it was in the day, Mabry was surprised by the news on Gwyn. Surprised and curious. But he knew not to probe further, not with this priest. He looked round and saw the new TV, turned off. "Any fresh word this morning?"

Tasker said "I turned it off at sunrise. They're still saying maybe six thousand people died—in New York alone, then several hundred at the Pentagon and maybe fifty on the plane in Pennsylvania. And nobody has the slightest idea how those few men hijacked four full-sized American planes, made them take off on time—very nearly on *time*; can you believe it?—and do what they did."

Mabry said "Any word on whether they've opened up lower Manhattan to traffic?"

Tasker said "I listened especially for that. It's roped off indefinitely—unless you've got an ancient dog or an aged parent trapped in a building with no food or water." He carefully straightened the creases in his trousers. Then he glanced up, smiling. "You're a lucky man, boy. Your aged parent is *here* and means to stay."

Before Mabry had to deal with the loaded implications of that, Audrey stood in the door, looking straight toward him, grim as Justice on any courthouse.

"Your breakfast is ready."

Those four words were also, plainly, loaded. Mabry looked to Tasker.

But all Tasker said was "Son, roll me forward."

*   *   *

Audrey's breakfast was as fine as her supper—impeccable scrambled eggs, crisp bacon, fried tomatoes, English muffins, and somebody's homemade peach preserves with coffee dark enough to power a drowsy platoon of combat marines. Tasker and Mabry talked a little—the day's outlook—but Audrey hardly spoke a word; and before the men were finished eating, she'd got up, set her dishes in the sink, taken a broom, and headed out to sweep the front porch.

So Mabry said "Audrey feeling all right?"

Tasker said "Did she look sick to you? Son, if you're going to have an employee in the house—notice I haven't used the word *servant* in thirty-odd years—you'll have to thicken your skin enough to bear the rapid changes of weather, the *indoor* weather. Audrey's peeved that you asked young Marcus to drive you to Raleigh, I think."

A genuine surprise. "Oh God. You know he waited up last night in the dark living room for me to get home?"

"No sir, I didn't. He's an energetic boy though."

Mabry said "So it appears. He told me how eager he was to meet me and that he was an artist—or hoped to be. So since I was tired to the point of stupefaction, I said the first thing that came to mind."

Tasker smiled. "Did he tell you he's got a full-time job? He delivers prescriptions for the drugstore in town."

"He didn't mention that. He sprang for my plan and said he'd be here by ten this morning."

Tasker nodded fast. "No doubt he will. He's never failed *me*. Are you riding down to see Will Green at the museum?"

It all but floored Mabry—*Is there some kind of spy system loose in the house?*—and his voice was all but hot. "That was the plan last night at least, but how—may I ask—does the whole damned household know my business so early?" He didn't mention that half the county seemed to know.

Tasker stayed calm. "Marc woke his mother up at three a.m.—he was that excited."

Mabry said "I guess I thought he was a grown-up man."

Tasker said "Grown enough to have a child of his own."

"Then why does he have to tell his mother every plan he's got?"

Tasker reached for Mabry's hand on the table.

Mabry withdrew it.

But his father persisted. "Son, consider this—first, Marc Thornton may have killed his brother a few years back (I'm not sure of that yet); and second, you may represent the best hope this young man has ever glimpsed."

So while he gathered himself for the trip, Mabry considered that.

When he got to the porch, it was ten past ten. The sunlight was strong but dry and mild, and a light breeze was rippling the high oak leaves. At first he heard nothing but that dim rustling. Then as he stood and looked back to the crossroads—a few pickup trucks parked at the store, the pool-hall beer sign already shining—he could hear a man's low voice off to his right. He turned and walked that way. There in the porch swing, Audrey was seated; and Marcus was balanced on the rail beside her.

He'd changed his clothes since 3 a.m.—a clean white long-sleeved shirt and navy blue trousers. And when he saw Mabry moving toward him, he stood up, smiled, stepped forward a little, and held out a hand.

Mabry shook it. "You're a man of your word, right on time." When he looked to Audrey, she was hardly smiling but not as grim as she'd been at breakfast. "Further greetings, Audrey."

"Still morning, Mr. Kincaid."

So we're back to last names. All right; keep talking. "Marcus, you ready to head for Raleigh?"

"I am, yes sir."

Audrey stood at that point, and Marcus looked toward her with some apprehension. But when she spoke, it was only to Mabry. "You plan to be back here by suppertime?"

Mabry said "After that handsome spread last night, I wish I could guarantee my answer is yes. But in case we get held up for any reason—this *is* a rental car—I'd better say no. If there's any leftovers though, I'd be mighty grateful."

Audrey said "We'll see what we can do."

Mabry and Marcus were down the steps and halfway out to the car before she spoke again. "Be careful with that boy. He's all I've got left."

Mabry turned to face her. "He'll be the one driving, but I'll take extra care. We're going to the museum and coming straight back."

With both eyes shut, she gave her permission.

The men walked onward. Mabry surrendered the keys to Marcus, who took no more than five seconds to acquaint himself with the workings of the Dodge; and then they were off, backing out of the drive.

When they made the first move forward, Mabry looked to the house.

By then Audrey was standing at the porch rail, with her hand up in farewell, as if she might not see them again. The forthright honesty of her gesture swept over Mabry. How many times had women bade him provisional farewell? His mother, his grandmother, Frances, even Gwyn, his daughter Charlotte when she was a child, a dozen others. And what guarantee did he have that his father would still be alive when he and Marcus came back this evening? His eyes welled tears and before they'd got to the main crossroads—against his effort to force it down—he gave a hard sigh. *Oh Christ, no.*

Marcus nearly stopped the car and looked over toward him. "You hurting, Mr. Kincaid?"

At once it struck Mabry. *He knows I'm sick. When did Pa tell him?*

He wouldn't ask for details now. So he said "I'm no more hurt than we all are, after this awful business in New York."

By then the car was stopped in the midst of the two-lane blacktop. Marcus said "You think those Muslim guys have ruined this country forevermore like they're claiming on TV?" It might very well be the gravest question he'd asked in his brief life.

Mabry said "No, I don't. But we can talk about that once we get a breeze underway." He pointed ahead with all the authority of Lewis or Clark. "Let's shove on forward."

Marcus said "And you're not going to scare me?" He was grinning by then but still entirely earnest.

Mabry laughed a little. "How could I scare you? You could bend me into pretzel shapes any minute you wanted."

Marcus said "I wouldn't want that. But your dad has told me you're maybe bad sick."

Mabry said "I see my dear pa has turned into a chatterbox in his old age. Marcus, here's exactly all I know. For a few months I've had strange symptoms that may be M.S.—tingling in my hands and feet, sudden flashes of light in my eyes, and occasional patches of double vision. My doctors are saying they need awhile longer to know for sure what's causing the problems. I asked you to drive me when I was flat worn out last night. You can bet your last penny I won't get scary. And I won't need any kind of nursing. I'm one of the safest adults you know." He gave that a few quiet seconds to soak in. "Any more questions?"

Marcus paused even longer than Mabry expected, but then he laughed frankly. "Just tell me what your upper speed limit is."

Mabry said "What's legal in the Tar Heel State now?"

"Sixty-five, most places."

Mabry said "Keep it just under seventy-four." It was only then that he realized Marcus's name was not on his rental car agreement. *Oh what the hell? This is dear old Tar Heelia. They won't give a damn, until we're both corpses; and then it won't matter, except to us two.*

*   *   *

In under two hours they were roaming the galleries of the State Art Museum, searching out various personal favorites and occasionally encountering one another by accident or at the will of Fate. At one o'clock Mabry asked Marcus if he was hungry.

"Mr. Kincaid, I'm hungry all *over* the clock. You could wake me up at three in the morning, and I'd scarf down a cross section of a cow and three baked potatoes decorated all the way."

Considering Marcus's rail-thin body, that seemed unlikely. But Mabry said "They've got a fairly nice café downstairs. Let's pause for a bite."

That sat comfortably with Marcus; and in the bright restaurant, he ordered a bowl of guaranteed original Cajun gumbo, followed by a mile-high turkey club sandwich.

Mabry also had the gumbo, then cheese and biscuits; and when they were near their last cups of coffee, he realized how little they'd said since leaving Wells—not quite what he'd expected, after Marcus's volubility last night. Despite the odd class session here and there and a few summer seminars in conservation, Mabry had never really been a teacher; but now he thought of a way that might trigger Marcus again and help him show his hand, whatever it was. "I need a short visit to the men's room now. After that, let's find our two absolute favorite pictures in this whole building and tell each other why."

For all the serious response on Marcus's face and eyes, Mabry might have proposed the hardest test invented by humans. Marcus said "It has to be my favorite in this one building, nowhere else?"

Mabry said "God, man, there are surely enough splendid pictures here. It's after all the single art museum in the country that's entirely state-supported. Show some in-state pride!" He was more than half joking.

Marcus's body still seemed to hedge, but he hadn't said no.

So Mabry left him alone at the table, found the men's room and was back in five minutes to discover that Marcus had called for the check and actually paid it—which was not the plan (he wouldn't hear of any reimbursement from Mabry). When they both stood at last, Mabry said "You rather head on home now?"

"Oh no sir, I'm ready. I just had to"—here at last Marcus paused to cross his eyes for comic effect (his first real levity of the day)—"*contemplate* my personal aesthetics and be absolutely sure of my choice."

In another three minutes, they were standing in front of Mabry's choice—the large circular Botticelli Nativity with a winsome baby, four months old, looking toward the painter; his worshipful mother hovering above him, St. Joseph snoozing in the middle distance and a long line of Magi winding through the far hills, bound for the baby.

When they'd both stood looking for a silent while, Marcus said "Now you get to tell me *why*."

Mabry said "You don't like it." It was not a question.

"Sir, I didn't say that. But you set the rules of this game we're playing—you got to say *why*."

Mabry went through a quick art-history lecture on who Botticelli was (a man apparently torn by a sense of sin for some unknown cause). Then he proceeded to a longer discussion of the surface of the picture—which passages were plainly in the master's hand and which were painted by studio assistants (maybe most of the picture), places where the surface had been overcleaned in the nineteenth century, the traces of near six hundred years of small repairs. He thought he was finished when he finally conceded. "To be sure, some experts don't think it's a Botticelli at all—just a big old handsome exercise in the Botticelli manner by some skillful lad in fifteenth-century Florence, maybe with the master's hands-on blessing." He paused, looked round for a guard and saw no one. So he gave a short stroke to the heavy handcarved gilded frame with his long forefinger. Then he looked round again and actually touched the canvas. Then he whispered strongly to himself "*Behave!*" Then he looked back to Marcus.

Marcus said "But that's *it*?" He wasn't laughing.

Mabry grinned though. "What else do I owe you?"

"I don't know—maybe more than a sermon."

"Gosh, was that a sermon?" Mabry moved a step closer to the picture.

But by then a guard had strolled in from the next gallery. He raised his voice—"Mister!"—then waved Mabry back.

So Marcus led the way to the main door. "I'll show you mine now."

Mabry followed him silently, still a little abashed (the guard was a black man). There were several good pictures by African-Americans in the upstairs galleries—Romare Bearden and Jacob Lawrence. Mabry thought they'd likely head for the elevator. But no, Marcus only led him into the next room and down a few yards to a very small picture—a favorite of Mabry's own, one he always visited on any trip here. Mabry didn't mention that; he waited for whatever Marcus might say.

First, Marcus said "I could lie down right here and sleep for a week. This is one happy room."

Mabry said "I agree but I doubt that mean-ass guard would let us even *kneel*, much less *lie*."

At which point Marcus fell to his knees in front of the picture. The glum guard had followed them, and maybe it was only because Marcus knelt three yards from the wall that he didn't make him rise.

Mabry moved toward the painting as though he'd never seen it. On a wall of big companions, it was only about fifteen by twenty inches. And its plaque said "St. Paul's Departure from Caesarea by Jan Brueghel the Elder." Though he'd known it at close range for years, Mabry studied its crowded surface silently. Once, with a reproduction in hand, he'd tried to count all the heads and bodies of the mob strewn along the harbor—he'd forgot the total, more than a hundred surely. Most of the city, anyhow, had plainly turned out—either to bid that eternally difficult guest St. Paul a hearty bon voyage or to hustle the wild-eyed apostle on his way with no return ticket or to see the four ships in various stages of arrival or departure. But where was St. Paul? Between his visits, Mabry always lost the star of the show; so now he bent, at sufficient distance, and tried to find the eloquent apostle among the many outsized noses that Brueghel had maybe provided as thigh-slapping amusement for his guaranteed audience of Northern European goyim. Mabry thought he recalled that St. Paul wore a halo, but after two minutes he still hadn't found him.

Marcus got to his feet with his broadest smile. "Give up?" Clearly he understood Mabry's present quandary.

Mabry said "Afraid so."

"And you're a certified licensed professional in the expensive picture business?"

Mabry kept his smile burning, a little surprised to be embarrassed. "I confess I am, yes."

Marcus took a long look at his watch. "You ready for me to show you right now? I can give you one last sixty seconds, by the minute hand."

Though he'd never had a son, Mabry knew enough about men — boys — to know he should let Marcus show him, a resounding trump of a hapless elder. To take another minute, and find Paul now, would be the cheapest kind of grown-up triumph. It wasn't easy, though, to say "I surrender. Show me the man please."

Marcus looked to the guard. Their eyes plainly met. Then Marcus stepped forward and all but touched the right man in the picture — Paul of Tarsus in his uncanny halo, escorted by soldiers, in the lower right corner, a tiny figure (maybe four inches high) to have altered the course of Western civ. Marcus looked back to Mabry — "Behold your man!"

The guard said "You gentlemen better move on now."

In all his years of museum-going, Mabry had never heard quite such an order; but the tone of voice was low and mild. Did it have to do with the African-American blood the man shared with Marcus Thornton?

Whatever, Marcus said to the guard "Can I just stand back and tell this white man what I know?"

The guard actually chuckled—another first for Mabry—and said "Bring him on up to speed, sure; but you keep your distance, man. *Behave* yourself."

So Marcus said to Mabry "I've got two reasons for loving this picture as much as I do. First, it's painted on *copper*—a sheet of copper, *metal*. Don't ask me how. Then second, the best thing is the way he's buried his one good man so you can hardly find him—just like in the world."

Mabry said "Good reasons, both. But of course you could spot St. Paul right off if you had eyes that could spot haloes in a big crowd of folks *without* them."

"*Right!*" Marcus said—he was truly excited—"but see, Mr. Brueghel" (he pronounced the name to rhyme with *frugal*) "rigged the whole scene to make you think you were the one soul in the entire world who could spot a good man. Nobody else in the picture can see him, nobody else in the whole museum, the guard can't see him" (Marcus waved to the guard, who gave a long wink). "Just me and—now—you."

So Mabry thanked him.

And Marcus accepted the thanks by patting his own left shoulder and bowing low from the waist toward Mabry.

They were out of the gallery and moving through the Greek and Roman sculptures when Mabry decided to act on at least a part of the reason he was here at all. He'd thought of consulting an old friend, who worked in the conservation lab, about his Adger picture. But this morning, just before he left home, he'd decided not to bring the picture and very likely—if he saw his friend—not to mention it today. His and Gwyn's hunch that some *small treasure* lurked beneath the boy's surface was still potent in him. He'd likely keep it private for now.

While Marcus was roaming through the book-and-gift shop,

though, Mabry asked the woman at the information desk to phone Will Green in the conservation lab. He and Will had studied the craft together at the University of Delaware, and Mabry hadn't seen him for maybe ten years. Hadn't he heard that Will had progressed to the top of the ladder, director of conservation here?

And so he had, though when a guard led them down to the door of the lab, Will looked like the same frazzled sheepdog of a boy he'd been long ago. And though they'd exchanged a few words on the phone two minutes before, at first he didn't seem to recognize Mabry. He spent five seconds squinting to take his whole face in — a recently excavated bronze.

Then, very oddly, Marcus spoke up in his mimicking voice from back-when. "It's your old buddy Mabry—you used to call me *Caid*, the only person ever."

That did it. Will reached out, took Mabry by the upper shoulders, and kept on hunting around his face. At last he said, "Caid, my God, I truly don't believe it. It's you, *intact*."

Mabry wondered of course *How the hell does this boy know my grad school nickname?* but he said to Will "I'm the actual last remains of Billy the Kid."

Will said "No, that's me. You haven't aged by so much as a *molecule*, except to get better."

Marcus said "Amen," as though he knew.

But Mabry said to Will "I don't know whether to thank you or run. Or maybe both." He gave a quick feint as though to flee.

And Will said "How long are you in town for?"

Mabry said "I'm visiting my father up in Wells—a few days more in any case."

"So you didn't suffer at all on Tuesday?" Will thumbed behind him as though this Tuesday were a tangible presence.

That reminded Mabry that Will had spent a night or two in Mabry's loft when he was in New York on museum business maybe four years ago, so he gave him a quick rundown on his European vacation and the Nova Scotian detour, but by now he'd firmly decided against any mention of the Adger. *Thank God I still haven't showed it to Marc.* He said "You're clearly busy right now."

Will literally wrung his hands before him, a forced sign of busyness; but he also said "Please let me take you to lunch almost any day next week. Right this minute, though"—he pointed behind him in the same direction as this past Tuesday—"we're setting a huge de Kooning behind a gigantic sheet of glass in a new frame we've made, and I've got to turn back and help with that."

Mabry said "Then maybe I'll call you tomorrow and see."

Will apologized for the rush he was in; but before he left, he looked to Marcus and extended his hand. "I hope I'll get to meet you properly another day."

Marcus said "My name is Marcus Dab Thornton—call me Marc or Dab. I'll keep the same hope."

The odd turn of phrase held Will for a moment. Then he grinned at them both and was gone back into the hubbub of a framing crew whom he'd left holding a broad sea of glass.

They were halfway up the highway to Wells, and Marcus at the wheel seemed in a kind of immensely careful but solemnly airborne trance whenever Mabry did more than make the occasional idle remark. At last Mabry said "I never knew anybody else with the middle name *Dab*."

That broke Marcus's trance. "And you still don't. I just told your friend that so he might recall me if we ever meet again."

Mabry laughed. "It might work. But maybe you ought to have said *Rembrandt*."

Marcus laughed even louder. "Damn, you're right!"

And they drove another quiet five miles before Mabry said "My father says you've got your own child."

That was a knot that Marcus needed a little time to loosen. After a while he looked at his watch—the timepiece old people often have, with an over-sized face and giant numerals. Then he said "Chief, it's still not but three p.m. Maybe it's a little early in the day to tackle such a personal question." He was partially smiling toward the road itself; he wouldn't turn to Mabry.

Mabry looked to his own watch—3:22. "I'm sorry. We've only known each other for twenty-four hours. I just thought we were Southern gents, and since the South specializes in telling the world its secrets within mere seconds of meeting a stranger—"

Still facing the highway, badly potholed, Marcus broke in. "Here's another game—how about it? One of us talks about his family for one solid minute. Then the other one gives out sixty seconds' worth of some private business that eats *him* up."

Mabry was more than mildly surprised at the man's inventiveness—maybe he should be a writer, not a painter. Anyhow he said "*Touché*," at once regretting the echo of Gwyn. "Who goes first?"

Marcus said "You went first in the museum, and it was piss-poor—you *owe* me something grand this time. So I'll start off, to give you time to gouge around in your deep *quick*."

Mabry wondered if something was getting out of hand here. *Is this young man as benign as he looks? And what's this news about killing his brother?* But he said "Fire away."

They went on another two rocky miles, passing a couple of trailer trucks about a mile long each, scary roadhogs. Then Marcus was ready. "You time me," he said, "sixty seconds flat. I'm nineteen years old. When I was fifteen, I'd waited as long as my dick would let me; and at the same time a cousin of mine was feeling the same about her pussy—she was seventeen and we were maybe too close kin. Anyhow the baby came with no complications. My cousin—Adeline—had it at her house with a midwife that was my mom's aunt. It's a girl, *way* the prettiest girl I know. And they tell me that this kind of child—afflicted—is mostly so beautiful you can hardly watch it. The girl's named Master—her mother named her Master after my dead brother—and at first we thought she was just not talking because she didn't have anything she needed to say. But now she's three years old, and the doctors say she's likely never going to speak. Everything she does is normal as daybreak, everything but her funny name (and she isn't guilty of that at all); but she won't ever make a sound. Not even when she hurts or when anybody hurts her."

When Marcus stopped he didn't glance to Mabry, but Mabry wondered *Who on Earth hurts her?* But he just said "You've got fifteen seconds."

Marcus finally looked. He was trying to smile, but it didn't resemble any smile he'd shown in all the past day. He said "Can't you tell I'm way past finished?"

Mabry said "All right. I was trying to be as fair as I could."

"Then you get a hearty round of applause." Marcus slapped the steering wheel with his right hand four or five times.

Mabry said "You ready for my bad minute?"

Marcus actually grinned, at the road this time; then he looked to his watch. "Ready when you are, O Mighty Chief."

So Mabry said "The mother of my one child was two years older than me. We were just barely married when the child was born, a girl named Charlotte—plain as a good shoe and smarter than any big handful of whips. The three of us tried to grow up together. The two girls tried—truly worked at it hard, my wife and my daughter. But my dick couldn't seem to wear itself out, however many women I took into bedrooms, closets, utility chambers, public *parks* even in broad daylight. And I mean, when I was a man full-grown in all other ways—I mean, up till I was way into my forties. What in Christ's name was I looking for? I had a fine type of work, my wife was more than a saint and beautiful and bound to be rich—I mean *seriously* rich—when her dad died, but I had to slide my slim piece of meat in and out of any girl that I could trick into joining me for five or ten minutes—sometimes a whole night, if I was out of town on a job or a workshop. I would pray to quit, I went to a doctor in hopes of some drug that would ease my hunger—nothing, no help. But it was my fault; I never doubted that. Then my wife had finally put up with all the shit I could shovel, and she moved me out when I was thirty-eight years old and our daughter was twelve. She died—my wife—five months ago; and wouldn't you know it?—she's left me more money than I can ever use, to spend on anything that's halfway worthy of her."

They rode in silence for maybe a mile, through a dense stretch of tall pines and sycamores and kudzu strangling a dry-goods store. Marcus concentrated on the road, which was smoother now. His face gave no hint of what he'd heard.

So Mabry said "How long was that?"

"Seventy seconds."

"Why didn't you stop me?"

"You hadn't finished and I needed to hear somebody else speak along those lines." He turned to Mabry, whose face was tormented.

Mabry was seeing a tumult of lights, assaulting him like inexhaustible demons pouring down the road straight at him.

Marcus leaned over and with his fist he knocked, very lightly, on Mabry's left knee. "Thank you—hear?—Chief."

Mabry put both hands up to cover his eyes, but he said "You're far more welcome than you know."

When they stopped in the drive at Tasker's place, it was four-fifteen. Mabry's eyes and mind had cleared up entirely, though his body still seemed bone-tired from yesterday—that and the New York horror and the three grand weeks in Italy with the final two maybe mysterious days in Paris (whatever they'd yield, if anything). So he sat in silence, a pleasant-enough brand of torpor but with no further plans for the visible future.

Marcus killed the engine and held the keys toward Mabry.

Then the first practical thought he'd had in a good many hours occurred to Mabry. "How will you get home?" He craned to look past

Tasker's old Chevy for another vehicle. There was only Audrey's even older beige Ford. "How did you get here?"

Marcus said "I walk. You know where Mom lives, by the white cemetery. I'm staying there now. I'll truck on down there and freshen my beauty—don't you know—and then I'll hitch my black ass to Sherwin. Then I'll use the broke-down drugstore car to deliver strong pills to elderly folks from now till the time to help your dad on into his bed. You ever read the labels on bottles those folks get? Scare you to death. *May cause seizures and leprosy. Do not drive or use heavy machinery.* What's heavy machinery—a fifty-dollar dildo?"

Mabry laughed. "Anything bigger than a cocktail shaker. You want to come inside—a cup of coffee maybe? I sure need a jolt of something to bring me back at least halfway across the wide Atlantic."

Marcus said "I envy that jet lag you got."

"I beg your pardon?"

"Jet lag—that feeling you get from flying so far in too few days."

Mabry said "You'll get it soon enough. Meanwhile, drop the envy." He reached for his door latch.

Marcus said "You want me to bring you something? You know, some kind of pick-me-up? The druggist is a good friend. How about a little mild-mannered speed, just a capsule or two?"

Mabry blared his eyes to their full stretch. "Noooo, I gobbled my share of drugs thirty-five years ago when drugs were the *thing*. I'll make me a cup of strong black coffee; then I'll risk a long doze. But thanks all the same." He looked again to Marcus, serious now. "For God's sake, don't get in any drug trouble. You'd kill your mother."

Marcus slowly agreed. "I would. And your dad—he's been good to me right on down the years."

Wait. What's behind that? Mabry said "How long have you known Reverend Kincaid?"

"Your pa, you mean?"

"Is there another Reverend Kincaid on the lot?" Once it was out, Mabry heard his meanness.

Before he could soften the sarcasm, though, Marcus said "I think I saw him in Baltimore when I was a child—we lived there then. And of course I'd see him sometimes when we'd come back home for visits."

Mabry said "But he didn't live here till a few months ago."

Marcus said "You'd have to ask my mom for details. My memory's a mess."

Mabry said "Well, I'm glad we had our trip. Maybe we'll think of some other possibilities."

Marcus said "That would be mighty fine. You just say the word."

Mabry smiled. "Is there anything we said or did that I'm not supposed to mention inside?" He pointed to the house that was now in deep shade.

Marcus said "Just don't stress how much fun I had. And how I sassed you."

Mabry said "You didn't sass *me*."

"Yes sir I did, there back at the museum with your favorite picture—how I said you didn't really tell me why you liked it." With that, Marcus opened his own door wide and was saying "So long."

But Mabry said "Wait."

Marcus sat back to wait.

"The woman in the picture—the Botticelli Virgin and Child? That long plain face, the straight blond hair, the long pale fingers— she looks more like my mother than any photograph I've got."

Marcus felt there might be the need for some lightness. "But you don't look a lot like Baby Jesus, do you? Not anymore."

Mabry said "I was telling you about my mother. I've missed her lately."

So Marcus backtracked. "I never met her, did I?"

Mabry said "I doubt it—but what do I know? She's been dead twelve years anyhow. Her name was Eunice Kincaid, and you've seen her now—in that big round painting." Mabry pointed toward where he thought Raleigh lay, more or less due south.

Marcus said "I'll keep her in my mind then."

Since Marcus wouldn't let Mabry pay him for the drive, now Mabry handed him a book he'd bought for himself at the museum—a catalogue of all the paintings they'd seen and a good many more. The Botticelli would be in there.

Marcus looked in the index, turned to it now, and held it up for Mabry to see.

All Mabry could do was nod at the sight. The thought of his mother—first in the line of women he'd hurt, over and over—was way too painful. He said "You take that book home with you."

"You giving it to me? Mr. Kincaid, you don't owe me one thing. I *enjoyed* this day."

Mabry said "Son" and stopped right there. *This isn't your son and he won't want a trace of condescension.* So he started again. "Excuse that *son* but—"

Marcus said "Call me *son* any minute you need to."

Mabry said "Son, I'll see you tonight."

Marcus said "If we live that long. You know what the old-timers up here say—'If the Lord be willing and we don't die.'"

Mabry said "Damned right too."

In another ten seconds they'd gone separate ways.

THREE

9 . 14 . 2001
9 . 17 . 2001

Inside, a minute later, Mabry had walked straight on to the kitchen—no lights, nobody. His father's door was open, but there were no sounds from him or the television or Audrey. Mabry quietly went to his door and looked in.

Tasker was dressed to his usual standard and up in his wheelchair but slumped to the side in a nap so abandoned he looked like a victim.

Mabry wanted to speak or somehow approach and gently close his mouth, but he knew that would wake him. So with the sense of abandoning a child—something he absolutely knew he'd done at the time of his divorce—he turned and went to his own old room. There was no sign of Audrey anywhere, though her car had been in the drive just now.

In his room, the bed (which he'd made this morning) had been remade to professional standards—hospital corners at all four ends. His towel had been folded, and the shirt he'd draped across a chair had disappeared. When he searched, he discovered that all the dirty clothes he'd brought from France were also gone. *Now she's laundering me* and *Pa. I'll stop that fast.* But no anger followed.

Somehow he didn't mind Audrey's rummaging through his things. At least there was no sign she'd unwrapped the painting, and that was the only thing that felt private.

He was almost about to open it once more, pop out the liner again, wet a handkerchief with plain saliva—the conservator's friend—and work on a chaste square inch of the wildness at the edges where the canvas had been covered for more than a century. That would at least remove a little dirt. But his tiredness overcame him, and he'd hardly lain down before he was lost in consoling dreams. He focused on them, and his resting mind told him that in Italy last week he'd bought, which he hadn't in actual life, the ravishing yard-tall nude Roman Venus, marble, second century AD (faked this past summer by his great-forger friend). In the room's warm air, she lay beside him at the edge of his pillow; and when he laid his cheek against her, he heard an ancient voice recite a Catullan poem in fine native Latin. Only two or three years ago, that would not have been sufficient to calm him and feed his desire. Now it was.

By the time Mabry got to the end of supper, though—Audrey's baked chicken and a deep banana pudding with real meringue—he was shaky on his pins; and he didn't know why. He tried to conceal it in talk about the museum and small jokes.

But Tasker saw his trouble. He rolled himself a few feet back from the table; and said "Son, let's step into my room for a minute." Before Mabry could fold his napkin and thank Audrey properly, Tasker looked straight to her. "Dear friend, please excuse me if I shut my door. I've got some dreadful old-man secrets to confess to this lad, old family business. None of them has the least connection with you. You get nothing but gratitude from my heart and soul."

Audrey seemed to take it calmly. "That's all right by me, Father. I've got some troubles of my own to bring you soon, but right now I need to drive out to Mama's and get a few things."

Tasker said "Please give her my best then."

Audrey looked up, smiling. "I'd be glad to do it, sir; but Mama's been dead since December twenty-first, shortest day of last year."

Tasker clapped both empty palms to his mouth, then tapped his skull. "She's very much alive in my old mind—see?" Then with more strength than Mabry had witnessed, he spun himself on into his room. "Son, join me when you can." He pushed the door half shut behind him.

Audrey had already risen and started clearing her place.

So when Mabry stood, he stacked his own cutlery and dishes and began telling more about the day—Marcus's Brueghel and the interesting things he'd seen in the picture.

Audrey couldn't smile. "That boy's got a lot more sense than dollars, but he's still dreaming of college somehow." She broke off there—no word about why she was studying at Duke but Marc was working a menial job. "You go to your dad. I'm in charge of dirty dishes."

Mabry said "You're taking on way too much duty. Let me wash these at least."

Audrey paused in place and began to speak in a genuine whisper. "You'll have a lot more time with dishes in your life than you'll have with Father Kincaid. Go – in – yonder – *now*." She pointed to the bedroom.

So Mabry thanked her calmly and went.

By then Tasker had the television on, and still there was nothing but obsessive news about the World Trade Center. By then the men delving in the mountain of rubble were gradually coming to the realization that however many thousands of men and women had died in the ruins, very little of any single person survived. As Mabry had guessed in Nova Scotia, the many thousand gallons of jet-plane fuel had cremated them all with the rare exceptions of a hand or leg here, a human face there.

When the news reporter, five hundred miles away, turned to face Mabry and Tasker and said, again, that lower Manhattan would be closed to traffic—wheel or foot—for several more days at least, Mabry stood and turned the TV off. Then he said "Oh, I'm sorry. You want to keep watching this?"

"Not at all," Tasker said. "It's where you live, though. I thought you'd care."

"I *care*, God knows, but there's nothing new apparently."

Tasker said "And there won't be, not till those smart Mohammedan boys strike again."

Mabry knew the answer but he had to ask. "You convinced they'll strike?"

"They'll have to—won't they? What else are they *for*, in their mobbed world, and sick as *we* are in all our money. You know what Jesus says about money, and he was just one more brown-skinned boy—barely more than a boy when he went on and died."

Mabry felt that was more or less correct but he suddenly laughed. "Pa, if you're telling me I need to move back down here and patch up this house, feel free to use the sentence I'm about to speak at this moment—*I'd need to be crazier than I already am.*" He laughed again, then saw he'd either confused his father or kicked him once more. But he sat back down, no apology.

His father's eyes were steady on him—not a mad hot stare but an unblinking gaze. So Mabry tried for at least a pleasant tone of voice. "You asked me in here a few minutes ago. Was there something you wanted to talk about?"

Tasker said "Maybe we ought to talk about guilt."

Mabry said "I'm mostly glad to oblige, but what brand of guilt have you got in mind?"

Tasker looked down and waited in silence a good while longer. When he realized he couldn't look up yet, he went on and said "Mine. I need you to hear my confession and forgive me, if you find it in your heart. Nobody but you can do the trick for me."

Of course it stunned Mabry. Confession and forgiveness—which till now he'd never heard called a *trick*—were not standard practice in the Episcopal Church, not in the branches Mabry had heard of. Hadn't even the Catholics more or less given it up, after Vatican II? But he said "Sir, you better tell me what you mean before I can answer. I'm no kind of expert in such dark waters."

Tasker looked up at last and searched Mabry's face, and then his lips moved as if they'd speak. But no sound came.

In another thirty seconds Mabry thought *He's having a stroke before my eyes*. And he stepped on forward, knelt beside Tasker, and touched his knees. "Pa, you want something else now? Should I call Audrey?"

But Tasker's hands came forward, right and left, and shoved Mabry back. When Mabry was in his own chair again, Tasker finally said "I failed your mother six or seven times—I've truly lost count. Honest to God, I've lost perfect count."

Mabry knew not to ask for further details. "She loved you, Pa, right down to the end. Any failures didn't matter then, whatever they were."

Tasker said "I know that much—but thank you anyhow. You want to know what they were, my failings?"

Mabry said "Since you're asking me—no, I don't. I can't see what good that would do either you or me, or Mother in her grave."

Tasker thought it through slowly, behind a face that looked self-possessed not unstrung. At last he said "You're the one I've got to offer this to, the only one."

Mabry actually pointed toward the kitchen.

But before he could even speak Audrey's name, Tasker shook his head. "She's a fine young woman but innocent, *innocent* so far as I know."

"She's had two sons with no visible father."

Tasker put a hushing finger to his lips. "She's not a priest. You noticed that, did you?"

Mabry said "I did." Then he held both flat palms out before his own eyes as if expecting the true stigmata to dawn in the room, like a phosphorus outburst, in utter silence. "I hadn't really noticed I was one though." He likely hadn't smiled so broadly since before he joined Frances, to wait by her deathbed.

Tasker repeated "You're what I've got. Remember Martin Luther's doctrine of the priesthood of all believers? Even Calvin believed it, I think I recall. So whether you like it or not, Old Sausage, you're *my* priest at the moment." Despite the cast on his ankle, Tasker swung his leg from the pedal of his wheelchair onto the floor and pressed up to stand.

Mabry said "Oh Jesus, you'll *ruin* yourself." And in two seconds, he'd gently seized Tasker by the elbows and seated him again.

Tasker said "It won't feel right if I can't kneel. I come from a kneeling church, remember?"

Mabry said "I seem to. But don't downgrade me now. If you've got something you need to unburden, I—and the Lord—will accept your words from any position. While we're remembering, remember the Last Rites."

Tasker's face had clouded again in a fresh confusion.

Mabry said "You can whisper or confess in your mind. You don't have to say one word I can hear."

Tasker waited again. "You've got to hear, fool. You're the only one concerned—only one still alive."

Mabry laughed. "*Fool?* Didn't Jesus say anybody that calls his brother a *fool* is in danger of hellfire?"

Tasker agreed. "I'm pleased you remember that much scripture still, but you're not my brother."

Mabry finally saw he was cornered. He looked down and straightened the legs of his trousers. He was part of that last generation of men who want their wash pants lightly starched and *ironed*. In Italy and France he'd washed his own shirts and trousers in the bathtubs of several hotels, feeling always more than a little grungy. Even now, though, he fiddled with the ghostly creases in the khaki on his thighs. It was the last delay he could think of before hearing his father out in the matter of guilt and forgiveness. Then he thought to listen for Audrey; was she still in the kitchen? No, no sound at least. He suddenly thought of the formula he'd heard in movies where priests unburdened other humans, so he took a deep breath and said it to his father. "How long has it been since your last confession?"

Right or wrong, Tasker said "Eighty-three years," his actual age.

From there on, Mabry was on his own. He said "Pa, what hurts?"

But Tasker couldn't speak. He said the word "I," maybe four times, before he shut down—no tears, no apparent confusion, just silence.

Mabry realized, in the next few moments, that he felt cut off, even disappointed. Somehow his visit had triggered this moment; and raw as his father's proposal had felt, now he wanted to hear the rest. He thought another moment, then said "That's fine. I'll make a confession of my own to you now. Then if you feel like you want to go on and say something to me, I'm here to listen."

At first it looked as if Tasker would refuse, but then he extended open arms.

And Mabry went toward him, kneeling as nearly as he could, almost touching Tasker. On the way there, he told himself *You can't lie now, you can't serve yourself. You don't know whether he wants details or just a list of the earnest sins you've already covered. Try that first, then see if he's satisfied.* By the time Tasker's hands were on his shoulders, Mabry felt that tears were bound to come shortly. Still he tried to speak and words came readily. "Father, I've never confessed out loud to a live human being in all my life. I can't even think of the names of all the Seven Deadly Sins, not now anyhow; but I'm sure I've committed every one already, except maybe murder—I don't recall murder." He grinned in an effort to lighten the mood.

Tasker wouldn't take the rescue. He only said "You're the one who would know that, not I."

So Mabry ducked under and plowed ahead. "The worst one, as you're bound to know, is adultery."

Tasker said "Not one of the seven. Try *lust* instead—illicit desire. Not that adultery's not bad enough."

Mabry said "All right—lust and all the other six and anything else you're likely to name, except child molestation, rape, physical hurt to others, and murder."

Tasker said "*Sloth*" and waited a good while, looking to the window opposite his chair. There was still clear daylight.

Mabry said "Why *sloth*?"

Tasker said "Because most theologians have claimed that pride was the prime of all dire sins, and of course it's bad, but my observation after sixty years of close sin-watching is that pure *laziness* tops the list. Most people persist in all the other wrongs just because they're too satisfied with lying motionless on their bed or their couch—or the couch in their *mind*—to stand up and change." Tasker waited, then laughed till actual tears poured. Then at last he could say "Just trying to help you along, Old Dog, or cheer you a little anyhow. You're not a lazy boy. Or you weren't, when I knew you."

Mabry said "I'm not now and thanks for the cheer." He thought he'd stop there and see if Tasker nudged him forward. His knees were hurting also; he rocked side to side.

But Tasker didn't tell him to go sit down or to stand and stretch his legs.

So Mabry said "You forgive my sins, sir?"

Tasker said "One minute, son. Don't tell me too much; but maybe just tell me the worst single thing you did, in lust, to another human being."

Mabry was baffled by the near-coincidence of this request and the serious game he and Marcus had played in the car, coming home. *Why twice in one day?* To the best of his knowledge, though, his father hadn't spoken with Marcus in the late afternoon. And if he had, surely Marcus wouldn't have brought up such a personal subject. Mabry wiped his damp lips and said to his father, eye to eye, "When I tell you, then will you tell me?" He'd tried to signal a touch of fun in his eyes and his tone.

But if Tasker caught the offer of fun, he didn't respond accordingly. He said "I told you I failed my marriage on either six or seven occasions. Let's call it seven." Then he took the time to look round the walls, plumbing his uncle's framed engravings and photographs as though he'd never see them again and must take their memory with him, wherever he was headed.

Mabry said "And the failing was lust?"

Tasker came back gradually but finally answered in a voice too loud for Mabry's hopes. "I fucked three women six or seven times—women in my churches who were meant to be in my spiritual care, though I all but ruined them. *Forevermore.* I stood one of them upright in the vestry and took her from behind. An altar boy was maybe ten feet away in that deep closet, fetching candles. If he heard a sound, he never told me so."

Mabry had never heard his father say *fuck*, and the word itself was more startling than the confession. But what Mabry said now was "The women were all grown—am I right?"

Tasker looked puzzled. "You mean were they minors? Of course they weren't. To the best of my knowledge, they were all over thirty."

Mabry said "Then I very much doubt you ruined them. Weren't they in charge of their own minds and bodies?"

"Son, a lot of women all but worship their priest. Or they did back when I was young enough to want them. So *ruin* is the word, and don't try to change it."

Mabry said "All right." He couldn't be sure of what should come next, but he said what he thought his father needed. "Then you're surely forgiven." He wondered *Is one single word of that true?*

And Tasker said "Who's the forgiver—you or God or all those women?"

Mabry said "I'm bound to say it's all the above."

Tasker said "You don't believe in God."

Mabry said "Have I ever told you that?"

"No, but you haven't told me a number of things. Do you act like you believe in—what?—what we used to call a Higher Power?"

Mabry said "Maybe not, sir. But neither does the pope, on a good many days."

Tasker said "You'll have to discuss that with him; he barely ever phones me. But don't slip out here now; I'm needy. What do you mean if you still claim your father is truly *forgiven?*"

Mabry said "Again, so far as I know, there's no human being who wants you in jail. Or in a torture chamber. Or naked in front of a firing squad." When his father didn't look up or speak, Mabry said "Am I truly wrong?"

Tasker's face began to shed years till he looked maybe a decade younger or the way he'd looked twelve quick years ago when his wife Eunice died and Mabry drove him home from the graveyard and heard him say "If you still pray, pray for me to go soon" and then burst out in the glorious laughter of a likable young man who's just won a race.

Here and now Mabry—still on his knees—lowered his head to his father's lap, and Tasker's hands took his son's big skull by both the ears and raised it to where he could meet the good eyes. Then he said "Thank you, boy. Maybe I can live with that."

Mabry waited as long as his legs could bear their squat. Then he rose and went back to the facing chair, and the first thing he could see were the bottles of Scotch and bourbon by Tasker's chair. He said "You ready for an after-dinner slug?"

Tasker said "*I'm* ready but I doubt *we* are." When he thought his son looked appropriately puzzled, he went ahead. "How long has it been since your last confession?"

Mabry said "Fifty-three years, Father." He made a move to kneel again.

But Tasker stopped him with an upright palm. "Didn't you confess to me just now? Didn't I sidetrack you in my usual roadhogging way?"

Mabry said "I told you my main sin was lust—adultery against Frances Kincaid, a kind of saint, almost as patient as one anyhow—way more times than six or seven."

As if he were asking the price of gas, Tasker said "Just give me a rounded-off number." He didn't smile.

Nor did Mabry. He knew the answer, almost surely. "With fourteen women in my thirteen years of marriage."

"How many times, total?" By then Tasker's face had the flat shining look of an automaton, some dreadful ticket-taker at the gates of Last Judgment.

Mabry tried to resist. "Is that figure necessary, Pa?"

The *Pa* didn't work. Tasker nodded yes.

And like many grown men, Mabry thought he knew the answer. "Depending on what you count or don't count as violations, a hundred thirty-odd" (he wouldn't have sworn to anything near, but the rough number felt true when he said it).

Tasker's face went even worse. Now the ticket-taker seemed near combustion. When he spoke, though, he said "Your sins are forgiven. Go and sin no more."

Mabry knew that the formula repeated Jesus' words to the woman caught in adultery, the one Jesus saved from a lynch mob by inviting "him who is without sin" to cast the first stone. Were those precise words appropriate for Mabry though? He said "Thank you, sir. One detail though—can an unmarried man commit adultery?"

Tasker said "With a married woman, sure—fool." He finally smiled.

Mabry laughed as if at a vast discovery. He slapped his forehead and said "Of *course*." He also rose for the Scotch bottle.

But Tasker had reached to the lower shelf of the table by his wheelchair. He brought up a small black box with a silver carrying handle.

Mabry thought he might remember what it held but no, not yet.

Tasker set it on the tabletop, opened it, and very carefully began to remove the contents—a small round silver dish, a small rectangular bottle, then a tiny box from which he took several circular objects that looked like goldfish food from thirty years ago—dry white wafers.

Oh Lord, it's his portable communion kit. It had been way more than twenty years since Mabry had taken communion anywhere, so it came out of him before he thought. "I haven't done that in years and years."

Tasker's delicacy in arranging the elements of the holiest sacrament in his faith absorbed almost all the attention he could muster. But he managed to say "This isn't something that you *do*, son. It's a living body that you eat and drink."

Mabry thought *He's really a crypto-Catholic now—that's plainly transubstantiation.*

But when Tasker faced his son, what he said was no part of the Catholic mass. He'd always known the old Episcopal prayer book by heart—ninety-nine percent—and now he cut to the chase and began the service. "'Ye who do truly and earnestly repent you of your sins, and are in love and charity with your neighbors, and intend to lead a new life, following the commandments of God, and walking from henceforth in his holy ways; draw near with faith—'"

At that, Mabry spoke again without thinking why. "You keep that little kit near at hand always?" He hadn't noticed it before this evening.

Tasker seemed untroubled by the intervening rudeness. "No, I needed it two or three days ago when your friend Gwyn Williams stopped in here on me."

Mabry had already heard of Gwyn's surprising visit here for communion; he also knew he could delve little further into Tasker's duties before he'd meet the thick wall of professional secrets. But he said "Has she been by here many times lately, since her latest trip home?"

Without looking up, Tasker said "You'll have to get that information from her, next time you see her."

Mabry said "I wouldn't dream of invading anyone's spiritual privacy," but he kept his place.

Tasker said "I mean to go on with this now, for my own sake. If you care to join me, you're welcome of course. If not, kindly leave."

The voice was as strong as it had ever been, in all Mabry's life; so he still kept his place.

And the voice went on. "'—Draw near with faith and take this holy sacrament to your comfort, devoutly kneeling.'"

Mabry knew enough to realize that his father would now omit the General Confession—likely on the grounds they'd confessed already—so he knelt again, this time for the body and blood of Christ. Or so the old man claimed. *And who am I to doubt it, miserable fucker that I am, my home city ruined and maybe my country and me stove up at middle age—maybe headed for a worse destination than a wheelchair—with no skill that anyone truly needs, with no one I really love and no one who loves me but (maybe, just maybe) this old fellow here?*

Yet the following morning—clear sun through oak leaves that had still not fallen and mild clean air through the open windows— Mabry was up and in the kitchen before Audrey had dressed his father. That door was shut. So he set the breakfast table for three and sat down to read the Raleigh paper with a cup of black coffee (Audrey had apparently made that early). He mainly avoided the front-page news. The headlines told him there was nothing fresh. The casualty figures were varying wildly from hour to hour, always in the thousands; the blame had been claimed by the Muslim group al-Qaeda; and the words *hero* and *heroism* were plainly in for the over-work they generally got when Americans came under fire anywhere. Were other peoples so proud of themselves? Weren't acts of strength and decency, in the face of whatever fear and danger, assumed to be the average brand of human behavior—from adults at least?

When his father's door opened, and Audrey rolled the old man out, Tasker also seemed ready for something better than what the current world was promising.

—So much so that, by just past eight, when they'd eaten their way through another big breakfast—corncakes with actual fresh white corn in the batter, bacon, broiled tomatoes, and a second pot of strong coffee—Mabry thanked Audrey with unmistakable sincerity and then asked his father if there was some place he could take him, some pleasurable drive to occupy the morning.

Tasker glanced first to Audrey, who showed no resistance; so he said to Mabry "Can you lift a man who now weighs maybe a hundred forty pounds?"

Mabry said "I'm an art conservator, remember? I can hurl around life-size marble statues of Hercules—and with no more damage than was done by the average Visigoth. Is that good enough?"

Audrey said "You saw Marcus built us that ramp off the back porch. Mabry, you bring the car right up to there; and we'll have no problem."

The sound of his first name in Audrey's strong voice was all but a shock. He said "Give me just long enough to visit the john, and we're on the road. Will you come with us, lady?" He hoped he'd get an hour alone with his father, but he tried to conceal it.

Audrey said "The lady thanks you but has to say no. I've got a few million chores right here." She was plainly glad to pass Tasker on to his son for the morning.

And when he'd got Tasker and the snazzy black wheelchair to the foot of Marcus's wobbly ramp, Mabry looked behind them to the door where Audrey stood watching intently. He gave her a grin and waved her away.

She managed a smile and went back into the kitchen.

Then Mabry said "Pa, you claim you weigh—what?—a hundred fifty pounds?" He was overestimating in hopes of jogging the full truth out of this sparrow-boned man who looked a little plumper after weeks of Audrey's cooking.

But Tasker said "One hundred thirty-seven pounds, to the *ounce*. Old Nelson checked it at the feed and seed store on their big scale just before I broke this ankle."

Mabry smiled. "How many meals ago was that?" He meant to be teasing his father gently.

But Tasker took it hard. "Look, son, this whole jaunt was your idea."

Mabry said "Still is" and moved in to lift the body that had launched his own tall body. It weighed no more than a small arm of firewood. When they both were settled and the engine had jumped into service agreeably, Mabry thought for the first time today *I hope my brain behaves on us now.* No double vision, no floods of light. A silent check of his checkable resources, and he seemed merely normal, so he turned to his father. "Choose your destination, sir. Or our first stop anyhow—we can drive to the *moon*."

Tasker said "I'm sorry it's no place new, but you're bound to know I need to visit the graveyard."

Mabry thought *Where else?* but he said "—My command" and off they rolled.

By daylight the cemetery's three piney acres had none of the weird weight he'd felt two nights before; and Mabry looped the car around the perimeter, passing again the stones of a few distant cousins and two or three dozen others whom even Mabry could place in the social order of their generations with a clean precision. There were whole families who ranged in station from the lowest category, which was "good country people," on up to the highest, "well-to-do" (interesting that the lower reaches were described rewardingly as morally good while the highest were merely rich). The worst of all stations, the dread "white trash," were not represented in this peaceful stretch by so much as a single corpse or stone; and of course there were no blacks. He even asked about the poorest whites. "Pa, is there some sort of dump way back in the woods for poor white trash? Where the hell *are* they?"

It got a welcome laugh from Tasker. "That's an excellent question. I'm afraid I can't tell you. When I was a boy they buried themselves, one at a time, in narrow graves at the edge of the woods on whatever ground they were tenant farming at the time—mustn't waste good cotton or tobacco land. Then when the Holy Roller churches moved into the county—Churches of *God*, they were usually called—I guess they could offer graveyards of their own. Now of course the trash can lie anywhere they want in the finest graveyards of Raleigh or Charlotte—they're all running banks now or at least selling cars." Mabry was almost passing the Kincaid plot without a pause. So Tasker said "Stop here. Right *now*." He was suddenly urgent.

Mabry stopped and even backed up a few yards so his father's door was neatly flanking the plot. Surely he wouldn't want to be lifted out here and rolled closer still. But Mabry waited in silence for Tasker's next wish. The window rolled down, and Tasker looked out for maybe two minutes—it was just before ten, and the light and air truly couldn't improve. When his father didn't speak, Mabry finally said "Who was buried first—how long ago?"

Tasker said "Bound to have been my father's father, old Walter Kincaid—in the late 1880s. My dad was a baby when the bastard died."

Mabry said "Was he that mean?"

"Mean as any six snakes, drunk by five a.m. most days and given to beating any flesh in his reach." But when Tasker faced Mabry, his rheumy eyes brightened; and he burst out laughing. "Let me show you some more." He actually opened the door on his side and tried to swing his gimp leg out.

Mabry said "Whoa! You can't walk, remember?"

"No, but *you* can—or so you promised. You backtracking on me?"

Mabry said "Not at all. We'll need to ration how many times I pick you up today though—once already. Is this our next venture? You sure about this?"

Exasperation, impatience, even a little anger swept over Tasker's face before he calmed himself enough to speak. "I'm entirely sure of myself, Dr. Kincaid; and I'll be most grateful for any amount of your ample strength."

Mabry nodded. "Just checking. And don't forget, it's *Master* Kincaid. I'm nothing but a simple Master of Arts, no PhD."

"You remember one thing too—I told you I'd gladly help you pay for a doctorate. You said you wouldn't need it." When Mabry tried to speak, Tasker held up a hushing palm. "*Master* Kincaid, kindly lead us to the dead. They've waited too long."

Mabry said "The Master is very much on his way." He swiftly stepped out of his door and hauled out the crutches his father had insisted on bringing.

Surprisingly nimble now, Tasker spent half an hour doing what he'd never quite done before—unloading on Mabry all he thought the next generation should know about these lost kinfolk. Two of them, he'd fairly recently concluded (from general hints on TV and radio concerning the nation's male population), were incestuous molesters of Tasker's own mother in her early girlhood. But then family sex was surely standard fare in the old rural and small-town worlds where your kinfolk were likely the only folk you knew; and genuine affection (not to speak of love or lust) could lead, soon enough, to a misplaced hand or other appendage. Tasker passed on beyond the molesters' stones with no sign of hate or even condemnation. He revealed what he'd never mentioned before—that his

own mother had shut his father off from any form of intimate contact once Tasker was born, though the marriage had lasted another
thirty years (who had told Tasker that?).

And perhaps most shockingly, he stood at the foot of his favorite
sister's grave and very calmly said "You know that Erma was all but
a strumpet—was almost surely one in her days in D.C. when World
War II was on? When she died of some kind of overdose, at age thirty-
six (we called it a very premature stroke), her landlady sent me a
packet of her leavings; and of course the main thing was four volumes of a diary. I made the mistake of gulping them down—nobody
else in the family but me could read her handwriting—and line by
line she got more obsessed with the bodies of men than anybody else
I've ever known. Just the young servicemen she found in bars and,
eventually, in Union Station where she'd pick them up and let
them rent a cheap hotel room where she could turn loose all she'd
learned about human skin and how to reward it—especially since,
as she wrote in the margin more than once, 'A high proportion are
bound to be slaughtered before they can even recall my name
much less my lips or how little I cost them.'" As Tasker tried to get the
diary quote right, he stumped up the length of her grave—right on
her body—till he paused, dropped his crutches and steadied himself
on her stone with both his hands. Then he looked to Mabry, suddenly as lost as a child in the woods (had Erma's memory stunned
him?). "Help me out here, boy. Where the hell am I?"

Mabry smiled uneasily. "You seem to be telling me all I never
knew—and more than I need—about our sexual history."

Tasker said "Then I beg your full pardon. They were all grand
people. Did I also say that?"

Mabry said "I've always assumed that much was true. You're a
great forgiver, aren't you?"

But by then his father had somehow managed to bend and
retrieve his dropped crutches, fending off any help from Mabry. He
hopped past two more stones and stopped again. Mabry thought it

had to be his own mother's spot, but Tasker said "One more time please—and I know it's as painful for you as for me—tell me what you know about his death."

Oh Christ, it's Gabriel. Can I somehow refuse him? Mabry walked on over. Tasker's back was turned to him, a small mercy; so he spoke to his back. "Thanksgiving 1970, my senior year in college. Gabe's freshman year and, as you recall, he was almost surely flunking out. I'd got home late the night before and had every hope of sleeping till at least noon—you know, repairing my almost infinite sleep debt. I'd also brought that girl you thought was the finest of all—Eileen Van Straaten—but Gabe wouldn't hear a word of refusal. I had to get up at dawn with him and that pitiful boy he brought from Davidson—Campbell McClain—and lead them out quail hunting with Hector Smiley's dogs. Maybe somebody could turn Gabe down, but I never could—God curse my soul—and so I joined him and that roommate for the gigantic breakfast Mother and Betsy had ready for us." He stopped for a long ten seconds. "Where were you, Pa?" Mabry meant it as a genuine question.

But Tasker stood in place, not turning, and shook his head. Did he truly not know?

Had he held some kind of special service on that Thanksgiving? Mabry still didn't know.

But Tasker said "I was in the house, with my mother and yours, all ready for you three boys to get back and eat the gigantic meal that was waiting."

Mabry said "All right. We scared up more than one covey of quail and even glimpsed a few wild turkeys—the dogs had a grand time— but though we more than halfway tried to bring home some birds, we hadn't hit a damned thing. Campbell came closest, and he'd never held a gun till that morning (or so he claimed). Then by noon we were chilled to the bone, and Gabe as always was starved for the next meal. So we gladly obeyed his order to start a great circle to the left and head on home. I'd long since noticed the sort of thing Gabe wouldn't have seen if you'd forced him to train the Palomar telescope right on the spot—Campbell was almost dead from the cold. So when he got the signal to head for warmth, he speeded up well ahead of Gabe and me and got to the old barbed-wire fence first. Gabe's bound to have known his city friend had slim acquaintance with the art of threading a human body, not to mention a shotgun, through that many strands of rusty wire. He yelled for Campbell to wait, then ran ahead to coach him through. But Campbell's ears were either frozen shut or he was showing off. Since the last strands of wire were almost on the ground, he'd got to his hands and knees and was just starting the crucial move—pushing his gun ahead to the far side beyond himself, as Gabe had surely taught him (or he ought to have never left Davidson College). By then I was near enough to see it plainly but maybe not near enough to do more than shout. And somehow I didn't even shout. But neither did Gabe. He didn't run either. He only loped in longer strides—I guess he couldn't imagine a fool as big as Campbell. But he got to his friend and dropped to his own knees. The gun was skewed toward them, and then it went off. I was no more than two feet behind him." Mabry had got that far with his voice in bearable shape. He thought he could reckon on a couple more sentences before breaking down, so he said more than he intended to say. "It killed the wrong boy." He meant himself of course; and at the moment, he believed his claim. But in another moment he realized he was waiting for a firm correction from his father, if only a merely polite refusal.

No words came from Tasker.

So Mabry said "You've understood that, all these years since?" What he meant was "I should have been the boy to die."

Still nothing from his father, though.

"Sir, I'd be very grateful for an answer."

Tasker had actually gone to his own knees, awkward and dangerous as that was. His back was to Mabry, and with both arms he was leaning his whole weight on Gabe's stone. He didn't look back, but finally he said "Honest to Christ, I don't have an answer."

"You wish I'd been the boy that got shot." Nothing in Mabry's voice indicated that he meant it as a question.

And his father only said "Gabriel Kincaid was the one human being I ever truly loved. I'm not proud to be telling you that, though he was a splendid boy—not smart enough and careless with his gifts but true gold to look at, and remember that laugh?" Mabry didn't speak and Tasker didn't wait. "I should have loved his mother at least as much and you too, Mabry. But I'm way too old, out here in the open day, to tell you or God-above a lie. And Gabe's been gone, as you can *see*, for very nearly thirty-one years. The end of the World Trade Center in New York is nothing—flat *nothing*—compared to the death of that one child. He very well might have saved the Earth with his plain goodness, if he'd bothered to last." Even Tasker was conscious that his final sentence might sound demented.

In any case, Mabry came up behind his father close enough to see the date on the nearly black granite. He didn't deny a word his father had said. In the dry fall light, as gorgeous as light got to be anymore, he might have concurred with the very strange claim, whatever it meant. All he did, though, was look hard at the date till he had it memorized. Then he said "Yes, sir, I can *see* it, way better than even you could guess. But I've known it forever anyhow. You didn't have to tell me." He even considered, for maybe three seconds, turning then and leaving this truthful old man alone at the grave, his crutches unreachable beside him on the ground. But then he bent to get them.

Tasker said "We need to hurry on home. I've got my appointment."

"What appointment?"

"With that contractor, the one I mentioned."

"No sir, you didn't mention any contractor."

Tasker then recalled the name. "Robo—something."

Mabry said "Robo Ketcham—the one that restores old local houses for millions of bucks?"

Tasker said "That's the man." He looked to his watch. "And hell, we're late."

To speed them onward, Mabry temporarily laid the crutches back on the ground and bent to hoist his father.

Robo was rocking in the green porch swing when they pulled into the drive. Audrey had staked him out with a paper napkin and a Coca-Cola. He'd poured a small package of salted peanuts into the bottle, and thus awarded himself a real treat—one Mabry hadn't thought of in thirty years but longed for at once (Robo had brought just the one pack of nuts). He was also reading the final pages of a thick hardback of *Anna Karenina*. Turned out he'd been a Russian major at Wake Forest and was reading the novel for the fourth or fifth time, this time in English because he'd heard the new translation was the finest of all. All Tasker had to say about *Anna* was "Mr. Ketcham, I've yet to read that book and may never get to it. It's the inside dope on adultery, though—right?"

For whatever reason of his own, Robo blushed ferociously—he was somewhere in his early forties, a genuine redhead with the naturally trim torso and hips of a boy who's never been near a gym, thank God, but is worth a moment's envy. When the blush began to fade, Robo held up the Tolstoy and shook it. "Yes sir, Reverend Kincaid. And it kills 'em all off—the lady anyhow and she's the one you care about."

Mabry said "You ever see the Garbo movie?"

Robo said "Never have but I saw Garbo." By then he'd joined the Kincaids in the yard.

Even Tasker, in his unworldliness, was mildly amazed. "Young as you are, you saw the most famous recluse of the twentieth century?"

Robo said "Thank you, sir. I'm older than I look. The first time I ever went to New York, about 1970, I forgot to take a raincoat; and a man on the street told me I could find a good cheap one at Alexander's department store, in their bargain basement. I admit I was fairly young at the time, but I'd already fallen in love with old movies, and I certainly knew who Greta Garbo was. Anyhow, soon I was roaming through a thicket of cheap raincoats—racks set so close together you could barely move between them. In no more than five minutes, this little short queer fellow struggled to reach me through the coats. When I saw him coming, I was so young and startled I thought I should run; but running was completely out of the question, so I held my own and when the little fellow got right up to me, he beckoned for me to bend down to him. By then he looked harmless enough to trust. I leaned way low and he whispered 'Don't look right now but we are in a *sacred* place.' I figured he might have lost his mind, but I whispered back 'What's sacred?' I was young enough to think the Holy Ghost might be smothered here in cheap rainwear. But he said 'Greta Garbo is right there behind us, not ten yards away. She's a notorious bargain-hunter.' I kept looking at coats for another two minutes while the guy wandered off; and when I looked around finally, Miss Garbo was standing no more than a yard from me. She had on a wide limp hat that nearly hid her face, but there was nothing she could do about her eyes—she had the best eyes I'd seen up till then, and she was staring directly at me."

Mabry said "Best eyes ever made."

Even Tasker agreed. "And the eyelids too. Ever notice her eyelids could have covered another two or three eyes?—they were that long and wide."

Robo said "You noticed just now I'm a terminal blusher. Well, I cut loose with a major blush. It felt like silent blood was pouring all down my neck and shoulders—and Miss Garbo actually touched me. Swear to God, she reached out and took me by the left elbow. And she said 'Child, are you all right?' I was sixteen already but plenty of people still called me *child*; so it didn't seem strange, not in her deep voice. But all I could think to say was 'Ma'm, have you seen any black raincoats?' What I was after was a romantic trench coat, real spy-movie style. And she said 'Oh sure, I just saw the *best*.' She pointed way behind her toward a dark corner, and I squeezed my way on over there. Found my raincoat too and it's still in my closet—can't bring myself to throw it away. My wife thinks I'm crazy."

Tasker said "Just leave her alone. You'll never change that. And keep your black raincoat. Bring it on over here if she tries to chuck it. I'll give you a closet all to yourself. But you'll have to build it first. All this house has got is a few old solid walnut wardrobes."

All three men were still in the yard—Tasker still on his crutches, refusing to sit.

Mabry said "I guess we need to step inside."

Before they moved, though, Tasker bowed his head to Robo. "I thank you for the story about Miss Garbo—makes me like the world better this dreadful week and likely explains why you're in the beauty business."

Robo grinned. "Is that what I do?"

Tasker said "That's what *I* hear."

Robo said "Maybe that remains to be seen."

Forty-five minutes later, they were back on the porch again—Tasker had asked Mabry to accompany him and Robo on the whole look-around. They'd hardly sat down when Audrey came out and said she could make a few extra sandwiches if Mr. Ketcham would stay for lunch, but he'd begged off—some promise he'd made to his youngest kid. So Tasker said "Mr. Ketcham, tell me the worst news first."

"Reverend Kincaid, I doubt there's any *worst* news. For a house this old, I can't see any damage of the kind you dread to find. No sign of termites, not to the naked eye. The floors feel solid. If any of the sills have started to rot, it can't have gone far. The plaster, as you've seen, is fairly hard up in a number of places—cracks and fallen patches. You know you've got that leak in the west bedroom. You likely need a few new sheets of tin, if you want to stick with an old tin roof—I'd recommend you do; they sound so good in a driving rain. And of course I'd need to send my boys all up in the crawl space to check for any trouble with the sills. But if they're in as good shape as I think, then once we'd taken care of the roof, the only big question I'd have for you is how much cosmetic work do you want? We could do everything from starting with your pine floors—a thorough sanding and a light coat of sealant—then coating the plaster walls with Sheetrock and a nice paint job."

Tasker raised a broad hand. "Stop there and tell me how much you envision in the way of hard cash."

Mabry burst out laughing and Robo chimed in. Mabry said "Pa, the man's not a lightning calculator."

Tasker said "I'll say you're dead wrong." He grinned at Robo. "Am I right, Mr. Ketcham?"

Robo said "It feels all wrong, you calling me *Mr.* Ketcham. Just Robo please."

But Tasker said "If you say so but—forgive me please—that's mighty peculiar. What does *Robo* stand for?"

"It started as *Robert*, sir."

Tasker said "Then Robert, give me three sets of figures—say, *total disaster*, then *rigorous facelift*, then *sufficient to see an old fart to his grave*."

Robo actually clamped his eyes shut and appeared to be trying to come up with three separate quotes.

When his eyes were still shut after thirty seconds, Mabry said "Robo, my father is well on into his eighties. He and I just returned from the local graveyard where all our family but he and I are stashed. To me, that suggests maybe two figures only—*total disaster* and *rigorous facelift*. And don't feel compelled to give the quotes now, not this minute."

Robo looked at Mabry and nodded calmly.

But Tasker also faced Mabry and said "Who in the goddamned hell called this boy and brought him out here, polite as he is, on a

day when he ought to be taking his rest?" He waited as if an answer
were due from Mabry Kincaid, nobody else, and when none came
Tasker turned back to Robo. "You recall I'm the fellow that called
you, right? And any work you do, on this lot anyhow, would be paid
for out of my pocket only."

Robo blushed again, fiercely indeed, and turned to Tasker.

So Mabry said to his father "I truly beg your pardon." Then he
looked to Robo, feeling more detail was relevant now. "My father's
eighty-three. I'm thirty years younger, almost to the day; but I've been
living in lower Manhattan for a long time now, and life up there
sounds maybe unfeasible for years ahead. Not to mention the fact I
may be coming down, fast, with the ruins of multiple sclerosis and
needing some kind soul's steady care—" He broke off there, unsure
of what came next, though his hands were on the rubber back grips
of Tasker's wheelchair.

Robo dug at the ground with the toe of his shoe, a boy's stage imitation of bafflement.

Tasker said "Robo, would a week be long enough for you to
come up with those two sets of figures? My beloved son here has
simplified your work."

Robo said "A week'll be plenty, Reverend Kincaid."

Mabry moved close enough to Robo to grip his left shoulder.
Then he pointed to Tasker. "He no more loves me than I love
myself."

Tasker said "Don't let that slow you down, son." By *son*, this
time, he seemed to mean Robo Ketcham.

Mabry thought *This is getting too scary for me. Scary*, he knew, was
not the right word; but then everything to do with love and family
had been past his reach or understanding—mostly, generally, all the
time.

As if somebody beyond them had fired a sizable cannon or snared
a mean stretch on a nearby drum, all three men suddenly burst into

laughter. None of them knew entirely what Mabry had meant about love, not to mention the chorus of all three voices. But it came on them all as a welcome relief.

And then from behind them, Audrey's voice came again. "It's way past lunchtime, way past *naptime*. I'm calling quits on all you gentlemen, whoever you are." Then she too laughed, not a common response from Audrey but thoroughly welcome. What she needed to say, but was holding back, was that the time for Father Kincaid's rest was over. Either Mabry would haul his father up the single step of the door jamb, or she'd come get him (she knew there'd be hell to pay in the evening if the old man didn't get his midday snooze).

So Mabry said "Come fetch him, Audrey. I'll walk Robo to his truck."

Tasker looked hard at Mabry. "I summoned him here. I'll send him off." Then he held out his right hand to Robo. "Whatever anybody else in this household may try to tell you—by phone, fax, telegraph, or tom-tom—I'm the man in charge of this one house and the land around it, for as long as I've got a conscious breath left. Don't take any private communications from anybody else."

For an instant Robo was understandably baffled. But then he grinned. "Reverend Kincaid, as you've likely guessed, this business of mine is one that sometimes puts me in the midst of family fights. As I understand it, you and I are doing business here—or agreeing not to do it. I'll get back to you in a very few days with preliminary figures. Then if you're interested, I can send my various experts in for a closer look." He and Tasker locked eyes, both of them grinned, and Robo bounded off the porch like a boy a lot younger than he claimed to be.

Audrey had disappeared from the door, leaving Mabry and Tasker alone on the porch with the bright day well advanced beyond them. So Tasker said "How many pardons do I owe you, son?"

"For what?" Mabry said.

"You're bound to know I went way too far in the cemetery. And many sons would feel insulted for that little moment I just staged with Robo."

Mabry said "The graveyard scene was hard, I'll grant—mainly because I know it wasn't a scene at all but a look at your heart. As for you and Robo and work on this house—you've got my blessing to do anything on Earth to these walls, including fire."

Tasker said "I doubt we'll burn it." But he said no more about the cemetery. He'd said what he meant there, and he wouldn't deny it.

In late afternoon Mabry roused himself from a long lie-down. It had been mixed in restfulness—more or less conscious stretches of troubling nostalgia and one or two patches of genuine dread for the city of New York, for his small place in it, and the only other resident who still ought to concern him deeply. When he'd eaten his sandwich an hour before and turned his father over to Audrey, she'd said "There's a piece of mail for you, back on your bed. Federal Express brought it while you were gone."

The thought of attention from Federal Express in a village as nearly abandoned as Wells was all but comic. "Who in the world knows I'm even down here?"

Audrey said "I'd be the last to know."

Tasker had all but shouted from his room. "That man who detoured you through Paris, your loving daughter, and—what?—maybe forty percent of the good-looking women on Manhattan Island."

Mabry had said "Pa, you lie down now and get the rest you clearly need—you're *hallucinating*, pal."

Tasker said "Very likely. But then I've hallucinated all my life— I believed in God, Lyndon Johnson, and you. Look where *that* got me." By then he was mumbling.

So Mabry had moved on off to his own room, and there on the bed was the large envelope with its detailed airbill, an unmistakable communication from his daughter Charlotte and charged to her account. Since he'd left the message with her roommate on the 11th, Mabry hadn't tried to phone her again. Learning about the huge deposit in his savings account had convinced him Charlotte would be foaming with rage, and now he took up the envelope with genuine reluctance. Why should her mother have left him a cent? Could he stand to take the bitter dose she'd no doubt aimed straight at his eyes (her marksmanship, like her mother's, was perfect)? *Go on and take it though.* He pulled the rocker toward the sunny west window, sat, and opened the envelope very neatly.

Dear Mabry,

I had a direct wire deposit sent to your savings account two days ago, then wondered if I had the right account number or even whether your bank was still standing and in business. Let me know immediately please if the money went astray in these wild times. Whatever you've had recent causes to think, I wouldn't want that.

Malcolm has just gone to work downtown, a kind of duty that's too sad to write about here and now. I'll tell you when we talk, if she can stand to do it for more than a few days. Thanks in any case for checking on us. We're doing OK and have lost nobody we really knew, but you can imagine that people in general are still a little dazed. I hope your luck has been as good as ours in avoiding harm. Up here New Yorkers, despite the daze, are thrilled with their new hero status, something they haven't had since the cover of Life *magazine at the end of WWII (that sailor kissing that collapsed trained nurse) and have always hoped the rest of the country would be forced to acknowledge.*

A friend of Malc's and mine is working downtown with the Salvation Army (she doesn't have to carry a tambourine; still, believe it if you can!). I gave her your address and asked her to drop by if she could. She phoned just now and said your block is waist-deep in silt and nobody's being allowed to wade through, not to mention drive by. But she also said the buildings in your vicinity look strong.

*Maybe we can all pitch in, down the road, and clean up your
loft?*

*Granddad says you're "ticking over," whatever that means.
Sounds like your heart's beating anyhow. Let me know if I can help
with the loft or anything else up here. Any plans for returning?*

Till when,
Charlotte

It was almost past belief—the whole letter, every word. He'd had
no such open-armed message from his daughter since maybe her first
year at sleep-away camp; and he read it through again and again, testing every word and phrase for irony. Since she was her mother's chief
heir, he assumed she'd known of the sum Frances had left him; and
while they'd never discussed it, he'd just assumed that—since she'd
bitterly and rightly resented the few things she knew about his infidelities to her mother—she'd begrudge him every penny. Maybe this
partly confirmed anyhow what he'd come to assume—that Charlotte's share of Frances Kenyon Kincaid's estate was so big as to leave
her no reason to envy his own. Even so, the suggestion that she and
Malcolm, her female partner, might help him clean up the no
doubt monumental debris in his loft was all but overwhelming in its
unexplained kindness. And it ushered him into a rest as deep as any
he'd had since those hours on the plane out of Paris before the pilot's
bad news woke him.

In late afternoon then, awake again (though still on his back),
strangely he thought of little but his work. If Baxter Sample truly was
dead, then that was the end of not just a likable acquaintanceship
but also a generous private client. He was lucky, lately, to have
turned down others, though; and more than one of them might still
want his services if he made contact. For more than a year, he'd
delayed a woman in outer New Jersey who claimed she had a large
Rubens portrait that "needed an overhaul." He'd never been asked
to overhaul any large picture by a world-class painter, and this

might be at least worth a day's drive out through the Pine Barrens to see what—in truth—she actually had. A friend who'd done some light work for her had said she wouldn't let him see the Rubens but that, in general, she was no fool at all. And more than a few young craftsmen lately had asked for private lessons—to work beside him on large and small projects instead of three to five years in graduate school. So quite aside from Frances's gift, he wasn't likely to starve, not soon.

He glanced at his watch. It was nearly four-thirty; and again he had no idea what an evening at home might hold, except TV with his father and Audrey (if Audrey would deign to join him and Tasker; so far she'd been skittish about their joint company except over food). Still, he should at least wash his face and check the paper for a movie maybe, in Henderson or Oxford or even a drive down to Raleigh or Durham. Maybe Gwyn would be game to drive them that far, if he'd catch her before she started downing the white wine.

It was Gwyn's name in his mind that did it. He was still lying flat, facing the ceiling, when he knew—truly *knew*—that her crazy-sounding notion two nights ago had to be true. Philip Adger's homely little daub lay on top of a Van Gogh sketch, both apparently in oils. Philip seemed to have painted a significant building atop a far more fluent sketch that had rendered a sky with clouds and a few bare trees, branches at least. *Let's say Gwyn's right. How on Earth did it happen?* He suddenly recalled, from the life of Van Gogh he'd been reading a few weeks back, a line from a letter Vincent wrote to his brother just a few days after settling in Auvers—the last place he lived before killing himself. It went something like "There are numerous painters here in the village—in fact, next door to me is an entire family of Americans who paint away, day after day."

Mabry had all but memorized the sentence because it seemed so weird. The whole possibility that a family of artistically hungry Americans, from (say) age five to fifty, should be painting away, cheek by jowl with one of the world's great painters—and one who was driven by madness, or whatever, to kill himself in a very few days—was more than a little past easy belief. So *try this. Philip Adger was the adolescent son in a family of well-to-do Charlestonians. They'd come to France and were living in rooms very near the café where Vincent had his own room. Somehow they all met and—unlikely as it seemed—Vincent took to young Philip, who was way more ambitious than his one surviving picture seemed to justify. Anyhow the boy and the tortured man wound up painting together—for a day or two anyhow—in the fields outside town. Vincent, who was known to speak excellent English, not only gave Philip a little encouragement, he also gave him a canvas that Vincent had used and discarded, unfinished. Philip painted on it—simple as that. When Vincent shot himself and died, Philip stayed on in France for whatever reasons through the rest of his life and wound up running the hotel in Paris where, long years later, Baxter heard of the picture from Philip's witch of a daughter-in-law and bought it, tipsy and sight unseen, for something like five hundred dollars.*

Now it lay in its wrappings ten feet from Mabry's right arm and Baxter was dead. He sat upright on the edge of the bed and thought he could take a clean T-shirt, wet it a little, wipe away a little more of the natural dirt of a century from the face of Philip's painting and test Gwyn's certainty. *Do I want to know now? Aren't there things I need to know first—like Baxter's whereabouts? And even if Baxter is truly dead, do I have any right to scrape away at Philip Adger's picture to get at Vincent's? Hell, if Baxter's gone—and he has no heirs—the thing could be mine. How would I know? Maybe nobody's left to ask but Miles the butler. And asking Miles would be telling him I'm holding something precious.*

Mabry stood, went toward it, and had the package in his hands—how precious did it feel?—when he thought he heard a knock at his door. It was barely closed and surely not locked. He looked down to be sure his trousers were zipped. Then he said "Who's there?"

"Just a sidewalk artist, not much else." The voice was frail and high.

But Mabry thought he knew it. So he lowered his own voice to the deepest best. "Shoot, I *collect* good sidewalk art; got some first-rate pieces from masters of the trade in New York and London, even *Rome*."

The hidden voice said "Mine's not first-rate, I can all but guarantee. But it's strictly for you."

Mabry cracked the door open, and yes it was Marcus.

He was in a clean shirt and pressed Levi's (did anyone outside the old Confederate states still press their blue jeans?), and both hands were holding a package a lot like Philip Adger's package.

So far as Mabry knew, Marcus had never seen Philip's package; but with Audrey in the house—and Marcus's apparent freedom to roam it at will—who knew what anybody understood about the dark picture? Anyhow, Mabry looked to his watch. Marcus was several hours too early to lay old Tasker down.

And he said "I know I'm early for your dad, but that's not why I'm here at the moment. I brought you this." He extended the package.

Mabry didn't know why but he hesitated to reach out and take it.

So Marcus laughed and shook it. "It's not a bomb, I swear to God."

Mabry said "A lot of things *are* these days, since I got home from Europe at least."

Marcus looked to the spotty ceiling. "This old house is the last place a bomber would aim at."

Mabry also looked up. Though he'd lain on his back a good deal here lately, he'd failed to notice again one of the favorite stains of his youth—the perfect profile of Alexander the Great created on the ceiling by nothing more sinister than the gradual inward creep of rusty rainwater long decades ago. He pointed it out to Marcus. "Ever notice that man?"

Marcus clearly hadn't but now he studied it slowly. "Kin people of yours?"

Mabry laughed, then thought it through. "Given what we've learned about human genetics and kinship lately, I'm trusting the answer is 'very likely.' It's an excellent profile of Alexander the Great."

Whether Marcus knew Alexander's features as fully as Mabry, he still said "It *is*."

Mabry said "You know a lot about him, do you?" He'd hardly said the last word before he was ashamed.

But Marcus merely said "I know he was a murdering drunkard who captured the known world and died at about the same age as Jesus."

Trumped! Mabry looked down again at Marcus's parcel. "So this is safe to touch?"

"Yes and it's for you."

Mabry took it. It was lighter than its size hinted at. "Do I open it now?"

Marcus said "It won't open itself. Need some help?" But he smiled.

Mabry motioned toward the rocker for Marcus to sit. Then he sat on his bed and slowly undid the very carefully bound-up parcel. At last he got down to what felt like a plywood panel, maybe ten by twelve, in numerous layers of green tissue paper.

Marcus said "I know Christmas is a long way off, but that's all the padding I could find for your gift."

Mabry said "My gift? Son, what have I done to earn a present from a man that works as hard as you do and has got a kid of his own to keep?"

Marcus took up a shirt of Mabry's from the rocker, laid it as gently on the bed as if it were a worthy living creature, and returned to sit. When he'd rocked himself a time or two, he looked to Mabry. "Two things about me to keep in mind, if you're keeping me there—first, my daughter Master lives in Durham with her sweet mother, that wants to know as little as possible about me and mine; second, I stabbed my baby brother in a bad piece of business, right on the street in Baltimore; and third, don't forget I'm a man that almost never had a father. Careful then about calling me *son* too many times a day. I might get out of line a lot faster than either one of us could handle—you or me."

The single phrase *almost never had a father* caught Mabry at once, even more than the word about Marc's young brother; but he felt he shouldn't lean on it, not yet—not after his own father's claim in the graveyard today. So he started on the parcel, as carefully as Marcus had laid his shirt down. When he reached further layers of white tissue paper, his left eye suddenly began to flash within—the yellow and orange explosions that he couldn't control. For the umpteenth time he thought a thing he mostly felt was silly—*Signals from somewhere.* But if so, he was a long way from knowing who was sending them and why and what they said. Mabry paused and looked up to the far wall—maybe distance would help him.

Marcus said "Don't stop. I got to know what you think here *fast.* Excuse me for not being able to wait." With both hands he shooed Mabry onward.

With the eye still beaming its likely meaningless but harmful beaconry, Mabry found the taped edges and worked them open with— by now—a lot of the expectation of a Christmas child, though a child in the grip of fear and pain which he knew he must hide from the nearest adult. What first appeared was the panel's blank side— blank except for four short lines of writing, apparently in normal fountain-pen ink. As Mabry tried to read it, the bursts of light began to fade; and he was so nearly sure of his vision that he said out loud what he thought he could see.

> *"Two grown men hoping they get better in time.*
> *From M. Thornton to M. Kincaid*
> *September 15th, 2001 with a lot of hope*
> *for help in both directions."*

He looked up at Marcus. "Did I read it right?"

Marcus grinned. "Word perfect." But when Mabry simply kept staring at the words, Marcus said with a quiet impatience "Turn the sucker *over.*"

Mabry did. At first it seemed almost like a monotone panel, three tones of blue on the light side of navy. He was all but certain he was missing something big but *why?* His eye wasn't beaming. *Am I going blind though?* Still, something kept him from looking to Marcus for further guidance. So he brought the panel closer to his face, ten inches from his eyes. *Ah there.* It was a picture, yes — entirely in dark blues, of two grown men from the crowns of their heads to just above their waists. Neither one of them seemed to wear a shirt or jacket. It could easily have been a Wanted poster of two grown guys, except that they were bare to the waist for some unknown reason. Not looking to Marcus, Mabry tilted the panel to catch the late light. *Oh Jesus, it's us — Marcus and I.* Then he did look up. "Christ, son, *thank* you. When the hell did you do this?"

Marcus was solemn but mainly pleased. "I sat up most of last night to finish it, after we got back from Raleigh — once I could think about what we said, the worst we had done in our whole lives. I figured I'd paint a kind of *police* picture of the two of us together — *Wanted*, don't you know?" He took a long pause, then burst out in helpless laughter.

Mabry joined him but returned to the picture. The likeness of each face was remarkable; and if anything, his own face was more like itself than Marcus's. *How'd he manage that?* He said "Were you working from photographs? Surely not just your memory."

Marcus said "No, my memory. I wouldn't even let myself go to the mirror. It just seems like my right hand can see things, long enough to paint the outline anyhow. Then I fill in the details mainly by guessing."

Mabry said "You don't need any help from me. You're off and running, man. And thank you indeed."

Marcus stood. "I guessed you would be leaving soon to head back north. So I wanted to show you a sample of what I can do in case you meet anybody up there that could use my hands. I also wanted to show you my thanks."

"For what? I haven't done a damned thing for you."

"No, but you gave me some faith in myself, just taking me seriously the last few days. And also giving my mom this good job, tending your dad."

Mabry said *"Faith?* Marc, I've known you—what?—seventy-odd hours? How did that help? And Audrey was hired by my independent pa, not me. I wish I could take some credit on either score but honest, I can't."

Marcus waited to think it through carefully. Then he shrugged as inscrutably as if none of his suppositions had really mattered, or as if they'd mattered deeply but that he'd somehow survive their collapse. His young face was suddenly that masklike.

Mabry hardly saw it; he was so genuinely interested in the painting. Nobody would call it brilliant, as a manipulation of acrylic pigments to produce a record of two men's heads and faces. Yet as a pair of remembered likenesses it was startling, and Marc's whole notion of producing a kind of *Wanted* image not only chimed with Mabry's own first reaction but was also witty and more spot-on accurate in its aim than was immediately comforting. Mabry said "I think I'd better leave it down here till I find out how I stand in New York. My daughter's letter, that I just got, says my neighborhood is in *bad*-looking shape."

Marcus said "I can take it back to Audrey's place for safekeeping. Or we could just prop it up here on the mantelpiece till you get back." While Mabry was grinning easily, Marcus was thinking again. Finally he lowered his voice as if any number of undesirable spies were just out of sight in the hall beyond them. "You're never truly coming back here to stay, right?"

Mabry couldn't speak for a while—no question of tears or other deep feeling. He just didn't know what answer was truest.

So Marcus filled in. "Not a damned thing down here for you but a grave, not once your dad has passed on to his earnings—right?"

His earnings? Mabry had never heard that phrase as a synonym for *just deserts* or *Heaven* or *Hell*, so he asked for a simple explanation.

Marcus didn't smile. "I think you know—whatever he's earned from God or maybe just the ground he'll lie in." He pointed precisely in the direction of the white graveyard. "That ground's mighty *acid*. I was down there one day when I was nine or ten and they were planning to dig a lady up and ship her to Philly where her grandson was living then. My uncle Whitlaw was one of the diggers, planning to get him a half a day's work. But once they'd dug to the six-foot level and still hadn't hit on any kind of coffin, they had no choice but to keep on going—it was mid-August and hot as cinders. Anyhow, they dug as far as eight feet down; and there was plain *nothing*. They'd buried that lady in a walnut box some thirty years before, and the ground had *eat* both her and the box. Nothing left but a handful of coffin nails and two gold teeth that the white man took—the boss that day. No bones nor *nothing*. So even if we niggers don't have tombstones on most of the bodies in the black graveyard, at least I *know* that yall disappear as fast as us—underground anyhow." When Marcus stopped, his face was lit in a way not shown in his painting.

If an actual flame had sprung from his forehead and licked upward now for a moment, it wouldn't have surprised Mabry at all.

But then Marcus laughed again, not as uproariously as before but maybe sincerely. Even he may not have known at the time. He stood up then, took the picture from Mabry, and leaned it in the absolute center of the heart-pine mantel. There was nothing else there, so it spread its own force to all sides freely.

Mabry said "A world of thanks, Marc."

Marcus couldn't meet Mabry's eyes at the moment; but he smiled to himself and said what came out more nearly as a thought than actual words—"Anything you say, Boss Man. It's *yours* now."

Before Mabry could even turn and look, much less reject the old-time name *Boss Man*, Marcus was gone. When he looked, the rocking chair was utterly still, as though no one had sat there for days. It seemed a huge vacancy—a hole—in the room. Mabry needed company right at once. He also needed to phone Charlotte but not in the front hall, no chance of any privacy there. He'd drive into Sherwin, for that long at least.

He left the house through the back-hall door, thinking he might get away unseen and maybe be back by suppertime—or maybe not. By the time he'd got almost to the car, he was more than half willing to hurt his father's feelings. Tasker's few words by Gabriel's grave had only distanced Mabry more, by the hour, from a parent he'd only been able to honor—not to mention love—in short and uncontrollable bursts.

When he got to the only pay phone he knew of in Sherwin, a black man was talking and a small mob of women were waiting to talk when the man was done (or were they yoked to him in some other way?—in his all-white wardrobe, he shined with a kind of magnetic chill, even in the warm late afternoon). It was five-fifteen; so Mabry decided to drive to the opposite end of town and loop back past his favorite houses, all ante-bellum and still in good shape, each no doubt housing a single white woman with just enough money to paint the white boards and the dark green blinds every five or six years and hire a black woman to fry her an egg and two strips of bacon by eight each morning, then make her an egg salad sandwich for lunch, then leave for the day once she'd washed a few "smalls" gently by hand and swept the porch.

Why hasn't the Holy Ghost burned every scrap of this town to the Earth, the way it burned Berlin and Dresden just three years before I was born? Alone in the car, Mabry laughed but then was far from sure the thought was crazy. Could anybody argue seriously that slavery had ended? And if not, then what about the devastation, four days ago, on Manhattan Island? Were we meant to read it—feel it, *taste it*—as partial payment anyhow on the nation's accounts? Of course we were but who the hell would?

Instead of turning back toward the pay phone, Mabry chose to roll on out of town; and in twenty minutes he was lying in deep grass by Dameron's Mill Pond—not another soul in sight and no sound at all but the sliding water as it reached the low falls and occasional birds, settling in for the oncoming night. With both arms stretched out wide beside him, he shut his eyes and tried to confirm a strong suspicion that this was the place—the virtual spot, within a few yards—where at age fourteen he'd lost his virginity. His mind had always been a setter-of-scenes from his sexual past—down to the actual slant of light, the temperature of the room or space, the taste of the girl (her skin or mouth or whatever deeper entrances he'd managed to plumb), and then the rate and final reward of his rush toward joy.

But lately he'd begun to wonder how honest his mind really was—with these scenes anyhow. As he lay there, though, with his eyes shut to the actual beauty on all sides, he told himself he was surely recalling the precise textures and feelings of that hour of elation and near-terror as Jeanette Walker—who was maybe four months older than he and whom he'd met in "daily vacation Bible-school" class—folded herself inward, step by step, to his ranging hand and the minuscule victories he steadily won.

Did he fall asleep? If so, no dreams disturbed his rest—not even the faintest whiff of Jeanette or any of the other rare early girls, including Gwyn. But once he thought he'd opened his eyes, he was blind—entirely blind. Even the darkest night would have showed him more than this. Now though the sky was an unbroken sheet of black, a great iron bell clamped down above him. And nothing moved or made the least sound. Sometimes, in his boyhood, he'd have a bad dream and know it was a dream. Then he'd roll himself side to side in the bed to wake up fast and break the terror. He tried that now—and rolled so hard that he felt real pain in both arms and shoulders. But still no sun. He had to believe he was fully awake and had either slept way on into night or was suddenly blind. Blind.

Not one of the doctors he'd seen in the past two months had warned of blindness as an early symptom of multiple sclerosis, if that's what he had. They'd barely warned him of anything, however, even when he told them of the trip to Europe and asked for advice on whether to go or what to do if any symptom should waylay him there. In their several emotionless ways they'd all said something like "Go right on about your business. Have *fun*. We'll see how you're doing when you're safely back and have worked off the ten pounds of pasta fat you'll have gained in Rome."

He lay on still another long minute. Then he tried to stand up; and that plain action seemed to work, at least he thought he appeared to rise. And soon he could sense a change in the nature of the air—high up, it was warmer and the odors from the surface of the pond were stronger there. He extended both arms and turned in place, two or more full circles. But the perfect dark was perfect still. He couldn't help laughing. *If I'm suddenly blind, then what the hell next?* Should he find some way to crawl to the pond and drown himself? *Can a skillful swimmer drown himself? If he wants to, bad enough, no doubt he can. But do I, here and now?*

And if he didn't, what next—alone as he was, at whatever hour of day or night, more nearly crippled than any quadriplegic in a wheelchair with two flat tires? For the first time ever, he saw the point in owning a cell phone. Now if he could manage to stumble toward his car and sleep in there, then surely somebody would find him somehow in the next twenty-four hours. *But that's assuming the traffic out here is as frequent as it was forty years ago, a shaky assumption.* This was a world where sweet Jeanette Walker was fifty-three years old (still at least a few months older than he) and likely weighed, oh, thirty pounds more than the last time he'd seen her and had four children older than Charlotte and way worse-tempered, not to mention six or eight grandchildren. Mabry opened his mouth and actually howled, while he turned an even larger circle—and this time, not in desperation or fear of being lost and blind at his age but in active loathing of the mind he'd made inside his skull.

Something behind him said his name, or a version of his name—
not *Mabry* exactly but more like *Maybe*. It was surely a child's
voice, girl or boy, before the gouging tool of adolescence had made
the choice. What child did he know, down here anymore? He
hardly knew a child in New York. Still, he froze in place and said "I
seem to have lost my glasses, and I can't see a thing."

Then a soft dry hand brushed across his left palm, and the voice
said one more word, maybe *Hurry?*

Mabry took a risky step and pitched flat forward to the ground on
both hands. He said "*I'm* sorry" and tried to rise but, for whatever reason, held a hand out and said "Can you help me stand up here?"

No voice, no help.

So he lay where he was and slowly guessed that the Earth was no
cooler than when he'd first lain down, however long ago. Had it all
been a dream? Was it a dream still? He knew that the nails of both
his hands were long (he hadn't cut them since his first days in
Rome), and he dug at the back of each hand with the opposite set of
nails—genuine pain. *You're awake now at least.* And slower than any
actual dawn, in vertical strips of hazy detail, he began to see—
through both eyes apparently and focused more clearly as true
evening rose up out of the pond and the trees beyond it. When he
looked to his watch, it said six twenty-eight (a little more or less).

He felt a strong need to give thanks to something—maybe to the
child, real or dreamed, that had brought him to life (if what had
touched him was a child, not an adult with a high tenor voice). Or
to his father's God, whom Mabry had never quite denied. Bereft
then of an immediate target for gratitude, he said the one word
thanks to his watch. If nothing else, time—a few scary minutes—
had brought him from total blindness to light, however temporary
or threatened.

But where next? He needed to get out of here before real night
fell. The nearest emergency room was fifteen miles away, Tasker and
Audrey were six or seven miles, the center of Sherwin was maybe two

miles. And Gwyn's house was ten long blocks from the center of town. Whether she was home or not, he'd better head there. If he made it alive, he could try to phone Charlotte, then phone his father to say where he was and then rely on Gwyn to know what he should do once night was on them (that would mean telling her about his fears, which he hadn't laid out truly before now).

He got to Gwyn's with no more blindness. She was cold sober, in a dark green dress (one of the few human beings Mabry knew who could wear green clothes and not look as though sprouts of ivy were waiting to flood from her lips); and she'd just started cooking herself a homemade dish of macaroni and cheese with country-ham bits. There was plenty to share, and she was glad to share it; so before Mabry told her about the blind spell, he made his two phone calls.

Audrey thanked him for calling, said his father was fine, they were watching *Rebecca* with Joan Fontaine and would leave the porch light on for whenever he returned.

Charlotte answered in New York and, at first, was not quite as warm as her letter; so he gave her a quick but honestly scary account of his ordeal at the pond, and that brought her round.

Most of his friends would have been alarmed and urged him to get to a doctor at once. Charlotte took a long pause and said "Are you in a safe place?"

"I just drove my rental car to Gwyn Williams's. She's making us macaroni and cheese."

Charlotte paused again. "That should cure you for a week or so anyhow."

There was no trace of meanness in her voice, and Mabry recalled how she'd loved macaroni as a child—her mother had also made it, from scratch. He said "It does smell promising, I'll grant you."

Only then did she say "You planning to get up here very soon, I trust?"

"For my doctor, you mean?"

"For him and me and the rest of the people who can take care of you."

What had softened Charlotte since he left for Rome? He had no time to consider the options before the undeniable fact of her present kindness swamped him (it had to be kindness; Charlotte was flat incapable of deceit). He'd wept only once before in her presence—when her mother finally asked him to leave and he had to obey her, walking out with one suitcase the week before Christmas when Charlotte was twelve—so he tried hard to keep her from hearing the fact that his throat had closed on him for nearly a minute.

If she noticed, she didn't mention the strangeness. She waited to see if he'd answer her assurance; and when he couldn't, she said "There's millions of hotel rooms going begging—all the tourists understandably scattered. I'll get you a good room. You like the Algonquin and so do I. You can check in there and then let your doctor tell you you're fine. If you aren't, he won't have much to offer; or so you've said. But Malcolm and I can take you under our wide wings for Temporary Long-Term Care, as they call it in the ads; and by then we can surely get down to your loft and start cleaning up enough at least for you to have your bed and shower and a few square feet for your tools and your table."

He decided on the spot. "I'll fly up this coming Monday then, assuming I can get a plane and a hotel room. I'll let you know tomorrow at the latest. And listen, darling girl—deep thanks." Nothing like that had passed between them for more than a year, since before he'd gone down to D.C. and sat by her mother in the last hard weeks. Charlotte had found it immensely unlikely that his motives were unselfish; and once he'd learned that Frances had left him a sizable sum from her own father's leavings, he'd expected even harsher treatment.

Now, though, she said "You want me to meet you at the airport?"

"Won't you be at work?"

"I can call in sick." That didn't seem too good an idea since she'd only just begun at the adoption center.

Mabry said "Let me call you if I think I'll need help."

With a little more talk about Malcolm's new job on the edge of the disaster site, they finished up just as Gwyn called from downstairs, "A fine dinner's *ready*."

It was—few in the number of dishes but fine, in the smallest details of preparation. Mabry was hardly alone, in the United States, in holding macaroni and cheese high on his list of favorite foods. Since he'd parted from Frances and Charlotte in '86, he'd eaten many a bachelor supper consisting of nothing but Stouffer's mac and cheese and the simplest green salad. Even Kraft's box version of the same dish (which tasted more like the cardboard it came in than anything else dreamt up by human minds) could see him through in a desperate pinch. Still, a chance at the actual homemade concoction was all but sufficient recompense for the whole day behind him—his father's painful words at Gabe's tombstone and then the blind episode at the pond. More and more, he was working to believe it had been nothing worse than a long intense dream—that eerie voice and the soft hand were surely the key.

So he sat not two feet from Gwyn's left hand—at a table set with all her mother's best in the way of china, silver, and glass—and ate what she gave him: the macaroni with its salty flecks of local smoked ham, old-fashioned cabbage slaw on a bed of Boston lettuce (a salad green his mother would never have known, dying as she did before it reached the South), and a glass of honest dry California Merlot. And they hardly spoke for the first ten minutes, politely wolfing down their late supper. When he'd said yes to Gwyn's proffered second serving, he also said "You're looking better by the day, old friend."

She was serving her own plate, as liberally as his. "Darling, it's only been two days since you saw me for the first time in three thousand years—am I truly that magic when it comes to bending time to my advantage?"

"You are, beyond doubt."

"Then maybe I can thank your visit two nights ago."

Mabry said "You know what Marlene Dietrich said?"

"On which of her many themes, the old bitch?"

Mabry said "'A good lay is the best facelift.'"

Gwyn set her plate down carefully, took a step toward Mabry, took all the fingers of his left hand (which was lying on the table), and bent them backward, very painfully. When he howled sincerely, she said "Are you claiming you're still the dispenser of excellent lays? Wouldn't I be the judge of that—around here at least?"

"Oh *yes* ma'm," Mabry said. "Far be it from me."

Gwyn sat at her place again and finally smiled. "Was it truly a *lay*? I was so nearly drunk, I couldn't swear to it, though I do recall we did lie down and both dozed awhile."

Mabry said "I'll confess that's my impression too. Whatever, it's a pleasant memory already."

She said "But, darling, you're peaked tonight. Are you bearing up?"

If I tell her, won't she panic and haul me off to whatever doctor saw her mother to the grave? But he wanted someone nearby to know, and Gwyn was the best possibility at hand. "No," he said, "I'm not bearing up."

"Tell Mama what's wrong?" She'd gone back to eating, and her mouth was working.

He gave her the briefest possible account of what happened at the pond.

Gwyn said "You're convinced it wasn't a dream?"

"No, I'm not," he said, "but it sure as hell seemed real. What's your guess?"

She shook her head firmly. "No guess at all. It was something real."

"What makes you think that?"

"A good many things—but mainly the child, if the voice was a child's. That doesn't sound at all like a dream *you'd* have."

Mabry laughed a little. *What does Gwyn Williams know about my dreams? We've never spent two nights in the same bed.* But then he understood she was right. Somehow she was right. The child's voice and hand was not a touch he'd have invented, asleep or awake—too sweet for his taste. *Whatever on Earth it was, it was there.* He nodded to Gwyn. "Now what do I do?"

"You want to go to New York tonight?" She glanced at her watch. "Too late to get you to Raleigh-Durham. But, darling, I'll drive you straight up the map—just eight or nine hours. If we get you to Wells within the next hour, you can pack. I never need sleep as long as I'm driving, and we'll be at your loft by just after daylight."

For maybe ten seconds it seemed entirely feasible. But no, that was way too much of a strut—too hard on Tasker, mean as he'd been, and too half-cocked in several other ways. He thanked her but said he had a few earnest chores before he could leave; he'd go on Monday.

"I'll drive you to the airport on Monday—what time?" Gwyn had all but lived on planes for thirty years; flying to New York, even in a catastrophic week, was no more to her than crossing the street.

Again Mabry thanked her but invented a tale. "I've already set up a ride with Marcus, Audrey Thornton's son."

"Is he safe enough for you?"

Mabry said "Meaning what?" *Does she think the boy might cut my throat for what's in my wallet?*

"Meaning can he drive safely?"

"He delivers prescriptions all over the county; I guess he can drive in a straight line to Raleigh."

"How'll he get back home? I can meet him at the rental agency and bring him back."

Has Gwyn ever seen him, kind-looking as he is? She might jump his bones, and he's way too polite to tell a white lady no.

"No, darling. He's got a girlfriend and a daughter in Durham.

Maybe, when he's eased the girlfriend's pain, he'll catch a bus home."

Gwyn searched Mabry's face like a burnt-out store. Then with what he thought was semi-affectionate exasperation, she said "You're the same old slop-eating chauvinist pig you've been all your life. You just think women sit on the porch waiting, every spare minute of their pitiful lives, for the next passing *peter*." When Mabry didn't speak, Gwyn said "Right or wrong?"

He chose his best Steppin Fetchit imitation. "Lawd, Miss Gwwyyyn. I reckons you's bound to be *right* about dat. Course, *me* — I ain't even *got* no peter, this late in life nohow."

Gwyn said "Precious man, don't ask my opinion on that. Like I said, I was floating on dreams the last time I saw you. Whatever may have happened or didn't, I'm still in one plump piece tonight — no major bruises and no important tissue lost." When she looked and saw that maybe she'd joked too close to the bone — that Mabry was truly losing himself by the day and here she was laughing at him and his pain — she reached out to cover the back of his hand.

He drew it away, gradually but firmly, with the sense that this was the awful moment — his final move as an intact creature before he retreated, or was brutally hauled by something like fate, toward one of the slowest deaths available to middle-class light-complected men (and even more women).

Yet he and Gwyn sat on calmly through the natural end of supper — very little more wine — and then adjourned to more comfortable chairs in her father's old office, a room off the kitchen. She offered him the sofa as a place to lie down. Mabry said if he took it, he'd be asleep fast; and he didn't want that.

Gwyn said she never meant to sleep another minute, the rest of her life.

Mabry said "That may be the strangest thing I've heard."

"And I'm the strangest woman." They both laughed at that, then kept quiet awhile.

Mabry finally spoke. "I'd drink to that, if I'd drink to anything else tonight—it's why I've sought you out here lately. The trouble is with me though. I'm the normalest man in the Western world and maybe the East—Katmandu has hardly got a duller soul. I think my eyes went blind today just to protect me from plain reality."

"What brand of reality is troubling you?"

"Did I tell you about our little ride this morning—mine and Father Kincaid's?"

"No you didn't."

"Well, after the customary fieldhand breakfast, I offered Pa a ride—anywhere we could reach and return from by dark."

"The cemetery." Gwyn said it before Mabry could even draw breath.

"How'd you know?"

"His age," she said. "Wait till you and I are ancient. Everybody we ever loved, or even liked, will be underground; so we'll want to go visit."

Mabry had hoped for more of a revelation than that, but he went ahead. "I complied and drove us straight there—it's practically on the back porch anyhow—and he insisted on leaving the car and limping over to all the dead Kincaids. I held back awhile, to give him privacy for what you mentioned—talking to the dead."

Gwyn seemed to be taking Mabry a lot more earnestly than he intended. "Some people can do it, I'm absolutely sure. My mother could. But your dad? I doubt it. He's more educated than is safe for graveyard conversation."

Mabry said "Absolutely. I'm sure he *can't* do it."

"You know that for certain?"

It seemed an odd question. Surely she hadn't been serious to begin with, so what could she mean now?

Mabry said "Ma'm, all I know is this. He stood at the grave of my dead brother and cut me *deep*."

"Something he said?"

"Don't make me repeat it." Then "He said my brother Gabe was all he'd ever loved."

Gwyn said "You sure he said *all?*"

Mabry nodded strongly.

"I thought he loved your mother."

When Mabry could speak again, he said "I'm telling you what the man actually said. Of course, I'd always known how he felt, long before Gabe died; but now Pa's gouged it deep in me just in case I ever need to check."

Gwyn said "Then that makes him at least half as mean as my dear mother—she told me, in every letter she sent me through her last twenty years, that I had utterly ruined her life. Just tell yourself your last surviving parent is a vicious shit and get on with your business."

Mabry laughed till he made himself sneeze. Then he thanked her sincerely. But at last he had to say "What made you come to him for communion then?"

"Who told you that—prissy Miss Audrey Thornton?"

"No, the high priest himself."

Gwyn said "I thought they kept their pastoral secrets, like doctors and lawyers."

"Wrong, darling girl. They chatter like lovebirds."

"There goes this girl's last illusion then." Gwyn got to her feet. "This calls for a thoroughly unsanctified drink. What's the worst I can get you from Daddy's old stash here?" She'd already opened the door of the cabinet where Walker Williams, a criminal lawyer as close to a criminal as small towns afford, had laid in an infinite stock of liquors going back to decades before his death in the eighties.

But Mabry said "Let's postpone Daddy for a while longer, could we?" He'd also risen by now.

Gwyn said "You want to go upstairs, I can tell—you feeling bad?"

Mabry looked down at his trousers—a plain boner, a rare occurrence in these troubled days. Being a man, he couldn't help grinning. The nation had entered dreadful straits four days ago, he was likely entering straits at least as awful for one human being, and his father had told him he'd hardly loved him ever at all, yet a hard-on proud enough to announce itself in a mighty protrusion as true as any schoolboy's ruler had cheered him sufficiently to yield a grin as goofy as Goofy. He managed to wrestle his grin back down to where he could whisper for the first time tonight—"No ma'm, I may just be feeling proud of myself."

Gwyn took a good look. It was hardly a welcome sight at the moment—the moment, the evening, or maybe the year. But she knew her part, and she read it well. "Oh sweetheart, please, let's *burp* that baby and put it to bed." As she passed Mabry, she whispered "Make him last till I lock up." Then she went to lock the doors.

He lasted all right.

—And lasted so well, so encouragingly, that at two in the morning Mabry drove himself safely back to his father's and entered the house as quietly as he could through the front door (the side door was always locked at bedtime). Again, despite Audrey's promise, there were no lights on anywhere; and again when he tried to creep down the hall and on to his own room, Marcus sat up on the sofa in the pitch dark and said "Sir, it's me. Are you bearing up?"

Mabry only whispered "Come on back."

In his room he swore Marcus not to mention one word of what he said to anybody, and then he told him of the scare with his vision.

Marcus said "I grant you, that's a first-class scare."

"It means I'll need to fly to New York on Monday and see my doctor. Any chance you can drive me to the airport and leave that rental car? I'll pay you and, of course, pay your bus fare home."

"You just say what time we leave; and Mabry, you've paid me five times over already for any time I spend attending to you." He said the *attending* phrase as naturally and coolly as though he'd been Mabry's footman all his life and only felt the dignity of the job.

It riled Mabry badly. "Christ, man, you're not *attending* to me.

I'm not a pure cripple—not yet apparently. It's just a piece of hauling I'm asking you to do, like hauling your prescriptions."

Marcus held up a hand and his eyes were hot, for the first time in
Mabry's knowledge of him. "Hold it yourself, man. I'm not into *hauling*—except my own ass. If you're not careful, I'll haul my own black
ass out of here in the next ten seconds; and you can find you a boy
of your own to haul you to the plane."

Mabry was scared, for the second time today. But still he said
"Wait, Marcus, before you get any hotter—what are you doing
here in my house this late in the night?"

Marcus said "So it's your house? Then I'll go right now. I thought
it was your dad's—the man I work for."

That calmed Mabry to the point where at least he could think
This is heading into waters I don't understand and never have. Late as
it was, he smoothed at the air with two flat palms. Then he said
"Whatever my mistake here, Marc, I apologize. I was trying to
respect your grown man's rights and reimburse you for the work
you'll miss. That's all I was doing."

And Marcus began his own calming down. "I can thank you for
that much. Sorry I sounded off. I must be tireder than I realized."

Mabry said "Were you waiting up for me?"

Marcus took a long moment to recall. "I was waiting to let your
father know you were safely home. He made me promise him I
would."

"He's not still awake?"

Marcus said "I can't tell you. When I laid him down at eleven,
though, he was worried sick. If you're asking me, you better go see
him."

"But then I'll wake your mother."

"Don't worry about her; that's why she's here."

Mabry held out his right hand. "I'll go see him right now. You get
your own rest."

Marcus shook the hand lightly, then turned to leave. "I'll see you

Monday, if you want me then. If you don't, tell Audrey; she'll cancel me out."

Mabry thought *I'll just bet she can*; but he said "Thank you, yes. I don't have a plane reservation yet. I'll call when I do."

Marcus said "I'm your man."

"That's all I was hoping." And then Mabry actually said to himself *I can see this fellow walking away. Even in dim light, I see him still.* His eyes worked that far.

And they took him straight on to the kitchen without the need to turn on lights. At the kitchen door he thought he should speak so as not to startle Audrey. He said her name clearly, then apologized.

And from her cot, she spoke at once. "I could hear you coming. Everything all right?"

"Pretty much so. And Marcus has gone. He said my father wanted to see me, whatever time it was."

In the faint starshine it was plain that Audrey was still lying down, but her voice was wide awake. "He said that, yes."

Before they could think or speak again, Tasker called through his open door. "Son, step in here. I need you for a second."

And when Mabry crossed the doorjamb, Tasker said "Let's stay in the dark, but close the door and sit down yonder in the Morris chair."

One thing about Pa, his orders have always been clear as knife cuts. So Mabry obeyed. But once he was seated, he could hear undeniable snoring from Tasker—soft but still a hint of sleep. He sat for maybe three minutes till he himself was drifting off. Then at last, for reasons he couldn't imagine, he started reciting a poem his father had always said was the best in the English language, Cowper's "Castaway."

> *"No voice divine the storm allay'd,*
> *No light propitious shone;*
> *When, snatch'd from all effectual aid,*
> *We perished each alone. . . ."*

As Mabry quit, he thought *Goddamn, those lines have likely caused more men to kill themselves than any brand of liquor.* And he got to his feet again. *Let the old bastard sleep.* He was at the door before he could think *Have I ever called him that?* Then his hand was on the doorknob.

Tasker said "This morning—" Then he paused again, so long it could have been another nap.

Mabry turned the knob.

"Hold on, son. I asked you to sit."

"Reverend, I sat for the better part of five or ten minutes."

Tasker said "That's got to be a lie."

"A *stretcher* maybe but not a real lie. I doubt you could prove I've ever lied to you."

Tasker said "I'll choose to believe you."

Mabry had gone to the chair again but was upright still.

"When you've sat down, son, I'll finish my business."

So he sat, exhausted now and on the verge of anger.

"This morning, as I told you, I made a real mistake." But that seemed to be it—no immediate sign he'd say any more, not tonight.

Mabry couldn't quite settle for that. "You're referring to what you said to me at my brother's grave?"

"That's it, yes sir—your brother, my son."

Mabry said "Your second son. But, sir, I think I've heard all I want to hear on that sad subject—you loved him, nobody else apparently."

"I hardly said that."

Mabry said "I can tell you every word you said; I wish I could forget it. You looked square at me and said 'Gabriel Kincaid was the one human being I ever truly loved.'"

Tasker was punching his pillows up beneath him, and Mabry could just see his tortured efforts to sit more nearly upright in bed. He didn't ask for help, and Mabry didn't offer it. Finally Tasker could breathe deep enough to say "I surely never meant to say that—or not that much, not then and there."

"You're a priest of God, sir—or so I've been told all my life, by every voice on all sides of me—and that's what you said: the *only* human being you ever truly loved."

Tasker said "Then forgive me please."

Mabry said "Is that why you wanted me to see you, this late?"

"I think so, yes,"

Mabry said "Then I can finally go on to bed?" and he actually stood. But when he'd got halfway to the door, he turned full-face to his father. "Forgive you for what—for not loving me and any other soul or for hearing you misstate your feelings this morning? Maybe you didn't love Gabriel either. From what I've seen of the human race—the male half especially—it wouldn't surprise me if you loved nobody. That's pretty much what most men truly feel."

Tasker said "All right. Then who have you loved? Not me surely."

Mabry started to take the question in earnest. His mother came at once to mind—and Frances, in her last agony. But he heard himself say what he must have felt. "I don't have any duty on Earth to give you that list, however long or short."

Tasker said "That's correct. You have no duty whatsoever regarding me."

Mabry said "I'll bury you surely."

Tasker said "I've made those arrangements already with Audrey Thornton and her able son Marcus. You've met them both."

Mabry said "I have." No other words or ideas dawned on him. And the only sound he heard from his father was the rustle of a body rearranging covers. So he said "Good night, sir."

Tasker said "The same."

As Mabry passed Audrey's dark cot, he wondered if he should pause and speak—a word of explanation or apology, maybe a word of comfort from her. She was likely to have heard, at least, some scraps of what had just passed between a legitimate son and his father; and in the past day or two she'd seemed more understanding of his setup—Mabry's, down here. But Audrey said nothing as he moved on through the dark, and slowly he took his silent way forward to the room he was born in (he thought of it that way one more time).

And in his own bed, he was shockingly calm in the face of what had happened. Was there anything left to speak of between Father Kincaid and himself? When he left here on Monday—and why wait till Monday?—would he ever come back? Why and for what? But before he could bring up even the vaguest answers to such questions, Mabry was asleep. Deep untroubled sleep, the best he'd had since his nights in Rome on the edge of the Villa Borghese gardens in the old pensione where he'd stayed since his first student trip to the city.

It was more than a long hour later when a sound at his front-porch screen slowly woke him. In the late summer warmth, he'd raised the nearest window; and now a hand scratched lightly at the wire. Or was he dreaming? With his tendency to spring to full awareness the instant he woke, Mabry lay flat in mild annoyance and thought "This Marcus needs a real talking-to." But when he called "Marc?" a woman's voice said "It's me." It seemed to be a stranger. He said "Who's me?"

"Your friend Audrey Thornton."

That's at least a step forward. Finally I'm her friend. He thought she was bringing bad news about his father. *Why to the window though?* Somehow he didn't wonder if she was offering herself. He'd slept in his briefs; so he stood now, fumbled for his robe, and moved toward the voice. He hadn't switched on a single light; but since it was pitch dark, he guessed they were still in the midst of night. And since Audrey didn't speak again, he stopped and asked if she'd called the ambulance. Almost before he'd said the word, he knew he had to be more than half asleep. He got all the way to the screen and raked his own hand across the dry surface before he managed to say he was sorry to be so groggy. *Anywhere else in the world, this late and a stranger at the window, I'd run the other way.*

Audrey said "No, Mabry, we don't need an ambulance. Since you left your father an hour ago, I haven't slept a wink; so I figured you might be in the same shape, and this might be the last chance we get to talk about things we need to settle."

By then he could see a little starshine on the backs of his hands. "What time is it?"

"I really don't know. Nowhere near morning."

Mabry said "You want to come in here? I guess we wouldn't wake Pa by talking." *But is that anywhere near a good idea?*

Audrey had thought the same thing. "Warm as it is, you could come out here; we could sit and talk."

He went out the side door and joined her on the porch. In silence she led them toward the front door. She'd left that open so she'd stand a good chance of hearing Father Kincaid if he called for her. She'd also brought out a bottled Coke in case Mabry might need something to wake him. They sat in two of the heavy old rockers.

Mabry took two swallows of the drink, thought *This meeting is somehow immensely peculiar,* then spent a whole minute hearing a whippoorwill call its quick three-syllable name again and again across the road in Edwin Russell's pasture. *Any human being that self-obsessed would get hauled off to the mental ward, no questions asked.* At last he said "You think that could be the same whippoorwill I heard every summer through my boyhood, right here in this spot?"

Audrey said "Don't forget I'm a big-city girl. I truly couldn't tell you."

Mabry said "Then I had far better luck." Before she could start reciting her luck, he said "And what brought you down here to stay?"

She wasn't eager to spell that out; but deep as the night was, she went ahead. "A hundred things. My mother had been staying with me up north, and she nearly died homesick for this place. I'd liked it myself, on childhood trips, but hardly enough to draw me here for good. The main thing was Marcus. He told me he's already mentioned to you that he might have stabbed his brother."

Mabry said "He didn't say *might* have. He just said he stabbed him and that's why his own daughter bears the same name."

Audrey held back a long while. She even leaned forward more than once—laying her head flat on her knees, then rising straight up like ancient Jews in prayer by the Wall. At last she said "Mabry, honest to God I know this is true. You can count on this. Marcus sometimes thinks he killed Master Thornton, his younger half-brother. I doubt they ever spoke ten mean words to one another, not in my hearing. But the facts are these. For all the love and attention I gave them, I'm sure you can guess I couldn't afford to raise them in the best part of Baltimore; and by the time they were into adolescence, both boys had started hanging out with older fellows that were doing drugs, selling drugs, even running full-time prostitutes— whores that were not a day older than my boys. Anyhow, one Christmas Day they were hanging out a few blocks from home (I was off at church, may God forgive me, when my own children were what needed me); and a scuffle arose involving a bad older man, an actual dealer. He was just a supermarket of every kind of drug. And it turned out I knew him. I'd taught him in grade school. Back then he was smart, handsome and smart and ready to please. But late that Christmas afternoon, a big fight broke out, as I said—pistols with the older boys, knives with the kids, cocaine on the sidewalk before it was over, strewn all around like common sugar. And two dead boys—my son, Master Thornton, and the fellow I mentioned, named Sadney Simmons. Sadney not Sidney, one of those strange names young mothers make up or get from TV. When the coroner finished his autopsies, and the police finished their billion questions, the truth seemed to be this—so far as my sons were concerned at least. Master had taken one shot through the chest, plumb through his aorta, and two deep cuts on his upper left thigh. Marc wasn't touched anywhere on his body. He was scarcely fourteen at the time, and he did own a knife. I knew about that and had begged him to sell it to some other boy or let me keep it till he

got a little older. He told me later that—once the fight started—he
had the knife out, protecting himself and Master, who loved to get
right down in the midst of a fight. But Master worshiped Marc
(maybe you've seen why), and Marc took every chance to stand
between his kid brother and any kind of harm. In the end, no
charges were ever filed on Marcus Thornton. He had never laid
hands on a gun; and when he's thinking straight today, he knows he
never harmed his brother. But as I told you, sometimes he convinces
himself he did. Sometimes I think he tells other people just to season his quiet life a little. But he's harmless as a rabbit, except for getting that wild girl pregnant. So you can rest easy; he would no
more hurt your father or you than St. Francis would, if he was
nearby."

Mabry said "Don't we wish he were?"

Audrey said "I'm no kind of Catholic, you understand; but if St.
Francis had any way of sending that boy to college, I'd scrub his stone
floors two times a day the rest of my life."

Mabry thought *I better not take that road, not now if ever; and I
surely won't probe into Marcus's innocence. If the Thorntons turn out
to be loyal to Pa, then maybe I can help.* What he said was "You've
finished up at Duke, right—your course work anyhow?"

"I have and they've been thoroughly generous to me with finan-
cial aid, but I still have various sums to pay, so I'll still need to hold
down a job for my own expenses. I told you I take my prelims in the
spring, and then I start work on my dissertation."

He felt bareboned in going straight to it; so he stood, watched a
single car pass down the road, then took a seat on the railing and
faced in Audrey's general direction. When he was sure he could see
the outline of her head in the dark, he finally said "How long do you
think you can stay with my father?"

"You mean will my studies draw me away? I've thought a good deal
about that already. Easy as he is to take care of, and interesting to know
(you've heard him helping me with my Greek), I can't imagine I'll

need to leave him often. The books I need, I can check out from Duke and bring up here. Once his ankle heals, he can ride down with me and read in the library while I hunt down what I need. Other times I can get Marc or somebody else to sit here with him while I go to Durham. If you and he want me, then I'll try to hang on."

Angry as he'd been with his father all day, Mabry's great relief surprised him. He told her so firmly; then he rushed on to say "Once his ankle's healed, of course you can stay in my bedroom. I'll get the roof fixed right away."

Audrey made the sounds of agreement and thanks, then she went so quiet that Mabry thought she might have lapsed into sleep.

Turning aside, he straddled the rail and finished his Coke, then finally asked a question in his normal voice. It should either wake her or prove she'd never dozed at all. He said "You're divorced from your husband?"

She answered at once, a little harshly. "Is that necessary to any agreement we're making here?"

Mabry said "Not really. I was only hoping to understand how free you are, what needs you may have at home or wherever."

Audrey said "There was never a husband or any kind of regular man in my life. When I was a girl, I lived like most of the girls I knew. So no, there was no one permanent man; and there's no one now, of any description. But long as it took, I put myself through four years of college at Towson State. That's some satisfaction; and maybe I'm a little sad to say it, but my life is fair enough now." There might have been more natural light by then, or the fury with which she'd told him that much might have lit her face.

In any case, Mabry could almost see her excellent eyes. He thanked her again.

"Is that enough?" Her tone by then was almost teasing.

"A gracious plenty, as my mother used to say."

Audrey said "Mine too." But though her voice had calmed considerably, she pushed on, fearless. "Maybe now you'll tell me something about your personal history—your daughter's mother, any partners you've had, anything in that line."

"My father hasn't told you?"

"Not a single word and I wouldn't dream of asking him. I've got at least normal human curiosity but I'm no detective."

Mabry said "Thank goodness." Then without thinking, he slung his empty Coke bottle way out behind him in the yard.

Audrey said "That'll be your first duty tomorrow. Is that a deal?" Though she chuckled, she meant it.

He thought through his options here and finally decided *The pure whole truth or nothing else.* And he said "I was married to a well-fixed woman, nearly two years my senior, for thirteen years. She was fine to look at, always beautifully dressed, way more intelligent than me, and a flawless mother to our only child. She was damned nearly flawless in our relations too, hers and mine; but she did tend to look at me more than I needed. I'd be at work in my studio or reading on the terrace alone; and then I'd look up and find her silently somewhere behind me, just watching me as if she thought I was some form of nourishment that I never was and couldn't become—still can't, to this day. Once I got my degree in conservation, we moved to D.C., the fringes of Georgetown—she was well-to-do on her father's side. I knew I could get steady interesting work there, and both her parents lived nearby (likely too nearby). A couple of good years passed—us together and Charlotte just born. Then I started the trouble. I couldn't be faithful and I've never known why. I kept my tracks clean, though; and if she found out, she never mentioned it, not for many years. Then when Charlotte was twelve, a friend of mine—an old friend at that, oddly a fun-loving male himself—filled her in at an April Fools' party one night. The next day we talked, and she asked me to quit. I said I would but of course I didn't, and eventually she asked me to leave. Wrong as I was, I had no choice but to pack my things. The day I left we sat in the breakfast room and told each other that, for Charlotte's sake, neither one of us would seek a divorce unless a perfect partner should come our way. I lived on in D.C. for a while; and for both their sakes, I kept my private life extremely private. I also saw both of them often, and we got along fairly fine. But after a while I knew I wanted a fuller life, so I moved north and did well there with a one-man business. No feasible partners materialized for her or me, though. Frances had a good job in real estate (her name was Frances Kenyon), Charlotte had good schools; and as I said, New York made a genuine home for me—till Tuesday at least. What changed everything actually came earlier this year, one calm Sunday night. I was in my loft alone, watching a movie, when the telephone rang. We'd called each other fairly often, right along, mostly to deal with some problem of Charlotte's, some trouble she was having in college or wherever. But this time Frances just outright told me the news was bad and was all about her. It turned out her doctor, a close friend of ours, had phoned her on Saturday to say he'd just got all her studies back; and she was well-gone with double breast cancer, stage four. It was completely typical that she said *well-gone*. Anybody else would have said the cancer was terminal, but Frances Kenyon said *well-gone*. I said 'Jesus, Frances.' Then the next thing I heard myself say was 'Can I come back?' I meant what the words meant; and just as fast, she said 'If you're free, I'd be glad.' I laughed and said 'Not *free* but *cheap*.' Then I told her I was utterly free of other women and would stay that way for as long as she needed my presence or even the sight of me. I kept my word. I stayed beside her, at home and in the hospice, for the rest of her life." When he stopped, he thought *That sounds too good. I'm claiming sainthood.* Then he said as much.

It brought Audrey out of her chair. She took a short walk to the steps, also faced the road (still dark as it was), then turned in place and said one word. "Why?"

"Why what?"

"Why did you go back to her; and why did you stay, rotten as you'd been?"

In full daylight, Mabry might have resented it, coming from the unwed mother of two boys by two separate fathers. But here and now he tried an honest answer. "Pure guilt, a great deal of pity, then eventually love. Frances was that good to know at last, and the main thing we learned was that we had a lot we could laugh at together. Why can't more young couples learn that, near the start? As time moves on, it may be the main thing—for middle age anyhow. And then we were ready to talk about how we'd failed and to understand. Frances wouldn't let me take what I knew I richly deserved—the entire blame for a broken marriage, a broken home, and the daughter I'd abandoned. In fact, two days before she died, just before the morphine overwhelmed her, she told me she took at least fifty percent of the blame for our failure. When I said 'Oh no,' she said 'Ah yes.' But when I asked how and why, she wouldn't say more than just 'I was not some body you needed, not steadily.' I'll swear she said it as two distinct words—*some* and *body*."

Audrey stayed in place but sat on the top step, hugging her knees, still facing him. "All right, two words. What did they mean?"

Mabry thought *Let up, Audrey*. But he said "Oh Christ, I've thought about that ever since. I have to think she understood that part of me long before I did. See, I'd started sex as a very young boy—fourteen years old—with willing girls my age and a little older. By the time I knew Frances, and before we were married, I'd been close to a good many bodies. Not that I thought of willing girls as *meat*. I truly didn't and a fair number of them are friends of mine still—Christmas-card friends, as my mother used to call them. Well-wishers anyhow. No, I honestly think the trouble was that, starting so early, I couldn't get over the pleasure of watching another face at my personal mercy. And I kept on doing it—"

Audrey rushed in. "God in Heaven, what's *wrong* with men?"

"Didn't I just tell you? That's one wrong anyhow. This week, in New York, we've seen other things. God can drive people crazy—maybe He's the main problem—but that's your department."

Audrey said "I'm far from a theologian yet. You may have a point, though."

It wasn't by any means Mabry's main point. "Audrey, you know we're the monsters of the Earth—men, upright humans with cocks and balls (most of us anyhow). Wherever this New York horror ends, we could just finish the human race sooner or later—men, just *men*, forget hyenas and hammerhead sharks. But one of the few things every man's had is a mother, right?"

Audrey wouldn't answer that. She waited awhile, then slowly rose and came back to her rocker.

Mabry leaned back in his; and they sat on in place, each dozing off, then rousing and asking an easy question or making a short remark about tomorrow or a bird that would wake and try a few notes (practicing for dawn) or a car that would pass, inexplicably late or early. It was all but dawn when at last Audrey stood and said "Father Kincaid will be waking up now in another half hour. I'll go back in. You need some coffee yet?"

Mabry thanked her but no. Then he said "Maybe we can talk a little more tomorrow, at least before I leave on Monday."

Audrey said "We can try" and moved on toward the door.

Mabry stayed in the rocker, dozing onward, till full daylight sent him to his bed. The whippoorwill had also quit, long since.

He slept through the normal hour for Sunday breakfast. The house had stayed quiet and no one tried to raise him. Then when he heard Audrey sweeping the porch, he put on his robe, stepped to the door to wish her good morning, and told her he truly wouldn't need breakfast—not to worry. He also told her he planned to leave for New York tomorrow and would like to have a little more talk with her this evening, if she could manage that.

She said she had no other plans than to be right here.

So Mabry made his plane reservation, then phoned the Algonquin and booked a small suite. The clerk was a man he recognized from older days; and the clerk claimed to recognize Mabry—"Come right on, Mr. Kincaid. You'll have the entire place to yourself, except for me and a bellman or two. All our guests have fled. I'll put you in the Dorothy Parker suite. At least the framed quotations on the walls can help cheer you up." Then Mabry left a message on Charlotte's answering machine to say he'd arrive, late afternoon tomorrow, and would get a taxi straight to the hotel and phone her from there. At least now he had the money to fund this mildly luxurious return to his home.

Toward midday, while Audrey and his father were at church in Sherwin, he found sandwich makings and a glass of buttermilk, then headed out. And through the next four hours, he drove himself—in what seemed all but perfect health and in surely perfect weather— up and down country roads, working hard to convince himself of at least one thing his father believed: *I could live somewhere besides New York.* Whatever his answer would be to that, if it came anywhere near the plain word Yes, then he'd need to ask himself *Where though? Would it need to be a city? Not if I could find a small stream of clients elsewhere. And however much body care I'll need if I've truly got M.S. And a woman I might just manage to live with, in whatever condition I wind up in—with however much or little my body and mind will have to give her through the years. Or months.* That led him on into wondering *Am I thinking of love? I can't have truly loved anybody but Mother and Frances ever—and Charlotte as a baby—and I wound up treating Frances like a rag doll after two or three years. If I'm badly sick, then won't I mainly be looking for a nurse? And what are my chances of finding a nurse I might manage living with, not to mention vice versa?*

By the time he'd thought his way that far, the rental car had got him to the pool hall; and though it was Sunday, the Cold Beer sign was on. So he went in—for whatever reason—in the hope of seeing Vance Scott. When he stepped on into the smoky gloom of the long narrow space, he saw only a single lanky biker planning the final shot of a personal pool game as gravely as if his heart would cease the instant he failed. Mabry knew not to speak; he couldn't ask for Vance. So he turned back to leave.

But at last Vance's voice spoke out. "Hell, buddy, you leaving without a kind word for the hopeless and needy?" He was nearly hidden behind the beer counter (beer and cigarettes, peanuts and girly magazines and out-of-sight rubbers—the proto-stock of all such spots).

Mabry smiled for the first time in nearly a whole day. "Oh, say an extra word to *me* then—*hopeless* and *needy* are my first two names."

Vance raised both giant hands far into the air above him and gazed to the ceiling. "I'd call on the Ancient of Days to bless you, if there was an Ancient of Days anymore."

Mabry said "What happened to Him?"

"Didn't He die this past Tuesday morning, with the rest of those lily-white Christians and Hebrews in New York City?"

Mabry said "Surely not."

"Then He sure as hell lost one major round in *somebody's* game."

Mabry recalled his father's line on the same event—very much the same line. But he only said "You must have lost a round yourself to be working back there. Is this your second job?"

Vance said "You forgot I own the place."

If Mabry had ever known it, he didn't now. But he said "Is it legal to sell beer on Sunday?"

"Jesus, Mabry, where have you been these past hundred years? Satan reached Dixie, on his swing down the globe, some forty years ago." Vance set a frosted Michelob on the counter.

Mabry took out his wallet.

Vance waved it off. "Don't insult the only friend you've got."

The last time they'd met—three nights ago—Vance had known way too much of Mabry's news. Was this another oracular finding from the mouth of his oldest sodden acquaintance? *But it's likely true—have I got another friend, a male anyhow?* So he sat on a stool, four feet down the counter, and asked a question he'd thought about often as he waited with Frances in her hard last days. "Vance, why don't American men have friends?"

Vance turned it over once. "After they're married you mean?" But before Mabry could agree, Vance said "For a start, American women won't *let* us."

Mabry slapped the counter firmly. "Right. But why the hell not? It would get us out of the house and out of their hair—*all* their various hair departments."

Vance said "Pure meanness or jealousy or mother-love. They birth you and raise you, so they want to give you all the love they've got and that takes forever." When Mabry nodded and drank a few sips of his beer, Vance said "So you got up with Miss Gwyn Williams."

The oracle, again, God damn his nosey soul. "You her social secretary, are you?" There was more than an edge of resentment in his question.

Vance raised both flat palms to say *Back off.* "No, Mabry, but this is a really small place—not even an honest town anymore. We've even shrunk since your prime days. Last census said we had eighteen hundred souls, give or take a few dozen—more than half of them black—so white folks know everything every other white folk does. We even know each other's license plate numbers."

Mabry said "I'm driving a rental car."

"And rental cars have a numerical prefix that tells you, right off, a stranger's in town—or an old local boy that went off, made good, and is gracing us po' folks with a visit. Some fellow the same age as you and me came in here the other night, *late* in the night, and told me he'd seen your rental car parked outside Gwyn's house. Congratulations. She's a serious looker still, so I hear (you know she and I were in grade school together, but I haven't seen her since she left here for Asia)." By then Vance had opened the ancient cash register and was counting a considerable stack of paper money.

Mabry said "Maybe you shouldn't flash that dough." When

Vance said nothing, Mabry tried it another way. "You ever been robbed?"

Vance set the money down on the counter and began to open the buttons of his shirt. After the first two, he continued downward with a comic imitation of striptease. Finally with a gentle shout of *"Whoa* there, boys!" he revealed his whole chest. It was not just surprisingly lean and well-muscled, it bore a long wide scar below the breastbone—fully the size of a man's giant hand. After five seconds, and no explanation, Vance slowly rebuttoned and took up the cash.

Mabry said "Looks like somebody dropped a big rock in a pool of lava."

Vance finished counting and stretched a rubber band round the stack. First he said "Eight hundred and twenty-two bucks—a right good take for an average week in a country village." Then he finally smiled. "You always could say what you saw, clear as any poet." Next he started wiping down the counter, as if the money had been human shit. Then again he smiled. "It felt more or less exactly like you said—but let's say a *boulder* got absolutely *flung* into *cooling* lava. Yeah, that was it."

"A pistol or what?"

"Just a sawed-off shotgun."

Mabry said "Progress comes to Peanut County."

"Wouldn't progress have called for a well-cleaned Kalashnikov at the least?"

Mabry said *"Right!* How long ago was it?" The center of the scar looked old, the edges fresh.

"Nine or ten months, not quite a year."

Mabry said "It looks amazingly healed."

Vance nodded but then he said plainly "It's been steady hell."

"Pains you still?"

Vance said "Every hour on the clock—the thing I saw. It never really quit me."

"What thing?"

Vance said "The living fellow that shot me—a white man I'd never seen before—was of course after money. I didn't try to fight; he'd unveiled his shotgun when he came to the counter. I just emptied the register and gave him the whole take, but then I tried a fool trick I'd heard about on TV back in the days when the streets of New York and D.C. were ninety percent muggers. I looked him in the eye—his face wasn't covered—and said 'I think I know your mother.' He looked as shocked as if I'd thrown two thousand volts through him. So I tried it another way. 'Don't I know her? Son, I think I went to high school with her.' I thought it might somehow change his mind about harming somebody that knew his mother. Turned out I was wrong. He must have hated every gut she had. That's when he raised his gun and fired."

Mabry was stunned. *"Jesus Lord."*

Vance smiled. "You got it, first guess. That's who he was—the true Son of God, come to wake me up, I'm damned nearly sure."

Mabry took a slow swig of warm beer and wished for about six ounces of Scotch. *Jesus—I knew this used to be the Bible Belt, but that's the last thing I thought I'd hear from Vance.* Before he could ask though, Vance bent way down, brought up a full pint bottle of Dewar's Scotch and an old tin cup, and poured a big drink which he pushed toward Mabry—an almost surely illegal transaction. So when he'd all but drained the cup, Mabry said "You want me to ask what he woke you *from?*"

Vance was smiling still. "Not especially, no, though you're likely the only friend I've got." Yet in the face of Mabry's hands, declining the question, he said "I woke up from the trance I'd been in forever. Now I just mainly think about every person I've ever done wrong by, especially the children—I've had four, you know, so far as I recall. I try to write at least two letters every week, begging all their pardons, one by one, enclosing whatever profit I've made since the last two letters. Some of them write to thank me, but that's not why. I'm a more or less happy man, standing here."

Mabry said "You do look good, considering our age and the wear we've taken." He finished the whiskey. "Did they ever catch the fellow?"

Vance shook his head. "Nobody to *catch*. You guessed who he was. They caught him once and nailed him up high. Then he came back for me."

Crazy as any bedbug. And it came as a surprise. Mabry had known a handful of old friends who fell in the holes they'd dug for themselves with the drugs and drink that had seemed such cushions in the longish dream of the 1960s; but though he'd seen Vance so seldom since boyhood, he'd have guessed him a good deal tougher than this. He slid his right hand forward on the counter, though, more than halfway to Vance.

And Vance looked down but made no move to meet the gesture. Yet when Mabry stood and offered to pay for the single beer, Vance looked toward the one boy still in his deep dream with the cue stick; and he lowered his voice to speak in private. He was speaking to Mabry. "That thing you mentioned—that sickness you dread? It's the grandest blessing you'll ever receive."

Mabry laughed. "You get that wisdom from your Friend Upstairs?" Despite his words, he'd wiped all irony from his face; and by the time he finished the question, he was all but serious.

Vance took it that way. He said "No, but lately I make very few mistakes, as you likely noticed. You know what I learn just by staying in this room, tweaking my ears."

Mabry said "I've noticed and I know." He gave a mute wave and walked toward the door.

He was almost out before Vance laughed, a great cascade of likable laughter. He was reaching behind him for the calendar—young Marilyn naked as any grand jaybird, stretched on her famous red velvet blanket. Vance said "Come here."

Mabry obeyed, took the calendar, and studied it closely. She was way more perfect than any girl should have been—or should be now. He'd only recently heard on the radio that, if she'd survived, she'd be seventy-five. Well, she hadn't survived and here she was in mere perfection. He offered it back to Vance. "Maybe if you'd handed this to Jesus, you'd have a smooth chest."

Vance said "Good idea but I didn't think of it. I doubt he's heavily into blonds, though." He wouldn't accept his gift back from Mabry. "No, you take it back to New York when you go — if there's a piece of New York left by next week. You could sell it on almost any street corner, I'll bet you anything. Or if not, just give it away to some needy man who's your and my age. He can take it back behind an old garbage can and whack off till his heart quits on him. Or his whacker falls off from radiation poison." The great stream of laughter poured out again.

How much of any of this has he meant? *Is it all a big joke on the godless City Slicker?* But Mabry knew not to ask, so he tried again to say a second goodbye and get to the door — with Marilyn safe for another few moments in his two-handed grasp — and this time he left.

By the time Mabry drove on through the few streets of Sherwin that bore any serious memories for him, it was nearly dark. He'd eaten nothing since the sandwich at home, and his stomach was starting to claw at itself, so he drove toward Gwyn. As ever, all her lights were on; but when he parked in the back yard and reached the kitchen door, there was a taped-up manila envelope labeled — in Gwyn's most elegant hand — *To Whom It May Concern (If Any Such Creature Should Materialize)*. Around the words, she'd drawn stars and whorls in green and red ink. All things considered, maybe he mattered as much as any other local; so he opened the envelope. A full-sized sheet of white paper said, in a smaller version of Gwyn's script,

I've gone to Randy Baynes's office in town. Even on Sunday he's meeting me there to finalize a plan to bring this Lovely Old Home back into some sort of use. Maybe that's a thing my parents could

tolerate anyway if either ghost should chance to drop in while I'm still alive and can hear their opinions. Back in time to offer a helpful beverage to any legal-aged friend.

Mabry thought *I'm legal but is this for me?* When he'd left her last night, he hadn't known firmly what his next plans were; but he'd said he might well see her today. So he added a P.S. in his own green ink.

I might try to find you later tonight, but now I need to get home and scrounge a little supper—my knees are weaker than any six kittens.

The note about food was not a white lie. His recent symptoms sometimes came in relation to hunger. He aimed for home, helplessly thinking of the Kincaid house as his actual home, whoever might live in those burdened walls.

It was deep dusk when he stopped in Tasker's drive. The house was even darker. If any light at all was on, Mabry couldn't see it. But then the kitchen side was hid, so maybe his father and Audrey were there. One car was in sight—Tasker's, not Audrey's. Had she gone off somehow and left Father Kincaid here alone? She no doubt had emergencies of her own, but leaving an ancient cripple in a wheelchair was borderline behavior for a paid caretaker, furthermore one in theological graduate school.

Even the front hall was pitch dark; and while he stood waiting for any trace of sound, he could hear nothing, not even the normal creaks and groans of so much lumber after so many years. It was too much like being blind again, and he'd almost turned back toward his car when he gambled on a last chance. "Anybody home?"

No immediate answer.

"It's Mabry. Who—?" *You're not an owl, fool.* But he couldn't say more.

Then a man's dim voice said "Tasker Kincaid."

Mabry was almost glad to hear it, and he felt his way down the hall till a faint light showed from the kitchen. When he stopped in the door, he could see two candles on the dining table and two sets of hands—his father's and Audrey's. They seemed to be near the end of eating. *Some sort of holy service here?* He said he was sorry if he'd interrupted.

Audrey said "Not really. The power's gone out." No invitation to step any closer.

He did, though. *I was born here.*

Tasker didn't speak and barely looked up from his seashell pasta with the Bolognese sauce.

So Mabry spoke to Audrey. "You must have had power to cook this meal."

By then she was at the stove, an empty plate in her hand.

"I did. It just went out—what, Father?—twenty minutes ago."

Tasker chewed on.

Mabry sat at his accustomed place, though no one yet had asked him to do so.

And in another minute, Audrey set a full plate down before him.

From then on, he ate—an excellent pasta, despite the iceberg lettuce in the salad (pale green wood)—and questioned Audrey about her work, a subject he'd hardly broached till now. If he'd had to guess, he'd have said she was working on something to do with Christianity and what it now meant in the wake of the various revolutions in civil rights. But no. She was aimed at understanding what Jesus' teachings about the family had done to subsequent human behavior in the Middle East, Europe, and eventually America.

When she'd talked for maybe three minutes about the subject of her dissertation, Tasker broke in without so much as a word of pardon. "Jesus said the human family was the biggest roadblock of all to anyone hoping to lead a good life—or his kind of life."

Audrey accepted the silence Father Kincaid had assigned her.

But Mabry said "Why was I never told?"

Tasker said "Told what?"

"—That your friend Jesus condemned the human family. I thought every church that ever existed all but worshiped the family—family life, family *values*."

Audrey nodded, still silent.

Tasker said "That's why you notice I've quit the church."

Mabry said "Please quote me some words of Jesus on the subject."

Audrey reclaimed her ground. Before Father Kincaid could cite any scripture, she raised both hands and made little quotation marks in the air—*Here come the true words*. Then she said "'If anyone comes to me and does not hate his own father and mother and wife and children and brothers and sisters, yes, and even his own life, he cannot be my disciple.'"

Tasker said "Gospel of Luke, chapter fourteen, verse twenty-six. We professional Christians conceal that as much as possible, along with everything Jesus says about rich folks—how they're *all*, every one of them, doomed to the blue-hot heart of Hell."

Audrey smiled at last. "Gospel of Mark, chapter ten, verse twenty-three and following. That particular passage always gives me extra pleasure, especially when I was a penniless child in Baltimore and all the lady-pillars of the church wore hats that cost at least a hundred dollars; and the few men who ever showed their faces in the sanctuary wore the finest wool suits—or pale cotton seersucker in the summer. I knew that saying and I'd think of them *frying* in a deep-fat cooker while Mama and I would be lounging in Heaven with a brand-new window-unit air conditioner and us in our own cashmere sweater sets and new leather pumps with heels so high we'd fall down and break our cotton-picking necks, except that we were in *Heaven*; and you can't fall there—or if you can, you don't break *nothing*."

Everybody at the table managed to agree in a round of unforced laughter for Audrey's memory.

But before they'd stilled, lights came on above them in a scary rush—the power was back, at an unwelcome moment.

Audrey even said *"Shoot."*

And quicker than he usually responded to anything now, Tasker said to Audrey "I'm finished, thank you, lady." He laid his knife and fork on his empty plate, then turned in a majestic arc toward his own room. Audrey rose to help him; but he said politely "I'm capable, notice." He even managed, once over his threshold, to reach behind him and shut the door nine-tenths of the way. In another few seconds his TV was telling the world the only news it had told for the whole past week—lower New York City in ruins, New Yorkers assuming the rest of the world cared as much as they.

Mabry wouldn't let Audrey shoo him off from helping with the dishes. But once they were done, she lowered her voice and said that Marcus would be here early this evening, to lay Father Kincaid down (being exhausted, he'd told her to call for Marcus early). With the preliminary bath and toilet chores, that could take a full hour. She asked if that would be too late to come to Mabry's room for the further talk he'd requested?

"Absolutely not," he said.

When he went on back, his imitation Rolex (bought on the Via Veneto from a cheerful black African for five dollars cash) said nine-fifteen. So he packed his one bag in the careful way he'd learned from his mother the first time he ever left home overnight— a summer trip, at the age of four, to this same house. It even occurred to him to wonder now, for the first time ever, if the conquest of such a meticulous skill might have set his otherwise unruly mind on the path to a lifetime's care for precious objects and damaged paintings. All the clothes he wouldn't need tomorrow morning were packed before he recalled Baxter Sample's painting, whatever it was. Should he take it north now? TV had said that airport security was screwed down tight; such a parcel might cause considerable delay. He could leave it here; and if Baxter turned up, he could send for it quickly (but if Baxter proved certifiably dead, then what?). Now, though, Mabry lit the overhead bulb and the bedside lamp, unwrapped the painting, and studied it patiently one more time.

In the past few days, the firm hints of a sketch he'd discovered by removing the liner and washing a few square inches lightly was tempting at the very least. Something else had lain, for a patient century, under a Charleston boy's awkward daub. He'd shown it to Leah in Nova Scotia and to Gwyn down here—nobody else, not even Marcus. Strictly speaking, it was not his to show to anyone. And now—whatever had happened to Baxter Sample—if Baxter's butler was still in the duplex, he could simply stop off and leave it with him, no further involvement.

Gwyn's certainty, though, that something by Van Gogh lurked beneath the surface had snagged immovably in his brain. Not that he thought Gwyn had any expertise in the matter, but her hunches about a number of not insignificant things had turned out true. For instance, she'd laughingly turned down his offer of marriage when they were fresh from college almost thirty years ago—an early bit of wisdom—and when she met Frances, shortly after he did, she'd only said "That girl's got your name all *over* her. Speak for her hand right now, and behave your mean butt."

In a sudden hot instant, Mabry was struck by an impulse to take the canvas to New York tomorrow, have it X-rayed and—if there truly was something under Philip's effort—then he could proceed with the painful process of removing the daub, millimeter by millimeter.

But Audrey's voice spoke at his shut door. "I'm free for a little while when you want to talk."

Well, maybe she's saved me. Or saved young Philip's whole legacy anyhow. He hadn't mentioned the picture to her, so he leaned it face-down behind him on the bed and went to the door.

When she was seated in the rocking chair, he returned to the bed. And she spoke first. "Father Kincaid says you were born on that spot."

To his amazement, Mabry couldn't answer—his throat had closed. Finally, though, he could say that was true.

In the unexpected silence Audrey said "Those old iron bed frames are mostly gone now. You know what happened—when they went out of style and white folks threw them out, black folks took them. My mother had two, and she tended to paint them both every spring—different colors each year. Even now, they're wearing thick *inches* of her paint; and I need to strip them back to the bare iron and start all over. You hang on to this one; your daughter should have it some day anyhow, to remember you by."

That freed Mabry to speak about Charlotte. "I'd have said you were wrong about that till just yesterday. Remember I got a letter from New York? Believe it or not, it was from Charlotte Kincaid, sounding kinder to me than ever."

Audrey said "Of course I've never met her, but I know she contacts her grandfather frequently, and he counts on her to buck him up. That was all that worried him this past Tuesday when the awful news broke on TV. He knew you were safe in France or on a safe plane."

"*Right*. For all he cared."

Audrey was wearing the same tan slacks she'd worn to church. For all the work she'd done today, they were spotless still; but she pressed at them now with both hands. "You and I scarcely know each other, Mabry; but let me say one thing I believe I have good evidence for—your dad has talked about you steadily, day and night, ever since I moved here. Every word of it is trusting, funny, curious, and loving. I'm a person who's had damned little love in her life, so little I could write down the whole story of it right here in my hand." She held up her left hand and drew a tight circle in the midst of her other palm. Then she brought that palm to her nose and mouth as if to smell and taste again the little she'd known. "He loves you more than anybody left."

Mabry thought *So what does that amount to?* and what he said was "Doesn't that just mean he's old and sick enough to think he may just need me soon—some close blood kin to find him a decent bed in a full-care place that likely won't beat him but will, after all, leave him snoozing out in a wheelchair before a TV next to other mindless abandoned folks that slobber all day and shit their pants?"

Audrey swallowed hard. "Partly, I guess. But don't forget I've signed on with him—not on paper, understand. We've got no contract but I mean to stay as long as he needs me. I've already learned a world of good from him."

Mabry said "That's welcome news but Pa could last another twenty years. His own father made it to ninety-eight, mean as pluperfect sin—he was 'too mean to die' as my pa used to say. I was with the old bastard once when he reached in his underwear, pulled out a turd the size of a black-marble Ping-Pong ball, and rolled it toward me, saying 'Eat that for dinner. Full of nutritious minerals.'"

Audrey said "Again, I've got my own evidence in that department—you mentioned old Cooter. She lasted forever and got mighty confused. We were all her enemies in the depths of what little mind she brought up north. We'd moved her to Baltimore by then. Nearly drove me crazy. Maybe it's why I'm working so hard to get a *partial* grip on God." Her face was wrenched but then she laughed somehow at the memory.

Mabry had to join her. "Teach me that grip if you ever learn it."

"It's a promise," Audrey said.

"Meanwhile, let us say—" It took Mabry a good pause to know what he meant to say. "I'll call you from New York as soon as I've got a permanent phone. Pa's got Charlotte's number, and I've left the hotel number here on the table. I have no idea when I'll get in my loft, if I even discover it's reclaimable. I think you know, too, that I may be ill—on a scale from, say, four up to ten and a half. If it's bad, who knows where I'll need to go and when? In spite of Charlotte's very kind letter, I doubt she's ready for the revelation that her dad's an invalid, failing by the day or the minute, even if she is the most sincere form of Buddhist alive."

Audrey said "Buddhists are the best—aren't they?—when they're not too hippie-dippie to *see*." Since Mabry couldn't answer at once, she said "Forgive me please—and don't think I'm asking in connection with my duty to your father; he and I've settled all that—but you said you're fairly well fixed for money: savings and insurance, I mean, and all such concerns—right?"

Mabry hadn't told his father, but now he said "Right. If I've got M.S., it won't last forever; but as long as my eyes and hands still work, I can pay the insurance. Surely they can't cancel me now that I'm sick." His word *surely* suddenly felt absurd. Of course they could cancel him—*could* and likely *would*.

"I doubt any heart as kind as yours is going to wind up alone aboveground."

Mabry thanked her. "But I'm not hunting a wife."

Audrey smiled slowly. "I wasn't proposing."

"Forgive me please. I hope you know I meant no offense, but you of all people can understand what I may be facing."

Audrey said "Thank you, Mabry. But *me of all people*? What does that mean?" In her face there was no clear sign of anger.

He waited, then said "You've mentioned your childhood in Baltimore, your memories of Cooter—"

Audrey raised a hand to stop him. "Friend, you're stuck with more guilt about black folks than I'd estimate is appropriate—for you anyhow, here and now in this one house. You are *not* your family, not your family a generation or two ago anyhow."

That much was a welcome stopgap at least. He had to push a step further on, though. "I have no idea what your salary here is, and I don't mean to ask you. But if you feel you're underpaid, please just quietly let me know. I can help out, for a while if not forever."

"Thanks but your father's being very fair to me."

Mabry said "Good. But let's stay in close touch. Tell me if you start feeling overworked or if you need something Pa can't help you with."

Audrey nodded and made the OK sign with her fine hand.

The morning was clear and warm before the sun had climbed above the oaks. Mabry skipped breakfast—he'd still not worked off his pre-travel nerves—and by nine he and Marcus had got his one suit-case in the trunk of the car and were ready to leave. Mabry's anger at his father had nearly subsided—even his disappointment seemed irrelevant—but once he stood alone in the midst of his oldest room, looking round for any last leavings, he faced a fairly surprising final question. *How much of a farewell do I owe here?* To be sure, he knew there was no way to leave without some at least brief visit to Tasker's room—or wherever he was.

He was back in his bedroom with the door half shut (Marcus and Audrey were out on the porch—Mabry heard them talking mildly). So he tapped on his father's door. No answer. More taps.

At last Tasker said "You're generally welcome. Presume I said yes. Step on in."

When Mabry crossed the threshold, his father's back was turned; and the TV of course was pumping out its endless repetition of no fur-ther news. Since he'd bought the damned TV only weeks ago, he took the sizable liberty of walking over and turning the volume almost off. When he looked to his father, he expected some sort of response to the liberty. But no, nothing.

In fact, there was something approaching a grin on the face that was still remarkably firm—no major sags. Tasker even gestured toward the screen. "Kill it all. I'm learning nothing."

Mabry obeyed and took a seat. When it was clear his father was waiting for him to speak first, he managed to say "Pa, I'm sorry to leave in the wake of this badness."

"You're referring to New York?"

"You're bound to know I mean the graveyard—what you told me there."

Tasker actually waited a minute, gazing at the room, then out the window. Finally, not turning back to Mabry, he said "Son, I'd flat forgot the cemetery." Then he looked to his one surviving son and was plainly honest. "What I said there seemed the truth at the moment— and even back here, later that night. But surely you're old enough now to know how the truth shifts and slides from hour to hour, if not by the instant."

"Yes sir, I am." When he'd sat through a loaded wait of his own, he still had to say "But aren't you in the business of *eternal truth*?"

"Oh I was," Tasker said. "I was, back when."

"And you don't believe it now?"

"On and off," Tasker said, "like most human beings. Or am I wrong?"

Mabry said "Don't ask me, Pa. I mostly gave up, thirty-odd years ago—believing, that is, in anything but beautiful objects, women included and occasional men."

"You ever touch a man?"

Mabry said "I didn't mean that."

Tasker said "I did, a thousand years back, before I was married. More than half the fellows in seminary were queerer than Uncle Harry's hatband, and even normal Christian ministers specialize in touching each other but you've noticed that."

Mabry laughed. "I have, here and there, yes sir."

Tasker said "Do rabbis?"

Mabry laughed harder. "You'll have to find you an observant Jew to ask."

Tasker said "Ask around up north for me, hear?"

Mabry said "I will and I'll phone you collect with what I find. I somehow doubt I'll have a whole lot to report on the rabbi end."

Tasker said "You do it. I'll pick up *fast*, to hear a dispatch from rabbi country." He was also laughing by then, more laughter than Mabry had heard from a parent in many hard years.

The ninety-minute drive to Raleigh—Marcus at the wheel—had been quieter than their recent meetings. There was no unpleasant charge in the air, chiefly exhaustion and Mabry's silent jangling apprehension at what he'd find in New York. Mabry did say, as the airport hove into view, that he'd left two important things behind him in Wells—the portrait Marcus had given him and another small picture. He didn't expand at all on the Philip Adger canvas, but he explained why he was leaving the portrait. When Audrey had left him the previous night, he'd finally decided it was safer for Philip's picture if it stayed here at Tasker's till there was some definite word on Baxter, life or death (Mabry did take Philip's small envelope, and its strange claim, with him). So he'd set the dim landscape on the left edge of the bedroom mantel with Marcus's double portrait on the right, and now he explained about the portrait to Marcus. "You know I can barely imagine what's waiting for me in the city. My daughter's already warned me to expect major chaos in my loft downtown. So I didn't want to risk any damage to our portrait. I'll send for it later."

"Or maybe come get it?" Marcus was literally turning off the highway at the airport exit.

"That may take longer than any of us knows."

"You'll come for Father Kincaid's funeral, won't you?"

Mabry said "Absolutely but, Marcus, you generally have to *kill* a Kincaid. We've got genes so tough the angels will have to slug us at Judgment."

Marcus said "I hope you last just as long as you want—a hundred and fifty."

"If I still know my name."

"But, Mabry, your dad isn't long for this world."

Even coming from a post-adolescent lad with slim education, that chilled Mabry. "What makes you say that?"

"He told me."

"When?"

"Last night, when I laid him down."

Mabry said "Remember his words?"

"Something like 'Marc, you've been a saint to me. But I won't be leaning on you much longer.'"

Mabry said "That was likely just old-man talk. He used it with me too."

"Did he give you five thousand dollars or more?" Marcus couldn't help smiling at the windshield before him.

Mabry said "Hasn't given me ten cents in years. What are you talking about?"

Marcus said "When he said what I told you, he reached down under the covers and brought up a brown envelope with my full name on it. 'Don't open this till you get to your car,' he said, 'and don't ever mention a word of this to Audrey'—and I haven't; so help me keep his secret please."

Mabry said "Wait. What was in the envelope?"

"Oh, sorry. Five thousand dollars in fifties, a wad big enough to choke a bull."

"A good-sized bull at that—any letter or message?"

"Just a note, in his hand. Something like 'This is all I can give you before I'm gone. It's way too little for what you've given me, but buy all the education it will afford.'"

Mabry could hardly have been gladder to hear it. "For God's sake, hurry on now and *buy* it."

Marcus said "I mean to, soon as you can advise me how. But don't you think that means he knows he's bound outward soon?"

Mabry nodded. "It could surely mean he thinks so." There wasn't time to speculate on when and how his father had got the cash (a visit to the bank, of course; but who drove him there except Audrey or Marcus or, a long shot, Gwyn?) or—most interesting—whether the gift had been planned for a while or had followed on the heels of the confrontation with his own blood son in the cemetery and in the two days since.

As they entered the airport grounds to deposit the rental car, Marcus said "I believe old people—even serious young people—can *think* themselves to death if they truly want to pass on."

Mabry could only say "You please help him as much as you can, anywhere he needs to go."

Marcus said "You too," which might have angered a son but didn't.

Then Mabry looked up toward Terminal A and saw the actual first sign of local fear—two uniformed National Guardsmen with rifles posted by a door. Many doors, many rifles, many very grim-eyed young men on duty—for days or weeks or likely forever, the rest of Mabry's life anyhow. Till this moment, here in clear fall sunlight two feet to the left of a young man more alive than any colt, Mabry felt dead, dead and forgot and halfway glad at least. Then he felt cold fright, like fingers kneading deep in his brain.

Then Marcus switched off the engine and said "Safe landing, Chief." He meant they'd landed at the car rental slot. A way more dangerous landing might yet lie ahead for Mabry, five hundred miles north.

FOUR

9 . 17 . 01
9 . 19 . 01

It had been five years since Mabry spent a whole night in the Algonquin Hotel; but he was still in the back seat of the taxi, paying his fare, when Mike—the chief bellman (a trim man with "the map of Ireland" all over his face)—came to the curb and spoke through the cracked-open window, "Mr. Kincaid! I heard you were coming. Did me a world of good this awful week." And Mabry was hardly standing on the sidewalk—two yards from the site of the famous heartbreaking photo of Scott Fitzgerald near the end of his life—before Mike was introducing him to the strapping young new doorman, Ed. In the lobby, he was greeted at once by a further cheerful clutch of employees who remembered him from the seventies and early eighties when he'd stayed here often on trips up from D.C.—more bellmen (Eddie and Kevin and Peter) and Jenna at the front desk to check him in with the effortless ease of a likable cousin, speeding through a few minor details before slipping him the key card to what was now called the Dorothy Parker suite.

In the wake of such a welcome, then, he was alone in the silent paneled elevator before he took a moment to reflect on why he'd chosen to stay here one more time, especially now that he could

have sprung for the Plaza or the Waldorf. Well, they *knew* you, whoever you were, once you'd stayed here twice; and they cared for the
chinless schoolmarm from rural Illinois with the individual care the
place had given to Faulkner and Welty, Olivier, and Yves Montand
and Simone Signoret (not to mention the less distinguished Round
Table jokesters whom the owner blazoned now on lap rugs and a
king-sized recent dining-room painting).

Once Mike had set his suitcase on the bed, and he'd tipped him
nicely, Mabry studied his long face an instant and said "Mike,
you're way too young to have known Mrs. Parker, right?"

"Right, I came here in '63; and she came in once about six
months later for drinks in the lobby with a gentleman friend. But I
didn't speak with her and—frankly, Mr. Kincaid—she seemed a sad
case."

Mabry could add a little to that. "Oh God, she was by then—or
so I've read—but I have one story that's not on the walls here. A
client of mine knew her husband, Alan Campbell; and shortly
before Campbell killed himself, he sent my friend a letter with a very
late Parker remark. It seems she and Campbell had gone to an
L.A. screening of a dreadful movie called *The Chapman Report*. It
was meant to be a comedy, based on the Kinsey Report, about a sur-
vey of American sexual behavior; and at the dreary end, as Campbell
and Mrs. Parker were trying to leave the theater without being
seen, a publicity flak from the studio spotted Mrs. Parker and raced
over toward her, pen in hand. 'Oh Mrs. Parker, we would be so honored if you'd give us a quote about the film.' Campbell said 'Dottie
never broke stride. She drilled the flak dead in the eyes and said, very
clearly, "In my opinion, *The Chapman Report* will set fucking back
fifty years."'"

Mike laughed, though with a slight professional reserve—respect
for a dead former patron, honored here in these three dark green
rooms, hung with her pictures and sayings and posters from the films
she'd written with Alan Campbell.

By then it was midafternoon. Mabry paused to realize how luckily he'd navigated the recent journey and the hours—no strangeness whatever in his body or mind and surprisingly little in the way of scary new security at the airports or on board his plane (he'd badly needed an airborne snooze). So he thought he'd try to track down Charlotte and see if dinner was a possibility.

As he lifted the phone, he felt another chill. What if her kind letter was an unreliable fluke and he met coldness now or the brush-off in which Malcolm specialized whenever Charlotte was out—or hiding out? *It would be a real setback.* But he dialed the number.

And Charlotte answered in the midst of the third ring. "Pa?"

She's taking this much of a dare—that it's me and that I'm still actually me. *But when did she start to call me* Pa? He could ask her that later. For now, he rolled with the name. "It's Pa, sweetheart." And then he choked, not so much because of the implicit affection but because of the reminder of the heartbreaking moment in *Gone With the Wind* when Vivien Leigh has waded her way back to Tara through Yankee hell-and-holocaust only to find her beloved Irish father in dementia. *Doesn't she lean to kiss his curly white head and say "Oh Pa, don't worry about anything. Katie Scarlett's home"?* Mabry even tried it on Charlotte now. "Katie Scarlett, dear child—"

And wondrously she got it. "Safe back at Tara. You're in decent hands, Pa. Are you at the Algonquin?"

"So I am—the handsome Dorothy Parker suite."

"Are they still publicizing that tiny sad drunk?"

"They are. And tiny she was apparently but not as sad as you may think. She wrote some crackerjack poems and one short story that *I* think's great. I'll defend her further, if you'll join me for dinner." The pause was longer than he intended. "You and Malc, that is."

"Malc's working a late-night shift downtown; and that's what I can tell *you* about, among a zillion other things. What time's good for you?" Her acceptance was as matter-of-fact, tinged with warmth, as the simplest agreement to sit for three hours at her Buddhist class.

Does she call it a class? Mabry glanced to the clock beside him on the table. "Fine but I'll need a quick nap. Wait, it's Sunday, right?"

"Monday, Pa."

"Sorry, I've been way off stride with dates ever since I left France last Tuesday."

"—You and the entire Western world, for now and maybe the rest of our lives." She waited, then imitated Vivien Leigh as Scarlett at her most balked. "Paw, O Paw, the Yankees have raised the taxes on Tara to where I don't see *any* way to pay unless I peddle my tender white thighs."

Mabry laughed but then couldn't help his true feelings. "You save those thighs, sweetheart. And better not mention them to Paw. Well-brought-up girls don't mention their intimate parts to Paw, not above the knee anyhow."

Charlotte laughed. "But whoever said I was well-brought-up? Still, aye aye, sir. Want to say I join you down there at six?—get an early evening."

"At six o'clock then. Call me from the lobby."

He was so tired he'd had the sense to set the alarm for five-fifteen. So he woke at five and lay, eyes open on the ceiling above him, and thought of what old Silvio had told him just before he retired some years ago after many decades as a bellman here—how he'd come into a lower room one morning, after getting a call from the mother of a young man to see if anyone at the hotel had seen her son. He hadn't come home, to Roslyn, for three or four days. He'd worked at the hotel off and on for several years, and sometimes they'd lend him a room when they had a vacancy on a weekend night and he was in town. Anyhow Silvio promised the mother he'd check; and then on a hunch he came to the lower room, looked it over fairly quickly, and noticed nothing but the unmade bed—a tangle of white sheets. It was the slack guest season, just after Christmas; and the maids hadn't got round to cleaning the room. It did seem strange, though, that the windows were open on a grim winter day; and the room was freezing. So Silvio closed the window; and just as he turned to head back out, he took a second look down at the bed; and there, after all, lay the man he was looking for—cold dead, snow white in the knotted white sheets, staring up open-eyed like Mabry right now. The lost man had brought the wrong friend home from some late bar, got strangled for his pains; and the killer had the sense to open all windows so the stench of dead meat could quietly escape.

Luckily, Mabry could chuckle now and even consider what secrets were sealed in the beds and walls of every hotel room, unless the hotel had opened for business that same day—and even then some wildness might well have gone down. *Far worse things can happen than whatever's loose in me now. At least one psycho killer is prowling the block at this moment.* He knew he was only hunting the feeble consolations that could ease him briefly. Well, he'd made himself laugh by then, a small cause for thanks. There on his back he checked his body, piece by piece, especially his eyes and the feeling in his hands, and found again that there seemed to be no problems since—when? Since his unfathomed blind spell forty-eight hours ago. In the morning he'd phone his personal doctor and try to see him soon. That could take a week; but maybe he could scare the kind man with his blindness story, true as it was.

The shower and shave went without incident. Then he passed up a look at the TV news. If the world had ended, Charlotte would tell him. He sat on the sofa and flipped through the past week's *New Yorker*—as out of date now as any issue of the *Police Gazette* from the 1890s. When he'd taken literally all he could manage, he couldn't hold off requesting a quick room-service Scotch.

It reached him seconds before the phone rang—his child in the lobby. *Child.* When had he last thought of Charlotte as that? *It feels right, though.* And when he'd opened the door on her smile, he said "Darlin' child." Her face was an almost alarming mixture of her mother and Mabry—the Kenyons and the Kincaids, two strong

Anglo strains: raven black hair (unaided by dye), very dark blue eyes (almost royal purple), and pale white skin without the least blemish anywhere in sight. He'd made then—or joined in making—a single beautiful thing at least.

Charlotte opened her arms and folded him in, as nearly as her arms could reach around him. "I am your child, sir. We know *that* for sure." When she moved back a step, of all things she said "We do *know* it, don't we? You're not going to tell me I'm adopted someday, or merely the bastard you may think I struggle to imitate at times?"

Honestly, it disturbed Mabry. "You want to test our DNA tomorrow?" When she didn't shake her head yes or no, he said "It would be a gigantic waste of money, I can guarantee."

Charlotte said "I believe you. Let's clutch every penny we've got to our bosoms till we find good ways to spend them on each other." By then she was walking up the narrow hall to join him in the green sitting room. Once she'd digested the Parker memorabilia on the walls—and the really quite lovely photograph of Dottie as a young woman maybe not much past thirty—Charlotte could see his indentation on the sofa, so she sat in the deep wing chair just opposite. Then she saw his Scotch. "You're one up on me."

"Not truly," he said. "It got here the instant you rang from downstairs. Let that one be yours, just to prove your pa is no hapless drunk; and I'll call for another."

Slightly to Mabry's surprise, she accepted.

An hour later, they were both still sober but relaxed enough to have got through accounts of where they'd each been and what they'd done since their last meeting a month ago. Aside from a few logistical questions—where would Mabry live till his loft was available (if it ever was), and could Charlotte and Malc be involved somehow in whatever solutions he'd find for his problems?—the only question on Mabry's mind at least was simple. *Why has my daughter*

*changed her tune about me so drastically? Why am I forgiven? Or why
am I not the master villain I was last month?*

The room-service waiter arrived with their own small table and
deftly sorted the army of plates and old-fashioned heavy bright
warming-lids (they'd both ordered burgers with melted cheese,
slices of purple onion, and tomato that somehow resembled a
tomato, even this late in the growing season). Mabry tasted the
accompanying Australian burgundy, pronounced it better than
drinkable, signed the astronomical check, and launched the question
before his first bite. "Darling, I very much hope I'm not staring down
a gift mule's throat too early in the evening; but help me with this—
you don't seem as mad with me as you were when I left for Italy."

Charlotte took a dignified swatch of time to ponder her father's
sneak attack—a huge bite, a long chew, two savored mouthfuls of
the Outback wine. Then she went for the giant shoulder bag she'd
left in the hall, sat back in the wing chair, and searched her possessions. What she found was a letter.

Or an envelope—long, white, no stamp, though it did bear Charlotte's full name in a script Mabry thought he knew. *Frances's hand,
no more than two or three days from the end. Oh Christ, please
don't make me read something new from those ghastly days. Or
nights.* The days were at least not scary, only flat-out tragic. So he
actually leaned toward Charlotte—he still hadn't eaten and wondered if he could now—and said "It might be better if you just sum-
marized. Or kept any really hard parts to yourself. For now at least.
I'm way too weak still to face that time again."

Charlotte gave the request a slow moment's thought. Then she
halfway smiled and held up a stalling hand. *Trust me here.* She took
out a single page and spread it on her knee as gently as if this were
even more precious than the last words of Gandhi or the Buddha's
last sutra. When she looked up a last time before her reading, she said
"I want you to hear this from *me*, not read it yourself. But I'm not sure
I won't break down."

This girl is as likely to sob as I am to spread gold-dusted wings and soar toward Newark. She'd stayed dry as Tangier, right through the funeral. But he smiled to help her onward.

She found the passage, toward the end of the page; and within three words, and without trying, she sounded uncannily like her mother. *"It was badly wrong, that I ever told you any of the grief I held against your dad. If you ever do marry, or live with anybody more talkative than a German police dog, I trust you'll learn this thing I've only learned now, too late. Unless your partner is a psychotic killer, any mistakes that drive you apart are no-fault wrecks. No human being can truly assign blame, not truly and fairly, unless one of them is harming children. Stop trying right now to punish your father.'"* Charlotte's voice had lasted. But she waited a good while, then held up the page. It was in a strong script, that had never been her mother's.

Quietly, Mabry said "Did you compose it?"

Charlotte had skin that could blush in an instant, and now it fired up, but she held her own against it. "No, Pa. It's not me. Surely you know I couldn't have managed anything that sane."

Mabry said "Oh girl, you got me wrong. Without my glasses I was only wondering if you'd been her secretary—did she dictate it to you? I wrote down a good many things myself in those days when she'd get an idea that she thought was important. She even dictated whole *wills* to me, some of them so convincing that I phoned her lawyer and asked if they had any standing in law. He assured me of what I already knew—that she had a fixed will already, and that anyhow you had full power of attorney by then."

Charlotte said "The handwriting here is from that good night-nurse with auburn hair."

"Adelaide Truesdale, a certified saint."

"Believe me now then?"

"Darling, I never disbelieved *you.* But it's useful to know that your mother truly said it."

Charlotte said "I agree Adelaide sports a genuine hundred-watt halo, but I doubt she could manufacture that much truth entirely on her own."

Mabry started on his dinner. When he'd swallowed the first taste (precisely as rare as he'd ordered it), and watched Charlotte fold the page and return it to her bag, he said "Would you kindly bring me a copy of that when you get the next chance?"

Charlotte said "Of course," then swallowed some wine. "And that means you now know what cheered me up—or made me less of a moral policeman than I've tried to be about what you did that ended yall's marriage."

Mabry noted the *yall*, realizing how he'd caused it. "I see it, yes ma'm; and I'm grateful for it—your mother made Adelaide look like a hooker when it came to goodness—but if you'd truly heard what she said, you wouldn't have just said *I* ended the marriage."

Charlotte bent again to reach for the letter, then saw the point in Mabry's objection and stopped herself. "All right, sir." She grinned. "It'll likely take me a good while yet for the full truth to sink in."

Mabry said "Thanks. But please don't abandon this thing she tried to tell you. In fact, while I was married to your mother—in the last three years we spent together—I outright cheated her with several other women and hardly tried to keep it a secret. That was my real crime, and I'll never deny it—"

She stopped him too soon. "But isn't Mother saying she takes an equal share of the blame for your unfaithfulness?"

Mabry said "Maybe so. What else could she mean? But then she wrote it, or spoke it to Adelaide, after I'd voluntarily turned up and stayed there beside her through her last weeks for right or wrong. Rat that I am, I came back to her with no hope for anything on this *Earth* but a trace of pardon."

As Charlotte sat on, silent, in her tall chair more or less facing her silent father—both of them eating still—her face slowly resumed its true age. So often lately, burdened with the sadness of her mother's last days and her anger at Mabry's last-minute return, she'd seemed a woman in her tired mid-thirties. She was twenty-seven, though; and by the time she'd consumed the huge burger and was eating her french fries, slow strand by strand, she began to look even younger still—twenty-four or -five. She almost felt it.

So Mabry said "Bear with me a second and don't get mad at an Old Dad question. Are you married now?"

She waited of course but her face stayed calm, true to its age. "To Malcolm—Malc?"

He smiled.

"Do you mean have we gone to some liberal foreign country and got legally wed?"

Mabry said "Either that or just in both your serious minds. To the best of my knowledge, you've lived together ever since your sopho-more year at Mount Holyoke."

Just the mention of her alma mater, and her mother's, helped Charlotte laugh now. "I guess you're saying we've proved we're more than 'four-year dykes.'"

Mabry joined her laughter. "Partly that. But maybe you're ready to go a little further. Do the two of you plan to spend your lives together?"

That sobered Charlotte's face. "Of course, we've mentioned the possibility. But both of us grew up staring at our parents' divorces; so maybe we're more spooked than necessary, by now anyhow. What do you think?"

God, when did she last ask me for advice—age nine or ten? "I'd say that, given your life expectancy here in the new millennium, there's no rush whatever for anybody to pledge eternal loyalty."

When she'd rolled that over, Charlotte finally said "Don't forget though—my life expectancy is balanced on the fact that my mother died of double breast cancer; and as of last week, I live in a city that feels as fragile as an ancient dead leaf."

Here and now, by way of reflection, that sounded wiser than anything Mabry had to offer. He gave their glasses two additional inches of wine and offered again to toast his daughter. At present she seemed all he had, and a very genuine prop to lean on, thin as she was and lithe as a slat.

She met his glass with no reluctance.

So he had to say "Charlotte, I'll bless any course you take from here on—you and Malcolm and whoever else feels right and worthy to your best mind. Don't forget you're your mother's daughter, Frances Kenyon's—exceptionally *worthy.*"

Charlotte said "Frances Kenyon *Kincaid,* remember? She never dropped that married last name."

"And I never knew whether that was meant as kindness to you and me or something more."

Charlotte said "It was love. She loved you, right on."

All Mabry could say after that was "Worthy," then "Worthy" again.

So Charlotte thanked him from the depths of her heart, real depths. Then she said "You're bound to be lonely."

He wouldn't deny it.

"Anybody in sight?"

He waited to wonder. *Nobody in New York—Blair Patrick backed out, long since. None in Europe. Not Gwyn Williams, trusty as she is and has always been.* "Not a soul. Ain't I a pitiful broke-down boy?"

Charlotte stood in place, took a step toward him, then stopped. She said "You're going through a brief bad patch, I can plainly see that."

"You said you'd help me turn that around." Mabry hated the catch in his voice on *turn.*

"I said it and I will."

Then it was his moment to thank her, and he managed to say it. Among the several reasons for gratitude, the fact that his eyes could see her clearly in the merciful light from a standing lamp was chief. No picture he'd ever cleaned or touched, no statue he'd stroked, had meant more to him; and now he was free to realize that.

*   *   *

The Algonquin had the expected physical merits and complications of its age, which was nearly a century. The rooms were small but the walls were thick as any Norman castle's. Provided no thoughtless guest slammed a hall door, and provided you hung your *Do Not Disturb* sign on the outside knob, you could sleep right through the day. And Mabry nearly did (he especially enjoyed the recent Spanish version, ¡*No Me Moleste!*).

When he finally woke, the bedside clock dimly said eleven-twenty. His first thought was that he'd missed breakfast in the dining room (with another of his old friends from the staff, Chuck, the Turkish Cypriot wrestler). Then he realized what day it was—Tuesday. The catastrophe had struck seven days ago. Would the passing of a week have improved his chances of getting to the loft? Last night Charlotte had thought maybe yes and had given him Malcolm's cell-phone number at her new job downtown.

But Malc's job consisted of sitting in a trailer and meeting the more or less desperate relations of people still missing; so Mabry thought he'd order a room-service breakfast, then see what else might need doing today. The order was under way and he was in the shower before the fear seized him—the fear that burned on the near-edge of terror and was surely natural to a long-term citizen of this vast huddle of human beings, all targets now in a way they'd never quite been before. *Why did it take so long to get me?* And he didn't know what he meant by *it*. What was the *it* that had got him at last?

When he'd shaved, eaten his muffins and marmalade, and drunk two cups of the riveting coffee, scalding and black, he was still badly rattled by what he could only identify as fear—not one of the symptoms of whatever plague had ridden him lately, the chance of M.S. And all he could think to do to cool it was face the monster—go straight outside and walk the streets.

Times Square was fewer than two blocks west of the hotel entrance, and the block between Sixth Avenue and the Square itself seemed entirely unchanged since his last time here. The welfare hotels had silently vanished, and he saw only one or two porno shops with their vaunted live peep shows. But the same swarthy men with enormous bellies, propped on the fenders of cars and engaged in ferocious debate, were thick on the ground. Then he was out in the strong sunlight of Broadway and Forty-fourth; and while the tourist crowd had drastically shrunk, there were still too many people on the sidewalks to make anything resembling a stroll possible. Yet in all the talk he overheard, all the faces he watched as he wove a path uptown, he saw no sign of fear to match his own. If terrorists of any stripe were planning a second assault on the city, wouldn't this be the site? Television had weighed, again and again in recent days, the likelihood of nuclear or biological weapons next time.

Before he could think his own way through the question, though, his shoulder was jostled by a man no more than twenty years old—a lean Hispanic with shoulder-length black hair and a laughing boy (red-haired somehow, maybe four years old) astride his neck—and that was all the help Mabry needed, for now at least. He stubbornly chose to walk as far north as Forty-seventh Street, the single block of the diamond district, with its dozens of ultra Orthodox Jews in their black suits, wide-brimmed hats, dangling sidelocks plus a sprinkling of gesturing old men with white beards. If hate-fueled Muslims could strike anywhere, wouldn't this block be as good a site as any in the Western world? As ever on the block, he failed to catch the eye of a single Jew (their own eyes apparently filtered out goyim); and when he reached Fifth, he turned back south and aimed for the hotel.

From his father's house Mabry had tried ten times to phone the superintendent of his building and had got no reply, though a phone seemed to ring. So sitting beneath the large photo of the young Miss Parker (Miss Rothschild in fact, her real maiden name), he called him again now—again no answer. He'd once even had the super's mother's number in farthest Rockaway; but when he dialed her now, he got a canned operator's voice saying no such luck. He called his doctor and made an appointment to come in on Friday. He called three clients for whom he'd been doing small jobs and said he was locked out of his studio now but would phone them the moment he'd found their pieces (he was fully insured). They were all either oddly uninterested or far more eager to reheat the past week's news than consider the fate of their semi-precious objects. So within an hour he was free again, back in New York with nothing to do—nothing he *could* do and no one he knew who was eager to see him. Why the hell hadn't he at least brought Baxter's picture, to tinker with whatever lay under young Philip Adger's attempt?

By then it was nearly three o'clock. Mabry dialed Baxter's home phone.

With unnerving speed a man's voice answered. "Miles Watson speaking."

Wait—another changed number? But no, the absence of Baxter's name had come as a shock, yet the voice was welcome as a mere sign of old life. "Miles, it's Mabry Kincaid back in town."

"Oh Christ, Mr. Kincaid. It's grand to hear from *you*."

Something had shifted drastically. Miles didn't sound remotely drunk or out of control in any other way except his words—*Christ? grand?* In the few days since Mabry had last spoken with him, Miles had gone from being the respectfully muffled butler to the man who managed, if not owned, the place. And when Mabry asked for any news of Mr. Sample, Miles only said "I'm right where I was, sir. I've not had a damned word that I haven't learned from the wireless or the TV or the trips I've taken down there at three and four in the morning, scouting the place and airing the dog."

"No word from the office?"

"There's no more office, just dust on the ground under all the other dust."

"And you said Mr. Sample had no known kin?" Grim as the outcome might prove to be, Mabry heard the TV detective in his voice.

Oddly, Miles took ten seconds for a deep yawn. Had he been caught asleep? "As you know, Mr. Kincaid, he had few friends. But no, he specifically told me more than once that he had no kin and was bloody glad of it."

"And no one at all has phoned you or written to ask about Baxter or anything to do with his life or his business?"

By now Miles had joined Mabry in the strange semi-police exchange. "I'm just telling you the painful facts, sir. Not one soul has rung this residence nor sent a flower, alive or plastic, nor asked if I needed any help at all. Nobody but you, Mr. Kincaid—thanks. Between you and me—and who else is there?—I've gone damned nearly mad more than once, not to mention lonelier than any camel at Alice Springs in the blistering Outback a century ago. Mr. Sample was excellent company, as you know."

"He was indeed. Look, Miles, could you get to midtown by five o'clock today? I'll buy you a drink."

Miles's loneliness burst into instant readiness. "I'll be there on the absolute dot, sir. And thanks in advance."

As he'd done with Audrey, for a different reason, Mabry asked Miles to drop the *sir*.

Miles said he'd try but reminded Mabry of his military past. "*Sir's* drilled into my noggin like nails, no doubt for life."

Mabry had hardly set the phone down before he wondered if somehow Miles could bail him out of any oncoming weakness—if he wound up needing steady care, say.

When he got to the lobby, the tall grandfather clock said four fifty-eight; but against the far wall, Miles Watson was posted on a sofa almost smaller than he (Miles was long and sturdily broad, not an ounce of fat). When he saw Mabry coming toward him, he unfolded upright—maybe six foot six—and extended a hand, no smile yet on his square brown face.

Big as Miles was, he was younger than he looked; and while Mabry was sure bad Australians existed, he'd never met one he didn't like, though some were rough-hewn in a fashion unlike any brand of American roughness he'd known. This young man was plainly in trouble, here and now. So with more confidence than usual, Mabry took the nearest chair, firmly staking a dim corner of the crowded lobby (not as crowded as usual, especially on weekends when its dozens of well-dressed but clandestine couples seemed to earn it the affectionate name that a friend of Mabry's had given it decades ago—the Adultery Lounge).

An hour later, he'd learned full details of what he'd hardly considered in the past week—how this young man had felt, alone in both a foreign country and in an employer's spacious and handsomely furnished duplex with the growing certainty that his employer was dead and had left no kin, nor even so much as a memorandum of instructions in the likelihood of any such occurrence. As the second round of drinks arrived—and neither Miles nor Mabry was a guzzler—Miles reached inside his double-breasted blazer and produced a white envelope. Carefully he drew out a four-by-six white card, which he examined for half a minute before handing it over to Mabry.

At once Mabry recognized Baxter Sample's script, the ideal hand for an honest lawyer—upright, assertive (though not aggressive), and legible in every particular. In an arrangement that seemed almost a poem in intent, it said—

FOR TONIGHT

A cold soup
A curry (you choose: maybe chicken or entirely meatless—
    say, eggplant?)

Basmati rice (which, in its native Indian dialect, means
   joyfulness rice — a splendid prospect surely!)
Your ice cream in my new machine (maybe coconut or
   something at least vaguely Antipodean — mango?)
Espresso
   And I'll be grateful if you'd join me at the table, Miles.

Though Mabry had never been a poetry scholar, he noted the interesting arrangement of pronouns — Baxter's initial and final *you* and, in between, a single *my* with a concluding *me*. Could four of his words be any more than random in selection; but as a good lawyer, wasn't Baxter an eagle-eyed guard of his words? When Mabry returned it, smiling, to Miles he said "Reads like a poem."

Miles gave the card another long study, then slid it back into its envelope — no comment on the *poem* suggestion; but he did hold the envelope up before him. "I put it in this for safekeeping. Could just be his last words to me."

Mabry said "What happened to Carlos?" Carlos had been the Filipino cook.

"Carlos moved on, about a month ago, more or less extra baggage."

"Are you a cook as well?"

"I cooked in the army, yes — the officers' mess. So I took on the kitchen work for Mr. Sample. I had the time really."

Mabry had noticed, on a couple of dinners at Baxter's, how old-world meticulous he was with his small staff — who did what and in what uniform, at what precise moment of the evening. Surely now he could ask the last question raised by the memo card. "Did you often dine with him?"

Miles nearly leapt across the brief space with his answer. "Oh bleeding Christ, no! — sorry, sir, I was Catholic. Lord, no. I'd never shared so much as dry toast with Mr. Sample. This would have been the first time we so much as sat down together." His gray eyes were puzzled, but he launched a quick smile.

Mabry smiled too. "So you're waiting for that dinner still?" By then it was nearly six-thirty. "We could move a few yards south and eat right here."

If the invitation surprised Miles, he kept his calm, though at once he got to his feet and waited for Mabry to lead them into the dining room.

By the time they were served the towering wedges of profoundly dark chocolate cake and cups of real coffee, they'd gone through virtually every subject they could possibly have shared. What hadn't been mentioned was the picture from Paris. Did Miles know of it and of Mabry's errand to bring it back? In any case, Mabry chose not to mention it. He said "Can a lawyer as careful as Baxter have kept the only copy of his will in his office?"

With peculiar assurance Miles said "Oh no. There's got to be a copy in the clerk of court's office in whichever county he filed it in, however long ago; or so Edna says — Edna's the clean-up and laundry maid."

Has this lad got expectations then? What has Baxter told him? Mabry said "He was from rural Indiana, right?"

"Right, a Hoosier I think he called himself."

Baxter had worked relentlessly to iron the Hoosier out of his bones, though he took some pride in sharing his native state with James Dean. What then if the will proved to be hiding in a small Indiana county seat; and what if it had a very late codicil that mentioned Adger's picture? *Nothing to do but wait and see.* Chances were likely, maybe, that the picture was nothing more arresting than two layers of work by a boy from Charleston, painting in Auvers on the afternoon Van Gogh shot himself. *The underlayer is a long stretch better, though, than the building on top.* And while he was fully involved with dessert, Mabry recalled the claim in Philip's note that the building portrayed was the château behind which Van Gogh shot himself. *That'll be easy enough to check. Didn't Van Gogh likewise paint the château?*

Miles went on in his fragile assurance. "I believe what's needed is for the executor of Mr. Sample's estate to take a certificate of death to the relevant courthouse and read the original copy of the will. Mr. Kincaid, I was wondering if you might be the executor?"

It ambushed Mabry in the speculations that shamed him now. "Absolutely not." *A little too fervent.* "If there's truly no family, what friends did Baxter have in New York or anywhere else?"

Miles reminded him one more time that he knew of nobody, that no one had phoned or made contact of any sort. And only then, on his second cup of coffee, did he say "I'm hoping you can help me then, sir. Any help could make it possible for me to stay on in the States."

The gravity of the young man's face and voice jogged two words loose in Mabry's head. "Terre Haute—Terre Haute, Indiana. As I'm sure you know, it means *High Ground* in French. Baxter was born and raised there, not in the country. I only just remembered."

Before either one of them could think what those two words might mean in Miles's future, or to Philip Adger's picture, a voice was at Mabry's elbow. It was Eddie, the ever-laughing and likewise long-term bellman from Cuba. "Mr. Kincaid, your daughter's been trying to reach you. Would you phone her at home?"

Mabry asked Miles to wait while he went to the lobby phone, but Miles produced his own cell phone and offered that.

In a corner of the lobby, Mabry managed the new device with remarkable ease (his debut on a cell phone); and before Charlotte answered, he had another spell of blindness. First, he was struck with double vision in both eyes. Then the left eye was entirely black for half a minute while the right eye cleared. Then both eyes began to clear. Since he'd had no trouble for three days, it hit him hard. Meanwhile, Charlotte answered calmly and Mabry tried hard to conceal his scare while he heard her out.

Apparently Malcolm had just phoned toward the end of her workday at the disaster site and said that if Charlotte and Mabry could join her down there by nine o'clock, a policeman friend might let them through a side barricade and on down to Mabry's street.

The blind eye cleared in the midst of her offer, so he didn't mention any trouble.

And Charlotte said she'd get a cab and pick him up in front of the hotel in half an hour.

On his way back to the table, though, Mabry feared another recurrence in his eyes downtown with the two young women—not that he doubted their competence to get him back to his own space here or the nearest hospital. He surprised himself, though, as he handed Miles's phone back to him. "How about a quick ride downtown with me and my daughter to check on my loft? Her partner thinks she may have a way to get us through." When Miles accepted, with almost stunned readiness, Mabry even went a step further. "For God's sake don't breathe a word of this; but Miles, I'm having trouble with my vision—brief spells of blindness. They could be symptoms of something bad. I'm seeing my doctor later this week, but I've barely mentioned the blindness to my daughter, so please keep my secret."

When Miles said "Right. If you feel the least patch of trouble while we're down there, just give me a sign and I'll stay near."

Good soldierly response. So that's why I asked him. Till then, Mabry hadn't quite understood his offer. They headed upstairs, fast, to use the john and to fetch Mabry's coat. It was raining by then.

In the cab Charlotte was almost invisible—all-black clothes, her long dark hair unbound and loose now at each side of her face. Yet the powerful hint of a beauty directly derived from her mother again reached Mabry in the dark. She showed no surprise or resentment at Miles's unexpected presence but kissed her father and gave the driver an address he balked at (oddly he appeared to be an American).

"Miss, you know I can't take you down there."

She said "But you can—" Then she changed course. "Let us off at the corner of Canal Street then."

When he still looked unconvinced, she said "Relax, I'm the mayor's bastard daughter; but he loves me a *lot*."

Mabry was proud to know her. He leaned back, shut both eyes— between a resourceful daughter and a strong young man—and rode where they took him. And before they were five blocks south of the public library, its recumbent lions supremely unaware that their home had been stormed, he was actually dozing. When he woke, Charlotte was out of the cab, waiting beside it; and Miles was beside him, paying the driver.

Ambushed as Mabry had been by the sleep (he hadn't felt tired), when he left the cab he seemed in reasonably good working order. He could see that Charlotte had pushed on well ahead and beckoned to Malc, who was standing just outside a long brown trailer. So when Charlotte came back toward him with Malcolm in tow, he could meet Malc pleasantly and introduce Miles. Then he lowered his voice to ask if Malc's friend, the helpful policeman, would have any problem with Miles's presence.

Malcolm sized Miles up. Of the four of them, he was way the tallest (Malc was second). She was also dressed right—a severe black suit, a small silver brooch, her hair caught back in a dark green band—and her face was almost beautiful here, almost a mirror reflection of Charlotte, though refusing to relent now. She finally smiled. "If you scrunch up, Miles, and look a head shorter, I think you'll be fine." She took them all in tow, as though deciding how likely they each were to pass through a barricade; and almost every barricade restrained small clutches of the big-eyed forlorn, the families or friends of missing men and women with unbearably naked signs of their grief—handmade posters with smiling photographs of a single missing man or woman (thank God, no children), occasional hand-lettered pleas for the slightest trace of hope: *Beatrice Hillman, last heard from at 8:36 a.m. on Tuesday, 9/11. We know she's alive but may be confused*. There was almost no talk, a whisper or two, a wistful smile as though any larger expressions of sadness or joy were being restrained for the dreamed-of meeting with whoever was lost.

At last Malcolm led them to a silent corner. "We can't get really near the chaos tonight, especially in this rain. You want to get a little closer, though, before we try to reach Mabry's place?"

Nobody said no.

The laminated photo ID, which was round Malcolm's neck, got them to the far west rim of the site—or a hundred yards short. They couldn't see more of the chaos than the tops of a wilderness of twisted metal under golden spotlights; but they were stunned by the huge fresh *emptiness*, the literal tall wide vacuum where the Towers had risen.

Mabry had to say *"Christ!"*

Miles said "Who else?"

Charlotte said "You might want to think of the Demon."

Yet the mild but steady drizzle on their heads and the chill air stacked around them like granite carefully sheared for buildings that would never rise were surely the perfect surroundings to close on four hapless guests of a giant absence that marked the scene of horrendous harm barely more than a week ago. Each of them— Malc, Charlotte, Mabry, Miles—felt something similar. For all the horror, though, they also felt the uncanny beauty of the light on the mist. Any sane creature might have felt itself in a space containing the lingering minds of thousands of other actual creatures—human beings—who died in fear and agony but were oddly peaceful now, this soon, this endlessly.

* * *

Farther south, Mabry's home block was lit only at the corners—no sign of even candles or lanterns in any windows—and the street and the sidewalks were silted way over Miles's ankle boots when he ventured a short way toward where Mabry pointed.

Mabry called him back. "Don't ruin your boots, Miles. The building's there. I can see that at least. What I need to do now is come back down here in daylight as soon as they'll let me come."

Malcolm said "I think I could get you through tomorrow."

Charlotte looked to her father. "But will Fredo be here?"

Mabry said "I've tried to phone Fredo a thousand times in the past week. His phone seems to ring but nobody answers. He lives with his mother, or so he always claims. I've seen her more than once, and frankly she's gorgeous."

Malc said "All the phones down here ring for some reason. They've never sounded dead, though most of them have been. But they're coming on slowly like everything else."

Having seen the dust around Miles's boots, Mabry decided he'd move no farther than where he stood. But he looked in the general direction of his door. Assuming it was there at all, it would be a wide gray door with a tattered bumper sticker some tenant had posted years ago—*Warning! I brake for hallucinations!* And funny as it still seemed, he told himself he'd never enter that door again nor climb those stairs to the loft he'd known for four years—mainly good times. Apart from the scary symptoms that had chopped in on him these past few weeks, he couldn't think why he felt so exhausted and unshakably grim. Was it simply that death hung enormous above him or, suddenly now, in actual human thousands, at his feet? Was his country's inevitable doom somehow inscribed around him in the air they were breathing?

And did Charlotte sense the same presence? She took her father by the left arm anyhow and whispered toward him. "Who is Miles and why is he with us?" Miles and Malcolm were ten yards beyond them in the midst of the empty street. From the moment they'd met, they'd taken to each other and were slowly trying to figure why.

Mabry said "Miles Watson is the butler for Baxter Sample— remember him?" He'd taken his daughter to Baxter's once when she first moved to town.

"Oh God, yes. Didn't Baxter work in the World Trade Center?"

Mabry said "He did, every day, and Miles is fairly sure he's dead. Anyhow when I spoke with Miles on the phone today, he sounded so sad that I asked him to join me for a drink at the hotel; and then you called so I couldn't quite leave him in the lurch with nothing but a slab of chocolate cake for company."

That reminded Charlotte. "Did yall finish eating?"

"All but dessert. You forestalled that." Mabry was smiling, though.

"Then it'll be my treat right now." She hadn't eaten since a lunchtime salad with a few nuts and seeds.

Miles plainly heard her. Still in the street, he said "Where the hell would we find a café or a bar in this devastation?"

Malc had heard the problem. She took Miles by the elbow like a suddenly blindfolded child. "There's *one* secret place."

So they all followed her.

Its frail light came out to meet them through what was now a denser drizzle. And they were no sooner inside the red door than Mabry declared the inescapable. "It's an *Irish* bar." And so it all but was. Surely no more than four blocks from his loft, and in a stretch of office buildings unbroken by other shops or restaurants, it was a long dark room—an almost scarily low ceiling with bulky dark beams—and no more than six or eight humans at the bar and in the three booths. *Is it real, though, or am I off in some fast dream?*

But Malc and Miles were already waving him and Charlotte toward them from a table at the back, by a well-banked fireplace; and the smiling barman said, as they passed, "The girl will attend to your needs in a moment." *My needs? Then how many years has the poor child got to haul them out to me?*

Still the girl appeared and, far from sounding like the Rose of Tralee, she had a broad stripe of New Jersey down her voice — low-pitched and friendly but, still, north Jersey. Her eyes were so dark blue that they looked almost entirely black from across the table; but when she reached Mabry, took his order for a single-malt whiskey, and heard him tell her "You're an answer to prayer," a smile escaped across the distance she'd attempted between them; and it made her an actual rewarding beauty near the end of a day he was feeling more than ready to finish.

All the same, in the next half hour they'd worked through several strands of interesting talk — Mabry's trip came first (both the European and Carolina sections, though with little reference to Tasker's hardness). It was plainly the subject that would let them avoid the obsessions of what was already known as 9/11. Charlotte and Miles both chimed in with travel tales of their own — a trip to Scotland that Charlotte had made in the wake of her mother's death and Miles's account of how he came from the deep outback of rural Australia through four years of army to upscale New York in under six months. When Malc asked about his job, he gave her the simplest possible story of his work for Baxter Sample, Baxter's disappearance, and the mysteries that had swarmed him in the past seven days.

The fact that Miles could still navigate his story with a likable dignity and candor and, yet, somehow spark a good deal of laughter at unexpected junctures was a help to them all. When he'd finally exhausted his stock of recent memory, though, they were silent for longer than they'd been since arriving in The Children's Pony. That was the welcome name of the bar, though it somehow offered the unreal promise which they all felt in silence — that this was a haven that wouldn't be here at all, not the slightest trace, if they came back tomorrow.

Actually, it was Malcolm's turn to talk; and she didn't much

want to. Her work was appalling and she'd had a long day. But neither Mabry nor Miles was clear on what she did down here, so she
felt some pressure to fill them in. It was Miles's forthright stare that
started her. She faced him and said "Last Thursday I volunteered for
what still seems an unimaginable job. When the diggers find what
we're forced to call *remains*—identifiable remains, however partial—
then I'm one of the staff who sits in that trailer you saw and, only
three or four times a day so far, phones the survivors and asks if they'd
like to collect their kin. Generally they don't force me to say that
what we've got are just *pieces* of their kin; but when we do, that's the
truly hard part. They mostly just say yes and come on down. If the
ones I've spoken with show up at the site, then I have the task of
meeting with them, trying to answer any questions they have, and
offering whatever help I can manage to provide."

Mabry realized how selfish he'd been with Charlotte last night in
asking so little about Malc's work. He'd even nearly forgot the fact
that she had some sort of religious degree she'd laid aside to pursue
her usual substitute teaching in ghetto schools that demanded her
visible strength and force. He said to her now "You must be overwhelmed with families. How big is your staff?"

Malc took a long swallow of her gin and water; and when she
could finally speak, she choked. Then at last she laughed. "Me and
generally one or two others."

Miles said "Holy hell! That's dreadful short change. Who's cheating us like that?"

Malc hadn't heard the details of Miles's ongoing dilemma; but
something in the broad placid planes of his face, his bowed hulking
shoulders, and his one word *us* told her to move ahead slowly. She
said "We have so little to give."

Miles kept the lid on but his voice warmed a little. "Little? Yet the
TV keeps saying many thousands died. Just this evening, they were
still saying maybe five thousand were finished."

By then Charlotte and Mabry were also fixed on Malcolm.

Where would this lead? With all her training, she wasn't known, among her close friends, for extremes of tact.

Malc took the time she needed, though. Then she closed her fist and, very lightly, tapped the back of Miles's great hand on the table.

His hand rolled over and took hers in.

She left that brief arrangement in place, and she said what Mabry had thought of days ago. "What the diggers are finding is that—with all that jet fuel—once it ignited, it left us very little in the way of human bodies. However many thousands died, they were *truly* cremated—vaporized."

The other three were as impressed as they should have been, but they said nothing yet. By then they all knew that Miles had prior rights here.

And at last he said "What could be better, once you've got to go?" He shook his head no as if he'd thought of an even better way of departing this one planet at least. But then they all waited half a minute till Miles finally turned them loose with an outright laugh. Then he faced the bar and signaled the barmaid, calling her "Miss" in a voice that was calmer and deeper than before.

When she came, she was also somehow subdued, as though Miles's discovery had worked through the intervening air toward her. Everyone joined him in further rounds of their first drinks; and Charlotte, Malc, and Miles each ordered toasted cheese sandwiches with lashings of home fries.

They were deep into wolfing down their food, and the second round of drinks, when Malc looked to the door. Three strapping men and a hefty young woman were entering. Malc touched Mabry's arm. "He told me he'd try to make it this evening and here he is." She pointed to one of the men—both were standing now at the bar, exhausted and dusty still, in denim jumpsuits that had the bartender wincing at the sight—and she said "That's Fredo, right?"

It was, though in the month since Mabry had seen him, Fredo had

aged a year or more and gained ten pounds, despite the fact that he'd
shorn his head almost to the scalp. Since Mabry was seated at the
only occupied table in the room, he waited for Fredo to make at least
a quick check of the space. Like most good supers Fredo had always
been a curious man and politely suspicious of all his surroundings
(he was not quite Sicilian, though he was from south of Naples, a
bone-poor boy in his mid-thirties maybe who'd immigrated with his
beautiful mother fifteen years ago). He didn't turn and, once his glass
of red wine was poured, he fixed on that as if it would be the central
magnet of the rest of his life.

Mabry said to Malc "I'll go speak to him." But before he stood
he said "Should you come with me? You made this arrangement
after all."

Malc said "Mabry, he's your super, remember?—he doesn't
know me except from that one meeting when Charlotte and I came
down to your party on the Fourth of July. I just ran into him yesterday evening as I was leaving work."

Mabry couldn't recall more than three or four times when Malc
had actually called him by his first name; so he took it as encouragement and went on forward, still feeling as burdened in the few
yards of space as any father approaching a son whom he knew to be
incurably hurt since their last encounter.

It was not the case; and in under ten minutes, Mabry confirmed
what Malcolm had learned—yes his loft was intact but way too
silted up to be a usable residence anytime soon. Nonetheless, Fredo
and his present companions were already hard at work in the building, and its neighborhood, as a clean-up crew. Again too polite to
state the cost, Fredo could only say "You need me to help you
soon, Signor Kincaid?"

Mabry said "Absolutely—and starting tomorrow if possible"
(surely his insurance would pay for the recovery or a hefty share).

He wasn't surprised to learn that three other residents of the
building had got on Fredo's list before him. Still Fredo thought that,

within another two or three days, the street barricades would finally come down; and Mabry could see the place at least. Then he might begin to know if he could stand to live there again, in that much nearness to so much fear, stopped only by death.

By the time he'd said good night to Charlotte and Malcolm, though—near two in the morning, back in his hotel—the city beyond his soundproof walls seemed his only home. If he didn't move back in his loft downtown, he'd sell it and find some less haunted place farther from whatever voices might linger that low on the island. *But still here in town. If I can possibly live alone.*

As the girls were leaving (he thought of them always as *girls*, however hard he tried not to say it), he thanked them for the help and the company; and not thinking hard, he craned to kiss Malc on the crown of her hair before he kissed Charlotte. They each tasted dusty but he didn't tell them so.

Nor did they tell him his own face bore the remains of something very much like ash. Who, though, knew the taste of human ash?

Miles stopped off at the hotel with him; and back in the suite, another drink later, Miles said "Aside from whether or not Mr. Sample left a will, it's fairly clear he left me jobless. Damned nearly broke too, though my tiny savings'll feed me for a week or so longer. So if you're needing a strong back and arms to help you dive into cleaning your loft, I may be your man."

Mabry thought *All right. It's clear he's writing Baxter off; and that triggers another bald truth, this much anyhow.* He said "Miles, so far as my work goes, I can't even think of diving into anything serious— nothing bigger than wiping a swab of solvent across two inches of a painting, and I've got no paintings on hand right now."

Miles said "You look really fit to me for heavier work then. And the guy down at your place can't start for—two weeks, was it? I need a job, as you can see; and I need it now."

Mabry's answer flooded him irresistibly. At first he said a mere "Thank you." But before Miles could race ahead, as he meant to do, Mabry put up a pausing hand. "Look, I think I could need you—or need somebody as strong as you—for a good deal more than you may have in mind."

Tall as he was, wide as his shoulders were, Miles by now was a little drunk. His eyes took awhile to settle on Mabry before he could say "Mind saying what it is?" He was vaguely suspicious of something more personal than he'd ever consider.

And Mabry saw that. He said "Oh *at ease*, pal. I've sometimes thought I'd have been really lucky to have a gay gene or two when ladies got scarce, as they've often done. But no, I'm straighter than any rail and have given *way* more than ample proof of my tendencies to pursue half the women that glance my way. What I mean is, I've almost surely got a genuine problem—multiple sclerosis. I'm seeing my doctor again on Friday morning. If he can confirm it— and it's hard to confirm; he's been testing now for several weeks— I may wind up with the need for steady company, steady strong care."

Miles clapped his hands once softly. "My mother's oldest sister, back home—she's come down with it recently too. No big problems yet, so far as they tell me."

Mabry nodded. "You planning to stay here for good?"

Miles said "In America? That was the main hope, yes sir. And Mr. Sample kept telling me there'd be no trouble about a green card. He knew a hundred immigration lawyers. Or so he claimed, and I never knew him to tell a lie. Not to me anyhow."

Mabry said "Nor to me. Amazing feat for a lawyer as endlessly successful as Baxter."

Miles's face looked slowly offended.

And Mabry hurried to mend the cheap offense. "Forgive me. But you probably know that, in the States anyhow, lawyers are the main profession that's joked about."

If Miles knew it, he didn't say yes. His face stayed solemn, but he leaned well forward. "This *help* you speak of—would it mean staying on here in New York or in North Carolina?"

Suddenly the wave that struck Mabry downtown rose powerfully again—his sense of the numerous dead on all sides, the chance of a desolating future. "It might be both."

Miles said "You understand that I'd need to know before I accepted any kind of offer."

Mabry thought *Whoa. Move carefully now.* He said "You recall I mentioned seeing my doctor on Friday? That's when I'll know if I need real assistance."

Miles got to his feet and asked again for the bathroom's whereabouts (he'd been there earlier).

His absence left Mabry with the panicky urge to phone somebody—just for quick contact with somebody calmer than this young man with his own dilemma—but who at this hour? He'd wake Audrey if he called about his father; and if he called Charlotte, what was there to say?

Before another name occurred to him, Miles was back and seated. "Could I take you to dinner this Friday evening?"

Few men or women as young as Miles invited older souls to dinner in a city this costly, yet it didn't seem wise to refuse him now. *Try a compromise.* "Thanks very much but let's call it a dutch date."

Miles grinned at last. "I'd rather not call it a *date* at all."

At which Mabry sniffed a recurrent problem. "Miles, I meant exactly what I told you. I don't have one scrap of interest in your body, except insofar as you look strong enough to lift me occasionally—if I prove to need lifting."

Miles said "Roger, sir."

"Roger, *Mabry*, please."

Miles agreed.

"And I may not have a job of any sort to offer."

"Roger, Mabry." Miles laughed, then suddenly leapt to his feet, moved right in on Mabry, and hoisted him up as easily as feathers, then tossed him three times very gently.

Mabry wasn't scared. Far from it. He felt a lot safer than he'd felt since leaving Italy; so he almost offered the job, here and now. But before he could speak, Miles set him back easily in his deep armchair and walked to the hall door. "See you Friday at seven—right?"

Mabry said "Right" and felt that it was. But once he'd proceeded through a calm half hour of minor chores and showered off the dust of his home street, climbed into bed, and read till the magazine fell on his face as sleep folded him in, he was chilled again. *I'm almost as young a man as Frances was a woman when she died in an agony I couldn't ease, couldn't even touch. She's anyhow out of it now; but I'm here and—with Tasker's genes—I could last another thirty years, blind and paralyzed and worse than that, if anything's worse. Who would be with me—Charlotte and Malc? Kind as they may be, they're weak-armed women; and whatever monster is burning inside me will strain them way past a normal quota of patience. They're women though and women can bear far more than men, God bless their hearts.*

True or not, he believed himself and was soon unconscious for a dreamless night.

Even as he dialed her number, Mabry wasn't quite sure why he was calling Blair Patrick. They'd spoken fairly often on the phone, but he hadn't seen her in maybe six months. She was one of his oldest New York friends; and as the sadness of last night's trip downtown lingered through the morning (and the prospect of his oncoming visit to the doctor was increasingly fearsome), he found himself hunting her number in his book.

A strange voice answered. "Renaissance Prints. Ms. Patrick's office."

Now she has a secretary at least. But almost before he could ask for Blair, she picked up her phone. He couldn't resist—"Wow, you're moving on up!"

She switched to her school-mistress tone at once. "That's not a secretary. It's Emmeline. You met her last time you were in here. She's just helping me today with a twelve-foot stack of Dürer wood-cuts. How many do you want?"

Mabry said "Put me down for a two-foot stack at least, assuming they're free."

Blair's old giggle flowered. "If they have to be free, I'll bring you twelve inches' worth. Will that be enough?"

"Never enough, darlin' child, but still—I take what I can get. And speaking of which, how about I buy you dinner tonight?"

"*Shit!*" she said. "I'm flying to Cincinnati late today—an ancient gent with, he claims, a houseful of Rembrandt and Franz Hals. And he says he 'just wants to clear the damned walls, at any price, and start over with Dalí.'"

Mabry had silently bridled at her starting with *Shit!* As he told his father, he'd broken more than half the Ten Commandments; but the fact that the younger generation said *shit* as easily as *sherbet* was still a hard fact for his ears. So he started with "Ugh," but then he said "I can get him a zillion fake Dalís by lunchtime."

Blair said "Every schoolchild could. And speaking of lunch, I'm free for *lunch* today."

He walked the few blocks then, a half hour early, to Christie's auction house, wandered through a show of several dozen soon-to-be-knocked-down eighteenth-century paintings from Catholic Peru (each Virgin and saint portrayed with the wholly convincing and magnetic plaintiveness of all the best American colonial art, South or North; didn't it all say *Oh bring me home?*—home of course being Europe).

Then he led Blair back to Torre di Pisa, the good Italian restaurant near the Algonquin. The midday was clear. Mabry had sent his clothes to the hotel's overnight laundry and looked halfway decent anyhow; but Blair looked fine—truly terrific—and the maître d' at the Torre registered the caliber of her power with an eyebrow lift in Mabry's direction.

He'd known her—what?—nearly twenty years, since a friend invited him down to Chapel Hill to demonstrate the mysteries of his craft for a class of art students. Blair was eighteen then, a dazzling girl, from up beyond Asheville; so he knew she was thirty-seven now. He'd behaved himself in Chapel Hill, despite the innocence with which she'd approached him after the master class and asked if he would come to her sorority for supper that night or just a movie with him and her only? That long ago, the gap between them seemed infinite—to Blair anyhow.

But once Mabry had moved to New York, they passed on the street once; and she recognized him—"You're Mr. Kincaid?" She was working way downtown, at a trashy gallery; and a fling ensued that broke both their hearts. Mabry honestly believed it had hurt him worse—the morning they woke in his loft and she said "Oh friend, I'm the wrong human being for you. I'm even the wrong human being for *me*. If we know what's likely to be good for us, we better jump out of bed right this instant, take separate showers, and forget we ever touched each other below the neck." Both of them had laughed; but at the moment, he hadn't asked what was wrong with her or him; and the years had passed so fast he'd never had the inclination to ask.

But they'd never lost touch, not quite, though sometimes the better part of a year might pass before one or the other would call for consoling company and mostly find it available. Mainly, they met to discuss Mabry's availability for a given piece of conservation that a purchaser might need on a picture. The restoration of damaged paper was one of his specialties, and Blair encountered reams of torn or discolored old paper. Occasionally, they'd drink enough wine; and then one or the other might venture on a confidence.

Recently, with Mabry involved in Frances's last illness and compelled to an unnatural degree of virtue, the secrets came mostly from

Blair. Lovely and smart as she was, with the passing of years, she was developing a genius for falling in love with awful heels. At first, her mistakes were largely comic; and both she and Mabry could manage to laugh as he offered suggestions for the best escape routes. But lately she'd begun to offer, without quite knowing it, a discomforting mirror of his own early caddishness. And even now, no more than eight days after the local calamity, as soon as she'd got her glass of Chianti, she launched—unbidden—into a detailed account of the latest adventure in self-abasement with a man fully nine years younger than herself and (according to the photo she produced from her wallet) no feast for the eyes, despite her assertion that their sex was phenomenal, aided as it was by his years of study in Tantric yoga which made him available for all-night sessions of mind-boggling gratification.

Today, when Mabry had heard much more than he enjoyed about Tonto's ongoing wonders (and *Tonto* was the Tantrist's actual nickname), he drained his own wine, set the glass down hard to change the subject, and said "Where were you when the buildings fell?" She lived in Chelsea.

The suddenness plainly shocked her; and prone as she was to sudden tears, her eyes nearly brimmed. She touched them with a napkin, then nodded deeply as though confirming Mabry's suggestion that she might have been present in the city on the bleak day itself. When she could answer, she said "I'm hoping we can talk about that."

Mabry said "Then what? God knows every other soul alive on Earth is babbling on about nothing else lately."

His meanness riled her slightly, enough to help her recall her age. She was very nearly as grown, and as sane, as this old friend. She said "Should we stay on?"

Laconic as she was, he understood she wasn't proposing to leave the restaurant. "I was going to ask you nearly the same thing."

"Is it home?" Blair said. "Is this big mixture of human beings *home* for either one of us?"

Mabry said "As recently as yesterday evening, downtown on Rector Street, I began to wonder."

"You got down there? How? Lord, I thought it was closed to all but the president."

"Charlotte managed it—Charlotte and her cowboy partner."

Blair actually touched him, the back of his hand. With her strong forefinger she all but drilled right through to his palm. "Cow*girl*, OK? But thank every star you've got that your blood daughter has found somebody as strong and kind as Malc."

He'd almost forgot Blair knew them. "You're damned right. In that one way, I'm a lucky man."

She finished her wine, refused his offer of a second glass, and said "What else is wrong?"

Before he'd left town for Europe, Mabry phoned and gave her a light account of his visits to various doctors—the baffling weirdness in his eyes and hands. He'd forgot, though, how he'd underplayed the possible badness of what might be wrong, other than just middle age and his own stark fears.

But by then their food had come. Both were having slightly different versions of shrimp and pasta; and for five minutes onward they managed to submerge in their plates with smiles of pleasure and occasional chatter about the very New Yorkish fact that, in an authentic-tasting Italian restaurant, most of the staff were plainly Mayan. On all sides now there were profiles as reliably aquiline as anything hacked into any pyramid in Yucatán—and as silent as they accomplished their duties. These genes had once been the kings and slaves who'd subjected each other to tortures as exotic as pulling string loaded with sharp-edged beads back and forth through holes in their lips and tongues, and Blair expounded on the details with the smiling over-elaboration to which most art experts were prone.

Beneath Blair's lightness and Mabry's, though, he felt himself pulled back strongly to the days when he'd been in intimate touch with all of Blair, all he could reach with two hands and ten fingers.

Yet some perverse flash made him feel the need to turn the moment against itself before he could dive headlong into teenage-lover foolishness. He couldn't remember precisely how much he'd really told her about his neuro mysteries, how scary they'd been and still were. And had Charlotte told her more while he was in Europe? He resisted the further urge to touch her, and he said "You know about my latest middle-aged fright?"

"I doubt I do," she said. "Which one?"

Mabry knew he'd asked for at least that degree of dismissiveness but it stung anyhow. So he made it hard. "The heavy chance I may have M.S. and will soon be leaning on my few real friends."

Blair completed an unusually long stint of chewing and swallowing, as solemn as if it were some professional test. Finally her face acknowledged his gravity. "*Friends* you've got. Who on Earth has got more?"

Mabry laughed. "I lie awake, trying to count. But *friends* are one thing, good *wives* are another."

She widened her eyes at his certainty. "Nothing to give you at this point but *Amen.*"

Far more than he'd expected, that angered him. He laid his napkin beside his plate and actually stood. No words came to him, but Blair's face quickly reddened.

The waiter approached them and waited in silence.

After what felt like numerous decades, Mabry sat back down. Then he said "I know you're Blair Patrick. No other expectations. *Continue,* as they say in Radiation, *to breathe freely now.*"

Blair pushed her own plate back the small half-inch that would indicate *finished,* but the waiter was gone again.

So Mabry said "Coffee, espresso, ice cream? They have ice cream almost as good as that place on Piazza Navona." He'd suddenly remembered the time Blair approached him and Frances in Rome, her junior college year, a whole year after he'd met her in Chapel Hill. All three had ordered hazelnut ice cream and sat outside in the chill March light till Frances shivered hard. Blair said "You're freezing!" and they went separate ways. Anybody you'd ever met up with in Rome had a special slot in your memory surely.

Mabry called the waiter, ordered their ice cream and coffee, then offered Blair a thoroughly genuine smile but no apology and no further medical information. "Here's a serious question, darling." He went on to give her a stripped-down story of the painting he'd fetched from Paris for Baxter. He ended with the fact that Baxter was very likely dead and that so far no will had been discovered, though surely a lawyer of his distinction would have filed a will somewhere. He thought that Blair would turn to some angle of that problem first.

But no, she said "Did you say Philip *Adger*?"

Mabry said "From Charleston. A friend of mine in North Carolina says she's kin to the South Carolina Adgers."

Blair fell on the news like a buoy in a storm. "That makes two of us. I've even been down there, to Adger's wharf where they made their millions—none of which percolated north to me."

"Nor to poor Adger apparently. For whatever reasons, he seems to have spent his whole life in France, ending up with a small hotel in Paris and a monster of a daughter-in-law who tried to cheat my client out of five hundred dollars."

"Did he finally get a bargain?"

Here and now, as with Gwyn and Marcus and his friend at the North Carolina museum, he pulled well back. But he wanted to know this much at least. "Suppose young Philip's boyish picture— a long dark building which may be the actual château in Auvers— lies on top of a Van Gogh oil sketch, at least a few quick strokes in Van Gogh's hand?"

At once Blair suspected the degree of cover-up. "You can tell me, Mabry. I've kept a great many secrets for you, recall. You know what's under young Philip's stumbling, right?"

Again he smiled. "I know what's under an ancient liner that lies around the whole framed picture—tree branches, I think, and a cloud or two."

"And clearly by Vincent?"

"Somebody a whole lot surer-handed than your young cousin."

Blair said "Exciting" and plainly meant it. Then she faced him, dead-on, and batted her amazing lashes fiercely (they were longer than the costliest camel's-hair brushes). "But of course you haven't *dreamed* of getting it X-rayed?"

Mabry batted his own in return a few seconds. Then with both hands in the air, he moved to damp her down. "The nearest X-ray machine to my father's is in a hospital packed with unwed mothers and people with blood pressure twice yours or mine from lifelong diets of pure salt pork" (he wouldn't mention his trip to Raleigh and the State Museum). "So no, it's never yet undergone any form of testing beyond my own eyes. And now, as I told you, my client Baxter is almost surely dead; and he seems to have died without a known relative. As I said, if he left a will, nobody's yet found it; so your cousin Philip's picture may well be an orphan. But the picture itself is still in my possession, in my father's house to be exact; and the last thing I need is an item in the *Post—Wonder Picture Discovered in Paris Cellar!*"

Blair said "Understood. Absolutely" and zipped her lips shut as the ice cream arrived.

When they'd both had spoonsful, Mabry finally said "Let's say—and honest to God, I don't know—let's say there's a fairly elaborate Van Gogh oil sketch lurking on the canvas. Properly cleaned, how much might it bring?"

Blair said "You know that's not my field, but you and I both read the daily art news. Wouldn't you say, oh, several hundred thousand?"

"Or with this provenance, the story of a young American boy who was with Van Gogh on the evening when Vincent stepped back of the building your cousin was painting and shot himself? Maybe you and I could do the research."

Blair was calmer now than Mabry. "If the story truly proves to be right, and if your client died with no known kin or anything resembling a legal will, maybe close to a million. But Lord help whoever gets involved. You can well imagine that a big auction house deals daily with exactly such problems—a valuable object and a complicated will, or none at all. If your client left a genuine orphan; and it's now in your hands with no known heir, you could be a zillionaire. Or you could be embroiled in a packet of nightmares for the rest of your life—almost surely would."

"A nightmare poised on a night-mare's nest," Mabry said. His dessert was gone that fast, and he'd already drunk his whole first espresso and signaled to the evident heir of a Mayan king for another.

When he'd walked her all the way back to Christie's door, they stood in a patch of light as pure as any in Iceland; and Blair thanked him for lunch in terms that would have served had he treated her to a coronation in a whole other country—no worries, no reminder of their city's ruin, no imminent choices of home or safety. When Mabry agreed that he'd phone on Friday once he'd seen his doctor, she apologized for her rudeness at lunch and said "You know how much your friendship means to me. You know I'd do anything on Earth. Just say the word."

So he said "Two words then—*eternal service.*"

She didn't understand him.

"Your presence beside me—whatever, whenever I'll need you. Nothing less." Even he wasn't sure of his meaning—his full request, if it was a request.

Blair tried to smile and failed, then pointed behind her at the whole Christie's building. "But you also know I've got this job. I'm not a rich woman."

"Exactly. Precisely. All friendships fail at that very point. And I'll wind up—where your parents likely will—in a nursing home, spoon-fed by strangers who wish I'd just die and free them up for a night at the movies or an unbroken snooze if nothing more." Then he could laugh, to free her so far as freedom was likely now that he'd fully explained himself.

Back at the hotel in midafternoon, Mabry sat at his narrow desk to list the chores that needed prompt attention. Since a return to his loft was days or weeks away, shouldn't he think of finding a temporary apartment or a less expensive hotel at least? He needed to see someone at his bank and, for now, move Frances's great largess to some destination that was both safer and more productive than the money-market savings account where it presently rested. He needed to phone down to Wells and speak with Audrey and Tasker. And — God! — he needed a small easy job to occupy him now, something to head off a crash into major blues or worse. How had he let Blair escape after lunch without asking her for something simple he could do with few tools? Or maybe he should phone some museum friend and scare up a similar uncomplicated errand.

When he'd noted down that many headings, he listened as a major fact dawned in his skull. *You'll do damned little till Dr. Brewer has lowered whatever booms he's got, if he's got a real boom yet.* And you won't see him for two more days. So there in the midst of Dorothy Parker's meager leavings, he let himself measure his own meager present.

It was Wednesday afternoon. Since coming to town, he'd seen his apparently likable daughter, her increasingly likable and admirable partner, Baxter Sample's baffled Australian butler (who might yet prove a sturdy rescue), the promising but burdened Italian super at his inundated home, and a helpless former girlfriend. None of them had phoned today. No one from North Carolina had phoned. The world was proceeding on its terrified or indifferent way, or so the television assured him. Yet barring Miles Watson, none of his friends or family seemed so much as mildly unnerved; and plainly no one needed him. No one on Earth.

He'd got to the age of fifty-three; he couldn't think he was truly a monster of self-entrapment or ingratitude. Yet here he sat, entirely alone, in the dark green walls of a famous hotel with nothing to do and no one to help. *Boo hoo. You could phone down to Malcolm, this minute, and offer to join her in her practical work—giving crushed human beings small bits of their dead. Or surely there's some other useful task you could volunteer to shoulder for a few days. No, you're paralyzed in your own tricky skin till Friday afternoon. Then you may just have the medical equivalent of a sizable rock set down at your feet to focus on, maybe something that real to circle around for the rest of your life.*

An hour later he'd walked a peaceful twenty-six blocks north to his favorite small clutch of paintings in the world, the Frick Museum. He hadn't called to see if it might have closed since the trouble, and yes it was open—no soldiers on duty and no unusual body search when he bought his ticket. As ever, on the walk he'd decided which picture he'd really try to *see*. Today it was the Rembrandt self-portrait in the long West Gallery; and it too was there, he could suddenly see at a glance through the door—unaltered, unspoiled, and golden as ever beneath its numerous layers of varnish that begged to be stripped off and no doubt should be if only the world possessed a conservator who'd know which layer was darkening varnish and which might just be an actual glaze of color laid on by Rembrandt's supremely knowing hand.

As he went toward the Rembrandt, Mabry paused in the prior room by two of his other favorites—the wide Bellini of St. Francis calmly receiving the ghastly stigmata from a vision in the sky and the Holbein portrait of steely Sir Thomas More, still in possession of the head he'd soon lose to Henry VIII. Each was a picture Mabry would have surrendered all his worldly possessions to own for thirty days. *Think of them hung either side of your bed.* Then he was ready to see the Rembrandt, a picture that was hard to see in any visit, hanging as it did in a room that likewise held one of the largest of all Vermeers and the now-disputed *Polish Rider*, which was either one of the grandest of Rembrandts or an utterly inexplicable event managed by yet another painter who'd never produced a surviving picture that could lay a finger on the glorious *Rider* (lately a small Dutch committee had assigned it to a modestly talented Rembrandt pupil named Willem Drost).

But today the huge nearby self-portrait—painted, Mabry knew, when Rembrandt was one year younger than he—came suddenly at him like a wide and tall heat-seeking weapon, with his own particular temperature precisely gauged as its present target. Then it passed on through him, from head to foot, and left its meaning, a thoroughly common message but remade now with the force of the painter's power of hand and his straight delivery of three plain truths made oracular today by inimitable genius—*You're no more lonely than any man or woman. Women's lives are tragic because they can seldom succeed in ceasing to love their children. Men's are lonely because they seldom truly love.*

Each of the three parts seemed dead true, true enough today to steer him straight back downtown past Tiffany and Cartier and the trashy dealers in pornographic Japanese ivories, that were often quite funny and could be bargained for, to his wide rented bed and deep on into the rest he awarded himself at sunset.

He'd only meant to sleep half an hour, then take himself to dinner at the Jewel of India, just up the block. The thought of their first-rate keema mattar with garlic nan and mango chutney had mingled with his memories of Rembrandt as his mind drifted out into dreamless sleep. But when he woke, the room was pitch dark; and he found himself in the midst of one more frightening failure to know where his body lay. In which direction was the door to the living room; where was the john and where were his own stinging hands and feet?

He thought he could move them. It even felt as if he was furiously waving his hands in the air near his face. He brought both hot palms down and aimed at masking both his eyes, but the dark was so thick he couldn't confirm he'd done what he meant to. So he lay still, hoping some slot of light would slice its way toward him or some surrounding nimbus from the street outside would gradually glow. In four minutes maybe a reddish flashing showed to his left. That might be the window wall. He swung what seemed to be his legs toward that red shine. His bare feet seemed to find a floor.

He seemed to stand and walk toward what had once been the john door. When his left hand reached out and fumbled beside him, he found a light switch; and yes, it was the bathroom. In pure gratitude he sat down on the commode, just to pee; and by the time he'd finished, he was so aware of thanks for the simple skills he'd called on in the past five minutes that he came near to tears. The only sign of a physical failure was the dryness of his eyes. They refused to weep.

Long showers had seldom been possible for Mabry, but this one lasted twenty minutes; and when it was done, for the first time he recalled in all his travels, he put on the terry-cloth robe that the hotel offered in his bedroom closet. Then—still in unbroken peace—he sat on the living-room sofa, faced the blank TV, and waited for the drink and the room-service supper he'd ordered. After an immensely long ten minutes, the phone rang for the first time in two days. An instinct told him that room service had discouraging news—they lacked the makings of something he'd ordered (he'd ordered a lot).

But room service mostly announced himself as *Chuck*. This was a woman. "Mr. Mabry Kincaid?"

"Speaking," he said.

"Just a moment, sir. I'll get your party." She sounded close by, no more than a few yards down the hall. Then there was the loud sound of a phone being dropped and a distant man's voice saying "*Christ Jesus.* See, I told you." It sounded like no one Mabry knew. Then a long wait. Then "Mabry?"—a woman.

"—Kincaid," he said again.

"It's Audrey Thornton, Mabry."

"Where the hell are you, Audrey?" *Watch your language now. She's almost a priest herself.*

"It's not Hell exactly. It *is* a hospital, though, in Roanoke Rapids."

Her house was in that eastern direction from his father's. "You been in an accident?"

"No, Mabry, but Father Kincaid has."

"Oh Lord, another fall?"

"A fall came first but—"

So Mabry filled her pause. "Are you in his room?" He thought she might be hiding some hard truth from him.

"No, I'm out in the hall at the nurses' desk, using Marc's cell phone. He forgot and left it with me last night. Small blessings abound—"

Mabry broke in. "Then start at the beginning please and tell me the story."

Audrey waited another few seconds before she chose to honor his request. "He either had a stroke and then fell down, or he fell and then had a stroke on the floor."

Mabry realized slowly that she hadn't yet said the word *alive* or *dead.* He also felt that he shouldn't say them, not to Audrey at the moment. So he said "Can he speak?"

"You want to speak to him?" Audrey had plainly reached the point where she wanted to end her role on the phone.

Mabry said "I didn't mean that. No, I'm wondering how you think he is."

"His whole left side is paralyzed at present. He's pressed my hand with his right hand though. I think he tried to say my name, but after a while he could say *Marcus* clearly." Her voice had stayed firm; she was not breaking up.

"When did it happen?"

"Five-fourteen, today. I looked at my watch when I heard him fall."

"Who took you to the hospital?"

"The regular men, paramedics from Sherwin, nice young fellows."

"Is his doctor nearby you?"

Audrey said "No, he's not in sight."

"Then tell me please everything else you know." She was proving less resourceful than Mabry would have guessed.

Audrey took a slow breath. "It's serious business, I know that much. I've told you about his left side and his speech. I truly don't think he's in real pain. He doesn't seem distressed at all. He's even smiled a time or two—I *think* it's a smile."

Mabry needed to say *Do you think he's dying?* But he couldn't make himself, for whoever's sake. He thought of his own appointment on Friday—that could surely wait. He said what he dreaded. "Has he asked for me?"

Audrey waited to think. "No, not yet."

"But you can't imagine him ever improving, not this far along?"

Audrey said "I'm trying not to think that."

Mabry said "Then you'll understand that there's nobody left but me to think it." When she didn't reply in five seconds, he said "I'll be there then. Can you or Marcus be with him till I come?"

"I'm signed on, yes."

"Is Marcus with you now?"

"He will be any time."

Mabry looked to his own watch—7:20 p.m. "Audrey, tell my father I'll be there just as soon as I can. I'll start calling airlines the minute we hang up. I may not make it before tomorrow morning. Give me a number where you are, and I'll let you know."

She read out the number. Then she said "Maybe you don't have to come now. He's in good hands."

"I don't doubt that, not at all; but Audrey, Tasker Kincaid is my only father." It was no attempt to trump her authority, only the truth and a truth he hoped his father might care to hear.

A half hour later Mabry had a reservation that would get him into Raleigh-Durham at noon tomorrow. Then just as he picked up the phone to call Audrey, his own mind crashed. *I can't fly down there alone this time. Maybe Audrey can count on me, but I sure-God can't count on myself.* He dialed Baxter's number and Miles answered promptly. It took no more than a hundred words between them for Mabry to realize Miles was politely bailing out of any thought of signing on for duty with a man who might be gravely ill, even for two or three days farther south. When he tried one further word of persuasion, Miles finally said "As you'll understand, sir, I need to be here if Mr. Sample rings this bell."

Increasingly impossible as that ring was, Mabry understood; and he sat through as much of his supper as he could manage to eat, trying to think of any escort—even a doorman or bellman from downstairs (Charlotte couldn't handle a physical crisis if one should descend; and though Malcolm could, he wouldn't ask for her this soon in their acquaintance, not unless everyone else should fail him). Marcus dawned on him next. Hadn't Marcus said he'd never been to New York? In any case, Marc was clearly the right man, if Audrey could spare him for the time it would take to fly up here, then fly back with Mabry and drive him on to Tasker's bedside or wherever Tasker would be by then.

FIVE

9 . 20 . 01
9 . 22 . 01

It worked. Mabry met Marcus at security in LaGuardia, pre-cisely on time. The passengers around them were much like any day's airport crowd, a little more nervous-eyed maybe than usual but surely not bizarre; and after a very smooth flight to Raleigh-Durham, they'd driven on the final two hours and were outside Tasker's door by midafternoon—Roanoke Rapids, North Carolina, a textile-mill town on the cruel Roanoke, a river that had flooded farmlands and houses for more than three centuries till a dam was built in the 1950s. Mabry set his one bag down by the shut door and asked Mar-cus to step in and bring Audrey out, if she was there.

She was but, when she came out to meet him, her whole body was dead-beat tired; and she said "Thank God" as her right hand came out and pressed Mabry's chest—the first time, surely, she'd ever touched him purposely.

Marcus walked past her on into the room.

But Mabry waited outside with Audrey, thinking she might have some news for him or at least a signal to follow her in.

She stood on, dazed, apparently waiting for the same thing from him.

So he said "Is it all right to go in now?"

She seemed to think it through. "I believe he already knows you're out here."

"You told him I was coming?"

Audrey said "I tried to. I haven't been sure he's understood a word I've said since he fell down yesterday."

"Has he said anything else, last night or today?"

"I don't think he's tried, no. Not while I was with him, and I've hardly left the room. But as I told you, he's been mainly calm."

Mabry said "Then I'll go in." When Audrey didn't move, he picked up his bag and gently moved past her.

The blinds were closed against the strong sunlight, but a single lamp shone over the bed; and Tasker was laid out straight as any parade-ground soldier with only the cover folded back above his bad ankle.

A sort of invisible clean glass wall stopped Mabry halfway toward the bed, and while he stood there silently—with Marcus smiling on the far side of his father—Tasker turned to face him. Mabry even took a single step forward, but again he was stopped. *What's stalling me here?* Then it came to him, something that seemed too absurd to be the answer. *He'll prove he can speak by calling me Gabe.* So still in place, five yards from his father, Mabry said "I'd have picked a cheaper place for a rest." When Tasker blinked hard, Mabry said "It's Mabry, Pa. Your main bad penny has turned up one more time."

Tasker blinked again, glanced backward to Marcus—Marcus tapped him on the hip—then set his still powerful eyes on Mabry. The eyes were half wild, but his voice was normal—"Alec, Alec." Then he freed his right hand and arm from the cover and beckoned slightly toward him. *Alec* was Tasker's awful father's name, from *Alexander.* Tasker had wanted to name Mabry that, but his wife had prevailed (Mabry was her own father's name).

Well, hell, it beats any other name but mine. The intervening wall dissolved, and Mabry answered his father's invitation inward. Only

when he got there and took Tasker's hand—it was warm as ever—
could he say "Mabry, sir. Anything on Earth you need from Mabry?"

The eyes had lost not one amp of power, but they filled with
tears.

Mabry slowly leaned and pressed his forehead against his father's
hand.

By then Marcus had brought a chair which Mabry could sit in
beside the bed.

It was no surprise that the doctor proved to be a *dot* Indian (as
opposed to *feather* Indian, a Native American). They were mostly
found in small hospitals now but were likewise frequent in towns and
cities—thirty years ago, Southern towns this size often had no doctors or only a single aging and impossibly burdened Anglo. Mabry
had asked for him at the nurses' station shortly after he arrived.

It was nearly sunset, however, before the young doctor entered
Tasker's room—white-coated, grave, darker-skinned than Audrey or
Marcus or more than half the Afro-Americans in the hospital and
almost alarmingly young in the face. Audrey and Marcus had gone
back to Wells to check on the house and collect a few things; and
Mabry was still seated close to his father, though Tasker seemed to
have drifted off. Every few minutes his eyes would open and search
round for Mabry; but since he'd said *Alec*, he'd tried nothing else.

Dr. Sharma, by his name tag, apparently didn't see Mabry's offer
of a handshake. Instead he made his own offer, a narrow smile so
quick it seemed to have flown in and out on hummingbird wings.
Then he raised his naturally soft voice and spoke to Tasker. "Reverend Kincaid, how is your day progressing, sir?"

Tasker's eyes were open and they found the doctor's face, but he
gave no sign, and he said no words.

Dr. Sharma said "We can be pleased that your son is here, can't
we?"

Before the doctor had even reached the end of his question,

Mabry could hear the note of exhaustion. This man was needing to get home for dinner, if he had a home; or was he an unwed medical resident who was working the usual forty-hour shift? So Mabry stood and nearly whispered "May we step outside?"

In the hall Dr. Sharma seemed even more drained. At best, he was half a head shorter than Mabry; but now he spoke first. "You know that your father has suffered a stroke?"

"I understand that, yes. His assistant, Ms. Thornton, phoned me in New York last night and told me. I got down as fast as I possibly could."

Dr. Sharma tried to look pleased at the news but offered nothing more.

Mabry said "How bad is the damage? What can we hope for?"

Before he replied, Dr. Sharma seemed to summon a powerful memory. *I'm the physician here. Stand fully upright and summon all your powers.* Then he said "Mr. Kincaid, I cannot answer that. Please remind me, how old is our father?"

"He's eighty-three." *I'll ignore the* our.

Dr. Sharma said, with the certainty of any Brahmin priest, "He could live another twenty years and move about slightly, if you have such genes in the family line. He could have another stroke in the next five minutes and die before morning or here and now. But so could I, Mr. Kincaid. So could you." At last he smiled fully—authority asserted.

Mabry wanted to slug the little man or, at the very least, welcome him to small-town North Carolina with a bouquet of the local racist epithets. All he said was "Is my father likely to sit up again? Will he speak freely?"

"Ah Mr. Kincaid, who am I to know? If you asked me to guess, I should say 'Not likely' to either question. But if you'd like me to hope that he will, then I'll hope for him—and your family—strongly."

Mabry had encountered more than several doctors in recent

months, all Anglo or Jewish. However smug Dr. Sharma's delivery,
though, his last few sentences were far more humane than any
other recent medical sentiment Mabry had met with. He'd offered
a half-amusing mix of Western hyper-certainty and Eastern fatalism.
So Mabry grinned. "How much longer can you help him here?"

Dr. Sharma didn't understand.

Mabry said "I'm asking, when should we take him home?"

"Ah." The doctor looked down at his hands, his almost tiny fingers,
beautiful nails surely armed with skill. Then he faced Mabry squarely
for the first time yet. "Please leave him with me another day or two.
Let him rest here with these very kind nurses. Then I will try to tell
you, very truly, where his best chances are."

In a mere three sentences, Sharma had further unveiled a human
heart. So Mabry came very close now to asking for this young doctor's attention to his own hard and pressing concerns.

That evening, which was September 20th—tired as Mabry was
from the sleepless prior night in New York—he wouldn't hear,
from Audrey or Marcus, of returning to Wells for a solid rest in his
old bed there. He sat in the dark of Tasker's room, in a crazily awkward reclining chair, and stole snatches of rest between the clatter-
ing entries of nurses and orderlies in search of necessary temperature
readings, blood-pressure levels, and taps on the intravenous bag that
was channeling some unlabeled liquid into Tasker's arm.

After each such maddening visit—Mabry had to assume Tasker
thought they were nothing but willful blunders—he'd go to his
father's side and speak to him quietly, explaining what had only just
happened and offering him a minute or so of calming talk. He
gave him carefully edited scraps of a cheerful account of his days in
New York—of his good time with Charlotte (omitting any mention
of Malcolm), his lunch with a woman as attractive as Blair, and the
fact that he'd found his loft in uninhabitable state (for reasons even

Mabry didn't search, he omitted the plan to have the super clean up his space).

He even offered Tasker stretches of verse that he knew his father was bound to welcome—odes by Keats, Shakespeare sonnets, poems of Tennyson with heavy stress on death and immortality: all of which Mabry had learned as a lucky veteran of the last generation of American schoolboys who'd had long hours of memorized verse drilled into their skulls. Whether his offerings reached deep enough into his father's brain to work even brief consolation, he'd never know. What seemed clear was that once he'd whispered his way through two or three sane minutes, Tasker's eyes would close and his breathing would slow to almost nothing.

The following day was hardly different—Tasker offered no other word to add to yesterday's *Alec*—so when Audrey and Marcus arrived in early afternoon, Mabry let them persuade him to drive to Wells and rest himself. He went to Tasker and asked for permission (Tasker gave no sign of refusal at least). He gave the nurses his best phone numbers and asked that Dr. Sharma be told how ready he'd be for news of any downslide in his father's condition. Finally he asked that Audrey and Marcus give him a minute alone with his father. They calmly agreed and again he went to his father's right side, the side that still worked.

Tasker's eyes were on him like searching black lasers; and his lips seemed, for more than a minute, on the verge of speech. But no words came, no sound at all.

So Mabry told his father where he'd be for the next few hours—either at the house in Wells or in Sherwin with Gwyneth Williams. And he said "Is there anything at all you want me to know or do? Just say the word, Pa; and I'll do my damnedest."

Next came a long preparation for speech; and this time actual words came clearly. "Good night, officer."

Pure late-summer sunlight was pouring through the window beyond the bed—it was just past one in the afternoon—and Mabry was wearing no sign of any officer's uniform, but he quickly decided not to alter his father's sense of time or his hope of identifying live faces. He couldn't conceal, though, his pleasure to hear that primeval voice—a father's, a priest's, the voice he'd hope to hear at the portals of any afterlife that might lurk. So he said "Pa, I plan to sleep till next dawn. But you get Audrey to call the house any instant you want me." He heard how much of the bitterness he'd carried north to New York had stayed up there. Well, he had no plans to flag it southward. He laid his hand beneath Tasker's hand, spread broad on the sheet. And Mabry would have sworn in a court of law that Tasker Kincaid tapped the back of his palm, very strongly, with one or two fingers but no more words.

Mabry found Audrey and Marcus in the little waiting room near his father's door. He told them he'd go straight to Tasker's house and try to rest there; they should phone him if there were any changes whatsoever in his father's condition. He could see, from the set of Audrey's face, that she felt two ways—a little offended that he took such a dug-in air of command but also mildly amused that such a prodigal son had returned so boldly.

Marcus himself was likewise amused, and he showed it more plainly. He even said "Since you're trusting my mom pretty fully, maybe I can get on back to Sherwin and do a little *lucrative* work of my own. I got my cell phone."

Mabry told them both he'd try to be back by midnight at least. Could one of them manage to be here till then?

Audrey said "I can be here till Hell freezes over. Father Kincaid's been too good to me to fail on him now."

So Mabry told them what he hadn't planned to tell—that his father had spoken one more time. He quoted the two first words— *Good night*—but for whatever reason he kept the third word *officer* to himself. And he asked Audrey please to write down anything else his father might say.

Audrey patted her big shoulder bag. "I've got pen and paper enough to write down the entire Bible if necessary."

There was a genuine pause in the room—was her voice truly angry?—but then all three of them broke out laughing.

An ancient woman, white and wearing a faded wash dress, had entered and was sitting in the far corner chair. At the laughter she dropped her magazine to the floor beside her and said "Oh please help an old country woman join your fun." Her eyes were as dark and bottomless as if she'd borne every human pain of the past thousand years.

Audrey and Marcus silently deferred the reply to Mabry. *Let the white man answer.*

Mabry was stumped, though. He stayed in place and tried to look away.

So at last Marcus felt someone had to speak. "Ma'm, we're just fools—so tired we're fools." He stepped on toward her and bent to retrieve her magazine.

She reached out, took his wrist, and found his face. Then she finally said, in a voice that might have come from any tobacco field in the eighteenth century, before the Revolution, "Son, I've met a fool or two down the years. You're way too smart, in the face and ears, to claim that title." Then she offered a curious laugh of her own, more nearly a strangling.

Marcus leaned and kissed the absolute center of her small head, right on the ruled-straight part in her hair.

She craned back and, once more, turned her bruised eyes on him. Then she said "I can thank you." But as Marcus turned toward his own mother, the woman said to the three people standing before her, "Do yall understand that my own daddy would have killed this boy for less than that?" When all three agreed, she said "Thank Jesus my dad's been dead and cold for eighty years, though he still gets to me some full-moon nights." And again she gave her terrible laugh.

Since Mabry was leaving, he thought he'd include the old woman in his parting. "Ma'm, is some member of your family a patient here?"

She nodded. "My son. Last drop of living blood I've got on the Earth."

Mabry said "Is he doing any better?"

"They won't tell you, will they? I been begging to know for four days now. They won't barely give me air to breathe, much less the truth. They think I'm just some rickety hick from back in the corn rows."

Mabry said "We can certainly see you're not."

She thanked him for that. "You reckon you could help that little Indian fellow give me the time of day? For a start, you could tell him my boy is the only thing I've got left aboveground today. Even that cold bitch wife of his is gone, took every cent of his money and ran— didn't leave us even a single food coupon. Not a single grandchild."

Audrey said "Then you live alone?"

"*Alone?* Christ Jesus," she said, "I'm so alone I can still hear termites clipping their toenails deep in the floorboards, not another sound anywhere *near* me and I like noise." But again she laughed.

So Mabry said "I'm going downstairs to the cafeteria right now, ma'm, to get me a bite. If I see Dr. Sharma, I'll mention we talked and that you need attention."

Again she thanked him but before he reached the door, she called again "Mister." When Mabry took a step back toward her, she lowered her voice. "We're talking about the same fellow, aren't we?—that gentleman with all the eye makeup on, that knows more about everything I can mention than I've ever known about anything, even having babies; and I've had four, three of them I buried: flu and whooping cough."

Mabry smiled. "I doubt it's eye makeup, just his natural shadows;

but yes he does seem highly informed. Named Dr. Sharma, a fine name where he comes from in India. To me he mainly seems homesick; but I'll make an extra effort to find him, next thing I do, and I'll mention you're feeling alone yourself."

"*Alone*, son! I feel like the last soul breathing, except for you and these friends of yours here."

Audrey and Marcus were still in the room. They made sympathetic sounds.

Mabry gave them all a small wave.

And he did have a chance to find the doctor — seated downstairs in the farthest corner of the dim cafeteria, alone with no more than a veggie burger. Quickly, he tried to explain the old woman's genuine woe.

Then Dr. Sharma's face begged him to sit, a sudden revelation of some immense solitude. "Yes, Mr. Kincaid, I know of those matters and am moving every mountain I can for her; but I'm gravely afraid I'll leave her alone — here on Earth, tonight if not sooner — with her son's dreadful wife." At the shocking word *dreadful*, Sharma blushed deeply. And at last he actually touched Mabry's hand. "You will not say a single word of this to anyone please." He pointed above him.

When Mabry stood he could only thank the young man, another lost creature.

Back in his father's house, Mabry made a pot of coffee, then realized coffee was his last present need. Every cell craved sleep. But some no doubt Scottish gene floating in him demanded he drink at least one hot cup of the coal-black brew. He sat at the kitchen table and let that fine drink take him. A few yards behind him, he could see that his father's room was still disheveled from the quick departure two days ago. Why hadn't Audrey straightened it up when she and Marcus were here yesterday? *Is she silently thinking he'll never get back? Maybe she's right and Lord help us if she's not.* Still the disorder bothered him. He walked in, neatened the white bedspread, and picked up his father's black-leather New Testament, "With the Words of Our Lord in Red Ink"—it lay on the floor beyond his wheelchair near the whiskey bottles.

Then the telephone rang. *Oh Christ.* Mabry couldn't think what to pray for, if he'd prayed for anything at all—a better few months or years of life for Tasker or an easy death. He trotted to the hall.

Right off, the voice was clearly Gwyn Williams's. "Mabry, sweetheart, you're here. I've been frantic to find you."

"I just this minute walked in from Roanoke Rapids. I got there yesterday afternoon."

Gwyn said "I'd have called a lot sooner, but I just heard half an hour ago. Tommy Waller at the drugstore said Marcus Thornton had told him several days ago."

"It was Wednesday afternoon. I flew down from New York yesterday morning and spent last night in the room with Tasker."

"And it was a stroke?"

Mabry said "A fairly light one apparently. I shared a cafeteria lunch in the hospital just now with his Indian doctor. Pa's paralyzed down his whole left side, but his right arm and hand still work occasionally."

Gwyn said "But can he speak?" From her tone, the importance of that was plain.

"He's said some three or four words to me. He's clear enough but it's obviously a struggle."

"He's bearing up, though?"

Jesus, Gwyn, bearing up *is not quite the phrase.* But he said "He seems sufficiently patient anyhow."

"So what's the outlook?"

Again, something in Gwyn's voice rubbed him wrong. Was it merely her lifelong officious air? *I own all the facts; I can solve this problem in under two seconds.* Mabry said "I doubt he'll be pouring you communion very soon."

Gwyn kept her silence for a full four seconds—she counted the time. Then gently she hung the receiver up.

Mabry knew he'd badly offended her and cheated on his father's confidence. *I'll call her back in another few minutes. Just give me some air.* The stale air in the shut-up house seemed a powdered dry poison, and he moved toward the front porch. But before he was there, great bone-dry heaves climbed up his throat like hands on a rope and stopped him in his tracks. He could tell himself, rightly, that this was no symptom of any disease but a poor-assed son's inadequate guilt for long stingy years with a parent who can never have meant worse than kindness.

Before he was even in full control, he returned to the phone and was punching Gwyn's number like a combination to the actual doors of Heaven or Hell—that urgent anyhow.

She didn't answer.

He dialed her again and, when he still failed to rouse her, he thought of driving straight to Sherwin and explaining himself. But then he might be out of touch with his father. *All right. I'll phone Audrey and tell her where I may be.*

Marcus answered on the third ring but hardly seemed to know him. Instead of addressing Mabry by any of his several names, he'd only reply to direct questions in a voice that seemed understandably exhausted. *He's a lot younger than Audrey and me though.*

So at last Mabry had to say "Is somebody there in the room right now?"

"Nobody but Father Kincaid, no."

Still polite, yes, but not as tired sounding. So Mabry's own voice hardened very slightly. "Then, Marcus, I'm his son—the man who's running this show or *paying* for it." The money part was not strictly true, though it might come to that.

Marcus took a long pause, then said "All right."

Something peculiar's surely going on. He asked to speak with Audrey.

Marcus said "She's gone to get her a Coke."

So Mabry had to ask straight out. "Then please take the pencil on my father's table and write this number down." He read him Gwyn's number, then said "You got it?"

"I do—Miss Williams, yes. We'll call you there, if anything happens."

Hell, does he know every number in town? Very likely yes—maybe from his business. Then I'm blocked on all sides. No point in denying the rumor that I've gone out now to find a woman. He had no time or strength at the moment to dig further down into Marcus's mood. *He's a very young man after all—nineteen.* Mabry sat in the front hall another ten minutes. Then he took up his bag and went to the bedroom he'd last occupied. The bed was made neatly—clean pillowcase and sheets. He'd stretch out there and beg for sleep. Oddly, it came.

Mabry thought he'd waked himself. He was lying on his left side, facing the window; but it took him awhile to realize that, again, his eyes weren't working, not normally. Before he could sit up and check on the problem, though, he heard a loud knocking at what seemed the front door and then a voice maybe calling his name. When he'd got to his feet, he nearly fell over. He could see fairly clearly; but when he paused to check, he realized that only his left eye was seeing. The right eye had gone fully blind again. Whoever had knocked, and called his name, called out again—some unintelligible string of words—a woman's voice most likely. So half blind and tattered from his nap, he walked to the front door.

Gwyn had given up and was halfway to her car before he opened on her. He literally couldn't think of words to say, but she turned back toward him and slowly came on.

By the time she could hear him, he'd remembered to say "Sweet lady, I'm sorry as I can be. I tried to call you straight back and say so, but not a soul answered."

That stopped her on the porch steps. "My soul got killed nine years ago in south Taiwan."

For at least five seconds, Mabry's good eye faded in and out of function. He didn't mention it but put both arms out beside him and braced his hands against the door frame.

It made Gwyn smile. "You posing as Samson in the Philistine temple? Victor Mature you ain't, baby boy; but—with this house being in the state it's in—go easy: you might bring it all down on us."

"Step here please, Delilah," he said, though still not saying why.

While he looked quite normal, Gwyn still caught the air of something wrong; so she went on to help him, if help was called for.

They'd found the makings of an early scratch supper—cold ham, burger buns, a big tomato, Swiss cheese, mustard, frozen green peas, two flavors of ice cream. And only when they'd eaten and pushed back to make fresh coffee did Mabry tell Gwyn more about anyone's physical shape than his bad-off father's. He began by pretending to realize that he'd missed today's doctor appointment in New York (in fact, he'd phoned and canceled the appointment yesterday).

That gave Gwyn the obvious chance to ask him how he was.

He mentioned this afternoon's patch of blindness, which had now almost resolved itself.

Being cold sober, Gwyn was smart enough to know she shouldn't light in at this point with a red-hot campaign to urge him back down here—a southern retreat in the face of age and weakness. She started by telling him about her talks with Randolph Baynes and his recent estimates for work on her homeplace. It seemed that the merest facelift on the roof, the floor joists, the plaster, and a good paint job would run her somewhere near eighty thousand dollars. Anything more ambitious would put her in deepest debtors' prison, but she'd almost decided to phone young Randy with the go-ahead.

"Hell, Mabry, I'm *old*. This was home at the start, and there's nowhere else on the planet to hide—or lean back on."

Mabry said "I hadn't failed to notice that."

"About me or you or the two of us together? God knows, nobody is calling for me."

Mabry made no effort to contradict her. He'd have thought his silence was an effort not to be stampeded into calling insistently for Gwyn; but he knew too surely that the same was true for him. Even then and there, with his vision very nearly returned, he knew he was rooted—here and now—in the safety of his birthplace, an entire house which might as well have been the first good rocket soaring past the planet Neptune with him as its single still-breathing occupant. As Gwyn leaned toward him across the length of the loaded table, he laughed at the image and again extended his arms at his sides, flapping them this time as if to add further power to his rocket.

Gwyn said "What's funny?"

"Oh me," he said, "—a billion ways. Shall we sit here and list them, one by one?"

"Darling, I've likely got no more than thirty years. Will that be time enough?"

Mabry said "I wouldn't have the least idea, but I think it's likely that we've got enough coffee to see us through."

After their coffee—which turned out to be decaffeinated, like all the coffee that was left in the house—Mabry asked Gwyn to walk with him back to his old bedroom. He didn't think of it as any first step in a planned seduction (otherwise wouldn't he have shaded the roadside windows?). He wanted her to see Philip Adger's picture once again in a peaceful house. He hadn't really noticed earlier, but it was still where he'd left it when he went to New York. He went to the mantel and took it up in both hands. Gwyn came up beside him, and in silence they both spent a good while studying it.

In fact the silence went on so long that at last Gwyn had to say "You know I'm right, don't you?"

"—About what you said the first time you saw it?" Mabry held it out for her to hold.

"I'm not about to put my invisible oils, or any mold spores I've brought from Tibet, on that precious thing and have somebody accuse me maybe a century from now of brutal behavior." She smiled but was earnest.

So Mabry kept it and when Gwyn turned as if to leave, he held her by liberally wetting the end of his right forefinger with saliva and stroking the upper right of the canvas.

That stopped Gwyn cold of course.

"Idiot! *Quit!*" She came back to him and at last took the picture. When she'd given the wet corner only a glance, she set the picture where it belonged—or had been for some days.

Mabry said quietly "The owner is dead."

"The lawyer who sent you to Paris is dead?"

"I told you he'd apparently been at his office when the building was struck and maybe when it fell. Nobody has heard a word from him since, not from him or anyone else on his staff. His likable butler, a lad from Australia, is hanging on to a few shreds of hope; but it's been ten days."

Gwyn said "He's dead. Or has chosen to change his name and reappear in East Borneo as some other man his wife will never find."

"He left no wife, no children, no family so far as we know."

Gwyn said "And *who* knows you've got this picture?"

Mabry paused to think. "A teenaged girl in Nova Scotia, a good friend in New York, then you and I. Plus Audrey Thornton and Marcus her son; but nobody knows about the Van Gogh connection except you and me, the New York friend, and the girl in Nova Scotia."

"The family you stayed with for those two days?"

"Yes, and she's likely forgot it by now."

"It was she, though, who found Philip Adger's note—right?"

Mabry said "Ah right." Then with exaggerated care he moved the picture into absolute center place on the mantel. "She'll no doubt barge in here any day now, with Interpol, and declare it belongs to La République française."

Gwyn said "Stranger things happen almost every week."

Mabry said "So they do." He realized that his eyesight had gone back entirely to normal; and suddenly he felt tired in every cell, enormously tired. He said "I haven't had a wink of sleep for two straight nights. I'll either have to collapse right now, for half an hour on that iron bed, or fall to the floor."

Gwyn looked toward the bed he was pointing to. Years ago he'd mentioned being born there, and nearly killing his mother in the process (an awful breech birth, with his gigantic skull refusing to turn and come out first as he had to do). What other boy she'd ever met knew the bed he was born in or thought to mention it? In any case she felt like saying "May I join you?" and she did.

Mabry said "By all means, pal, but I doubt I'll be good for one damned thing but literal *sleep*."

She waited a moment to see how insulted she ought to feel. *Hell, not at all*. So they both stretched out.

And sleep was very nearly all that happened in the next two hours, very nearly all.

When Mabry woke it was dark at the nearest window; and though Gwyn's body was turned away, he could hear from the even rate of her breath that she was still asleep. There was no way for him to get up without waking her, so he lay in place on his back another good while. He was mainly consulting his own assaulted body. At the moment his eyesight seemed to be working, but the whole length of his spine and both legs were jangling hard—rattling so fiercely that Mabry could scarcely believe they weren't truly audible to Gwyn. An honest assessment of the past month would have to conclude that—whatever any hundred doctors might say, American doctors, not counter-culture shamans—he'd taken, or had forced down upon him, a huge slow course of wide curves in his path.

So far they were crazily unpredictable. So far the jangling wasn't quite definable as *pain*. Again, it was a kind of horrifying music played by his nerves—or played by his brain on the million-stringed instrument provided by his neurons. And again, the horror lay mostly in the fact that no one but he could hear the music. He could lie in this bed, on his ample back, for another long century and try to help another human being—however sympathetic—comprehend the nature of what might yet drive Mabry Kincaid mad or lead to his imminent total paralysis, requiring total round-the-clock care from another human being (if not more than one); but even he couldn't ask for that. Couldn't or wouldn't—at present the choice seemed meaningless.

Whenever, Gwyn spoke without rolling toward him. "How does New York feel?"

"Ma'm?"

"Your city. Can a human being with natural feelings live there, ever again?"

Mabry turned to his left side and laid a hand on her broad upper hip. "Gwyn, don't human beings still live at the North Pole and on the garbage dumps of New Delhi?"

"Not quite the Pole but, close, I'll grant you—and the garbage dumps, sure. I've climbed all through them, hunting antique Shivas—found two at least and a gorgeous Ganesh, four feet high with a lovable belly."

Mabry said "Then what did you mean?"

"I meant can you visualize your particular soul and body staying on now in a place that's the number-one target on Earth, for every form of punishment that any band of psychopaths can muster?"

"Wells could be hit by a moon-sized meteor an hour from now."

Gwyn thought about that, then surrendered to laughter.

Mabry's hand came up under her breasts as he joined the fun, but then he said "I may have to flip a coin."

Gwyn could finally say "You mean you're flipping for your favorite bozoom of the two you're holding or for whether or not you can live in Gotham, our Latest City of Dreadful Night?"

"Maybe both," he said and laughed again, though it seemed to him he might very well mean it. *But alone. Remember, it would be* flat *alone. Forever after?* He didn't say that. He glanced to the window again—full dark. "Shall we scrounge up a supper from whatever's left?"

To Gwyn it seemed they'd eaten big sandwiches minutes before, but she said "We could drive into town and find something decent."

Mabry said "I promised Pa I'd be here, waiting by the phone."

Gwyn said "Then let me run to the store." It was said in a tone of pure selfless help.

Mabry told her he'd never stop that. And though again he didn't explain, he was close to believing he wouldn't manage to spend a night alone in this house, not tonight anyhow. Fear was likely the main reason, unfocused fear; but he told himself it was owing to the danger of getting an emergency call about Tasker and finding that his own eyes, or hands or mind, wouldn't let him drive to the hospital safely—not alone and maybe never again.

At half past nine Gwyn served a good supper, and Mabry tried to tell her about his days in New York. Understandably, she wanted to know about the state of his loft and what he'd seen on his downtown visit with Charlotte and Malcolm. He barely mentioned Miles, and he held off stressing the awful presence of so many dead lives in the air, not one of whom could have died at peace, not to mention the desolate living kin with their Xeroxed photographs and hopeless handouts. Gwyn had after all been to North Vietnam and Cambodia; but even she could see that, despite more quantities of double-strength coffee (real coffee), Mabry was craving a long night's sleep. When he said he'd help her with the dishes, then scoot for bed, she told him to scoot right then. She'd handle the cleanup. He was at the hall door before he could make himself turn and ask for what he'd hoped to avoid. He said "Dear pal, is there any way on Earth you could manage to stay here tonight?"

She was already drawing water at the sink; but she turned, mildly curious as to why she was needed. "I didn't really shut down my own house but—"

So he gave her an absolute honest plea. "I wouldn't ask you if I thought I could handle an emergency call in the midst of the night."

She hadn't yet asked and it seemed a hard time to raise the question, but she went ahead. "Did your own doctor warn you?"

"I told you I was meant to see him yesterday but then Audrey called."

"So no word yet on all those tests you took?"

Mabry waited till he'd choked down the bulk of his anger. His voice was low. "*Jesus*, friend—there's no word, no. In my experience, very few doctors' secretaries tell you on the phone about your M.S. or your cancerous womb. Maybe you found otherwise in the Orient?"

"Call it Asia," Gwyn said, "that's the new polite term. No, Mabry, they'll hardly tell you when you're truly on the last day of your deathbed. My cancerous womb was all but hanging between my knees before they told me." With her voice still solid, low in the air, she turned back to the sink to draw water.

That was news to Mabry. "Oh Gwyn, I didn't know a word about this. I beg your pardon."

She wouldn't face him. "You've got it, friend."

"Want to tell me more?"

"Please go on to bed. I'll be here tomorrow. We can talk then— or five years from now—if your interest survives."

He said "Of course my interest will be here. Right now I'm just swamped, far more swamped than I expected to be. In another few days, I'll be a better friend. Meanwhile, I checked and Audrey has got clean sheets on the other bed in my room. Will you please be there?"

"I will. Guaranteed."

He held his place another whole second.

Then just as he turned to leave, Gwyn thought of something. "You want to phone Audrey now and check on the state of things before bedtime?"

"Please let's don't. She and I've got a strong understanding—she'll call if the least thing goes wrong with Tasker."

"Then sweet dreams," Gwyn said. "Rest deep anyhow."

Just before he sank, Mabry raised his head. "Oh girl, did you ever marry a Signor Becchi? You mentioned him once, if I remember rightly."

Gwyn waited in hopes sleep would overtake him. When his eyes stayed open, she had to say "Not *married* exactly. Not on this planet. Anyhow he's no concern of ours today."

Mabry's eyes shut finally. "That's a major relief."

Gwyn said "Glad to be of service, old friend, however small."

Both of them laughed.

He rested so deeply that, when the only phone rang in the front hall at 5:43 in the morning, he didn't hear it. When Gwyn had answered and come back to rouse him, she was forced to shake him hard. And when he lurched up and faced her with blurred—crazed—eyes, she said "Mabry, be calm but get up now and speak with Audrey. She's on the phone."

"Pa's dead," he said.

"I don't think so. I honestly don't. But get up now. Audrey's waiting for you."

So she was, wide awake at Tasker's bedside. "Mabry, I'm sorry to trouble your sleep; but your father's been terribly restless all night. He hasn't said a word, but he plainly wants to have you nearby. I waited till daylight at least to call you."

"He hasn't had another stroke?"

Audrey said "Oh no. Just sleepless, as I said, and tossing in his sheets. When I try to ease him—Marcus *or* I—he waves us off. The same with the nurses. He's bound to want you."

Even groggy as he was, Mabry couldn't think that was bound to be the case. When, in the past five decades anyhow, had his father ever wanted him urgently? Yet he said "Tell him I'll be there in less than an hour."

He managed a shower, clean underwear, and a cup of fresh coffee. Then Gwyn drove him in his rented car to Roanoke Rapids. He'd told her that Marcus could drive her back to her car in Wells; but once they'd parked outside the hospital, he asked her if she'd mind walking in with him.

She said "I've come close to loving your father for my whole life." That was her answer and she walked in with Mabry. When the elevator doors opened on the top floor, he actually put his arm through hers and led her beside him into his father's room.

Both Audrey and Marcus were there, and Tasker's head craned up and either grinned or winced hard at the new sight. His skin was flushed a purplish red; the restlessness which Audrey mentioned had plainly been real work.

As Mabry moved toward him, Gwyn tried to pull back but Mabry kept hold of her arm.

So Tasker studied them both, like complicated texts he must shortly explain or at least comprehend. His lips even parted; but if he meant to speak, he chewed the words with a terrible groan. Then he looked back at Gwyn and maybe tried to smile but ended by shaking his head—a seeming *No*. Then his right hand came up and waved her and Audrey and Marcus toward the door. They must leave the room. Only Mabry seemed welcome to stay for a while or maybe forever.

As it was, here and now, Mabry felt nearly ready—a clean room, light enough, room to stand and turn in, a white enamel sink with hot and cold water, paper towels, a small bathroom with a shower and commode and of course the bed with this old man. *Do I love him at all?* Maybe that was irrelevant, now at least. He didn't plan to leave him. Anyhow he thought of Gwyn and the Thorntons. They were likely outside, at the door or in the lobby. So he said to his father "I'll step outside for thirty seconds and get young Marcus to drive Gwyn home. Should Audrey stay with us?"

For a long time that seemed too much for Tasker, too many words or too many choices. But then he shut his eyes and signed an apparent yes to all the options.

When Mabry went out and met with the others in the waiting room, they were plainly ready for a little relief. Marcus would ferry Gwyn to her car, then go about his regular plans for a Saturday morning. But when he told Audrey that his father had agreed she should stay, Audrey said "Let me tell him I need to run home—his house and my house—to bathe and change and tend to a few chores. You can mostly reach me by phone, and I'll be back in under three hours. Will that suit you? You saw he wanted you." It clearly caused her no pain to say it.

Mabry said "Please come back as soon as you can." Then he went to Gwyn, hugged her close, and said he'd call her later in the morning. "A billion thanks."

Gwyn said "Should I just say goodbye to your father?"

She hadn't said *farewell* so Mabry figured she might be assuming she'd see his father sometime in the future. He said "He seems to have something to *do* with me. Let's leave him to it now."

Gwyn didn't ask for more explanation; and when she turned to Marcus, ready to leave, Mabry said "Marc, I'll no doubt see you later today. You know I'm grateful."

Marcus said "I know it" and led the way out.

When he entered Tasker's room, Dr. Sharma was there at the bedside, talking very quietly. He turned to Mabry and smiled. "Ah, you're here, sir. We were missing you."

Mabry smiled but said "I had to go missing. I was tired to the bone. Ms. Thornton knew exactly where I was."

Dr. Sharma heard the offended note. "I meant no criticism at all. Your father has been hoping for you, however."

By then Mabry was also at the bed, his hand on the blade of Tasker's shin beneath the cover. "Has he asked for me? I haven't heard him speak since I got here."

Dr. Sharma said "I couldn't say precisely. I think he may have called you by your Christian name late in the night when I was away."

"Ms. Thornton told you that?"

"I think it was her son."

Marcus hadn't mentioned that to Mabry, so he stayed in place and asked about his father's progress. Tasker's eyes were fixed right on him.

Dr. Sharma looked to Tasker, not Mabry, and said "I think we're doing the expected."

Mabry said "And the *expected* is that my father can go to his own home tomorrow or Monday?"

The doctor's eyes were reluctant. Did he recall ever saying such a thing? At last he said "Let's rest a little longer. We can speak tomorrow maybe." With very few more words, he ducked and left the Kincaid men, both generations.

They were there, alone, till late morning except for mumbling visits, every few hours, from a nurse's aide with a blood pressure sleeve and a fever thermometer. Audrey phoned in midday and asked if she could wait awhile longer. She was babysitting Marcus's daughter, "a treat and a relief" as she said with welcome candor. She'd never mentioned her grandchild before, not to Mabry anyhow. Mabry said "I'm all the job seems to need till bedtime. Pa's quiet now and the doctor says what he needs is rest."

Did Audrey let it slip, or was she truly near some ending? In any case, she said "Rest—pure rest—is what we all need." The sound of a young girl's clamoring voice was clear behind her.

And Mabry thought *Whatever you do, just don't leave us.* But all he said was "Come when you can."

She said she'd do her best, or she'd try to send Marcus.

*   *   *

When he looked back to Tasker, for the first full time Mabry felt a
rushing return of what his father might have likely called love.
Like any decent boy, brought up kindly, he'd had moments of real
delight with this man, waves of thanks as drenching as water, and
the need to loop up his small-framed father in embraces that silently
promised to honor and protect him forever or at least a lifetime. The
human race would surely have vanished long centuries ago without
such returns, and so it should have. What did the hugely successful
attack on New York buildings and lives eleven days ago, three
blocks from his loft, represent but the momentarily triumphant
assertion by nineteen young men that people should *cease* (millions
of people, maybe all Americans, surely all infidels) since those
young men had simply lacked fathers? Or adequate fathers. Absurd?
Well, maybe. But maybe not. The longer Mabry looked at Tasker,
the more he thought *maybe not*. He took the hand that lay on the
sheet and held it closely. Then he said "Father Kincaid, tell me
something to do" (he heard himself say *Father Kincaid* for the first
time). "Anything you need that Mabry can get?"

The old head, smaller now by two or three sizes, shook a hard *No*.

There was nothing here to read but the pocket New Testament
Audrey had brought. Mabry took it up from beside the phone and
showed it to Tasker. "Anything I should read?"

A long wait, Tasker's eyes loosened their feverish grip on Mabry's
face and looked to the window. Full sun had won its scuffle with fog
and was streaming in. Then the old man turned his whole body
toward Mabry; and for the first time since his son had come back,
Tasker managed to raise his head five inches above the pillow.

Mabry leaned forward, to catch the head if it tumbled back (he'd
seldom seen his father's bare thin neck before today).

Tasker again shook his head no.

Mabry stayed in place but smiled, ready now for whatever might
come.

Then Tasker said, clear-tongued but very slowly—word by word as if they were polished stones he was handing out to be laid carefully by his only son—"She. Gets. A. House."

Mabry's head was nodding. Whatever it meant, he knew he ought to reward the mere words and the effort they took. *But what does he mean? What women does he know? Who's he seen lately?— Gwyn Williams and nurses. He hasn't talked to Charlotte. It's bound to be Audrey.* He spoke as clearly as Tasker just had. "Audrey Thornton you mean?"

By then, though, the head had settled back on the pillow; and a blurring screen was lowering between the face and Mabry—Mabry and anything Mabry could see, beyond or around them. Had his own eyes failed again, or was his father truly leaving? When Mabry reached out, the same cool hand was there—Tasker's, on the sheet. The eyes seemed open still and trying to follow him as long as they could, against strong odds.

When Tasker actually left at last, it was more than two hours on into midday; and he took his last breath so calmly that Mabry, sitting no farther than three feet away, heard nothing at all, surely not the final breach in the wall of the softest artery in the brain that had thought this first son to life—had actually *thought*, one bright afternoon on the porch beside his warm but childlike wife, three years into a marriage that was cooling fast, *It's almost certainly time to put a child between us*; then had stood and told her "Eunice, let's rest." Tasker, as a young man, had napped no more than twice a year; but Eunice had looked up, studied his whole face, understood him, and risen to take his larger hand. These fifty-four hard years later—and with Eunice in the grave for twelve years—by the time that elder son touched it again, the hand was colder than the room around it.

It was midafternoon before the Kincaid house was plain to see as Mabry turned the last curve, alone in his car, two hundred yards off. His father's car was parked where he'd left it the day he broke his ankle, in the old horse shed. And though no other car was in sight, he could see Gwyn Williams rocking in the porch swing. *Oh Christ, I told her I was already here—that I needed quiet time till sundown anyhow.*

As he stopped beside the tallest oak, Gwyn stood and came forward to the steps. Since morning she'd changed into a navy-blue dress and pulled her hair back in a dark red ribbon.

Mabry paused halfway to the house. "Gwyn, thanks but I thought I mentioned *quiet* time."

"You did and I mean to be out of here fast, friend; but listen, I've buried two people in this town in recent years, and I think I know a few things that can help you."

He said "Such as what, pal?"

"I can call the best mortician and get him under way (the only other white one's a knee-walking drunk). I can ask for the church on whatever day you want—the church and the priest. I can book the florist and specify the live blooms (otherwise you may get the finest Hispanic plastic). I can notify your father's chosen pallbearers and book motel rooms as nearby as possible—"

Mabry's hand came up to stop her. "*Touché*, my darling." Then he moved on toward her; and after a nearly silent half hour of puttering in the kitchen, they were drinking real coffee at the table.

Gwyn had finally understood that Mabry had almost no strength left for a verbal grilling, but there was a single thing she knew that needed bringing up. So she finally said "Beg pardon, friend, but this may be crucial when it comes to funeral plans and whatever—"

Mabry touched her wrist, smiling. "I can guess where you're headed—did Pa leave a will?"

Her turn to say "*Touché*—but you know what I mean: did he name his pallbearers or the priest or the music or the scripture or whatever?"

"Not to mention whether his elder son is now a billionaire."

"Exactly." Gwyn laughed.

Mabry said "I believe Pa told me, two or three years ago, that he'd made a will; and that I'd find a copy in his underwear drawer 'when the need arises and in whatever house my underwear resides in at the time.'"

"Should you look there now?" Then she felt she'd pushed a step too far. She took her empty cup to the sink, rinsed it carefully, and said "I'd better get on back home. Randy Baynes has got paint samples for me and said he'd drop by the house before dark. Phone me the minute you've got any job for me to do."

Mabry stood to hug her. "You'll be my main help, and I'll call you very soon."

Then she was on her way, giving him the time and emptiness he needed.

First of course he went to his father's old bureau; and yes a long white envelope was there, under the dozen pairs of dark gray socks and inscribed in Tasker's strongest large script—*To be opened at my death by my beloved son, Mabry Kincaid.* The word *beloved* was unexpected, even in this particular place; it slowed Mabry down. Instead of returning to the kitchen and cutting the envelope open with a clean knife, he knew he should wait a few minutes at least. He hardly anticipated revelations, but yes he must wait till the moment was right.

From the hospital he'd phoned Audrey and Charlotte. Charlotte said she'd fly down tonight or tomorrow morning. Audrey said she'd be there when he needed her. He had a hard time persuading her not to send Marcus to get him—even though she had no notion of his blindness—so again he told her he needed a few hours quiet time and she finally understood. Alone in the house then, he went to his room first and sat on the bed.

What else did he need to do? Who else must he call? There were no other close relations in fact, no professional colleagues whom Tasker truly honored, and very few of the friends from his father's

era who were still alive and lucid. There might be something in the
white envelope he'd need to act on soon; but it lay by his leg on the
bed, not ready. Not scary quite but imposing in its plain demand to
stay shut.

Mabry's vision had held up, but now as he sat and waited for what
seemed bound to come—some sort of breakup, some genuine trib-
ute before the presence of watchful others would leave him frozen—
what he felt was neither tears nor the choking he'd felt awhile ago but
a slow return of the maddening jangle down his spine and both his
legs, a scalding electric assault from every nerve. For the first time
since he left New York, even after yesterday's blind spell, he felt real
fear. *This is something dreadful that won't go away—no detour round
it.* He was right and would be for the rest of a long life; yet when he
stood and brought Philip Adger's picture back to the bed and studied it two minutes, then he could lie back—holding the picture on
his chest with the white envelope untouched at his side—and fall
straight asleep.

A little more than an hour later, he gradually swam up to sounds
from the kitchen. He'd locked the front door when he saw Gwyn off,
so it had to be Audrey or maybe Marcus—did Marcus have a key, or
had Audrey lent him hers? He knew he should go and check on
whomever, but the jangling in his body was louder still, and he lay
in a drench of self-pity for maybe another ten minutes before he
heard firm steps coming his way and then Audrey's voice.

"Mabry, are you in there?"

The sound was more welcome than he'd ever have guessed.
"Oh yes ma'm, come in please." He drew the envelope up under his
left flank but stayed in place, the picture on his chest.

And then Audrey stood there, tall in the doorway in the mild lamp-
light. She was in a black pants suit, handsome attire; and for the first
time since the day he met her, Mabry thought again *She's a fine-
looking woman.* And now he thought *I'm proud to know her—*

exactly the thing his father might have said, and in Tasker's words (though Tasker might also have phrased his opinion as "a well-set-up woman" or "a handsome woman"). Audrey had conveyed her sympathy on the phone, but again she said "I've lost my own parents, so I may know how you feel."

Mabry thought *Lord God, then you know the full contents of a major mare's nest.* But he said "I think you very likely do. I'm a true orphan now." He smiled, then found he almost meant it.

Audrey walked on into the midst of the room and turned to face him fully. "Yes, Mabry, you are—you and me both—and it's bad hell, ain't it?"

She'd heard him use country language with Tasker, but Mabry had never heard Audrey indulge herself that far. He'd slipped the envelope under the picture, so he sat upright now. "You look mighty fine."

She looked down at herself. "I bought it this morning. I wasn't babysitting all this time, but I didn't want to tell you I was shopping for mourning. I somehow knew, though, we'd be having a funeral." Steadily her voice was assuming trained dignity.

Mabry said "That's something I've got to do myself. Maybe Marcus can help me find a good store."

Audrey said "He knows every white and black men's store between here and Richmond. But you sure you can't wear your father's suit?"

Mabry realized she'd almost surely never seen his father upright in recent years. "No, child, I can't. I'm way taller now."

She said "We got a world of plans to make then. Or you surely do. I'll be in the kitchen when you're ready to tell me what I need to do next, if anything. I understand my employer's departed."

Mabry hadn't thought of that. "Oh please don't say it. Help me forever." He'd spilled it out without an instant's forethought. *And I mean it, don't I?*

By then she was heading back toward the door. "I bought us some groceries—not a whole lot but I'm glad to cook your supper."

He was suddenly hungry. "Please do. I'm starving." When Audrey was almost out of sight, he thought to call behind her. "We won't be having any drop-in company here tonight, will we?"

Audrey said "Not unless you summoned somebody. Father Kincaid barely knew another soul but you, me, and Marcus. Said all his boyhood friends were dead."

Maybe Gwyn will be back. But he didn't say that. He said he'd shower and join her very shortly. He quickly stripped and took his towel, but then the sight of the envelope stopped him. He found the knife in his trousers pocket and carefully slit the white flap open. As he'd thought, right off he could see it was a will—his father's last testament, entirely handwritten and (as Mabry knew from his mother's death) legal in the state of North Carolina so long as two friends of the deceased would witness to the fact that the actual script belonged to the dead man. It wasted no time with a florid preamble but proceeded simply.

My beloved and sole offspring, the Master of Arts Mabry Kincaid, is herewith executor of my estate and will at once inherit my desirable holdings. They amount to the Kincaid family home in Wells, N.C., a decrepit Chevrolet, my personal effects (such as gold watch and wedding ring) plus my bank account, the capital in my insulting pension fund and any other inconsequential sums of money that he finds strewn around at my death.

I trust that Mabry will absorb whatever amount he can employ for his own good purposes and then will consign the remainder to the Salvation Army, whom I respect a great deal more than the Red Cross, who seem mainly interested in posters and publicity.

I have given my life to the church I served, so they can hardly be expecting any money from me now.

To my lovable granddaughter, Charlotte Kincaid, who has been her own mother's fortunate heir, I leave her grandmother Kincaid's Bible, her favorite cookbook, and her cameo brooch of the boy

Antinous, who served the Emperor Hadrian in duties I leave for Charlotte to discover as she moves on upward through time and learns the endlessly curious ways and means of the world from long before the Roman Empire till now and no doubt forever beyond. I never had the nerve to explain the meaning of the brooch to my wife, who had got it in turn from her own grandmother who had got it as a gift from her uncle Bootie who visited Rome in the 1880s. It would just have ended Eunice's enjoyment of an admirable piece of Italian artistry, and why do that? Anything else I may have neglected here and now will go to my son and his understanding of where any overflow should run.

In conclusion let me put in writing this one more thing I failed to do till now. I have loved the world. I may even have loved it, and its attendant beauties, too much at times, and leaving it—whenever I do—will be hard. But I die in gratitude to every soul who has been kind to me. There are hundreds of them and they know who they are.

(Signed) Tasker James Kincaid,
December 31, 1999

There were no additions from later dates, no crossings-out. So Mabry was left to wonder again—as he folded the spotless pages, put them back in their envelope, and set it behind Philip Adger's picture on the mantel—*Who's the* she *he mentioned in the four-word codicil I heard him speak a few hours ago?*

In the distant kitchen, a pan clattered down, which reminded Mabry that an audible shower now would give him a quarter hour to think. He moved that way.

Audrey had put a red smock on top of her new good clothes, so when Mabry appeared she felt she had to apologize. "This redness is no sign of disrespect; it's just to protect me."

Mabry said "By all means. And by contrast, don't I look a lot like Huckleberry Finn toward the end of his misery?" But he stood in the doorway in clean khaki trousers and a long-tailed black shirt.

Audrey looked and smiled a little. "Mr. Finn deserved something better than misery, don't you believe?"

Mabry hadn't thought. But he said "I'm glad you feel that way. I'll join you, if we ever get called to jury duty when he turns up outside the Pearly Gates."

Audrey didn't turn back from the sink again—she was peeling shrimp—but she said "You estimate you and I will be inside those Gates?"

Mabry said "Don't ask for an estimate on *me*. You and my pa will surely get in, assuming you don't have a burning crime I haven't heard about."

"Not a one," Audrey said. She waited while Mabry sat at the table; then she said "Wish I'd had a little more fun."

"God knows you've earned it." That felt like the truth, and it forced Mabry to speak out sooner than he'd planned. He said "Did my father promise you anything I need to know about?"

She still didn't face him, but she spoke right back. "Meaning what please?"

"—Among other things, I've just read his will. He wrote it by hand in December 1999, the night before the millennium; and there are no recent codicils or changes."

Audrey still felt no compulsion to turn or even look up from the sink. "So anything he promised me wouldn't be legal, would it?" When she turned back now, she laughed awhile and that revealed a beauty she'd somehow kept hidden in her face since Mabry first met her—beautiful for the first full time since Mabry met her nine days ago.

He rushed onward then. "All right. We want you to have this house."

Her question came as fast as his offer. "Mabry, who is *we*?"

He asked her to join him at the table for a minute; she came and sat at the opposite end. He said "*We* is Tasker Kincaid and his one living child. This morning, not long after you and Marcus left, Pa looked straight at me and spoke four words." They were hard to repeat, dredging up so much feeling; but he got them out clearly, then needed a pause.

In the silence Audrey said "Who'd he mean by *she* and which *house* was it?"

Isn't she reaching too far now? But no, I asked her to tell me everything. He said "I've been thinking hard ever since Pa spoke. At first I thought *she* couldn't be anybody else but my daughter; but Pa knew that, with her mother's wealth, Charlotte won't need a cent if she lives to be a thousand. In his will he takes precise note of that fact. He was also bound to know that, good as Charlotte is, this house has never mattered to her. She never spent any real time here in her childhood, which is when you mostly come to love places—don't you? And that was my fault. I never brought her here. She went to her mother's family home, as most children do. No, Audrey, my father admired you a very great deal. You and I know how grateful he was for all you've done—"

Audrey had to break in. "Mabry, it's nice to hear you working through this whole process; but don't forget, I only came to know your father less than one full month ago."

Mabry knew that his age could trump her here firmly; he knew the single relevant truth. "Love, thanks, reward—all the truly good things are measured by heat and depth, not endurance. So Pa's word *she* is bound to mean *you*."

Audrey waited a long time, then agreed but was silent.

Mabry said "All right?"

She felt no ease yet, if she ever would. "You know I thank you; but Mabry, which house was he talking about?"

"This one surely, the Kincaid place. You don't know of any secret place he owned, do you?"

She sat on, silent, looking down now.

Mabry said "What's the trouble?"

She finally said "I owe both of you a world of thanks; and I know that, up till I moved in here, Father Kincaid meant you to have this house for the rest of your life. But you understand, better even than I do, that this house needs a lot of work—call it *conservation*, which is your trade after all—and I simply don't have money even to fix the roof."

Mabry said "I do. Charlotte's mother—Frances Kenyon Kincaid, the wife I did so much to harm—has lately left me sufficient funds to bring this place back to proud condition."

At last Audrey looked up; the beauty had lasted. She said "This place is your family's old home, the only one you've got. Surrender this now and you truly are an orphan." But she was plainly waiting to hear more. "Tell me this please—if this house should be mine, as of now, why on Earth should you be the man to fix it?"

Mabry finally said "All right, how's this? I told you I just now read his will, not more than half an hour ago. At the present moment, as I've just learned, the whole place is mine—house, trees, sheds, land, birds, squirrels, blind possums. Pa left it to me, free and clear. Now once the will's probated, I'll consign the deed to you. But then I'll fix it. Call it a gift. Say I'm giving it to Cooter." He was trusting she'd understand his equation with its sub-inclusion.

She was plainly baffled, however, and moved to stand from the table and go back to planning the supper she'd promised.

So Mabry saw he was forced to lay out his beggar's proposition. "You know I may be in bad shape. I had to cancel a meeting with my doctor to rush down here; but frankly I'm sure, from various signals my body's giving, that I've almost surely got multiple sclerosis or something as bad. Sometimes apparently M.S. is mild, but I've already had bad pain and worse—real spells of blindness. I have to think that, sooner or later, if I live awhile longer, I may turn out to need steady care."

Audrey kept her seat then and began to draw geometric figures on the table with her long forefinger. They were complicated as any cat's cradle, and they slowly stacked up on one another. "Father Kincaid told me that much anyhow. He knew it before you ever got back down here from Nova Scotia."

"I told him on the phone before I left for Europe. You likely guessed that I very seldom pray, but I wanted his prayers while I was gone—and ever after, I guess."

Audrey nodded. "You got them, from him and me both." She pointed to the dark bedroom behind them. "More than once he asked me to come in there and sit beside him and ask God to lead you."

"Pa didn't ask for healing?—that I'd get well, I mean."

She thought it out, then shook her head gently. "I noticed that too. Then finally I figured he was only asking for what we could *get*— what we *might* get."

Mabry said "So I got led to this table here tonight."

Audrey searched his whole body, all she could see. Then of all things she laughed, a deep splendid over-spill.

But Mabry could feel his face flushing red. "What, please ma'm?"

"You're trapping me, boy." She'd never come near to calling him *boy*. It was at least as shocking as *honky*, as comic as *boss man*.

"Trapping you in what?" He was partly confused, partly disingenuous.

"Mabry, first you tell me your father gave me this house outright, in his very last words. Then you say it's yours but that you'll fix it up and hand it over to be mine forever—mine and my own heirs once I'm gone. *Then* you say you'll hand it over in turn-key condition but that I'll need to nurse you the rest of your life. Tell me, boy, is that much right?"

It was Mabry's turn to think through her deductions and her final question, which he hadn't done till then. At last he imitated the figures she'd drawn on the table and then gave his own laugh, though not as deeply delighted as Audrey's. He was managing to meet her eyes, all the same.

She said "How wrong am I?"

"Dead right," he said, "—speaking of dead." And in the next thirty seconds, which were mute between them, he understood, with real amazement, that of course he meant to give her the house. He had no trace of a wish to disobey his father; but he also desperately hoped that Audrey would give him his own room and help him as needed, as long as needed, which he also knew might be hard as hell and might last a long while.

By then she'd stood, rebuttoned her red smock, and gone to the sink to assemble the dinner of shrimp and grits which she'd planned for the two of them and whoever else might hear the news and turn up, uncalled for.

Later that same night—a Saturday—Mabry had found, in Tasker's checkbook on the face of a blank check, this further list of simple requests—that his body be "inexpensively burned" and interred between his wife and Gabe, that there be no service in any church, no presiding clergy but that *"my son Mabry and my granddaughter Charlotte stand in the graveyard on the brightest day convenient and read aloud, to one another and whoever else might care to be present, whatever words from the Book of Common Prayer seem beautiful to them and have some chance of being true, since John Keats and I both understand that anything beautiful is bound to be true. They can be sure anyhow that Tasker Kincaid will hear them from whatever mansion he's in, in the place of many mansions, as Jesus names the place he intends to go when he dies."*

SIX

9 . 25 . 01

On the Tuesday then—conveniently bright in late afternoon—they delivered Tasker's wishes to the absolute letter with
Mabry, Charlotte, Audrey, Marcus and his child, Malcolm, Gwyn,
and Vance Scott from the Sherwin Pool Hall (of all unexpected but
welcome guests) in attendance at the graveyard. Then all returned
to the Kincaid house for the lavish spread of funeral provisions,
arranged for by Gwyn and hauled in by the best providers in easy
reach. There were actual caterers now in the county; and the best,
thank God, had not forgot how to cook and present the rewards of
Mabry's childhood—fried chicken that was somehow not greasy but
succulent and tender all the same, the salty smoked ham sliced
paper-thin and served between the crumbling halves of beaten
biscuits no bigger than a quarter, pickled watermelon rind, baby
cauliflower and okra, and of course the upper-quality echelons of
whiskey, wine, and even beer that Tasker Kincaid would have been
proud to serve the souls he valued, including Vance Scott (who
arrived unasked but cold sober, though he'd leave as pickled as any
gherkin under the roof).

The refreshments had largely been laid out before the family left
the house with the ashes in their stout Chinese urn—a handsome
eighteenth-century vase which Charlotte had found, at Mabry's

request, in a SoHo shop; and which she and he had sealed with molten wax the night before. So when they all re-convened at the house, there was little work for anyone; but with no prior coaching, the younger inhabitants—Charlotte, Malc, and Marcus—pitched in with calm pleasure, replenishing plates and glasses and keeping up a quiet dishwashing concern back in the kitchen (Gwyn had brought a thousand dishes and bowls that had been her mother's). That left the four older people to talk in the living room and out on the porch. The whole day was warm; and even as dusk began to gather, the porch was fine (with Marcus's daughter Master running safely and silently among them).

That was where Mabry and Vance talked alone for the last twenty minutes before Vance realized he should get on the road now or plan to sleep a few hours in the swing. Soaked as he was, though, he managed to warn Mabry of an oncoming danger which he himself— Vance—had suffered not all that long ago. In a great many looping and slow-timed paragraphs, and despite the existence of his wife Betty Ann, it came to this—*Both your parents are finally gone (and gone forever), you're as alone as any old turtle in the depths of a cold pond, don't go crazy now the way I have and turn yourself into something no two other creatures can manage to stand beside.* When Mabry had thanked him for the useful alert, walked him to the car, and got him safely seated and belted in, it turned out Vance had one last thing. He reached his left arm out of the window, took Mabry's wrist, and held it as tight as he'd held him that day in the camp swimming pool. "Son, you don't ever plan to live in that goddamned hell hole called New York again?" When Mabry smiled but didn't respond, Vance said "Answer me."

Mabry said "It's been my home a long time now."

Vance forged ahead. "Don't you *hear* me? It's ruined—stove up and drowning, as of two weeks ago today. I was talking to Charlotte just now in the kitchen. She said if she wasn't attached to that

husky friend of hers, she'd be right down here in this old house. And
Christ knows, she could fix it up now, couldn't she?"

Mabry signed yes. Then he said what he hadn't intended. "So
could I, as I think you know. At least you know what Frances left me."

"No I don't."

"In the pool hall twelve days ago, you told me you'd heard I was
now well-heeled."

Vance said "I don't recall that but then I seldom even know what
I mean, even once I say it. I must have been trying to cheer you up.
You looked so damned sad. And son, you still do. Let an old friend
tell you, you look in the worst shape I've ever seen you in. I won't
guess why, beyond the things I've already said; but I'm estimating
you're smart enough to know what a sane man would do at this hard
point."

Mabry said "Tell me."

Vance said "I just have."

Mabry said "All right. How likely are you, old underwater buddy,
to be reliable all these years later?" He was partly joking, partly dead-
earnest.

Vance cranked the engine, gunned it twice, turned on his radio
(hillbilly music of the ancientest sort, the kind they'd both dodged
steadily through their boyhoods—Homer Briarhopper and the Dixie
Dudes, on fiddles so mean they could peel the last scrap of bleeding
hide from a panther's face with the panther near you, bearing the
pain). Over the racket, Vance said "I never meant to tell you one single lie in my life, mine nor yours." Again he reached for Mabry's arm
and again he pressed it. "I've missed you, buddy, and I trust to see you
soon. If nobody else'll guard your damned ass, just hope to find
Vance. He's right up the road."

Mabry almost believed it, even as the car nearly ditched itself ten
seconds later, a hundred yards onward. And he even felt the need of
at least a few minutes alone, if he could steal the time.

But when he opened his bedroom door, Marcus was already there in the rocking chair, both eyes shut, though he still wore his jacket; and his necktie was knotted. Beyond him on the far bed lay young Master, exhausted from her play outside in a yard as safe as the sky and deep asleep but turned to face Mabry—a face no judge on Earth could find less than lovely and worth every act of human mercy the Law or life itself might afford. Yet Mabry was on the verge of quick anger to have had his room invaded, unasked, when Marcus opened a single eye and spoke out clearly. "We were waiting for you, sir." He didn't rise but he leaned far forward. "I've been guessing how hard on you these last days have been, especially today."

Mabry sat on the edge of his bed. "Not as hard as I feared."

"But you miss your dad already." It didn't seem to be a question. Had Marcus ever known a father, though? Neither he nor Audrey had mentioned one.

So Mabry told what seemed the truth. "I doubt I've had the time to tell how I'm going to feel. I'm not a child, you know."

Marcus let that settle on the room's warm air, then blared his eyes in calm amazement. "I doubt I understand you."

Mabry laughed. "I'm a monster. I told you that before." He craned his head and neck up and sideways. "Notice the scales— snake scales on my neck."

At last Marcus grinned. "No you're not. You've been too good to me."

"Monsters have their personal favorites, don't forget."

"Apparently so." Seated as he was, Marcus reached down and fastened a button on the jacket of his excellent blue suit.

Mabry thought he might be asking for attention to the suit, a recent purchase. He said "When you buy a suit that fine, it lasts you forever."

Marcus said "Could we talk about something else?"

Mabry said "Shoot," then heard how wrong that sounded.

But Marcus moved past it. "My mother said that when Father Kincaid passed, he was asking for her to get this house."

So she's already told him—well, natural enough. Mabry said "That's correct, right down to the actual verb Pa used in his last few breaths. I was the only other person in the room; and the last words he ever said to me, very slow and clear, were 'She gets a house.' He had to mean Audrey, and this has to be the house."

Marcus shook his head hard, as though it were drenched. Then he faced Mabry. "And you hope to stay in this room when you have to?" His face was as neutral as such an active face can be.

Any day before now, that might have angered Mabry—an assault on his actual property; it was his house still. Today, though, it might be an easy chance upward. "I'd hope to repair the whole house, yes, and stay in this room when I come on visits. Then if my illness leaves me helpless someday—it may or may not—I could dream this house would still be a place where I could get care. I'd be a paying guest of course." The progress of those three plain sentences—they felt nonetheless like the densest argument Socrates, Plato, or St. Paul himself had laid on a listener—had drawn a smile to his lips. "—As long as I have a cent to my name."

Marcus's face had the calmest gravity possible in a man still so young. He said "And what then?" Next, he was almost trying to smile.

It had been three days since Mabry underwent any signs of whatever had harrowed his body in the past two months. Maybe now he was free. Maybe his father's *passing* (in Marcus's ongoing effort to dodge the word *death*) had somehow carried his son's sickness with him. *Not a chance on Earth. Get real again, boy.* Taking the remains of his latest smile with him, Mabry got to his feet and walked toward the mantel. No trouble with his legs, no audible jangling. And his vision was clear.

He went to the center, took up Philip's picture (first reaching for the envelope on the back again) and walked toward Marcus. Marc also stood but Mabry said "Please sit back a minute." Then he said "I don't think this is too dusty for your perfect suit." He wasn't mocking the young man, who was slightly tense; but he took real care as he handed Marcus both the picture and the small envelope. "If you read the note first, I think you'll enjoy it."

Marcus must have read it through two or three times before he looked up. "I had no idea you got this too—same time as the picture?"

Mabry said "Yes, but of course *I* wasn't the one that got it. It belongs to the man who hired me to loop through Paris and collect it."

"You figure he's dead, though?"

"All but certainly."

"So it's yours forever now." Marcus rubbed a clean hand across the muddy face of the canvas. Then he grinned up at Mabry, who was still standing near. "It's kind of an ugly sucker, ain't it?"

Mabry laughed and sat back on the foot of his bed. "Young Philip was surely no Vincent, was he?"

Marcus waited a good while, staring at the surface as though it would yield some useful fact. Then he said "But he knew poor Vincent Van Gogh—think about *that*!"

Mabry nodded. "So it seems. I doubt he's lying. He had nothing to gain by saying what he does on the back of a picture he had to know would lie in a cellar or be flung in a furnace." He pointed to the note in Marcus's lap.

Marcus said "Course not."

Then Mabry had to say what came upon him as a potent demand. "Marc, you must know this—that picture's not mine now and may never be."

Marcus looked rightly puzzled.

"Even if Baxter Sample is dead deep under those ruins, there may yet be some distant relation who'll eventually rise up to claim his things. He may have left a will. None's been found yet but that doesn't mean there's not one somewhere. He was a fine lawyer, never forget."

Marcus said "Then all the more reason to think he died with no arrangements. Don't they say the cobbler's children always lack shoes?"

It seemed a strange claim, if proverbial, till Mabry thought it through. Then it had its own strength. When he looked back to Marcus, the clean hand was stroking the surface again. Mabry had to say "Careful. No matter how clean any human hand is, it's got its own oils."

Marcus lifted his hand but continued to stare. "Mr. Van Gogh is bound to have touched this—don't you think?"

Mabry said "What makes you feel that?"

Still not looking up, Marcus said "Oh, just my sappy old soul, I guess. I want to believe it."

Mabry said "Me too. It's likely what made me take up my job—all the graduate work I had to do, all the absolute silent lonely time I spend on one small canvas even now, more than twenty years into a career."

Marcus stood, walked over, and laid the picture by Mabry on the bed, then returned to his rocker. When he spoke, he slid into a black minstrel comic voice. "Boss man, I sho hopes it's *yours* someday."

Mabry took the same voice—"*Thank* you, Rastus"—then knew their volume might well wake Master from the sleep she needed. He returned to his own voice and spoke very softly. "I can hope it will be mine for some brief day and, after that, yours. I can *hope* for it all." He stood from the actual iron bed, took Philip Adger's picture, and moved toward the mantel—his eyes swam fiercely with wild gold spikes of light and a deep seizing darkness—but he managed to set the frame in its place, this time on the left edge with Marcus's portrait of the two of them four feet to the right. In their dark blue world, they looked even better than they had last week when Marcus produced the picture, a welcome surprise.

His eyes were still beaming, swimming, flaring; but Mabry turned then slowly toward the door, laid a hand on Marcus's shoulder as he passed, and headed for the kitchen, through a house he had owned for a few hours only (in fact had never owned, since the deed was still in his father's name). He was aiming to see mainly Audrey and Charlotte and Gwyneth Williams, the friends he'd likely need even more than the young Marcus Thornton whom he'd just now left alone with a child as lovely as daylight and a picture that might prove hopeful down the road or might be no more than what it seemed to some people now—a dim souvenir of a lone American boy's hard afternoon by his easel in a field in France, long years ago, when a painter who'd been mildly kind to the boy had excused himself, walked straight on past the house the boy was trying to paint on a cast-off canvas and shot himself, then staggered back to his room above the café near where the boy's own prosperous parents had rented rooms and died with a loving younger brother beside him only two days later, having sold one painting in his solitary life.

REYNOLDS PRICE

Reynolds Price was born in Macon, North Carolina in 1933. Educated at Duke University and, as a Rhodes Scholar, at Merton
College, Oxford University, he has taught at Duke since 1958 and
is now James B. Duke Professor of English. Fifty of his short stories,
ranging from his first work in the early 1950s to the early 1990s, were
published in his *Collected Stories* in 1993. His first novel, *A Long and
Happy Life*, was published in 1962 and won the William Faulkner
Award. His sixth novel, *Kate Vaiden*, was published in 1986 and won
the National Book Critics Circle Award. *The Good Priest's Son* is his
fourteenth. Six of the novels take their places in separate trilogies
concerned with two families—the Mustians of eastern North Carolina and the Mayfields of eastern Carolina and the mountains of
Virginia. Among his thirty-six volumes are further collections of fiction, poetry, plays, essays, and translations. Price is a member of the
American Academy of Arts and Letters and the American Academy
of Arts and Sciences; his work has been translated into seventeen
languages.